Birder,
She Wrote

ALSO BY DONNA ANDREWS

Birder, She Wrote

A Meg Langslow Mystery

Donna Andrews

MINOTAUR BOOKS

NEW YORK

First published in the United States by Minotaur Books, an imprint of St. Martin's Publishing Group.

www.minotaurbooks.com

Title page illustration by Gabriel Guma

Library of Congress Cataloging-in-Publication Data

Names: Andrews, Donna, author.
Title: Birder, she wrote / Donna Andrews.
Description: First edition. | New York : Minotaur Books, 2023. | Series: Meg Langslow Mysteries ; 33
Identifiers: LCCN 2023015447 | ISBN 9781250760241 (hardcover) | ISBN 9781250760258 (ebook)
Subjects: LCSH: Langslow, Meg (Fictitious character)—Fiction. | Women Detectives—Fiction. | LCGFT: Detective and mystery fiction. | Novels.
Classification: LCC PS3551.N4165 B57 2023 | DDC 813/.54—dc23/eng/20230407
LC record available at https://lccn.loc.gov/2023015447

Our books may be purchased in bulk for promotional, educational, or business use. Please contact your local bookseller or the Macmillan Corporate and Premium Sales Department at 1-800-221-7945, extension 5442, or by email at MacmillanSpecialMarkets@macmillan.com.

First Edition: 2023

1   3   5   7   9   10   8   6   4   2

To Angela Lansbury,
for giving us Jessica Fletcher

Chapter 1

"This is the life," I said, as I wriggled into an even more comfortable position in the hammock.

I wasn't talking to anyone in particular. As far as I knew, there was no one within earshot. But just in case there was, I was going to do my best to look—and sound—like someone who was deeply contented and should not be disturbed for anything short of an actual emergency. Although the people most apt to interrupt me were safely occupied elsewhere—Michael, my husband, was teaching his Friday classes at Caerphilly College, and my twin sons, Jamie and Josh, were at school until three.

My notebook-that-tells-me-when-to-breathe, as I called my comprehensive to-do list and calendar, was nearby, but I'd already checked, and nothing in its pages had to be done right now. For the next hour I was on hammock time. I could read. I could put on my headphones and listen to some music. Or I could just lie here and enjoy the balmy May weather, the masses of blooms in our flower beds, and the fascinating aerial ballet of hummingbirds darting to and from the nearby feeder.

The hummingbirds. I sat up with a frown. The last time I'd found the time to watch them, there had been half a dozen of them, impossibly small, their iridescent jewel-toned bodies sparkling in the sunshine as they paused, sipped, and darted away. Now there was only one, flitting around the feeder. And he didn't even seem to be feeding—just darting about.

Was there something wrong with the latest batch of sugar water? This little guy and all his fellow hummers had been keeping us busy refilling the feeder—sometimes they went through two batches of sugar water a day. And if the feeder ran low, they could always turn to the vast quantities of pollinator-friendly blooms we'd planted in the yard. Every year we added more flowering perennials—multiple cultivars of bee balm and columbines, salvia and milkweed. Great ropes of native honeysuckle covered long stretches of the fence around our yard. And while I preferred to spend my energy on perennials—if you're going to all the trouble of digging, why not plant something that will stay around for at least a few years?—Rose Noire, our nature-crazy cousin-in-residence, had gone overboard with the annuals and biennials—foxgloves, hollyhocks, cleomes, petunias, nasturtiums, zinnias, and who knew what else. We had almost as many flowers on display as Flugleman's, the local garden supplier. We even had baskets of jewel-colored fuchsias hanging from limbs and poles at various spots around the yard, and a vast field of purple clover just across the fence in a pasture that was technically part of Mother and Dad's neighboring farm.

The sight of all the flowers cheered and calmed me. Maybe this hummingbird just wasn't hungry at the moment.

Just then another hummingbird flew toward the feeder— only to jerk back as the first hummingbird attacked, making a sort of buzzing noise and stabbing with his needle-sharp little bill. The newcomer fled, and the first hummingbird resumed circling the feeder, like a sentry patrolling his station.

Was this dog-in-the-manger act normal hummingbird behavior? Did our beloved little pollinators bully each other away from the feeder? I should ask my grandfather. Sometimes it was useful to have an eminent naturalist in the family.

Then again, did I really want an hour-long lecture about the feeding and reproductive behavior of hummingbirds? I'd ask my grandmother Cordelia. When it came to backyard ornithology, she was just as knowledgeable and a lot more practical.

I'd film a little of the suspected bully's behavior first. I was reaching to pull out my phone to do this when it rang. Okay, that was convenient. But when the caller ID showed it was Randall Shiffley calling, I sighed. Randall might be trying to reach me about any number of things, but the odds were that he was calling me in my role as his part-time assistant in charge of special projects. Or, as I sometimes called it, the Mayor's Special Assistant for Headaches and Nuisances.

"What's up?" I asked.

"The NIMBYs are at it again."

I winced and stifled a groan. The NIMBYs—short for "Not in *my* backyard!"—was our shorthand way of referring to many residents of Caerphilly's ritzy Westlake neighborhood who were constantly filing complaints against their neighbors. Not, usually, their fellow Westlake residents. Unfortunately, their neighborhood was on the outskirts of town and bordered by several farms. And most of its residents were, as Randall put it, "not from around here." Affluent retirees. Businesspeople who either didn't mind a long commute or managed their far-flung empires remotely. The occasional distinguished professor recruited by Caerphilly College. Not, for the most part, people who had any previous experience of living cheek by jowl with working farms.

Those of us who were locals, or at least long-term residents, could almost predict when newly arrived Westlake residents' raptures over the lack of traffic noises would give way to complaints about the roosters waking them up at dawn. When they'd notice that the green, unspoiled landscape they liked to gaze out upon contained not only cows but also cow pies and muddy pig wallows. When they'd realize that the fresh country air they'd been rhapsodizing over was often scented with manure.

And that's when they'd suddenly become Caerphilly's problem. Or, more accurately, my problem.

"Who's in their sights this time?" I asked.

"Edgar Bortnick and his bees."

"Oh, good grief," I muttered.

"Yeah. Apparently, Edgar had another big dustup with Wally the Weird."

I knew Edgar well, because last year Dad had gone in for beekeeping in a big way and Edgar was his guru. And Walter Inman, aka Wally the Weird, a retired businessman from the D.C. area, was my personal candidate for the worst of the NIMBYs, mainly because on top of harassing the neighboring farmers he frequently picked fights with his fellow NIMBYs.

"Supposedly Edgar promised he'd move the hives that are right across the fence from Wally's patio," Randall continued. "But it's been a week now, Edgar's bees are still dive-bombing Wally and his guests, and Edgar's nowhere to be found. Hasn't answered his door, and his voicemail's full."

I felt a brief twinge of anxiety but reminded myself that this was normal for Edgar.

"Remember," I said. "Beekeeping's a sideline for him." Even in my own head I was careful not to repeat my mistake of calling it a hobby. A passion, an obsession, a vocation, a calling—but not, according to Edgar, a hobby.

"Yup, I know the wildlife photography's his main gig."

"Which means he's always going off in the woods for days or even weeks with nothing but a canteen and his camera," I pointed out.

"And normally I'd assume that's what he's doing now," Randall said. "But there are a couple of people he usually asks to keep an eye on his place when he does that—my cousin Sam, who has the farm next door, and your dad. I checked with both of them, and he didn't say anything to either about being gone overnight."

Definitely worrisome.

"It's always possible that something happened to delay him," I said. "The other day Dad was telling me about how Edgar once sat in a tree for three days, trying to get some good pictures of a nest full of newly hatched screech owls. And you know how spotty cell phone coverage is the second you get a few miles from town."

"Odds are that's what's happening," Randall said. "And that if he did agree to move his hives, he'll be doing it when he gets back—although I kind of doubt that Wally the Weird is telling the truth about Edgar agreeing to move the hives. But there's not much use in *my* trying to explain any of that to the NIMBYs. Could you maybe go over and work your diplomatic magic?"

Under most situations, I'd have said Randall was at least as diplomatic as I was. But he was right—I usually had better luck soothing the savage NIMBYs. Of the three people whose farms bordered Westlake, Edgar was the one the NIMBYs hated the most, but they complained almost as often about Randall's cousin Sam, who specialized in organic, pasture-raised pigs. Wally the Weird and the rest of the NIMBYs seemed to confuse "organic" with "odor-free" and resented having the pig pasture visible from their elegant, upscale backyards. And they also assumed that Randall's refusal to ban his cousin's pig-keeping was due to nepotism rather than common sense.

"So you want me to go over and calm Wally down?" I asked.

"No, actually it's the Brownlows complaining today," he said. "Apparently Wally was bragging about winning his argument with Edgar, so they were all expecting the beehives to be gone by now. Though if you can track down Wally, that would be a good thing, too. Mr. Brownlow seemed to find his absence downright suspicious. We don't want poor Horace having to dig up Sam's pig wallow again."

"Right." Last year Wuzzums, the Brownlows' pampered Maltipoo, had gone walkabout for a few days, and Wally swore he'd seen Sam burying a Wuzzums-sized something in his pasture. My cousin Horace had been halfway through a forensic excavation of Sam's pig wallow when another deputy apprehended Wuzzums on a farm ten miles away, covered with ticks, fleas, and mud, and looking as if she'd been having the time of her life. Which apparently she had—when her pregnancy became visible, the horrified Brownlows had dumped her at the county animal shelter, asking to have her "put down." Luckily, Caerphilly's shelter is a no-kill one, and Wuzzums—aptly renamed Wild Thing—was now living the good life, protecting the hens on a nearby poultry farm. But the whole episode had left me with a very low opinion of the Brownlows.

"So, pacify the Brownlows and verify that Wally the Weird is still among the living," I said. "And Edgar, too. Or if I come across any evidence that Wally has done away with Edgar, I'll call Chief Burke. Will later today work? My grandmother's coming over pretty soon to take me on an expedition. We're helping Horace and Deacon Washington look for the old Muddy Hollow graveyard."

"Oh, good idea," he said. "Finding that's more important— it's such a vital part of the county's history. The NIMBYs can certainly wait till you're back. Or even till tomorrow if it takes you all day to find the cemetery. If the NIMBYs call again anytime soon, I'll tell them I've assigned you to track Edgar down. Which wouldn't be a bad idea, if you can manage it. I'd like to hear his side of the argument with Wally."

"Roger. You don't ask much. I'll put it all on the list for today if possible, and I'll let you know what I find out."

We said our farewells, and I settled back in my hammock.

I tried to recapture my earlier relaxed mood. Focused on the flowers. On the sun glinting off the bright copper feathers of our Welsummer hens. On our llamas' gentle, contented humming.

But I feared I wasn't going to recapture my relaxed mood quite so easily. I pulled out my phone again and checked the time. Almost ten o'clock. Cordelia was supposed to be here by eleven for our expedition. Technically I had enough time to get over to Westlake and back with five or ten minutes to spare. But there was no way I could placate even one of the NIMBYs in under an hour.

So I scribbled a couple of items in my notebook. Calm the Brownlows. Calm the Griswolds if necessary—they were the other Westlake denizens with a view of Edgar's beehives. Find Wally the Weird. Find Edgar. And then after a moment of thought, another two items I'd been too relaxed to write down earlier. Ask Grandfather about hummingbirds. Ask Cordelia ditto.

I gazed sternly at the offending hummingbird, now perched on a flowering dogwood branch near the feeder, presumably so he could guard it with less energy expenditure.

"Your time's coming," I muttered.

I tucked my notebook away under the hammock pillow, lay back again, and closed my eyes. Usually, writing something down in my notebook as a future to-do item enabled me to get it off my mind and concentrate on what I was doing in the present. Of course, it sometimes took a little time.

I concentrated on the distant, erratic tinkling of the wind chimes. On the smell of the nearby lavender. On the—

"Hey, Meg." My brother, Rob. "You busy?"

"So much for hammock time," I muttered.

Chapter 2

I glanced over to see what Rob needed help with. He was carrying a small sturdy packing crate and had an assortment of tools and objects wedged under his arms, including a flattish crowbar and what looked like a prop from the set of *The Wizard of Oz*—the head of the Tin Man, with a small silver accordion soldered to it. What the—?

I rolled out of the hammock. Right-side up, I realized that what I'd mistaken for the Tin Man was actually Dad's bee smoker. You lit a fuel source in a cylindrical container—the head—and used the accordion—actually a small bellows—to pump the resulting smoke out through the spout that looked like the Tin Man's upside-down funnel hat. The smoke was supposed to calm the bees and keep them from attacking.

And the flattish crowbar was what beekeepers called a hive tool—used for popping off the top of the hive, scraping out debris, and other arcane bee management chores.

"Don't tell me," I said. "Dad's new shipment of bees has arrived."

"Actually, he thinks of them as your bees," he said. "Since they'll be moving into the hive here at your house. Can you grab all this stuff while I carry the bee box?" He lifted his arms. The smoker, the hive tool, and a small collection of other items fell to the ground.

"Dad can't carry any of it?" Not that I waited for an answer to begin picking up the scattered instruments he'd dropped.

"He's putting on his beekeeping outfit," Rob said.

I wasn't quite sure how this would keep Dad from helping to carry at least some of the equipment he'd be using when he approached the hive. Then again, I'd long ago figured out that it was hopeless to expect Dad to perform mundane chores while wearing a costume—and however useful and practical it was, his beekeeping outfit was definitely also a costume.

The screen door slammed, and I turned to see Dad emerging from the kitchen, ready for action. Last year he'd done his beekeeping chores in some rather scruffy gear handed down from Edgar, but this year he'd invested in a new outfit. His beekeeping hat, which was rather like a pith helmet, supported a long veil of netting that pooled around his chest. He wore a baggy off-white shirt and matching pants—I assumed the loose fit reduced the chance that any bees who landed on the cloth would get close enough to his body to sting. The pants legs were tightly strapped around the tops of his knee-high white PVC boots. His shirtsleeves disappeared into the tops of his elbow-length white-and-tan leather gauntlets. What the well-equipped apiarist will wear. You could tell by his jaunty manner that he thought he cut a very dashing figure. I would never spoil his fun by suggesting that he looked less like Indiana Jones than the Pillsbury Doughboy.

"Your bees are here!" he exclaimed as he drew near, walking carefully because his new boots were on the large side.

"So I gathered," I said. "Are you going to put them in the hive now? I thought the boys were all excited about helping you."

"Yes." His face fell. "But your mother put her foot down. She doesn't want the boys anywhere near the hive until the bees are safely installed and have calmed down. She's completely over-reacting."

Overreacting? Or demonstrating the common sense we all knew Dad often lacked. I had to confess, I felt a sense of relief, knowing the bee installation would be over with by the time the boys came home. Especially since Dad was doing it without Edgar's expert help.

"Don't start till I get my camera," I said. "I want to document this."

"Great idea!" He beamed at me, and then continued clumping toward the back of the yard.

I thought it was a pretty nifty idea myself. Having a lot of photos might help console the boys for missing all the excitement. And besides, if I was in charge of documenting the bee installation, I'd have a perfect excuse for keeping my distance from the action. I'd noticed that one of the items Rob had left in my charge was what Dad called his Bite Bag—a specialized first-aid kit for treating family and friends who fell afoul of bees, wasps, hornets, and other stinging pests. While I very much approved of the Bite Bag, whose contents included everything from antihistamines and topical steroids for itching to epinephrine injectors for ana-phylactic shock, I wanted to avoid anything that would require my getting treatment from it.

I jogged to the barn, which housed both my office and my blacksmithing shop, and located my digital camera. When I emerged from the barn—

"Meg? What's going on?"

I turned to see the tall, jeans-clad figure of my grandmother Cordelia emerging from the kitchen. Right behind her was a young woman I didn't know. The newcomer was dressed in what she probably considered casual clothes—or maybe busi-ness casual: beige linen slacks, a beige silk blouse, low-heeled beige shoes that were probably more expensive than sensible. Her wheat-blond hair was caught up at the nape of her neck with a pair of chopsticks in the sort of artful arrangement that only looked easy.

Cordelia glanced back at her, and a brief flash of annoyance crossed her face before she composed herself.

"This is—" she began.

But the young woman interrupted her, stepping forward and holding out her hand.

"Britni Colleton," she said. "That's B-R-I-T-N-I. *Sweet Tea and Sassafras.*"

"Meg Langslow," I said as I shook her hand. It sounded incomplete—was I supposed to add something? Surely she could spell Meg, especially since I used the plain-vanilla version. Was "sweet tea and sassafras" a beverage order? Should I tell her that we could provide the sweet tea, but I couldn't promise the sassafras? Unless my cousin Rose Noire had some in her herb and natural medicine collection.

Cordelia noticed my puzzled look.

"Britni is the reporter who's interviewing me for the *Sweet Tea and Sassafras* magazine," she said.

I nodded and braced myself to pretend I'd actually heard of the publication.

"She wants to meet and perhaps interview some of my family for the article," Cordelia went on. "But if this is a busy time—"

"Dad and Rob are busy at the moment," I said. "The bees came."

"For your hive!" Cordelia exclaimed. She looked more cheerful and strode toward the back of the yard where Dad and Rob were heading. "This could be fascinating," she said over her shoulder, presumably to the reporter.

"Actually, I prefer to think of it as Rose Noire's hive—since it's right in the middle of her herb fields." I began picking up the things Rob had consigned to me. Cordelia circled back and held out her hand, and I gave her a few items to carry. Then I fell into step beside her as we headed for the far end of the yard.

I glanced back to see the reporter following us. She had her phone out and was busily taking pictures of anything that caught her eye. Of our copper-and-black Welsummer hens, who mobbed her just as they did anyone who entered the yard, on the assumption that they must be planning to scatter chicken feed. Of our five llamas, who had sensed that something exciting was about to happen and were already gathered at the end of their pen closest to the herb field. Of our barn, which was still an unconventional pale pink, with elaborate painted garlands of roses and lilies—the supposedly temporary paint with which it had been decorated for last summer's wedding festivities had proved to be a lot more durable than expected.

"They'll be pollinating your flowers along with her herbs," Cordelia said. "I'd call the hive just as much yours as hers."

"Ssh," I said. "I'm hoping to avoid taking on any of the extra work the bees will cause."

We arrived at the fence separating our backyard from Rose Noire's herb field. Rob was waiting on the other side, so we handed over the various beekeeping implements we'd been carrying and settled in to watch, leaning on the top rail of the fence. On the outside. Away from the hive. Cordelia and I—and Britni the reporter, of course—weren't wearing head-to-toe protective gear. If the bees emerged from their shipping container in a bad mood, we'd be better off if we didn't have a fence with a narrow gate blocking our path to safety. After taking a few dozen photos of the hive and of Dad in his beekeeping outfit, Britni joined us.

"I do wish Edgar was here," Dad said.

"Who's that?" Britni asked.

"Edgar Bortnick," I said. "Dad's beekeeping guru."

"He's not coming." Dad was laying out his various tools and gadgets as methodically as if he were a surgeon getting ready to perform an operation. "I can't imagine why he's not here. I called yesterday, when the bees came, and got his voicemail. So

I dropped by his farm, and his truck was gone. He must be off on one of his expeditions."

"Expeditions?" Britni echoed. So while Dad sorted out his tools, I explained about Edgar's wildlife photography.

"I think he'd have let me know if he was going out of town," Dad said. "A couple of days ago he mentioned checking out a possible sighting of an eagle's nest, but that was someplace here in Caerphilly County. Meg—could you ask Randall to have his cousins keep an eye out for Edgar while they're in the woods?"

"They won't be spending all that much time in the woods this time of year," I pointed out. "If it were hunting season, yeah, but this time of year they're all busy at their farms and construction sites and whatever."

"True." Dad looked concerned.

"And anyway, Randall's already got his family keeping an eye out for Edgar," I added. "In fact, this morning Randall asked me if I could help with the search."

"Wonderful!" Dad looked completely relieved.

Nice that someone had such confidence in my Edgar-finding skills.

"And meanwhile we can't afford to wait for him to come back." Dad's good mood had returned. "These bees need to be hived immediately! But don't worry! I know exactly what to do. I helped Edgar last time."

"Last time?" Britni asked. "I thought this beehive thing was new."

"This will be our second try at getting bees established in this first hive," I explained. "Edgar brought over a batch last spring when some of his bees swarmed, and he and Dad set up the hive, but a few months later all the bees were gone."

"They all died?" Britni looked alarmed and drew back, as if afraid whatever had killed the bees might be contagious to humans.

"No," Dad said. "If they'd died, we'd have seen a lot of dead bees. They disappeared. Flew off and set up their hive some-where else. I spent some time looking around in the woods, but I never did find them."

He looked sad, as if still wondering what he'd done to cause the bees' desertion.

"They do that sometimes," Cordelia said, in her most consol-ing tone. "And it's rarely something the beekeeper has done. They just get notions."

"Edgar would agree with you," Dad said. "But I want to do everything I can to prevent it from happening again. I have some ideas about what might have caused it. I've been doing quite a bit of reading about apiculture over the last six months."

And doing his best to get the rest of us to share his fascina-tion. He'd even given Michael and me spare copies of what he considered the most interesting and useful books for beginners, on the theory that we should know at least a little about the lat-est additions to our household.

"Meg, are you ready?" Dad asked.

For a second I thought he was expecting me to pitch in with whatever he and Rob were about to do. Then I realized he meant ready to take pictures. I lifted my camera and nodded.

"Hmm." He frowned. "You can do either photos or video with that, right?"

"Yes—which do you want?"

"Both." He sighed. "But I suppose photos are more practical."

"I can take some video for you." Britni held up a digital cam-era that was almost the twin of mine.

"Great!" Dad beamed at her. "I think we're ready to get started. Let me know when you're ready."

Britni and I each took a few moments to find a strategic po-sition, with a good view of both the hive and the small packing crate, which was humming gently. Then, once we assured Dad that we were ready, he began talking.

"Okay," he said. "We're going to get started. Let's open the crate. Don't worry," he added. "There's an inner cage."

He reached for the hive tool, but Rob was already holding it.

"I'll pry it open," he said. "So you can keep telling them what we're up to."

Actually Rob knew what a bad idea it was to trust Dad with any kind of tool. Of course, Dad was fully qualified to patch up whatever damage he did to himself or bystanders, but that didn't mean we should trust him with tools if we could help it.

Rob began prying open the crate. Dad turned back to the cameras and continued.

"These are Italian bees," he said. "*Apis mellifera ligustica.*"

"Italian bees?" Britni echoed. "What's so special about them that you had to have them shipped all the way from Italy?"

"We didn't." Dad frowned slightly. "We got them from a bee-keeper right here in Virginia. That's the common name of the subspecies. Italian bees are reasonably productive, and they're known for being comparatively calm and gentle. Much less apt to sting."

I could tell by the look on Britni's face that she didn't find "comparatively calm and gentle" all that reassuring.

"This box contains approximately three pounds of bees," Dad said. "That's between ten and twelve thousand bees."

Rob was lifting the top off the small crate and the sound of the bees became louder, and more like buzzing than humming. Was that just because we could hear them better? Or did they resent having their crate opened?

I had no desire to be any closer to twelve thousand resentful bees. I used the zoom lens of my camera to get a closer look at them. The top and several sides of the box were filled with a heavy wire mesh, through which I could see bees—some clinging to the mesh, others crawling over and under and around each other in a writhing mass of furry black-and-yellow bodies.

Should I put a little more distance between me and the hive that would be their new home? Britni leaned over slightly, then pulled back as if having the same thought.

"They don't sound calm," Britni said.

"Neither would you if you'd been cooped up in a tiny little box for a few days," Cordelia said. "Not to mention being slammed around in a delivery truck."

"Only one day," Dad said. "I paid extra for overnight delivery. I'd have gone to pick them up myself if I could, but—"

"But you've had a lot on your plate," I said.

"And we'll be taking steps to calm them down. Rob, the smoker!" He held out his hand and Rob slapped the smoker into it.

We watched—and I took multiple pictures—as Dad opened a little door in the cylinder and tried to set its contents alight. It took him six tries before he managed to keep the match lit long enough to ignite the fuel. Rob decided to fill part of the lull by continuing the explanation.

"Once we get it lit, we'll puff smoke on the bees," Rob explained. "It calms them."

"What's in the fuel? Will it affect us?" Britni sounded as if she planned to report us to the DEA.

"Cotton scraps and pine needles," Dad said over his shoulder. "Aha!"

He had finally managed to light the smoker.

"Rob will handle the smoker." Dad pressed the bellows to produce a sample puff of smoke before handing the smoker to Rob. "We'll also dampen the bees, to temporarily inhibit wing function."

"So they'll all be too wet to fly and too stoned to care," Rob said. "Which will make it easy for Dad to run up, pour the bees into the hive, put the top on, and retreat before the bees get riled up again."

"But don't forget the queen!" Dad peered down. "She's in

there, in a little separate cage, so they can't get at her—because she's not their queen yet. She was raised separately, and she will smell alien to them, and they'd kill her if they could get to her. But they can't. We'll pop her into the hive, still in the cage. They can see her and smell her, and in a few days, they'll get used to her."

"Then I guess you go back in and let her out," Britni said.

"No, the queen cage has a hole in one end that's filled with a plug made of candy," Dad said. "The bees eat the candy, and by the time they've consumed it all and can get at the queen, they'll probably have accepted her as their queen."

"And if they haven't?" Britni sounded skeptical. And way too focused on possible negative outcomes. If Rose Noire were here, she'd probably be shaking her head over the gloomy and pessimistic color of Britni's aura.

"Then they'll kill her, and I'll have to get a new queen."

"I'm sure it will be fine," Cordelia said. "Queen bee breeders have got the whole candy plug thing down to a science. Let's not borrow trouble."

"You're right." Dad's face reverted to cheerfulness. "And I'm sure these bees will do fine. They look very calm and industrious."

Calm? Industrious? I wasn't quite sure how he deduced that. Energetic, maybe. If you looked closely enough, you could see individual bees crawling. If you half closed your eyes, all you saw was a fuzzy mass of yellow and black that writhed ominously. And their buzzing sounded pretty angry to me.

"Time's a-wasting!" Dad exclaimed. "Let's get started."

I glanced around to make sure my escape route was clear.

Chapter 3

Dad reached over to his stash of tools, picked up two plant misters, and handed one to Rob. Then he squatted down beside the bee box and began misting the bees.

Rob sat down cross-legged beside Dad and joined in. Cordelia, Britni, and I watched them for several minutes. Every so often Rob would pick up the smoker and pump a few dozen puffs of smoke into the cage.

"Shouldn't they be getting quieter?" Britni asked after a while.

"I think they are, actually," Dad said. "It's just happening so gradually it's hard to notice."

This sounded like wishful thinking to me. The bees seemed to be buzzing and crawling just as vigorously as ever. But Dad would be the one getting up close and personal with them, so maybe what he thought was what mattered. And he would be wearing his beekeeper's outfit.

"Okay," Dad said to Rob. "I'm going to take them in. You stand by with the smoker. If they start getting aggressive, you could try darting in and puffing at them."

Rob didn't look very cheerful about the darting-in idea, but he nodded. Dad put on his gloves—he'd shed them for the misting portion of the program. Then he picked up the bee box and carefully carried it toward the hive.

"Damn, but I wish Edgar was here," Rob muttered—too softly for Dad to hear, I hoped.

"He'll do fine," Cordelia said.

Dad set the bee box down right beside the hive. He fumbled with the lid of the hive for a few minutes, then remembered his hive tool. Although he still seemed to be handling it rather awkwardly.

"Those brand-new leather gloves are too stiff," I said to Cordelia, in an undertone. "I was planning to break them in for him, the way I do with the boys' baseball gloves, but I didn't know the bees were coming so soon."

"You had bees last summer," she said. "At least for a few months. Didn't he already have a set of gloves?"

"Yes," I said. "And they were nicely broken in, too. Unfortunately, Dad left them lying around where the Pomeranians could get to them. There were only a few scraps of leather left by the time we found them."

"A good thing those pups are cute," Cordelia said.

Dad had gotten the top of the hive off and was using the hive tool to pry open the wire mesh inner lid of the bee box. It finally popped open—

And the bees began swarming out. Not all ten to twelve thousand of them—in fact, the bulk of them were still writhing and crawling in the box. But more than a few. Dozens at first. Maybe hundreds. They were buzzing in a cloud around Dad.

Dad reached into the box with both gauntleted hands, scooping up a double handful of bees.

"Coo-*ul*," Rob murmured.

"Oh, gross," Britni said.

Gross? Not really. But maybe a little alarming. The bees seemed to be clinging to each other, and a lot of them were clinging for dear life to the wire sides of the inner cage.

Still, Dad picked up a moderately large clump of them and deposited them gently inside the hive. He then reached in and held up something—the queen's cage—and set it down on the ground beside the box. Then he continued scooping up hand-fuls of bees.

And the bees weren't cooperating. More of them kept flying up and buzzing around Dad. Others couldn't fly yet, but they could still crawl. And they did. Out of his hands and up his arms. Out of the box and onto the ground, so Dad had to be careful where he stepped, lest he crush some. He bent over, ob-viously having trouble seeing the grounded bees because of the thick beekeeper's veil.

"Oh, great, what's he doing now?" Rob muttered.

Dad had flipped up his veil.

"Dad, no," Rob shouted. "Put your veil back down."

"James, be careful," Cordelia called.

Dad was now bending over, trying to brush the crawling bees aside. He began trying to pick them up but was stymied by the thick leather of his gauntlets.

"Oh, God, no," Rob muttered.

Dad was pulling off his gauntlets—carefully, because there were still a few bees crawling on them.

"This is getting very interesting," Cordelia said. "Let's try not to startle him. Or them."

Dad was picking up bees with his bare hands, both from the ground and from the bee box, and putting them in the hive. A few seemed to fly up as soon as he deposited them in the hive. Occasionally he'd stop to pick off the bees that were crawling up his arms and pants legs, and fish out the few that had wormed their way inside his sleeves or the neck of his shirt.

"I can't look." Rob was covering his eyes with both hands. "Tell me when it's over."

"Shouldn't you be dashing in to puff smoke at them?" I asked.

"I'd stay away for now," Cordelia said. "The bees don't seem to be acting aggressively. If Rob got closer, it might alarm them. They seem to be accepting your dad."

She was right. If any of the bees were stinging Dad, he was too absorbed in his task to notice. And as far as I could tell, they weren't stinging him. Crawling all over him, flying in an increasingly dense swarm around his head, but not stinging. If Rose Noire were here, she'd be full of interesting theories about this. That the bees liked Dad's aura, perhaps. Or that by trusting the bees not to sting him Dad had won their trust in return. Maybe Dad was right about Italian bees being calm and gentle. Maybe what sounded to me like angry buzzing was actually the bees' song of joy and delight at being released from their prison into the middle of an organic herb field by a keeper who wasn't afraid of them. Or maybe these bees had evolved enough intelligence to figure out that they should exhaust all other means of repelling invaders before resorting to their stingers, since by doing so they were actually committing suicide.

"James," Cordelia called out. "You don't actually have to place every single bee in the hive. Just tuck the queen inside. The rest will all find their way in."

Dad didn't seem to pay any attention at first, but after a couple of minutes he picked up the little queen cage, placed it inside the hive, and began turning around, carefully watching the ground in case he'd missed any of the few remaining grounded bees. And then, almost tiptoeing, and occasionally bending down to pick up a stray crawling bee and move it to safety, he began slowly making his way back toward us.

"Dad," Rob said. "You do realize you're still wearing some bees, don't you?"

Britni gasped in alarm and began backing away from the fence.

"James, why don't you stop right there?" Cordelia was heading for the gate. "And we can pick the remaining bees off of you while you're still near the hive."

"If you're sure," Dad began.

"I've worked with bees."

Dad followed orders and stood obediently still in the middle of the path. While Rob and I watched with gaping mouths—as Britni was doing, for that matter, though she had retreated almost to the back door—Cordelia went through the gate and approached Dad. She was walking a little more slowly than her usual brisk, businesslike pace, and there was definitely something fluid and catlike in her motion. The bees that were crawling on Dad, and occasionally taking off or landing on him, didn't seem to react to her. Using her bare hands—just like Dad—she carefully picked up the remaining bees and set them gently on the brilliant purple flowers of Rose Noire's early-blooming lavender.

"Awesome," Rob murmured. "It's like they're bee whisperers."

Was this a family superpower that I might have inherited? I wasn't sure I had the nerve to find out. Or the nerve to use if it came to that.

"Meg," Dad said. "You haven't seen any more skunks lately, have you?"

Dad was the king of the apparent non sequitur.

"No," I said. "Not since you and Grandfather removed the one that had taken up residence under the llama shed. Why?"

"They could be a threat to the bees," he said. "They eat the bees whole and spit out the inedible bits. Bears are worse, of course, but we don't often get them here."

He continued to list all the things that could harm our bees, everything from murder hornets and bee wolves—a type of wasp—to mites and spiders. I was starting to wonder how any bees ever survived. Should we post sentries over the hives?

"Done," Cordelia said finally, when she'd finished examining every inch of Dad. I was relieved that her interruption brought

Dad's lecture on bee predators to an end. The two of them strolled toward the gate.

"That was great!" Dad enthused. "I'd forgotten you've had bees."

He'd seen the row of hives at the back of her garden only a few hundred times. Perhaps he assumed she hired someone to take care of them. I'd have pointed this out, but Cordelia merely smiled enigmatically.

"Wonderful." Dad was surveying the hive with a look of great satisfaction. "The first of many, I'm hoping."

A hope I didn't quite share. Not yet, anyway. I wanted to see how well the bees coexisted with the llamas, chickens, cats, dogs, and (of course) humans already resident in the yard before we added to their numbers.

"After all," Dad continued. "We have plenty of room!" He waved his arm in a half circle and smiled as if already gazing on row after row of busy hives.

"Well, that was pretty exciting." Rob was glancing at his phone. "But it took longer than I expected. We should go. Grandfather is expecting us out at the zoo."

"Oh, yes!" Dad turned to go, then whirled around again and looked at me and Cordelia. "Do you want to come with us?" he asked. "We're going to help out with filming a new documentary about animals and their offspring."

He looked hopeful and apologetic. I wasn't sure if he really wanted us to come, or if he was merely being polite. Cordelia appreciated the Caerphilly Zoo, but if there was documentary filming going on, Grandfather would be in the thick of it. And while Grandfather and Cordelia had once gotten along well enough to produce Dad, nowadays they recognized that the less they saw of each other, the more enjoyable life would be, not only for them but for everyone around them.

"Sounds lovely," Cordelia said. "But I already have plans for today. Tomorrow, perhaps?"

"Right!" Dad's face cleared, and he and Rob dashed off toward where Rob's car was parked.

"That was interesting." Britni's tone of voice suggested that she used "interesting" the same way Mother did—as a polite thing to say when you couldn't think of anything nice. She glanced toward the house, and I suspected she was trying to think of a tactful way of suggesting that we go back inside.

Cordelia was leaning against the fence and watching the bees explore their new backyard.

"Horace should be here any time now," she said over her shoulder.

"Another of your grandchildren?" Britni asked.

"No," Cordelia said. "Horace Hollingsworth is one of Meg's cousins on her mother's side. He's a Caerphilly County deputy, and also the county's lone crime scene investigator."

"Ah." Britni sounded unimpressed. Maybe even dismissive. Annoying of her. Didn't she find it interesting, the idea of meeting a crime scene investigator? I thought I would. Then again, maybe some of Dad's fascination with crime and crime fiction had rubbed off on me.

"Have you filled Britni in on what you and Horace are planning?" I felt an immediate twinge of guilt when I realized I was half hoping Britni would decide to opt out of Cordelia's planned expedition.

Chapter 4

"I haven't really had time to brief Britni." Cordelia turned to face the reporter. "We're going to help Deacon Washington, one of Meg's neighbors, find his long-lost family graveyard."

"Long-lost family graveyard?" Britni sounded puzzled. "How do you lose a graveyard?"

"Deacon Washington's family has an oral tradition that a great many of their ancestors from the eighteen hundreds were buried in a graveyard near the southern end of the county," Cordelia said. "Up until a few years ago, the land down there was owned by someone who wasn't very receptive to the idea of people exploring his woods and trying to find their ancestors' resting places. But the land changed hands last year and the new owner is okay with our doing the search."

"So you're going to wander around in the woods looking for a bunch of headstones?" Britni's tone suggested that she didn't think the expedition would be a whole lot of fun. Dare I hope that she'd decide to stay behind? I wasn't yet entirely sure why, but I hadn't taken an immediate liking to Britni. For someone who was supposed to be writing a profile on Cordelia, she seemed strangely uninterested in what interested her subject. Not just uninterested—slightly dismissive. Although she visited often, Cordelia lived an hour away in Riverton, a small town in the foothills of the Blue Ridge Mountains, where she ran a thriving craft class center, tended her extensive garden, and was the leading light of the local bird-watching community. If Britni wanted to shadow Cordelia as she went about her daily routine, why were they down here in Caerphilly?

"There probably won't be any headstones to find," I said. "This would be a very old African American cemetery."

"A slave cemetery?" Britni wrinkled her nose slightly, as if puzzled by our interest.

"It might date back to pre–Civil War times," Cordelia said. "In which case some of the occupants could have been enslaved people, who didn't usually get headstones. At least not anything the modern eye would recognize as a headstone. And in that era, it would be much the same for free people of color. But even if it's from the second half of the nineteenth century, the people buried there would have been poor—many of them sharecroppers. And again, headstones would be unlikely. Wooden ones, maybe, but those might have deteriorated over time. Often there would be nothing more than rough field stones."

"Then how are you going to find this graveyard of yours?" Britni asked.

"With dogs," I said. "Scent dogs. Horace has been training his dog—and several others—as cadaver dogs. Historians and archaeologists have been having a lot of success using dogs to help locate lost burial grounds."

"Well, that might be interesting." Slight emphasis on the "might," and her tone sounded rather grudging. Clearly she was disappointed at Cordelia's choice of projects. Or maybe of *Sweet Tea and Sassafras*'s latest choice of interview subjects.

"You said something about Randall asking you to find Edgar," Cordelia said. "Is that going to prevent you from joining us?"

"No," I said. "Just let me get my hiking boots."

I ran inside to find them. When I reemerged, it sounded as if Britni was trying to talk Cordelia into a different agenda.

"Well, no," Cordelia was saying. "I can't say I've ever been to the Frilled Pheasant. I'm happy to try it if you want to go, but I thought you said you wanted to get a sense of what my daily life is like."

"It's just that it's such a nice place." Britni's disappointment showed. "But yes, the whole point is to go someplace where you usually go."

"When I'm here in Caerphilly, I usually eat with the family," Cordelia said. "Here with Meg and Michael, or with my son and daughter-in-law—their house is a few miles away."

Britni couldn't suppress a slight sigh. Evidently the Frilled Pheasant was the kind of place she expected her profile subjects to patronize. I had nothing against the Frilled Pheasant, actually. The excellence of their pastries almost made up for the fussy decor. But both the local bakery and the town diner had pastries that were just as good—in fact, probably better—at half the price.

"Of course, I do go out sometimes." Cordelia had obviously noticed the disappointment on Britni's face. "If you like, we'll hit one or two of the best places while we're here."

Britni perked up.

"Muriel's Diner can't be beat," she said. "Or Luigi's, if you're fond of pizza. And I do hope we can catch at least one of the New Life Baptist Church's fish fry picnics before I leave."

Britni's face fell again.

"Or the restaurant at the Caerphilly Inn," I put in. "That's always nice."

"Oh, yes." Britni liked the sound of that. "I'm staying at the Inn, you know."

Sweet Tea and Sassafras must give its employees generous travel allowances.

"We could do that," Cordelia said. "And—great! Here's Horace now." Cordelia turned to wave as Horace emerged from the back door with Watson, his Pomeranian, on a leash. Three other Pomeranians were scampering loose behind him. I immediately recognized Widget, who lived in our basement with my cyber-savvy nephew Kevin, and Winnie—aka Winter Solstice—who belonged to Rose Noire. The third Pom was probably Willie Mays, who'd been adopted by Chief Burke's grandson Adam. The chief often dropped Willie off on days when the boys were in school. The Poms, originally a litter of seven, tended to pine when left alone, and were never happier than when running in a pack with some or all of their siblings. And for that matter, Adam and my twin sons, Josh and Jamie, were also happier as a pack, and picking up Willie from our doggie daycare was always a good excuse for the boys to get together.

Britni seemed unimpressed with the Poms.

"You're not serious," she said. "Don't tell me those things are cadaver dogs."

"You were maybe expecting bloodhounds?" I asked.

"Or some kind of real working dog." She sniffed derisively.

"Any dog can do scent work," I said. "It's a natural ability. Show me a dog with the worst sense of smell in his species, and he'll still be a wizard compared with the most talented human nose."

The Pomeranians yipped joyfully when they saw us and ran forward to be petted. Britni drew back slightly, as if fearful that the dogs would leap on her neatly pressed linen pants with their admittedly muddy paws.

I always have a hard time warming to someone who doesn't like dogs.

Or someone whom dogs do not like. As if well aware that she wouldn't appreciate their charms, the Poms raced right by Britni, dashing back and forth between me and Cordelia.

"Are you bringing just Watson or the whole pack?" I asked Horace.

"Only these four," he said. "They're all getting pretty good at the scent work. But we'd probably better leash them all if we're going into the woods. You know how they are when they spot squirrels."

"Or deer, or rabbits, or gently falling leaves." I ducked inside the barn and grabbed three more dog leads. When I emerged the Pomeranians saw the leads and recognized them as a sign that they were going someplace—possibly someplace exciting, but at any rate, they'd be going together! With people! They grew so excited that they began running around in circles, yipping madly, making it ten times more work to leash them up for the trip.

"How about if I take the dogs in my cruiser," Horace suggested. "And you and Cordelia can pick up the deacon?"

That made sense to me. We stowed the Pomeranians in the back seat of his cruiser. It was designed for securely transporting even the most recalcitrant human prisoners, so it would probably keep the dogs from interfering with his driving. Cordelia, Britni, and I piled into the Twinmobile, as Michael and I had dubbed our SUV, and we caravanned the mile or so down the road to Deacon Washington's place.

Every time I visited the Washington farm I went away determined to go home and do some work on our own house and yard. Or, more likely, call Randall to have Shiffley Construction come over and do the next batch of overdue repairs and improvement projects. Over the past two centuries the huge, rambling Washington farmhouse had obviously been expanded four or five times in as many styles by workers who cared more for comfort and sound construction than architectural consistency, but it was in perfect condition, freshly painted, and almost hidden by flowering plants. Pink and white azaleas, pink and white dogwoods, a profusion of roses and daffodils—somebody had a green thumb. As I stepped out of the Twinmobile I inhaled the strong, sweet scent of a nearby lilac.

I spotted Isaac Washington, the thirty-something grandson who'd taken over running the farm about the time the deacon turned eighty. Isaac was standing beside a large, bright green John Deere tractor, gazing thoughtfully into the open engine compartment with a wrench in his hand. His face broke into a smile when he spotted Cordelia and me getting out of the car.

"Meg! Ms. Cordelia!" He tucked his wrench into a toolbox at his feet and gave each of us a firm handshake. "I can't tell you how grateful I am that you're doing this for Grandpa. We went out a couple of times over the winter, but there weren't a whole lot of days when it was warm enough for him to be out there for very long. And now that it's warm, every time I offer to do it, he just tells me I've got too much to do around the farm."

"And I'm sure you do, to keep the place looking like this." Cordelia gazed around the farmyard with obvious appreciation and approval.

"Grandpa is in his cottage," Isaac said. "I can go fetch him."

"Let Horace and Meg do that," Cordelia said. "And you can talk to me while you work on your tractor. Talk to us," she corrected. Britni had apparently reconsidered her initial decision to stay in the car and was slowly approaching, eyes never leaving her feet, as if expecting to encounter cow pies or other unsavory obstacles. Clearly she'd formed her impressions of rural life at less meticulously maintained farms.

Horace and I let the Pomeranians out so they could greet the Washington dogs—two very mellow hounds who seemed amused rather than annoyed by our little fur balls. So we were still nearby when Cordelia introduced Britni to Isaac.

"Have you worked here for very long?" Britni asked, in a very sweet and condescending tone.

"The Washingtons have owned this farm since Reconstruction times," Cordelia said. "Eighteen sixty-seven or thereabouts."

"And worked it as enslaved persons for several generations before that," Isaac added. "We have a long history on this land."

His voice was proud rather than angry or confrontational, but Britni seemed to find his words unsettling.

"Oh! I see!" she said. "Uh . . . how nice."

Something about her tone of voice reminded me of Mavis Anstruther, a longtime member of the Caerphilly Garden Club who was one of Mother's particular bêtes noires. Mrs. Anstruther still didn't understand why the club kept vetoing her annual suggestion of having a southern plantation theme for its annual spring garden show.

What did Cordelia actually know about *Sweet Tea and Sassafras*? Had she ever seen the magazine? I knew I hadn't. What if its notion of southern lifestyle was full of genteel nostalgia about antebellum plantation life and the Lost Cause, complete with respectful articles praising Robert E. Lee and soft-focus watercolors of the Stars and Bars?

Horace had gone over to greet Isaac, so since I had a moment, I pulled out my notebook-that-tells-me-when-to-breathe. My hand paused over the page. "Find out more about *Sweet Tea and Sassafras*" was a little vague.

Aha! I wrote down "Call Ms. Ellie to ask what she knows about *Sweet Tea and Sassafras*." When in doubt, ask a librarian. Then I tucked my notebook away again, and Horace and I headed toward the deacon's cottage—which looked almost like a doll's house, tucked into the far end of the back garden.

"My great-grandfather built it around 1910," the deacon had once explained to me. "When he realized that sooner or later there'd be murder done if his wife and his widowed mother kept trying to share the same kitchen." And now it was the perfect solution to the deacon's desire to be near the support he needed while maintaining as much privacy and independence as he wanted. Staying on the farm while making it clear that Isaac now held the reins. And seeing his four lively great-grandchildren as much as he wanted while having a quiet place to retreat to when his energy flagged.

He was sitting in a rocking chair on the cottage's tiny front porch but leaped up when he saw us.

"Meg! Horace! I'm all ready." He reached down to the floor beside his rocker, picked up a roll of paper, and turned to Horace. "I've been working on that map I told you about. Talking to some of the other old folks to see what they remember and trying to set it all down on the map."

He unrolled the paper and held it up. Clearly it had started life as one of the U.S. Geological Survey's detailed topographical maps—apparently of the southeast end of the county. But it was now covered over with scribbles and squiggles in different colors, representing buildings, roads, and farms, past and present. If you spent enough time studying it, you could get at least some idea of what that portion of Caerphilly County had looked like at various times in its history.

"This is amazing!" Horace exclaimed.

The two of them put their heads together over the map, and almost immediately lost me in their discussion of which back roads, logging roads, and hunting trails would get them closest to the area the deacon wanted us to search. Horace's work as a deputy had given him a knowledge of the county's present-day geography that almost matched the deacon's eighty-odd years of living and farming here. I left them to it and focused on appreciating the sights and sounds of the farm. Like a growing number of Caerphillians, Isaac had found that the best way to make a living as a small farmer in the twenty-first century was to target the thriving locavore and organic markets. His pasture-raised chickens and pigs seemed to be happily co-existing in the nearest field, and I could smell that he'd probably just spread a new layer of well-aged organic cow manure on his vegetable gardens.

According to Randall Shiffley, being able to appreciate the smell of a farm was the first step toward becoming a real local.

I couldn't help wondering if any of the NIMBYs would ever get to that point.

More likely they'd get fed up and leave. At least I hoped they would. Although so far, the Brownlows and Wally the Weird had lasted three whole years. And the Griswolds, the other most frequent callers on Caerphilly's complaint line, had been making our lives miserable for at least five years.

I resolutely shoved the NIMBYs out of my mind. I'd have to deal with them—but not just yet.

Horace and the deacon seemed to have reached agreement on our route.

"Meg, could you bring that?" the deacon asked, pointing at a large, old-fashioned picnic basket. "A few goodies in case we get a little peckish while we're out there in the woods."

From the size and weight of it, the basket probably contained the makings of a complete picnic lunch, and in quantities that would feed our whole expedition several times over. And since the deacon had never taken up cooking, I expected either his daughter-in-law or his granddaughter-in-law, Isaac's wife, had done the packing. They were both notably good cooks. Any doubts I had about enjoying our expedition disappeared.

So we ambled back to our vehicles, stashed the picnic basket in the cargo area of the Twinmobile, and headed south. Horace and the deacon led the way in the cruiser, and I trailed along behind them.

We followed country roads for a while, then took off onto a gravel road and finally a series of dirt roads that were little more than a pair of tire tracks that often disappeared into the grass, dirt, or—increasingly—mud.

That was the point when Britni tried to jump ship.

"This is much farther out of town than I was expecting." She looked anxious. In fact, she'd been looking increasingly anxious ever since we'd left town.

Cordelia and I exchanged glances.

"I'm sorry," Britni said. "This really isn't very useful for my article. Can you take me back to town now?"

"Sorry," Cordelia said. "But no, we can't. We really need to stick with Horace right now."

"But—"

"He's due back on duty in a few hours," Cordelia went on. "And he gave up part of his time off to do this. At this point, taking you back to town would waste a whole hour of the very limited time we have for this search."

"Then just drop me off someplace where I can get an Uber," Britni said. "I can— I'm not getting any cell phone service. How can I call an Uber if I can't get a signal?"

I was tempted to say that I wasn't even sure we had Ubers in Caerphilly, but I suspected saying this would not have a calming effect, so I bit my tongue.

"If you don't want to join our search, you can wait in the car," Cordelia said.

"Or we can have Horace radio dispatch," I suggested. "Maybe one of the deputies on duty can come to pick you up."

Britni stopped complaining at that point, but I could see her eyeing our surroundings with unease. Sometimes we traveled through fields, but more often we wended our way through the woods. Horace finally came to a stop in a small clearing. I parked beside him, and we all hopped out.

"Are we still in Caerphilly County?" Cordelia asked.

"Just barely," Horace said. "Well, we haven't got all day. Let's get to work!"

Chapter 5

We let the dogs out, allowing them to sniff and answer any calls of nature. Then we set off. Horace and Deacon Washington led the way. Cordelia and I followed, each holding the leashes of a pair of Pomeranians. Every so often Horace and the deacon would stop and study the well-annotated map, and then steer us off in what they'd decided was the right direction. I had my suspicions that Horace might be stopping a little more often than was absolutely necessary to keep us on course, to give Cordelia and the deacon plenty of time to catch their breaths. But if that was his idea, he was very subtle about it. Cordelia sometimes used our map-and-rest stops to get in a little bird-watching, and the Poms were always happy to have enough time to stop and smell every square inch of the surrounding scenery. I relaxed, and breathed the fresh, pine-scented air. This was almost as soothing as the hammock.

The only person not enjoying our expedition was Britni. I was a little surprised that she decided to accompany us into the woods after all. And she seemed fine at first. Her anxiety seemed to have eased, and she didn't seem overly tired. She was bringing up the rear, but that was mainly because she was picking her way carefully, to avoid getting her elegant shoes messy.

She started off wearing the sort of polite expression that didn't do much to hide the fact that she was bored. Bored and maybe still just a little bit nervous.

But the farther we went, the more nervous she got. Maybe she'd been traumatized in childhood by someone's overdramatic retelling of *Little Red Riding Hood*. She kept glancing around and frowning, as if expecting the Big Bad Wolf to jump out from behind every tree.

Eventually she began trying to quibble with the path we were taking.

"Why don't we try looking over that way?" she suggested, pointing to her left, in almost the opposite direction from the one Horace and the deacon had chosen.

"That's pretty much the direction we just came from," Horace said.

"We've gone so far already," she said. "Maybe we've overshot this graveyard of yours. Besides, the way you're going is downhill. It's already getting pretty muddy around here. The farther we go in that direction, the muddier it's going to get. That way looks a lot drier."

"We're not looking for the most delightful path," Cordelia said. "We're looking for the graveyard."

"But it wouldn't be in the middle of a swamp, would it?" Britni's voice no longer sounded bored. Querulous, with just an edge of panic. Did she have a phobia about swamps?

"I don't think we're going to run into any actual swamp," the deacon said. "Not here in Caerphilly County. And if the ground gets a little marshy—well, if you ask me that's just the kind of ground they'd have put it on. If a piece of land was good, well-drained, fertile land, they'd have been farming it, back then, not burying Black folks in it. We're looking for someplace people would have considered wasteland. Useless land. Too marshy or too steep or too rocky to farm."

"And didn't the old-timers call it the Muddy Hollow grave-yard?" Cordelia asked.

The deacon nodded, as if to say, "I rest my case."

"Let's keep going this way a little longer." Cordelia pointed in the direction Britni objected to. "I have a good feeling about it. Deacon, didn't you say the old church was by a creek? Give a listen."

We all stopped, and I, for one, held my breath. Was that the sound of running water, off in the distance? Or was I only imagining it because Cordelia suggested it?

After a minute or so of listening, Horace and the deacon exchanged nods and set off again. Downhill.

Britni was right about the path we were following getting muddier. I half expected her to pipe up to say, "I told you so!" But so far she'd confined her commentary to the occasional heavy sigh, designed to communicate that she was exercising almost superhuman patience. I made sure to glance back often enough that I'd notice if we were leaving her behind, and the rest of our party just ignored her.

Maybe I was starting to see why my grandmother had brought Britni down to Caerphilly. Cordelia didn't suffer fools gladly and was probably already getting impatient with her interviewer. Having her family around would help. We'd buffer her against Britni's annoyingness.

Or maybe we'd just help her keep her temper and avoid lashing out at someone she hoped would write a positive article about her. Or, more to the point, about her beloved Biscuit Mountain Craft Center. I suspected that was the only reason Cordelia was putting up with Britni.

After a while, Horace called another halt.

"We're in the general area where we might want to start searching," he said. "Why don't we let the dogs get used to being in the lead?"

So Cordelia and I forged ahead, each with a brace of dogs. After a little while, the dogs seemed to be getting excited. If they were fully trained cadaver dogs and Horace had already given them the command to indicate they were working, that might be a good sign. A sign that they had detected the hidden grave-yard. But since they were only partly trained, and Horace hadn't ordered them into working mode, there could be any number of reasons for their excitement. We could be approaching the graveyard. Or following the recent steps of a deer. Or nearing some delightfully smelly bit of carrion. They might even be excited because we were letting them choose our path.

They seemed to be leading us off to the left—away from the faint path Horace and the deacon had been following. Which meant the footing was just a little more treacherous, and we had to slow down, which the Poms found exasperating. But we followed their lead. And even over their excited yipping and pant-ing, I could tell that the sounds of running water were definitely not my imagination. They were leading us toward a stream. That was a good sign, wasn't it?

After a few more minutes we stepped into a clearing. At its far edge we saw the silvery glint of sunlight reflecting off the water of a small stream. The clearing looked as if it might be a little soggy. A couple of low places held small puddles of water. A thick layer of leaves and leaf mold covered most of the ground, deep enough that you could only barely make out bumps that were probably small tree stumps.

The dogs were still pulling, but we halted them. Horace took Watson's lead from Cordelia and told him to sit. All four Pomer-anians instantly obeyed and gazed up at him eagerly. To them, scent work was a glorious game, and Horace had just given the signal that they were about to play it.

Cordelia turned over Winnie, her remaining charge, to me, and began brushing the leaf mold off the nearest stump.

It wasn't a stump. It was a jagged lump of stone, stuck into the ground in a way that seemed more indicative of human purpose than an accident of nature.

"This could be a headstone," she said.

"It's just a big rock." Britni was mincing along, trying to find the driest path.

"It's a fieldstone," the deacon said. "In slavery times, like as not, that was all they had to mark a grave with. If we look close, we might find a trace of carving on it. But even without any carving, it's a headstone, all right. Looks as if there're several of them."

He gestured at the rest of the clearing, indicating the several lumps covered with leaf mold or vines that I'd assumed were stumps.

"And look!" Cordelia pointed in another direction. Following her finger, I spotted two small clumps of orange daylilies.

"Ditch lilies," the deacon almost whispered. "Graveyard lilies."

We all gazed around for a few minutes, spellbound by the peace and beauty of the clearing. It was a little eerie to think that perhaps, over a hundred years ago, there had been a church nearby—that there still might be ruins to be found. Not to mention the graves of dozens of its congregation. The clearing had a strange air—not so much haunted as . . . still inhabited.

Of course the mood couldn't last. And of course it was Britni who broke it.

"The flowers couldn't be, like, just growing wild?" she asked.

"They're not native," Cordelia said. "They tend to naturalize after being planted somewhere. And here in the South, they're most often planted in graveyards."

Then one of the Poms whined softly, and we got busy. Horace gave Watson an encouraging pat. Cordelia took back Widget's lead. I kept Willie's and let the deacon take Winnie, the gentlest of the Poms.

"I see *dead people*," Horace said. Britni looked at him oddly, but those were the words Horace was training Watson to recognize as the command to start looking for graves or bodies. All four dogs began sniffing industriously.

And almost instantly all four of them began pulling to the right of the path we'd entered on—away from the stream, and into a slightly denser area of woods.

"I hope they're not after a deer," Horace muttered. "They're still in training, you know." But he let Watson have his head and followed.

Watson, sniffing busily, was trotting along in a straight line, occasionally going through—or under—a thicket or bramble patch, which was hard on Horace, but easier for the rest of us, since we could take advantage of the trail he was blazing. That was one of the few disadvantages of having such small dogs for scent work, I mused. They could get through spaces much too small for humans. Would a larger dog—a German shepherd, for example—just plow through and make a trail for his handler? Or would he go around obstacles like brambles?

The other dogs were definitely on the trail of something, too, alternately snuffling the ground and lifting their noses to sniff the air.

Then Watson barked once in a curiously authoritative tone.

"Oh, damn," Horace exclaimed.

I was the closest to Horace and Watson, so I followed Willie through another thicket of brambles to emerge in another small clearing, eager to see what they'd found.

They'd found a dead body. A very recent one.

Chapter 6

"Everyone stop exactly where you are!" Horace shouted. "Don't come any closer!"

Behind us, the sounds of dogs and people crunching their way through the underbrush stopped.

"What's wrong?" Cordelia asked.

"Standing by," the deacon said.

"Is there some kind of danger?" Britni sounded on the edge of panic.

"No danger," I called back. "At least not if you stay where you are."

Not that she'd be in danger if she came closer, but I thought that would be more likely to keep her where she was.

Horace was staring at the body while petting Watson.

"Good boy!" He fumbled in his pants pocket to pull out a treat for Watson.

"This isn't exactly what we were hoping they'd find," I pointed out.

"No," Horace said. "But they did exactly what we were asking them to do—they found the nearest dead body. We need to reinforce that."

He handed me a treat, and I gave it to Willie, along with several hearty exclamations of "good boy!"

"A good thing they're so food motivated," Horace said—a little absently, since his eyes were on the corpse. "Makes training them easier."

I turned to study the body. Male, and either stocky or chubby. It was hard to tell, since he was lying facedown in a tangle of Virginia creeper. And it was equally hard to estimate his height. He had salt-and-pepper hair, shaggy rather than long. He was wearing jeans, hiking boots, and a long-sleeved pale green cotton shirt.

Anxiety flooded my mind as I remembered that Dad hadn't been able to find Edgar to help with his bees. That no one had seen Edgar in several days. I'd recognize Edgar's face, but I wasn't at all sure I'd know the back of his head. And I couldn't see anything about this body to prove it wasn't Edgar.

"Can you tell who it is?" I asked.

"Not yet."

"Shouldn't you be checking to make sure he's actually dead?"

"No." Horace shook his head and glanced back at me. "No need. Odor of decomp. And maggots. But even before I noticed either of those signs, Watson told me he was dead."

"Told you how?"

"By the way he reacted. If the guy had been merely injured, Watson would have run up to him, tail wagging, and started licking him. Watson didn't do that—he just sat down, barked once, and looked back and forth between me and the body until he was sure I'd seen it. All business. Whoever the guy is, he's dead, and probably has been for some time."

"Damn," I muttered. "What do you mean by 'some time'? Hours? Days? Weeks?"

"A day or so would be my best guess. Here." Horace handed me the end of Watson's lead. "Hang on to him. Break the news to the others. Keep them away for now. And see if you can get a signal to call nine-one-one. I'm going to start documenting the scene in case this isn't just a sad accident."

He had pulled a camera out of his pocket and was already taking pictures of the corpse and the surrounding clearing.

I retraced my steps—with difficulty, since both Willie and Watson would much rather have stayed to watch what Horace was up to. After I pushed through the brambles, I came out in a small clearing and found myself face-to-face with Cordelia. Evidently Horace's warning had found her about to tackle the thicket I'd just emerged from. Both she and Widget looked at me with impatient curiosity. The deacon was sitting on a fallen log, gently scratching Winnie's head. Britni was half crouched and standing on the balls of her feet, giving the impression that a single loud noise might send her fleeing into the woods, screaming her head off.

"Horace and Watson have found a dead body," I said.

Britni uttered a small yelp and swayed slightly on her feet. Then she seemed to recover. Or maybe—cynical thought— she'd thought better of fainting dramatically once she realized that no one would rush to catch her if she fell.

"What do you need us to do?" Cordelia said.

"For now, stay here. And take charge of Willie." I handed over the leash. "I think Horace wants as few people as possible near what could be a crime scene."

"A crime scene?" Britni's voice held a note of panic. "Does he think it's a murder?"

"He doesn't think anything yet," I said. "It's an unattended death. Probably an accident, but until we know for sure, he's treating it as a potential crime scene."

"Keep us posted," Cordelia said.

"You're in charge here," I said.

She smiled.

I returned to the clearing with the body, leading Watson and pulling out my cell phone as I went.

I only got one bar, but with luck I could get through. I dialed 911.

"What's your emergency, Meg?" Should I worry about how matter-of-fact Debbie Ann, our emergency dispatcher, was about seeing my cell phone number pop up?

"We've found a dead body in the woods," I said.

"A dead body where? You're breaking up."

"We're in the woods," I shouted. "Near—"

"In the what?"

Then the call dropped entirely.

Horace looked up from where he was taking photos, on the far side of the body.

"We might need for you to go back to civilization to make that nine-one-one call," he said. "Not to mention leading the chief and everybody back here."

"Maybe," I said. "Let me try something first."

I opened up an app that calculated GPS coordinates. It took a little longer than usual, but it eventually showed our latitude and longitude, down to about eight or nine numbers after the decimal point. I took a screenshot and pondered for a few moments. Texting took much less bandwidth than a call, but texting 911 didn't seem to be doable, and I didn't have a cell number for Debbie Ann. But I had Chief Burke's cell number. Hardly a day passed without my calling or texting him or his wife, Minerva, to coordinate the boys' social life.

"Can't get through to 911," I texted to him. "Let me know if you get this."

I heard the familiar *whoosh!* that signaled a departing text. A few seconds later a ding announced the chief's reply.

"What's wrong? And where are you?"

"I've got the chief on text," I said, as I typed in the GPS location. "Shall I tell him we have a suspicious death?"

"You can tell him we probably have a murder," Horace said.

"From this angle I can see that there's a gunshot wound smack dab in the middle of his forehead."

"Dead body," I typed. "Horace sees gunshot wound."

A few seconds passed. Then several texts appeared.

"Copy. Sending Vern to bring your father. Can Horace give directions on best route to your location?"

"Working on it," I typed.

"The chief wants directions," I said to Horace. "Can you help him? And would it help if I sent him some pictures of the deacon's map?"

"Yes, and yes, assuming the pictures would go through. But even if they didn't, seeing the map would help me give him directions, so yeah, take some pictures of the map." Horace began circling around, keeping his distance from the corpse. He took Watson's leash back from me, sat down on a large nearby rock, and began texting at lightning speed. Watson curled up at his feet and seemed to be settling down to keep an eye on the body he'd found.

I waded back through the brambles to where the rest of the party was waiting.

"What's going on?" Britni demanded.

"The dead body has a gunshot wound," I said.

"Oh God," she moaned. "There could be a killer on the loose."

"We have no idea if it's murder, suicide, or accident," I said. "But whatever happened, it's not that recent, so if there's a killer on the loose he's probably long gone from here. Horace is giving the chief directions so he and his officers can find their way here."

"And your father, of course," Cordelia said.

"Why would we need him?" Britni asked. "Does this murder have something to do with bees?"

"Of course not," Cordelia snapped. "Dr. Langslow is the local medical examiner."

But did it have something to do with bees? If the dead body was Edgar Bortnick, maybe it did.

Although if Edgar was dead, the NIMBYs would be the prime suspects. Almost the only suspects—Edgar was widely liked by nearly everyone else in the county. If one of the NIMBYs had done it, why here, though? I found it hard to imagine any of the NIMBYs finding their way out here. Most of them behaved as if they were leaving civilization when they ventured outside of Westlake.

I focused back on the problem at hand.

"Deacon, it might help if I took some pictures of your map," I said. "Horace could use them to help explain where we are. Can you show me?"

He did, and I took several close-ups.

"I figure we should all stay here until the chief arrives," I said. "In case he has questions."

Cordelia and Deacon Washington nodded. Britni shuddered slightly. I suspected that if she had any idea of where she was, she'd have found an excuse to leave already.

I returned to the clearing where the body lay. Horace was still seated on his rock, texting. I opened up the most useful map picture and held it up so Horace could look at it. Horace nodded his thanks and glanced back and forth between his phone and mine as he texted.

I realized that I was standing with my back to the body. I'd have thought that would be a good thing—it's not as if the dead guy was going to sneak up on me. But somehow it was unsettling, knowing it was behind me. I shifted so I could see it out of the corner of my eye if I wanted to.

"I suppose we have to leave him where he is until Dad has declared him dead and you've done your forensic work," I said.

Horace glanced up and nodded.

My curiosity got the better of my discretion.

"Do you have any idea who he is?" I asked.

Chapter 7

"Oh, sorry," Horace said. "I forgot you didn't get a good view of him. Pretty sure it's Mr. Inman."

"Wally the Weird?"

Horace nodded.

"Damn." Should I feel guilty that my first reaction was a sense of relief? That it wasn't Edgar or any of the other local residents I actually liked?

"Yeah." Horace's tone was flat. "This could be a tough one."

"Really? Why?"

"A lot of people disliked him." He nodded in Inman's direction. "The way he was always complaining about people and hassling them. Even his fellow NIMBYs weren't too fond of him. Then again, is any of that something you'd kill a man over? Punch him in the nose, maybe—but shoot him? Plus he hasn't been here all that long. In Caerphilly, I mean, not here in the woods."

"Only three years," I said. "Feels like longer."

"Yeah." Horace smiled.

"Time enough to make enemies," I said. "He had a positive knack for that."

"Of course. But what I meant was that he's lived someplace

else most of his life. A guy like Inman didn't start making enemies three years ago. He could have a lot of them from his old
life somewhere else. Could be one of them caught up with him.
That's going to be harder for the chief to investigate."

I nodded.

"Okay, thanks." He stood up and handed back my phone. I
took that as a signal that he'd finished using the map. "They're
on their way. Make sure the rest of our party all stick around at
least till the chief gets here. But keep them where they are. This
is obviously a crime scene."

"You think he was killed here?"

"Can't tell yet, but even if he was only dumped here, that
makes it a secondary crime scene."

"Roger." I made my way back through the bramble thicket to
the others.

Cordelia and the deacon were seated on the fallen tree,
studying his map. Britni was standing nearby. She was fidgeting,
occasionally starting to take a step and then stopping herself.
I suspected she'd chosen one of the driest spots she could find
and was trying to stay there.

They all looked up when I appeared.

"Nothing new," I said.

Cordelia and the deacon went back to their map studies.
Britni sighed and went back to picking at a place where a thread
had snagged on something and been pulled out of her otherwise still pristine linen pants.

I found my own spot on the fallen tree.

Suddenly the faint splashing noises of the stream grew louder.

"Someone's coming." Cordelia pointed toward it. "From that
way, not the way we came."

Her voice sounded a little tense. I could understand why.
If the chief and his forces were following Horace's directions
they'd come in the same way we had, wouldn't they? And for

that matter, it would take them a lot longer to get here. So who was this?

Something occurred to me. Horace had said we were still in Caerphilly County, but just barely. While still peering in the direction of the stream, I turned on my phone and pulled up one of the pictures I'd taken of Deacon Washington's maps. I hadn't noticed before—or, more accurately, hadn't paid much attention to the fact—but we were very close to the county line. On the other side of that line was Clay County. I sometimes joked that as a citizen of Caerphilly, I was honor-bound to dislike and distrust anything and everything from our benighted neighboring county. But it wasn't entirely a joke, and I couldn't help feeling that it wasn't exactly good news, having someone from Clay County show up at the murder scene.

Or would that be return to the murder scene?

"I'm going to let Horace know they're coming," I said to Cordelia in an undertone.

But just as I was turning to flounder through the brambles to the crime scene, one of the approaching figures shouted.

"Horace! Meg! That you?"

I recognized the voice of Vern Shiffley, Randall's cousin and Chief Burke's most senior deputy.

"Over here!" I shouted back.

I relaxed again, and so did Deacon Washington and Cordelia. Even Britni looked cheerful at these signs that we were back in touch with the outside world.

I pushed through the brambles to let Horace know about the new arrivals, then returned to greet them.

Vern was moving slowly. Slowly for him, since he had long legs and an easy, ground-covering stride. But the figure with him turned out to be Dad, who had shorter legs and wasn't as much at home in the woods. Vern was visibly trying not to leave Dad behind. And he was carrying Dad's black bag.

We all greeted them with enthusiasm.

"That was fast," I said when they reached our clearing. "You must have figured out a great shortcut."

"Oh, there's a real fast way to get here," Vern said. "Just across that little stream you can pick up a logging road. But the road mostly runs through Clay County, so I don't recommend it. Under ordinary circumstances, I wouldn't take it myself. Too much chance of running into some hotheaded local."

"I've never learned the back roads in Clay County," Deacon Washington said. "And I have no intention of trying."

"We'll go back the way we came," Cordelia said.

"But it's such a long walk." Britni wasn't quite pouting, but her tone suggested she wanted to. "And I don't want to have to wade through the stream." She pointed to Dad, who was wet to the knees.

"Oh, you don't have to wade," Dad said. "Not unless you want to. There are plenty of stepping stones—I just lost my balance."

"Don't worry, miss," Vern said. "We'll have a few vehicles coming and going that way. Once the chief gets here and has a chance to talk to everyone, we should be able to save you the long walk."

"Better a long walk than a short one through Clay County," the deacon muttered.

"Meg, why don't you show your dad where Horace and the body are," Vern suggested. "I'll start getting statements from these good folks."

He handed Dad his black bag—which only looked like an old-fashioned doctor's bag. It was actually a very modern medical kit, designed to help him deal with both emergencies and the dead bodies he encountered as the local medical examiner.

"This way." I led Dad through what was starting to become a reasonably pain-free path through the bramble thicket.

"Oh my." Dad stood for a few minutes, studying the body. Watson whined softly and wagged his tail. Dad went over and scratched the dog's head, rather absently, eyes still on the body. Then he seemed to snap to attention. He set down his black bag and reached into his pockets for gloves.

"How about if I take Watson back with his siblings?" I said. "And leave you two to get on with this."

I'd seen Dad doing his preliminary examination on a dead body before. I could watch if I had to, but I didn't want to.

"Good idea," Horace said. "Could you get word to the chief to have someone bring my forensic gear? Which is locked in my cruiser, of course. Normally that would mean it was handy—"

"The chief already sent Aida to collect your gear and bring it here," Dad said. "Do we have an ID on the deceased yet?"

"I was waiting for you before I dug into his pockets," Horace said to Dad as he handed me Watson's lead. "But it looks like Walter Inman."

"Poor man." Dad was pulling on his gloves. He was still studying the body with a thoughtful expression.

Watson and I left them to it.

Back in the other clearing, Vern was poring over Deacon Washington's map while the deacon explained how he'd happened to hit on this particular part of the woods for today's search.

"This wouldn't have happened if we'd gone the way I suggested," Britni said. "I *knew* this was a bad way to take."

I saw Cordelia open her mouth, then close it and purse her lips. Probably worried about offending the reporter. But I could see she was dying to say something.

No reason for me to keep my mouth shut.

"If we'd gone the way you suggested, we wouldn't have found what could still turn out to be the old cemetery," I said. "And it would have meant that the poor man's body would be lying out here for who knows how long. Maybe that doesn't matter to you, but he was someone we knew."

Both Vern and Deacon Washington raised their heads expectantly.

"Walter Inman," I said.

"Wally the . . . right," Vern said.

The deacon just nodded. He closed his eyes briefly, and I suspected he was saying a silent prayer for Wally the Weird.

"I can't wait to get back to the Inn and take a long hot bath," Britni said, almost to herself.

"The Caerphilly Inn? Nice," Vern said. As everyone in town knew, the Inn was elegant and relaxing and ruinously expensive.

"Oh, yes." She simpered. "*Sweet Tea and Sassafras* always takes good care of its content providers."

I nodded. I was just glad she hadn't come to town without booking a place to stay, as so many visitors did. The Inn was the only hotel in town, and both it and the several dozen bed-and-breakfasts in town were often booked months in advance. More than once we'd ended up sheltering people when there was no room at the Inn or no room in their budget for the Inn's room rate. Encouraging to know that at some point, Britni would leave us to go back to the Inn.

"I'm looking forward to spending time there." Was she reading my thoughts? "So much nicer than that ghastly place I was in last night."

"I did warn you," Cordelia said. "She was staying in Riverton, at the Ghillie Dhu," she added, to me.

"The place where the landlady believes she's also hosting fairies in those tiny thatched cottages in her backyard?" I asked. "And never met a Scottish plaid she didn't like?"

Cordelia nodded and rolled her eyes.

"It sounded so quaint on the website," Britni said. "And by the time I got there and realized how horrible it was, I couldn't find a vacancy anyplace else in town."

"You were welcome to stay with me," Cordelia said. "I did offer."

"I'd have loved to if it wasn't against company policy," she said. "But thank goodness we decided to continue the interview in Caerphilly." She smiled, closed her eyes, and seemed to retreat into herself. Perhaps thinking about the civilized delights awaiting her at the Inn would help her cope with the stress of our current situation.

Vern appeared to notice some noise and turned to stare in the direction of the stream. Was it just my imagination or did he seem unusually alert. Almost tense.

Did the Poms sense danger, or were they only picking up on Vern's body language? They were all stiffening and staring toward the stream. I found myself wishing we'd brought the rest of the dogs. Tinkerbell, Rob's Irish wolfhound, was better protection than an armed guard, and even Spike, the Small Evil One, could be surprisingly effective against evildoers.

Chapter 8

Then Vern visibly relaxed.

"Is something wrong?" the deacon asked. Clearly being this close to Clay County was making him uneasy.

"Just keeping my eyes open," Vern said. "Chief's here."

Now I could see the stout figure of Chief Burke hiking sturdily through the woods from the direction of the stream. He nodded when he came near.

"Please tell me I'm back in my own county," he said, sounding slightly irritated.

"You are," Vern said. "Near as I can tell that little creek's the boundary along this stretch of the county line."

"Good." The chief looked around as if puzzled by the lack of a body.

"Crime scene's over there." Vern gestured toward the bramble thicket that separated us from the body. "We're giving Horace and Dr. Langslow a wide berth so they can work the crime scene in peace. You want to join them, or at least take a gander?"

"Please."

Vern led the chief to the path through the briar patch and they disappeared.

"Does this mean we get to go home sometime this year?" Britni asked.

"Probably," I said. "Unless the chief thinks you might have useful information about the crime and wants to interview you first."

"Useful information?" She rolled her eyes. "What useful information could I possibly have? I don't even know whoever it is that got killed, and I have no idea where I am, and obviously I've never been here before in my entire life."

"And when the chief hears that, I'm sure he'll let you go." I found her lack of interest in the murder curious. Wouldn't most reporters get excited at being on the scene for the discovery of a homicide victim? Even if they were on some other beat, like sports or social news, the idea of getting a byline on a breaking news story tended to excite most journalists.

But then maybe she didn't consider herself a journalist. She'd called herself a content provider. Clearly a profession with different priorities.

The chief reappeared.

"Meg, I'd like to interview you first," he said. "Horace tells me the rest of your party haven't even seen the body, so I'm going to have Aida take them home. One of my deputies," he added, for Britni's benefit. "Her cruiser is just a little ways away from the far bank of that stream."

"Thank goodness," Britni exclaimed.

"Chief, I expect that will be fine for Ms. Colleton," Deacon Washington said. "But if it's all the same to you, I'd rather go out the way I came in."

"I'll go along with the deacon and keep him company," Cordelia said.

"I'm not walking back all that way." Britni didn't stamp her foot like a toddler, but I suspected she was tempted.

"Don't worry," the chief said. "You can ride out with Deputy Butler."

He gestured in the direction he'd come from, and I could see a tall figure in a khaki deputy's uniform striding toward us. My friend Aida. I wondered if it would make Britni feel safer if I mentioned that Aida was a star pupil in the martial arts classes we took together and had won medals in the statewide police marksmanship contests. No, probably best not even to suggest that her stellar self-defense skills might be needed.

Aida was carrying two heavy cases. When she got closer, I recognized them as part of Horace's forensic gear.

"Where do you want these?" she asked, looking around with obvious curiosity.

"Take them through there to Horace," the chief said, indicating the path through the thicket. "Get yourself a good look at the body while you're there, and then you can give Ms. Colleton a ride back to civilization."

She nodded and pushed through the thicket.

"Vern, why don't you see Ms. Cordelia and Deacon Washington back to where you parked," the chief said. "I'll have Aida meet you there. She can take them back to town with Ms. Colleton."

"Can do, Chief." Vern stood and gave the deacon a hand up.

"And the dogs?" Cordelia asked.

"I think they've earned their keep today," the chief said. "How about if you take them with you and drop them off at Meg's house."

Aida emerged from the shrubbery, and she and Britni headed toward the stream.

"I gather that unfortunate young woman didn't know you were planning to drag her out into the forest primeval today," the chief said, when Britni was out of sight. "Just who is she, anyway? One of your city cousins?"

"A reporter, doing a feature on Cordelia," I said.

"And ironically, she arranged to do her interviewing while I was here visiting the family," Cordelia added. "Since, as she put it, Caerphilly was so much closer to civilization."

"Let's hope today's experience doesn't discourage her from doing the feature," the chief said.

"Actually, I wouldn't be heartbroken if it did," Cordelia replied. "I don't really know much about the magazine she works for, and I'm starting to wonder if I should have checked it out first. Well, no time like the present." She, Vern, and the deacon set off to retrace our path from the cars, leading the excited dogs.

"I suspect Ms. Colleton will not be a particularly useful witness," the chief said. "Still, I'll need to interview her, if only to confirm that."

I nodded. I'd long ago noticed that when working a case, the chief had to worry not only about finding the culprit, but also about crossing his t's and dotting his i's so the culprit's defense attorney would have no opportunity to claim he'd overlooked other potential suspects.

"Tell me what happened," he said, taking out his notebook.

So I told him, from when Cordelia had recruited me to go along with the expedition to the point when Watson had given his official body-finding bark and Horace had shouted at us all to stay back.

"A bit of luck, having Horace find Mr. Inman," the chief said. "So often well-meaning civilians manage to contaminate a crime scene."

"It's definitely Inman, then?"

He nodded.

"Well, then I get to tick off one of the chores in my notebook." Noticing his surprised expression, I elaborated. "And no, bumping off Wally the Weird was not on my to-do list. Randall called this morning to tell me about the latest kerfuffle over in Westlake."

"Another manure complaint?"

"Another bee complaint," I corrected. "When I got back from this expedition, I was supposed to go over there to soothe the

Brownlows, and then find Wally and keep him from picking another fight with Edgar. I guess I still need to see the Brownlows, but at least Wally is taken care of."

"And won't be picking any more fights, poor soul."

"But I was also supposed to find Edgar and get his side of the story," I said. "And now I'm worried."

"About Edgar?"

"Dad's been looking for him since sometime yesterday," I explained. "Calling, texting, emailing, and even dropping by, with no luck."

"Which is actually not that unusual for Mr. Bortnick," the chief said. "He often disappears for weeks at a time."

"But not without getting someone to take care of his farm while he's gone," I said. "And you know what conclusion all the NIMBYs are going to jump to about his disappearing right now. They're going to claim he killed Wally and then went on the lam, and they'll all be lining up to testify about all the bitter arguments the two have had." I decided it would sound downright paranoid if I shared my worry that Edgar might also be a victim of whoever had shot Inman.

"You could have a point." The chief looked ever-so-slightly harried. "I can't really spare the bodies to do much of a search for Edgar right now—I need everyone I have to work this case. Not to mention the fact that only a couple of my deputies would really be very good at searching the woods. For now we'll just have to hope he turns up soon."

"Vern might be able to recruit some of his cousins to do a search," I suggested. "Some of them know the county's woods like the back of their hands."

"But how do we know he's even in the county?" the chief countered. "What if he's off taking pictures of bears in the Blue Ridge, or cypresses in the Dismal Swamp?"

"True," I said. "Although the only expedition Dad knew about was here in the county. Looking for an eagle's nest—the Shiff-leys might have noticed that."

"I'll get Randall to ask."

Just then Dad came galumphing through the briar patch. He didn't seem to have much luck sticking to the path and was starting to look as if he'd been dragged through the original trackless thicket several times.

"We might as well transport the body now," he said. "And I'll see how soon I can schedule the autopsy."

"I've already sent for transport," the chief said. "I assume if you'd managed to come up with a closer estimate on the time of death, you'd have told me already."

"Sorry!" Dad looked as if it pained him greatly to disappoint the chief. "At the moment, somewhere between twelve and thirty-six hours is as close as we can get. The body's still in full rigor, so it can't be much longer than that, or much less. Thank goodness Meg and her expedition found him when they did!"

He beamed at me as if I'd done something remarkable.

"The Pomeranians deserve the credit," I said.

"Normally we'd be able to get a tighter estimate from the in-sect predation," Dad went on. "Horace and I will be working on that, but there's a complication—let me show you."

Dad plunged back through the thicket. The chief followed and I tagged along. I wasn't all that keen to hear more about insect predation, but neither was I eager to be left alone in the woods near a murder scene.

The body was now lying faceup. A quick glance told me that it was, indeed, Walter Inman—and that I didn't want to take more than a quick glance. Inman had a bullet hole in the middle of his forehead, and Horace had reached the stage of his crime scene evidence collection where he was busily plucking entomo-logical evidence off the body. I averted my eyes and tried not to think about it.

"So what's the complication?" the chief asked.

"That!" Dad appeared to be pointing to a giant anthill.

"Ah." The chief thought for a moment. "How do the ants complicate your time of death calculations?"

"Just look at them!" Dad exclaimed. "They probably started collecting eggs and larvae from the body within an hour of Inman's death. And they're still hard at it."

Yes, I could see what looked at first like a slightly wobbly black line leading from the patch of Virginia creeper in which Inman had been lying to the anthill. Peering closer I could see that the line was made up of hundreds of ants, racing along in both directions as if following an invisible superhighway.

"It's a big colony," Horace said, his tone gloomy. "They could have hauled off enough eggs and larvae to have a significant effect on our time of death calculations."

The chief nodded and waved away some flying insect that had buzzed near his face.

"In theory, we could excavate the anthill," Dad suggested. "And inventory the eggs and larvae. . . ."

He trailed off when Horace shook his head.

"But I suppose that wouldn't be very practical." Dad sounded as if he'd been longing all his life to excavate an enormous anthill full of fly eggs.

"I doubt if this case will hinge too much on the precise time of death," the chief said. "Don't worry about it."

But from the expressions on their faces, clearly Horace and Dad were going to worry. I could already see them fretting. And Dad was probably going to repeat his suggestion of excavating the anthill.

"Do either of you have any idea where Edgar Bortnick has gone?" the chief asked. "Meg's worried about him. For that matter, so am I."

"He told me he was investigating a possible golden eagle sighting," Dad said. "Of course, it will probably turn out to be an immature bald eagle. They're hard to tell apart, and we don't often get the golden eagle here in Virginia. Although—"

"Where was the sighting?" the chief asked. "Here in Caerphilly County?"

"I think so." Dad frowned in thought. "He mentioned that he was going to drop by to check on the hives he has at our cousin Festus's farm on the way to look for the eagle's nest, and I doubt he'd be doing that if he had a very long drive to wherever the eagles were."

"Why not check on his social media?" Horace said. "He's always posting what he's up to."

"Edgar's on social media?" I asked.

"Oh, yes." Dad pulled out his phone. "Why didn't I think of that? He's bound to have posted some photos there of whatever he's doing."

"Even when he's out in the middle of the woods?"

"Well, not always from the woods," Dad said. "Sometimes he has to wait till he gets back to someplace that's got cell phone service. I suppose that's what we'll have to do to check on him. I'm not getting any signal here."

The chief, Horace, and I also pulled out our cell phones, but unsurprisingly none of us could get a signal, either.

"I had signal when I left my car," the chief said. "And then I lost it when I went into the woods after crossing the stream. Maybe we could pick up a signal back there."

Which is how Dad, the chief, and I ended up standing on several large, flattish rocks in the middle of the little stream, waving our cell phones in the air. If, as the chief suspected, denizens of Clay County were watching us from places of concealment, they must have had a good laugh at our expense. Or maybe gotten a little paranoid, wondering what we were up to in the middle of the stream. But we were, just barely, able to get enough signal there to inspect Edgar's social media—although we didn't have enough bandwidth to see the actual photos, only the captions.

"Aha!" Dad exclaimed, pointing to Edgar's most recent caption. "As I expected. Immature bald eagles. And I'm sure he's right. Edgar's very sound on raptor identification."

"Posted yesterday afternoon at five fourteen," the chief mused. "And you haven't been able to reach him today."

Dad shook his head. I wondered if the chief was thinking the same thing I was—that knowing Edgar had posted a picture from somewhere eighteen hours ago did nothing either to reassure us that he was alive or to eliminate him as a suspect for Inman's murder.

"I find it hard to imagine Mr. Bortnick as a prime suspect in this case," the chief said, as if reading my thoughts. "But I have to consider the possibility. On the positive side, considering him as a suspect almost certainly gives me scope for taking what steps I can to locate him. We can get his cell phone records. See where he posted this from, and when and where his phone last pinged a cell tower." The chief began typing on his phone— probably texting one of his deputies to start drawing up a warrant for Edgar's phone data.

"And maybe Vern or one of his cousins would recognize where the picture was taken," Dad suggested.

"We don't need the Shiffleys for that," I said. "We've got Kevin."

"He doesn't exactly spend much time in the woods," Dad pointed out.

No, Kevin, my tech-savvy nephew, was probably as unfamiliar with the great outdoors as Britni. Although to his credit, when we occasionally evicted him from his computer-infested lair in our basement for things like picnics or cross-country skiing trips, he joined in with good humor, or at least an absence of whining and sighing.

"Edgar's pictures are digital, right?" I asked. "Which means that the picture file also includes the date, time, and location. Let's get Kevin to go onto Edgar's social media and see if he can figure out where Edgar is. Or was the last time he was heard from."

"Good idea," the chief said.

He and I both texted furiously for a few minutes—he to someone back at the station about the warrant, while I sicced Kevin on the digital photos.

Predictably, Kevin protested at first that he was swamped with work—and yes, as a senior programmer and department head at Mutant Wizards, Rob's software company, he did have a lot on his plate. But as soon as I explained that the photos might be connected with a murder, he managed to overcome his scruples about shirking his job responsibilities and agreed to inspect Edgar's photos.

"Thanks," I typed. "Because I have this nagging feeling Edgar is in some kind of danger. I know that sounds like superstitious nonsense."

"No," he texted back. "Sounds like maybe your subconscious could be adding up clues faster than your conscious. Don't worry—we'll find him."

"I hope so," I muttered as I tucked my phone back in my pocket.

Chapter 9

"I'm going to head back to the station soon," the chief said when he'd finished his own texting. "Meg, I can drop you off at your vehicle if you'd like."

"If it's not too much trouble, I'd appreciate it," I replied.

"No trouble at all. I need to go there anyway, to drop off Horace and his evidence bags. Let's go see if he needs any help carrying it all."

"Any idea when the ambulance will be here to collect Mr. Inman?" Dad asked, as we headed back to the crime scene.

"Actually, it will be the funeral home's vehicle," the chief said. "No sense tying up the ambulance for someone this long dead. And they should be here anytime now. You'll go back with it, I assume?"

"Of course. And I'll let you know when I can arrange the postmortem."

"Good," the chief said. "And here comes Vern. He's going to keep watch over the crime scene for a bit, until Horace is sure he's collected everything we're likely to need."

We made our way single file on what was rapidly becoming a well-worn path through the shrubbery. Horace had filled a remarkable number of evidence bags. We were divvying them up and trying to figure out if we'd have to make two trips when Vern stuck his head into the clearing.

"Maudie's here for the body," he said. "She could use some help with the stretcher."

Dad, Vern, and Horace each took an armload of evidence bags and trotted out to meet Maudie, manager of her family's funeral home, leaving the chief and me to watch over the crime scene and the rest of the evidence. The chief was gazing around the clearing, but I wasn't sure if he was studying his surroundings or just letting his eyes rove while he thought.

"It's weird, don't you think?" I said. "The body being dumped out here, right next to what might turn out to be the old graveyard?"

"It wasn't just dumped here," he said. "According to Horace and your dad, he was killed here."

"Ah. But still a weird coincidence, don't you think? That he was killed here, right next to the graveyard?"

"Probably a coincidence he was killed by the graveyard." The chief glanced around as if looking to make sure there wasn't anyone eavesdropping. "Not all that surprising to find someone killed in this particular stretch of the woods."

"Because of how close it is to Clay County?"

"Because of how close it is to a spot people in Clay County use for selling dope and conducting other illicit activities that they'd rather not be caught doing." His jaw tightened at the thought. "Which would be Clay County's problem, except that we're more and more seeing folks from Caerphilly coming out here for the same reasons."

"To buy drugs?"

"Sometimes," he said. "We've always had a little bit of that. But lately it's mostly underage kids coming out here to buy moonshine. A few from Caerphilly High, and a whole lot more from the college. There's been a real uptick in that lately, and we haven't had much success shutting it down. We can't really do anything across the county line without cooperation from the Clay County deputies, and it's not as if they're going to do anything about it."

"Given that the moonshiners are probably cousins of theirs."

"Not to mention all the bribe money that's probably changing hands." The chief looked thunderous. "Those . . . clowns are the kind that give law enforcement a bad name. It might even be Clay County officers who run lookout for the dealers and moonshiners. All I know is, if my officers spot someone they think might be crossing the county line with the intention of purchasing something they shouldn't be purchasing, it's no use trying to stake out the road to catch them when they're back on our turf. They always seem to find out we're there and they take another route home. They're being warned."

"Frustrating," I said.

"We don't have a big drug problem here," he said. "But what we have, you can mostly blame on Clay County. And remember that incident last fall when three students from the college showed up at the emergency room with what turned out to be methanol poisoning?"

"From Clay County moonshine?"

"They'd definitely been drinking moonshine," he said. "And we could never prove it, but the odds are they bought it just across the stream there, or in one or two other places like it in Clay County. So I'm not the least bit surprised to find a dead body in these parts. A little surprised it's a gunshot instead of an OD. And a whole lot surprised it's Walter Inman. I wouldn't have taken him for a drug user. And moonshine? The man used to turn up his nose at the wine selection available in the fancier local restaurants."

"Maybe he wanted to buy some moonshine as a kind of joke," I suggested. "To provide a unique taste sensation for some of his out-of-town guests. I can hear him now. 'Look! Authentic back-woods hillbilly moonshine!'" I did my best imitation of Wally the Weird's high, nasal, overly precise voice. I'd heard it often enough while dealing with the NIMBYs.

"I can actually see that." The chief chuckled softly. "You think he'd serve it in champagne flutes or shot glasses?"

"Antique sake cups."

"Yes." He gave a snort of laughter. "He was a bit of a fish out of water here in Caerphilly, and a thorn in all our sides sometimes, but there was no real harm in him."

"So you say, but then how'd he manage to get himself killed out here near one of Clay County's better-known drug and moonshine markets? And maybe I'm off base, but isn't it more usual for drug dealers and moonshine sellers to keep shifting around where they do their dealing? Keep the authorities guessing?"

"Under normal circumstances, yes. But when the authorities themselves might be involved, or at least tolerant of what the moonshiners are doing . . ."

Vern reappeared.

"Body's on its way to town," he said. "What's that you were saying about moonshiners?"

"We were discussing the incongruity of Mr. Inman being killed in such close proximity to a location largely associated with the illegal sales of drugs and moonshine," the chief said as we began picking up the rest of the evidence bags.

"Good point." Vern shook his head. "How'd he even know it was there? I mean, Meg, you didn't know about it, right?"

I shook my head.

"And you're local. Just not plugged into the college kids' grapevine. Same with Inman. Not only would it be weird for him to know about it, I can't think of any reason why he would want to."

"Meg and I were speculating that perhaps he wanted to serve it to some of his party guests," the chief said.

"Still wouldn't explain how he found out about this place."

"The same way I would if I wanted to buy some moonshine," I said.

They both looked at me curiously.

"I'd ask someone I'd expect to know," I continued. "In my case, probably one of you two. Or Horace or Aida. I'd ask a cop. Someone who could steer me away from anything either unsafe or illegal."

"Smart," the chief said.

"Making moonshine is legal these days, you know," Vern pointed out.

"Legal, but controlled," the chief added. "Like most everything connected to alcohol."

"True," Vern said. "In Virginia you need a permit to even own a still, and a distillery license to use it. By the time you get to that point you're already out a few hundred dollars and you better not even think about selling the stuff unless you've dealt with all the federal fees and permits and taxes. If you ever do want some moonshine, just drop a word to Randall or me. Couple of our cousins are doing it—just as a hobby, for family consumption, and they haven't poisoned any of us yet. Their stuff is good enough to sell, but they decided it wasn't worth the red tape to go into the business. Over in Clay County, they just ignore the red tape."

"I'll keep it in mind," I said.

"So the chief will probably have us asking around to see if Inman's been looking for a moonshine connection." Vern glanced at his boss, who nodded.

"I can think of another way he might have found his way out here," I said. "Knowing Inman. He was always reporting people, usually for minor things like not cutting the grass as often as he did or leaving their trash cans at the curb too long."

"And he has yet to realize that it's not our job to enforce his homeowners' association rules," the chief said.

"And I guess now he never will realize it," I added.

"That stolen car report a couple of months ago wasn't minor,"

Vern said. "'Course, I guess you could say his heart was in the right place."

I remembered the incident. Inman had called in to report that he'd seen someone steal one of the Griswolds' several cars. When one of Vern's fellow deputies tried to stop the car to check, the driver fled, leading to a dramatic cross-county police chase and the arrest of seventeen-year-old Shane Griswold—not for stealing the car, which he had his parents' permission to drive, but for possession of the cocaine found in the glove compartment.

"That's exactly what I was thinking about," I said. "What if Wally the Weird now fancies himself a hotshot vigilante anti-drug crusader? What if he thought he'd found another neighborhood teen on his way to buy drugs and followed them out here to get the goods on them?"

The chief nodded.

"I can see it happening." Vern shook his head. "And even if the kid wasn't dangerous, the drug dealer might be. Then again, I bet we're going to take a close look at the Griswolds. They might still hold a powerful grudge against Wally."

"Do they ever." I sighed. "They want to put up a spite fence."

"The Griswolds?" Vern's mouth twitched as if he found this amusing.

"Yeah," I said. "Eight-foot solid wood fence. About five minutes after they filed the building permit, they got a registered letter from the Westlake homeowners' association. Wally the Weird's doing. They need their neighbors' permission to put up anything taller than a six-foot fence, and Wally's not going for it. Claims it would block the light to his yard and reduce the value of his property. I got dragged in to help mediate."

"How'd it turn out?" Vern asked.

"It hasn't," I said. "Still dragging on."

"Figures." He grimaced. "They've been calling nine-one-one

on each other pretty regularly. Those two and the Brownlows. I've been telling the chief we should charge all of them with abuse of it."

"Is that a crime?" I asked.

"Yes, ma'am." Vern was known for having memorized large portions of Virginia's penal code. "A class one misdemeanor, punishable by up to a year in jail or a twenty-five-hundred-dollar fine or both."

"I like the sound of that," I said.

"I'm not rejecting the idea completely," the chief said. "But I think we should wait until we have a blatant and completely unassailable case."

"Yup," Vern said. "So believe me, I'm watching out for one."

We fell silent for a minute or so.

"You think any of this gives any of them a motive to bump off Wally?" I asked.

The chief shrugged as if unwilling to speculate.

"Not a single thing he's done sounds like a rational motive to me." Vern sounded tired. "But it adds up to all of them being pretty fed up with each other. Maybe fed up to the point that one more thing would make them snap. I can see that happening. Maybe it's selfish of me, but if one of them did snap, I'm just glad it was Wally they went after. Could have been my cousin Sam. He's done a few rounds with them. Or any of Sam's neighbors."

"Like Edgar Bortnick," I said.

"Like him, yes," Vern said. "I've already spread the word for everyone in the family to keep their eyes out for him. And Chief, I bet you're going to want us to look into those allegations Inman made about the library."

The chief frowned and nodded.

"Allegations about the library?" I echoed. "The Caerphilly Library?"

"Mr. Inman was under the impression that it was a hotbed of

drug-related activity," the chief explained. "Not a venue for drug use, of course, but the place where dealers sold their wares."

"With Ms. Ellie in charge?" I said. "I'd like to see the dealer who dared."

Vern chuckled at that.

"Yeah," he said. "Always a lot of teens hanging out at the library. Inman seemed to think all teens were automatically suspicious characters."

"I admit, I regarded his ideas about the library with a great deal of skepticism." The chief sighed. "Now I wish I'd tried harder to make him tell me what in blazes gave him that idea."

"Kind of a weird coincidence that he got a bee in his bonnet about discovering what sounds to me like a pretty implausible drug mart," I said. "And then gets himself killed near a real one."

"Possibly not a coincidence at all," the chief said. "Let's get the rest of these evidence bags to the car. Horace is waiting for us."

The chief and I managed to pick up and carry the rest of the bags. Actually, we mostly held out our arms and let Vern pile the evidence bags into them.

"I won't make you stay out here too much longer," the chief said to Vern. "But keep your eyes open while you're here."

Vern nodded.

The chief and I began hiking back to the stream.

Chapter 10

"Were you still planning to visit the Griswolds today?" the chief asked as we approached the stream. "Or was it the Brownlows?"

"I usually end up having to deal with both of them when I go over there," I said. "And Mr. Inman, though obviously that won't be a feature of my visits to Westlake anymore. You want me to hold off going there until the news about his murder is out?"

He pondered that.

"I'm probably going to send Horace over to secure Mr. Inman's house and begin examining it for evidence," he said finally. "And I'd rather not send him there alone, but we're going to be dreadfully shorthanded. If you were planning to go over there anyway in your role as Randall's emissary, perhaps you could coordinate your schedule with Horace. Use your diplomatic skills on the neighbors. He'll be there to work a murder case, not answer questions or hear people's complaints about the height of their neighbors' lawns."

"Run interference so he can do his job," I said. "Can do."

"And of course, if you notice anything of interest, I can rely on you to bring it to Horace's attention," he added. "Or mine. And while he's over there in that part of the county, I'll have him do a welfare check on Mr. Bortnick. Be embarrassing if we sent a whole bunch of Shiffleys scouring the woods for him, only to find he was tucked up in bed with a bad cold. Or lying on his basement floor with a broken leg."

My mind added "Or lying dead on his floor with a wound from the same gun that had killed Wally the Weird," but I decided that was way too melodramatic to say aloud. Why had the thought even occurred to me? A reaction to finding a dead body, I assumed.

"I think Dad has a key to his house," I said instead. "He keeps an eye on the place when Edgar is away, remember. Would that make Horace's welfare check easier?"

"Much easier," the chief said. "Good thought. You can help with that, too. If Randall had anything else in mind for you to do today, tell him I'm borrowing you."

We'd reached the little stream and began carefully crossing it. There were enough reasonably large, flat rocks to make crossing possible, but there wasn't a single obvious safe path, so crossing with our arms full of evidence bags required paying attention. Horace waited on the far side and was visibly relieved when we both reached dry land without dropping any of the bags in the stream. He hovered protectively over us as we stowed them all in the trunk of the chief's sedan. The trunk and much of the back seat.

"I'll be happy when we get all this safely back to the station." Horace looked up and glared at something. "And happy to leave this place. Getting tired of being spied on."

I glanced around. On the Caerphilly side of the stream the woods came right down to the edge of the water, but on the Clay County side there was a reasonably large open area—nothing but grass, weeds, tree saplings, and, in the distance, a vine-covered mound that could be the remains of an old tobacco barn. Or maybe even the remains of a house. The clearing was the right size to have held a house and garden and maybe even a small pasture.

I couldn't see any watchers. But the woods loomed up around the clearing, and there were plenty of places for watchers to hide.

Just then I saw a small flash of light from the edge of the woods.

"See that?" Horace said. "Reflection of someone's binoculars."

"Careless of them," I said.

"I suspect it's deliberate," the chief said. "Let's get moving."

I climbed into the back seat of the chief's sedan, beside the stack of Horace's evidence bags, and Horace handed in a few more bags for me to hold in my lap.

"Just until we get to my cruiser," he said.

On our way back to where Horace and I were parked, the chief briefed Horace on his mission to search Mr. Inman's house and check on Edgar.

"And while I'm there, I'll see if I can find out any information about his next of kin," Horace said.

"Maudie doesn't know?" The chief sounded surprised. "Didn't she handle the arrangements when his wife died last year?"

"She did," Horace said. "According to her, there were a couple of grown kids, but they didn't come. Or maybe weren't even invited. Inman didn't want any services. Just had his wife cremated and picked up the ashes a few days later."

The chief shook his head as if baffled. I could understand why. A few weeks ago we'd all been to the funeral of an elderly member of the New Life Baptist Church, where the chief's wife, Minerva, had led the choir and congregation in at least half a dozen rousing hymns and the Reverend Wilson had preached an hour-long combined sermon and eulogy that had everyone alternately laughing and weeping. "A proper send-off," Michael had said. I felt more than a little sorry for Mr. Inman's frail, wheelchair-bound wife. No proper send-off. And she'd been— well, one of the nicest Westlake residents was probably a bit of an exaggeration. But a solid contender for the least annoying.

When we arrived at the back road where we'd parked—it felt

like at least a week ago—we managed to fit all of Horace's evidence bags into his cruiser. As we were finishing up, my phone dinged. I glanced down to see who'd texted me.

"Kevin figured out where Edgar's last pictures were taken," I said.

"Here in Caerphilly?" the chief asked.

"Yes," I said. "And northwest of town." Almost the opposite end of the county from where we were now, and as far as you could get from Clay County.

"Makes sense," Horace said. "Festus's farm is out that way, and your dad did say Edgar was planning to drop by to check on the hives he has there before looking for the eagles."

"According to Kevin, Edgar posted a dozen pictures yesterday afternoon." I was continuing to read my nephew's texts. "The eagle picture was the last one, and he posted it shortly after he took it, so even if he was in the woods, he was in a part of it that got cell phone signal. But he hasn't posted anything since that eagle photo at five fourteen yesterday afternoon."

Horace and the chief both looked grave.

"Kevin points out that he rarely posts anything but wildlife photos," I added. "And often goes for days without posting. Though he hasn't yet figured out if the silences happen because Edgar's not finding anything interesting to photograph or because he's out in the middle of nowhere with no signal."

"If we took a couple of the Poms out to the location of that last photo, we might be able to track him," Horace suggested.

"I appreciate the enthusiasm," the chief said. "But isn't it a little premature to start searching for Edgar with cadaver dogs?"

"They're not all turning out to be cadaver dog material," Horace said. "Watson and Willie are pretty good at it, but Winnie is much more interested in finding live people."

"I'm sure it will do Rose Noire's heart good to know that her dog chooses life," I said. "What about Widget? What's his talent?"

"I don't think we've really found Widget's talent yet," Horace admitted. "So far he mostly finds squirrels and deer droppings. But Winnie shows definite signs that she could do search-and-rescue work, and so does Whatever."

Aida, his fellow deputy, had adopted Whatever, and would doubtless be proud to hear that her pup was showing such a useful forensic talent. Although I wasn't sure how Pomeranians could be expected to perform the rescue part of search and rescue. Then again, I supposed even larger SAR dogs concentrated on the searching part and left their handlers to organize the rescuing.

"Go and do the welfare check on Mr. Bortnick's house first," the chief said. "If you don't find him there, you can borrow something of his to give the dogs his scent. But I'm thinking we should have you process Mr. Inman's house, or at least seal it before you go wandering out into the wilderness."

"Seal it, for sure," Horace said. "Probably better to process it after we have some idea what you might want me to be looking for."

"True," the chief said. "Then I'll go over and do a cursory examination. Put seals on the doors. Break the news to the neighbors. Observe their reactions."

I felt a sense of relief. While I was curious to see how the Griswolds and Brownlows reacted to the news of Inman's death, I had no desire to be the one to break it to them. Horace's face suggested that he felt the same.

"And I can take that nephew of Randall's with me," the chief went on. "The one who's doing that summer internship with us so he can see if he wants to major in criminal justice when he goes up to Tech this fall. What's his name—Brady? Brandon?"

"Braden," Horace said. "Nice kid."

"Braden, Braden," the chief said. "I'll get it soon. Anyway, I'll leave him there to keep an eye on the place. With orders to call nine-one-one if anyone does try to get in—no vigilante heroics.

So if Edgar's not at his house, then yes, see if you can find him out in the woods."

Looking happier to have sorted this out, he got back in his sedan and drove off.

"Does the chief really want Braden guarding Inman's house?" I asked. "Seeing that there's still a killer at large, couldn't that be dangerous?"

"Not really," Horace said. "Last week we had Braden guard a stolen car out by the zoo until I could get there to process it. The chief mentioned it to Randall, and you've never seen so many Shiffleys driving up and down that road the whole time he was out there. So by sending Braden, the chief's basically deploying the entire Shiffley clan to guard the place."

"That's good." It occurred to me that having so many Shiffleys in trucks cruising up and down the streets of Westlake would also greatly annoy the residents. A plus in my book. "And come to think of it, I expect most of the houses in Westlake have security systems with cameras, so Braden will be doubly watched over. What's next?"

"I've got to take the evidence down to the station and start logging it all in. How about if you get the key from your dad. I'll ask Aida if we can borrow her pup, and you can bring her and Winnie down to the station. And Watson, too, of course. He won't be much use for the search part, but he'll enjoy the outing."

"Works for me." I was delighted that helping Horace might give me yet another reason to postpone tackling the NIMBYs, at least until tomorrow. Curious that the notion of visiting Westlake sounded so much worse than an undetermined number of hours spent hiking through the muddy woods, dodging ticks, snakes, and spiders. "Will that give you enough time to log in all the evidence?"

"No, but enough time to get it all locked up," he said. "And to get a couple of the most important things ready to take down to Richmond to the crime lab tomorrow."

"It's a plan, then."

When I walked back to the Twinmobile, I noticed that the enormous picnic hamper was still in the back. Should I return it to the Washingtons? No, I decided, they'd be insulted. I'd pass the contents around, giving the Washingtons credit for its deliciousness, and brainstorm with Rose Noire about what we could take them as a return present.

I texted Dad to ask for Edgar's key. Then I headed home.

Chapter 11

Back at home the house was quiet. Apparently empty. I took the hamper back to the kitchen and began unpacking it onto the kitchen table. Cold fried chicken. Slices of ham. Burritos, including several marked as "veggie." A baguette and a tub of whipped butter. Croissants. Carrots and celery sticks with two kinds of dip. Two large thermos bottles of homemade lemonade. Brownies. I liked the Washingtons' definition of a proper picnic.

I arranged some of the goodies on platters, refrigerated the rest, and texted a couple of family members who might be nearby that there was free food for the taking. I grabbed a chicken breast and took a bite before strolling out onto the back porch to give our triangular iron dinner bell a quick whack. Cordelia was leaning on the fence at the back of the farm, apparently watching as Rose Noire did something near the beehive. She turned at the sound of the dinner bell. I lifted my chicken piece. She saluted, said something to Rose Noire, and headed for the house. I went inside, and by the time Cordelia came through the back door I'd put out a supply of plates and silverware to achieve at least some semblance of civilized dining.

"Did Rose Noire even notice the dinner bell?" I asked.

"Probably not." Cordelia glanced back. "She's performing some kind of welcoming ceremony for the bees."

"Do the bees appear to appreciate it?" I asked, as I set half a dozen glasses on the table.

"So far they don't even appear to notice it," she said. "Which is all to the good."

"Where's your shadow?"

"Britni?" She closed her eyes briefly and took a breath as if summoning patience. "She went back to the Inn to recuperate. With luck that will take her the rest of the day. Oh, good; a cold lunch—I assume that means you won't mind if I change out of my hiking clothes and freshen up a bit before I eat. Don't wait for me."

Since I already had another mouthful of fried chicken, I only nodded and waved in answer.

But as I chewed, I remembered the item I'd jotted down in my notebook. I pulled out my phone, called the library, and asked if I could speak to Ms. Ellie.

"So," she said, after we'd exchanged greetings. "Is this purely a social call, or were you calling about something in particular? Because while I'd love to chat—"

"You have a million things to do," I said. "No, it's not entirely a social call. I was wondering if the library had any back issues of *Sweet Tea and Sassafras*."

"*Sweet Tea and Sassafras*?" Her voice sounded puzzled.

"It's a magazine," I explained. "I gather it's kind of like a wannabe *Southern Living*. What they call a lifestyle publication, focusing on Southern culture and—"

"I know *what* it is," Ms. Ellie said, with a touch of asperity. "I'm just trying to figure out why in the world *you'd* want to read it."

"Is it that bad?"

"Bad isn't the word, really." She sighed. "Just . . . insubstantial. Insipid. Reading it's rather like trying to fill up on cotton candy. Not that you'd have to do all that much reading—it's heavy on the photos. Pretty pictures of fussy, over-decorated houses. Recipes that are either bland and boring or downright peculiar. Puff pieces on socially prominent ladies."

"I'd like to see a few of those puff pieces," I said. "Because they seem to be doing one on Cordelia."

"Cordelia?" she echoed. "Your grandmother Cordelia?"

I nodded, then realized she couldn't see me.

"Evidently," I said. "Is that odd?"

"Very. I wouldn't have thought Cordelia would be the kind of person they'd want to profile."

"Why not?" I felt a little defensive at what sounded like a slight on my grandmother. "She's interesting. And prominent. She runs one of the top craft centers in the country plus her own Renaissance Faire, and she's very well known in bird-watching and conservation circles, and she played in the All-American Girls Professional Baseball League when she was young and—"

"And I can't imagine why *Sweet Tea and Sassafras* would care about any of that," Ms. Ellie said. "Maybe I'm wrong, but they seem to favor a more traditional view of a woman's role in society."

"Ick," I said.

"Yeah. They usually feature women who start out as debutantes and grow up to give big dinner parties and charity balls. Women who appear on their town's best-dressed lists and host snooty teas for each other. Women who are polite, well-spoken, and haven't had an original thought in their lives."

"That doesn't sound like Cordelia," I said. "Now I'm starting to worry. Why *are* they interviewing her?"

"You never know." I could hear the rattle of a keyboard. "Let me do a little sleuthing. Maybe they have new management. Or maybe their circulation is slipping, and they've realized they need to cover some more interesting topics. More diverse people. I'll see what I can find out. And meanwhile, yes, we have some copies. I put my foot down on buying a subscription, but Mavis Anstruther gets it, and donates her copies when she's finished with them—all of them with a label plastered across the cover that reads 'Made possible through the generous donation of Mrs. Virgil Allerton Anstruther'."

Of course. It would be Mrs. Anstruther.

"And I bet she wants a receipt," I said. "For tax purposes."

"Of course. And you might be the first person to look at them, other than Mrs. Anstruther. Nice that they might finally serve some useful purpose. I'll gather up a few and have them held at the desk for you."

"If it's no trouble," I said. "And tell whoever's on the desk that I'll get in as soon as I can. Not necessarily today—busy afternoon."

We said our goodbyes and signed off. I was tempted to tell her why my afternoon was going to be so busy, but it would be hard to explain any of it without mentioning the murder, and I wasn't sure if Chief Burke would want me talking about that, since he hadn't yet publicly announced it—probably wouldn't be announcing it until he'd located and notified Inman's next of kin.

Besides, Cordelia had returned, bringing Aida with her. Aida and another lively furball.

"When Horace asked me what I was calling her, I just said 'Whatever,'" Aida was explaining as she turned her Pom loose to join the pack. "Turned out to be a great idea. For the first few months, every time my daughter said 'Whatever' the dog came running, expecting a treat. Kayla hardly ever says that these days."

"A happy ending," Cordelia said.

"I need another dog, though," Aida said. "One I can name As If. Hang on." She pulled out her phone and glanced at it. "I need to take this."

She stepped outside for privacy. I glanced at Cordelia, who was also looking wistfully at Aida's departing back. Clearly she was wishing Aida had stayed put so she could eavesdrop. I came by my curiosity honestly.

"Should I find it ominous that Horace is planning to use the Poms to search the woods for Edgar Bortnick?" Cordelia asked.

"No," I said. "This time we're using the ones that have shown an aptitude for finding live people. We'll be taking off as soon as Horace is free. I'd ask if you want to go along—"

"But it might be a little more strenuous than this morning's outing," she said. "Which was tiring. Besides, I already have plans. I'm going to bee-proof your hummingbird feeder."

"Does it need to be bee-proofed?" I asked. "I mean, can't they just share?"

"Not easily," she said. "If you get too many wasps and bees, it tends to contaminate the sugar water—not sure why, but it does. Plus it tends to scare off the hummingbirds. The bees will just overcrowd the feeder and make the birds feel unwelcome, but the wasps will actually become aggressive and chase the birds off."

"Most of the poor hummingbirds are probably used to that by now," I said. "Have you ever heard of one hummingbird chasing all the others away from the feeder?"

"Oh, so you have a bully bird," she said. "Yes, it's quite common. They're very territorial, the males in particular. Not surprising, given how much they have to eat to simply stay alive. If one male hummer finds a good food source, he'll try to keep all the others away."

"Will he eventually figure out that there's going to be enough for everybody?" I asked. "Since we will rush out to fill it as soon as we notice it's getting low?"

"No," she said. "It's hard-wired into their tiny little birdbrains. But don't worry. I know a few tricks to take care of your hummingbird problems."

"And any bee problems that arise, I hope." I'd finished the main course of my lunch and was deciding whether to have a brownie. No, actually I was deciding whether to have one brownie or two. "This is disillusioning. Nature's supposed to be . . . restorative. A way of forgetting about all the problems we humans cause. But the hummingbirds and honeybees are behaving just like the residents of Westlake—quarreling and trying to grab the lion's share of everything." And maybe even killing each other? I hoped not.

"It's hard-wired into us as well," she said. "And the bees aren't quarreling—just the hummingbirds."

"That's a relief," I said.

"Of course, it's not unheard of for one hive of bees to fight with another," Cordelia added. "But it doesn't usually happen if there's enough nectar to go around."

I filed this away to use as ammunition the next time Dad suggested that we needed additional hives.

Aida stepped back inside.

"Sorry," she said. "But that was good news. The Riverton police have checked with Mrs. MacGilleBhrìghde. Am I pronouncing that right?"

"I have no idea," Cordelia said. "It was Gibson before the Gaelic bug bit her."

"The owner of the fairy-infested bed-and-breakfast?" I asked.

"Yes." Aida was eyeing the food. "She alibis your friend Britni for all of last night."

"I didn't realize Britni was a suspect." I shoved several of the food platters in Aida's direction.

"She wasn't much of one." Aida helped herself to a burrito. "Especially considering that she can't keep the name of the dead guy straight—keeps referring to him as Edgar. But she's an odd duck, and we don't know a whole lot about her, so the chief asked me to check her out. And apparently trying to keep up with Ms. Cordelia yesterday was so difficult that she took to her bed with a migraine and had to be nursed with hot tea and cold compresses and whatever else Mrs. MacWhosit thinks is good for a migraine."

"I could almost feel sorry for Britni," Cordelia said. "Being left alone's the only thing that helps me with a migraine."

"I hear you." Aida held up her burrito. "Mind if I take this for the road?"

"Take two," I said. "And don't ignore the brownies. And if you like the spread, tell TJ Washington when you see her."

After bidding Aida goodbye, Cordelia and I dug into the feast. We ate in silence for a few minutes. Then Cordelia set down her burrito.

"I want you to do something for me," she said.

My mouth was full, but I nodded.

"I want you to check that magazine out."

"*Sweet Tea and Sassafras*?" I asked, after swallowing my mouthful of brownie.

"Yes. I'm beginning to wonder about them. When Britni first contacted me, I got the impression that they were interested in profiling me because of Biscuit Mountain."

That made sense. In only a few years, Cordelia had turned an abandoned pottery factory into a nationally respected center for art and craft classes. That was a good enough reason to feature her from my point of view.

"And I thought it would be good publicity for the center," she went on. "But Britni doesn't seem all that interested in it. Or in crafts. Well, she was rather hoping she could get a picture of me doing something dainty and feminine, like embroidering tea towels or crocheting toilet paper roll covers. Once she found out that was a no-go, she lost interest. She actually shuddered when I suggested the photographer could take pictures of you giving me my next blacksmithing lesson. And she clearly thought having to stay for any length of time in Riverton was cruel and unusual punishment, which is why I suggested we come down here. So why is she so keen on doing a profile of me?"

"No idea," I said. "But I'm on it. Checking out the magazine, that is."

She nodded her thanks.

Rose Noire came through the back door. She was dressed quite nicely in a gauzy pink flowered dress and pink ballet slippers with little ribbon roses on the toes. A little dressy for working in the garden, but no doubt she'd gussied up to make a good impression on the bees.

"I think the bees are taking the news quite calmly," she announced.

"What news?" I asked.

"About Mr. Inman's death." She floated over to the table and sat down. Her eyes brightened when she saw the burritos marked "veggie."

"No reason they shouldn't take it calmly," Cordelia said. "Since they'd never actually met him."

"But members of the household were involved." Rose Noire had taken a plate and was busily removing the foil from her veggie burrito.

"Only in finding his body," I said. "I'm sure none of us had anything to do with his death."

"But finding a murdered body is so traumatic!" She clasped her hands, forgetting she was holding the burrito, which disintegrated under the pressure.

Should I reassure her that I wasn't particularly traumatized? Or would it upset her more to think I was the kind of heartless person who took murdered bodies in my stride?

"And we will all deal with that in our own way," Cordelia said, her voice solemn. "Of course, Deacon Washington and I have seen a great deal in our long lifetimes. It's easier for us. And Meg will, as usual, cope through action."

She had me pegged there. Nothing like a long to-do list to help me snap out of a down mood.

"Good." Having crushed her burrito, Rose Noire was now arranging the remnants on her plate to make a sort of taco salad. "And luckily the dogs also seem to be taking it well. That's the beauty of living in the moment, the way dogs do. They tend not to brood."

I wasn't sure the dogs had anything to brood over. Not only had they gone for a very long walk in a woods full of exciting new smells, they'd had the excitement of finding a dead body—and received treats for their trouble.

"Rose Noire is going to take me into town to run a few errands," Cordelia said. She turned to Rose Noire. "Can we return the picnic basket to the Washingtons on our way? I'd like to make sure the deacon's doing okay after this morning's excitement."

"Oh, yes," Rose Noire said. "And I'll take them a thank-you present. Some lavender, I think. And some of the sugar cookies. And maybe a sample of the new soap I just made."

"I do hope you're planning to make candles with some of the wax the beehive will produce," Cordelia said.

We spent the rest of the meal discussing plain and scented beeswax candles and the potential usefulness of honey in Rose Noire's organic cosmetics. I refrained from pointing out how premature all this discussion was. According to what I'd read in all the beekeeping books Dad had been showering us with, a new hive might need every drop of honey it made during its first summer to survive the rigors of the winter. But I was relieved that at least we'd found a topic of conversation other than murder.

Once Rose Noire and Cordelia had taken off, I wrestled the large dog carrier into the back of the Twinmobile—it was big enough to hold Tinkerbell, Rob's Irish wolfhound, so it should be fine for any number of tiny Pomeranians. Then I packed some of Deacon Washington's picnic bounty for Horace, made sure I knew where the relevant Pomeranians were, and was actually contemplating spending a few blissful moments in the hammock when a ding announced a text from Horace.

"Your dad dropped off Edgar's key," it read. "Can you round up the dogs and meet me at the station? I should be finished soon."

Chapter 12

I texted Horace to let him know I'd be on my way soon. Then I rounded up Winnie, Watson, and Whatever and coaxed them into the carrier—clearly they thought me a big meanie for not letting them be free-range SUV passengers. I texted Michael and the boys, in case Horace and I were still hunting for Edgar when they came home. And then I took off for town.

It occurred to me that Horace had said he should be ready soon—not that he was already poised to leave. Which meant that if I hadn't had the dogs in the back, I could with a clear conscience have dropped by the library for a quick look at *Sweet Tea and Sassafras*. Of course maybe . . .

I pulled over in the Washingtons' driveway and called Ms. Ellie's cell phone.

"Were you just holding those magazines for me to look at?" I asked. "Or were you going to let me check them out?"

"Actually, I was just going to let you take them home and hope you'd forget to bring them back," she said. "If you're still interested."

"Definitely interested," I said. "And I might want Cordelia to see them, too. I'm on my way to town—I'd come in to get them now, but I've got a car full of dogs."

"Come around to the back door, just beyond the book drop," she said. "I'll have our intern bring them out. I'd do it myself but I'm running errands at the moment."

So I pulled up behind the library and found the intern standing just outside the back door beside a book cart that contained a two-foot-high stack of magazines. I wanted to protest that a handful would have done just fine, but I didn't want to seem ungrateful, so I helped her load the entire stack into the back seat, since the cargo area was fully occupied by the dog crate. I thanked her and she scurried back inside.

Was it shallow of me to be glad that we'd done this handoff behind the library where, thanks to all the surrounding trees, no one could see us? That only Ms. Ellie and her intern knew I was interested in *Sweet Tea and Sassafras*?

Maybe not. The cover of an issue on top of one of the piles caught my eye, and I picked it up. June of last year—a wedding issue. The cover photo featured three young blond women in low-cut antebellum hoop-skirted dresses. The middle dress was white, the flanking two almost—but not quite—Pepto-Bismol pink. The young women stood in front of a mass of azalea bushes in a sort of salmon color that didn't seem to go at all with the dresses, and in the background were the white columns of what could be a historic plantation house, or maybe just a replica, like Walter Inman's McMansion. Even a casual inspection suggested that the azaleas and columns had probably been added into the picture by someone whose Photoshop skills weren't much better than mine. Along the right side of the cover were teasers for some of the articles inside: "Dresses Any Deb Would Die For!" "Collecting Doilies and Antimacassars!" "Congealed Salads Make a Comeback!"

I flipped through. Ms. Ellie had been right. Heavy on the photos, and not always very good photos at that. Not a lot of interesting articles—I'd have been hard-pressed to occupy half an hour in my dentist's waiting room with the magazine. And

Sweet Tea and Sassafras had probably used up its lifetime quota of exclamation marks in this one issue.

I stuck the wedding issue into my tote bag. If I had some downtime later, I could study it. Try to figure out why they wanted to interview Cordelia. I moved the rest of the magazines off the seat and onto the floor. I wasn't quite sure why. Was I embarrassed to be seen reading them? Or did I want to make sure there was no chance of Britni figuring out that I was checking up on her and her publication? Assuming, of course, that she rode in my car before I'd finished with the wretched things. I covered them up with an old blanket we kept in the car in case of unexpected picnics and climbed back into the driver's seat, still thoughtful.

I had a hard time imagining Cordelia in these pages, among the congealed salads and the antimacassars. She had a point. Why did *Sweet Tea and Sassafras* want to interview her?

I'd worry about that later. I left the library and headed for the police station, a few blocks away.

Horace was out in the parking lot with Sammy, another of the deputies. They were loading evidence bags into the trunk of Sammy's cruiser. Evidently Sammy would be making the run down to the crime lab in Richmond.

"And have them call me if they have any questions," Horace was saying.

"Right," Sammy answered.

"But remind them that I might be out of cell phone range at times."

As usual, Horace having to part with his carefully collected and neatly labeled evidence looked a lot like a mother dropping her only child off at nursery school for the first time. But after half a dozen more bits of completely unnecessary parting advice, he let Sammy drive off with his precious cargo.

"Time to find Edgar," I said, to distract him from Sammy's departure.

We decided to caravan, so Horace wouldn't be stuck with me if he got an urgent call. And to leave the dogs in the Twinmobile for the same reason. We probably wouldn't need them at our first stop, the wellness check at Edgar's house, but if anything dog-worthy came up, they'd be available. And it was probably useful to bring Watson along in addition to Winnie and Whatever. We were hoping not to have to use Watson's corpse-finding abilities, but you never knew; and having him along would make the other dogs happy. Even happier than they normally would be at getting to ride in a car.

Although I was envious of the way Horace wouldn't have had to bother with the giant crate. Could I install something in the Twinmobile that worked the same way as the barrier Horace's cruiser had between the front and back seats? That would be an excellent thing to have: the ability to stow the Poms in their own secure compartment, where it didn't matter that so far all of the humans who had adopted them had been spectacularly unsuccessful in their efforts to train them to settle down in the back seat of the car and not try to crawl into the driver's lap.

Before long, Horace's cruiser turned off the main road onto a dirt-and-gravel country lane. On our left was a field of corn, row after row of young plants already a foot and a half high. On our right, a broad green pasture, empty except for a cluster of forms at the far end, under the trees. Cows lying down? No, pigs, I decided. Yes, definitely pigs—a minute later I passed a driveway with a neatly painted sign that read:

S. SHIFFLEY.
PASTURE-RAISED PORK.
RED WATTLES.
GLOUCESTERSHIRE OLD SPOT.
BOARS, SOWS, GILTS, BARROWS,
AND SHOATS FOR SALE.

From which I deduced that Vern's cousin Sam was a full-service pig farmer, selling both live pigs of various ages to fellow farmers and finished pork products either wholesale or to consumers. Probably both, if he operated like most local livestock farmers, seizing every opportunity to stay afloat. And, evidently, Sam raised two well-known though endangered heritage pig breeds—even I had heard of Red Wattles and Gloucestershire Old Spots. Dad would approve. In fact, given Dad's fascination with heritage animal breeds and the frequency with which he'd been visiting his friend Edgar, whose farm must be nearby, I'd have made a bet that Dad had long ago visited Sam Shiffley and met his entire pig collection.

To my left the corn continued. On the right, another pig pasture, followed by a fence with trees on either side of it. Probably the dividing line between Sam Shiffley's farm and Edgar's. Another pasture—this one with goats. Dad could have told me what breed they were—in fact, he would insist on doing so and explaining the strengths and weaknesses of the breed and whether they were meat goats or dairy goats.

I just noted, with pleasure, that apparently Edgar raised goats. Or rented his front pasture to a goat farmer. I rather liked goats. Not enough that I wanted to add them to our menagerie, but I liked watching them. I could see big goats grazing. Little and presumably young goats frolicking. I rolled down my window. Now I could hear the occasional bleat and inhale the air, which smelled of rich, moist, fertile soil with grace notes of lilac and manure.

I spotted Edgar's mailbox. Right after passing it, Horace turned in to a tree-shaded lane. We followed the lane for a long way, with goats to the right of us and sheep to the left. A very long way—clearly whoever had chosen the site for building here had valued privacy. Eventually we pulled up in front of a long, low, comfortable-looking farmhouse. While not as pristine and beautiful as the Washingtons' farmstead, it was definitely well maintained.

But something had started to bother me. I parked the Twin-mobile in the shade, hopped out, and hurried over to where Horace was getting out of his cruiser.

"Are we sure this is the right place?" I asked.

"His name's on the mailbox," Horace said. "And this is the address the chief gave me."

"Yes, but where are the beehives? I didn't see a single beehive on our way back here."

Horace blinked, looked around, and nodded.

"Maybe he keeps them in the backyard?" he said. "Although I guess out here it would be more like the back pasture. We'll figure it out—we'll need to search the whole place. You brought the key, right?"

"I thought Dad gave it to you."

Horace paled and began slapping his pockets. Luckily, he found it in one of his back pockets.

"Here," he said. "You hang on to it. I'm going to try knocking."

He marched up the steps to the front door and knocked. I noticed he was standing slightly to the left of the door, rather than planting himself in front of it. Force of habit for him, I suspected, but it reminded me all too well that a killer was still loose in Caerphilly.

We waited in silence. No one answered. I could tell he was listening, head cocked.

He knocked again.

"Mr. Bortnick," he called.

Nothing.

"Mr. Bortnick, it's Horace Hollingsworth. Dr. Langslow asked me to check on you. He's worried about you."

We waited in silence for a couple more minutes. To the right and left of the door were pairs of large side-by-side windows—

probably one set each for the rooms that flanked the entrance. Horace peered into both sets. He rattled the doorknob, but it was locked.

"Stay here," he said. "I'm going to knock at the back doors. And any side doors I find."

He took off. I sat down on the porch steps. Sideways, so I could watch both the front door and the driveway, where the Pomeranians were still snoozing in their crate in the Twinmobile. And I kept my ears open.

Sheep bleating. Goats. A chickadee. Several other kinds of songbirds. But no sounds from inside the house.

Eventually Horace emerged from the other side of the house.

"Nothing," he said. "Let's use that key you're holding."

"See any beehives?"

"At the far end of his back pasture."

That was reassuring.

"Let's make sure the dogs will be okay," I said.

I went back to the Twinmobile and raised the cargo door so they could get plenty of air. Horace brought over a bowl of water, and we tucked it into the crate. I slipped three chew toys in beside it. The dogs looked content.

Then we returned to the front door. I opened it up and stepped aside to let Horace go in first.

"Mr. Bortnick?" Horace called.

I followed him into a front hall that was refreshingly uncluttered. It had ten-foot ceilings, white plastered walls, and mellowed oak woodwork. The only items in it were a large stoneware umbrella stand and a few wall-mounted coat hooks. To the right an archway led to a large living room with wall-to-wall bookshelves and not much else except for a few old but comfortable-looking easy chairs. To the left, another archway revealed a small dining room, containing only a plain oak table and four chairs. A stairway led up the left side of the hall to the second floor, and at the back was an open door that revealed an old-fashioned linoleum floor. Probably the door to the kitchen.

"Lock the front door," Horace said. "We don't want anyone barging in unannounced. And stay here while I check things out."

I suspected that if anyone came within sight of the house, the dogs would alert us. But I nodded and, after locking the door, stepped into the living room and inspected the nearest bookshelf. Fiction, mostly, and mostly old and well-worn volumes. Dickens, Austen, Conrad, Hemingway, Shakespeare. I could see that the next bookcase was full of books on the natural sciences—the birds and the bees, plus plants and minerals and geology and meteorology. I suspected Dad had enjoyed himself browsing Edgar's library. I'd enjoy it myself.

Upstairs I could hear Horace's uniform boots clacking on the bare wood floors. Edgar didn't seem to bother much with rugs. He didn't seem to bother much with anything apart from books and a few basic, no-nonsense pieces of furniture. I wondered if he put down throw rugs for warmth in the winter and then took them up in summer when they'd be just another thing that needed cleaning.

Horace came clumping down the steps.

"Not upstairs," he said.

I followed him back to the kitchen. A big, old, roomy farmhouse kitchen that appeared to date from the nineteen-twenties. Clearly the occupants had replaced the appliances periodically over the years, but the high glass-fronted upper cabinets were so old they'd come back in style again.

"Not here," Horace said. "I'll check the basement."

While he did, I snooped around the kitchen. I wondered if Edgar had someone come in to help with the housework, or if he did it himself. The spotless condition of all the rooms I'd seen suggested he had help. But then again, he'd made it easy for whoever did the cleaning by being so minimalist. Only a few things left out. A coffee maker and a toaster on the counter. A cast-iron frying pan on the stove. Of course, he had plenty of cabinets to keep things in—though even the cabinets weren't overstuffed. Yes, I peeked.

The only non-minimalist touch was a white-painted glass-fronted bookcase in one corner, filled with cookbooks. Mostly cookbooks.

A pair of binoculars and a well-thumbed Peterson's bird guide lay on the kitchen table, which was in front of a large bay window with a view of the backyard.

I went over to check the view outside. Near the house was a profusion of what I suspected were bee-friendly flowering perennials. Beyond that I could see his vegetable garden. Corn, beans, and squash grown together, Three Sisters fashion, with the beans starting to climb the corn stalks and the squash vines shading the ground around them. And lots of tomatoes, peppers, onions, carrots, and who knew what else. Beyond that were a dozen fruit trees—apples, peaches, and cherries. And yes, there were beehives nearby, a whole row of them. They were in the center of a field of purple-flowering clover that sloped down to the small stream that had once formed the border between his farm and his neighbor's. Now it was the border between farmland and the Westlake neighborhood. It was jarring to see the huge houses seeming to loom over the stream and Edgar's yard—though at least I could see only three of them, thanks to the hilly terrain and the fact that they had reasonably large yards. The Griswolds' mock Tudor to the right, the Brownlows' faux Colonial on the left, and in between, Walter Inman's house, which was a dead ringer for Tara in *Gone with the Wind*.

I thought of picking up the binoculars to get a better view of the beehives and the NIMBYs, but I stayed my hand. If Horace emerged to report a body in the basement, the whole house would suddenly become a crime scene. Until he gave the all clear, I'd work on leaving behind as few fingerprints as possible.

Just then Horace popped out of the basement door.

"He's not down there," he said. "Not in the house at all. Of course, he could always be somewhere outside or in one of the outbuildings. I need to search there. And he's got a sort of combined workshop, photo studio, and office down there in the basement. I should look there to see if I can get a clue about where he went."

"I can help," I said. "You want me to look for clues in the basement or search outside?"

He frowned as if the decision was hard.

"Probably less chance I'll contaminate any evidence outside," I said. "Since it's already out there being contaminated by goats and sheep and passing birds."

"Good point," he said. "Outside, then. But if you find anything—"

"I'll back away and call you."

Horace nodded and disappeared into the basement.

Chapter 13

I went out the back door and used my key to lock up behind me so no one would sneak in while Horace was busy and distracted. Horace occasionally alarmed the family by sharing tales of criminalists who had come to grief at the hands of evildoers when working solo at crime scenes. Not surprising, actually, if many of them shared Horace's tendency to focus on the evidence in front of him and shut out the rest of the world.

I explored Edgar's outdoor domain. Not many potential hiding places, either for a dead body or a live intruder. The goat shed. The tool shed—unlocked, which probably meant they didn't get a lot of petty crime thereabouts. I looked in those, and under and behind any shrubbery anywhere near large enough to conceal a human form. He didn't have an actual barn, which made sense, given the small size of his property. His neighbors probably thought of it as a farmette, or maybe just a really big yard, although they'd have been too polite to say so aloud—at least not in his hearing. He had spring peas and strawberries ripe for the picking in his vegetable garden, and at least one early-variety cucumber that would turn into a yellow submarine if someone didn't pick it pretty soon. Enough ripe vegetables to convince me that he hadn't been here since yesterday morning.

As I neared the far end of his property, I kept my eyes on the beehives. There were ten of them, forming a fairly regular line in the middle of the clover, about ten feet away from his back fence.

Edgar was fond of explaining that honeybees were essentially slow and gentle, with no interest in stinging anyone unless they thought their hive was in danger. But Edgar had had many years of working with bees. Managing to look mostly harmless was probably second nature to him, at least around his hives. What if the bees took exception to something I did? What if they were one-man bees and would resent any intruder? Was there such a thing? If only I'd spent more time reading those bee books of Dad's.

As I drew closer, I began to worry about something else. I wasn't seeing bees. A few visiting the clover field, but when they flew off they didn't head for the hives. They headed in the direction of the house. There were no bees flying in and out of the hives. I was no expert, but we'd had bees in our hive for five or six months last year. I knew what a busy, occupied hive should look like.

These hives didn't look like that. They looked the way our hive had looked after the bees had decamped: empty and more than a little forlorn.

There weren't any dead bees lying around. There hadn't been around our hives, either—a good sign, according to Dad. I assumed that meant that we hadn't managed to kill our bees— just annoy them enough that they left in a huff.

I approached the nearest hive, moving slowly. And I tried to think calm, bee-friendly thoughts, as Rose Noire had so often recommended last summer when people appeared nervous about passing by our hive to visit her herb drying shed. What if I happened to approach at bee-siesta time? What if they were all snoozing away the heat of the day inside, and would awaken cranky at having their nap interrupted?

Okay, that didn't sound very realistic. But neither did the idea of Edgar, the bee guru, having nothing but empty hives on his farm.

I tried to lift the lid of the hive, with no luck. Evidently there was a reason the hive tool was a beekeeper's best friend.

I peered in through the small entrance near the bottom of the hive—something I would never have done if the hive had been buzzing with activity. Even now it made me nervous to have my eye so close to the opening. And it wasn't the least bit useful—I couldn't see anything inside.

I hiked back to the tool shed and surveyed its contents. Aha! A hive tool. I grabbed it and returned to the hive.

The top came off easily, and the inside was empty. Not just empty but scrubbed clean. Since I'd helped Dad assemble his hive when it first arrived, I knew most modern beehives were modular, made up of a stack of several interchangeable wooden boxes. With the help of the hive tool I removed the top box. The second box was also empty. Neither box even had any frames— rectangular trays designed for the bees to build their combs on. The frames slid vertically into the hive boxes like hanging file folders into a file drawer, and were removable, so the beekeeper could easily inspect and maintain the hive—and harvest the honey. All of the frames were gone from this hive.

And then it hit me that the hive also smelled wrong. I hadn't often gone near enough to smell our hive during those few months it had been inhabited and operational, but when I did, it had smelled like wax and honey, with a slightly earthy under-tone. A pleasant smell that had lingered, more faintly, even after its occupants had flown away.

This hive had a nasty chemical smell. And a slightly familiar one. I closed my eyes, took another sniff, and tried to stop thinking about the smell and just react to it.

Wasps and hornets. A few weeks ago, a couple of visiting cousins had been badly stung, and we found that a colony of hornets were diligently building a nest under the eaves of the llama shed. The spray Michael used to zap the hornets' nest had smelled just like this.

I put the hive back together and checked out the next one in line. It was also clean and empty, and smelled of insecticide.

They all did.

I could think of only one reason for Edgar's beehives to smell like this. Someone had sprayed them with insecticide. Someone other than Edgar. It wasn't anything he would ever have done himself.

I looked up from the last of the hives and turned to scowl across the stream at Westlake.

Of course, there was no one there to scowl at. All three of the visible McMansions had elaborate outdoor areas in their back-yards. The Griswolds had nearly half an acre of wooden deck, most of it roofed with pergolas. The Brownlows had nearly as much deck space, though instead of pergolas for shade they'd gone in for patio umbrellas, wooden planters, and large potted trees. Walter Inman had done up his backyard in stone. Stone pa-tios, stone retaining walls, stone steps, stone benches—enough stone to build a small pyramid if they'd stacked it up instead of spreading it out all over most of his backyard. He even had a stone outdoor kitchen with built-in grill, sink, and pizza oven.

Yet none of the NIMBYs were outside. None of them ever seemed to spend much time outside unless they were entertain-ing, from what I'd heard. The Brownlows' elaborate teakwood outdoor furniture was all neatly swathed in protective water-proof covers.

No—wait. There was someone outside. Someone was slouched in one of the Adirondack chairs on the Griswolds' deck. I couldn't see much except for a large pair of the sort of brightly colored sports shoes that probably cost the moon. Shane Gris-wold, I assumed.

I studied the houses again. I had nothing in particular

against colonial style, and I rather liked mock Tudor. Even In-man's Tara clone wouldn't have been bad if it really had been a faithful replica of the original Georgia mansion. An uncom-fortable reminder of an unenlightened and arguably evil era in the South's history, perhaps, but at least not an aesthetic blight on the landscape. But these houses . . . they were overlarge to the point of becoming awkward and ungainly, the graceful lines and proportions of their inspirations distorted in the service of grandeur and sheer square footage. It was as if someone had taken several well-designed houses and overinflated them with a bicycle pump.

I leaned on Edgar's back fence and rested my eyes on a more congenial sight—the little boundary stream. This time of year, especially after as much rain as we'd had, it was flowing with reasonable speed. Even so, you could safely wade across it—or, if you didn't want to get your feet wet, you could use the rough bridge made of a well-worn two-by-eight plank, which crossed the stream at a spot near the middle of Inman's backyard. The flowing water was relaxing to watch, and its gurgling, trickling noises made a pleasant background sound. Later in the year, the stream probably made a less picturesque addition to the landscape—especially in a dry year, when it would shrink to a thin trickle of water surrounded by a lot of mud and rocks, and even a child could step across it with impunity.

If Rose Noire were here, she would point out that even then it would be running water and would symbolize prosperity and abundance. And she'd probably be full of all kinds of ideas about how to enhance it.

The three nearest NIMBYs were also eager to enhance the stream, though they all had different ideas about what they wanted done. The Griswolds wanted to replace the plank with an elegant arched Japanese-style wooden bridge. Wally the Weird had favored a substantial stone bridge. The Brownlows advocated digging out the stream bed, installing a large drainage pipe, directing the stream into it, and then dumping a few hundred tons of fill dirt over it, so you couldn't even tell that there had once been a pleasant little stream there. So for the time being, both the stream and the little plank bridge were safe. Even if the NIMBYs could manage to come to a consensus about what they wanted done there, any project would need agreement from Edgar and permission from the county, and I didn't see either of those happening.

But at the moment, I studied that little plank bridge with suspicion. If, as I suspected, someone had sprayed insecticide on Edgar's hives, it would take a bold person to drive or walk all the way down Edgar's lane and sneak from the front yard past the house to the far edge of his property. But it would be remarkably easy for one of the NIMBYs to wait until dark, then walk to the bottom of the hill, use the plank bridge to cross the stream, and sneak into Edgar's yard a mere ten feet from where the hives were. There was even a back gate to save them the trouble of climbing over the fence. If they were careful enough to choose a time when his house was dark, odds were no one would see them, and he'd never know who'd murdered his bees.

Murdered his bees? Was I overreacting? Maybe. Then again, I knew how vital bees were to the environment. Grandfather was fond of reminding us that at least a third of the world's food supply was directly dependent on bees and other animal pollinators.

And not only were they important, they were beautiful. I realized that I was actually looking forward to having bees around again. Watching them—from a safe distance—dart from flower to flower. Maybe even finally getting to enjoy the homegrown honey that we'd been looking forward to before our bees had flitted.

The NIMBYs probably weren't the only people in Caerphilly stupid and vicious enough to poison a neighbor's beehives. But it would be a very short list, and they'd be right at the top of it.

Especially the Griswolds and the Brownlows, who'd been so persistent in their complaints about Edgar's hives.

And Walter Inman, of course. Of the three, he had the easiest access to the plank bridge. If he was the one who'd killed the bees, Edgar's future hives were safe. But Edgar would be that much more of a suspect.

I turned and began trudging back to the house, thinking furiously. I needed to tell the chief about this. Find out if Edgar had reported the incident. Because it was a crime, wasn't it?

I had no idea. But I knew how I could find out. As everyone in Caerphilly knew, Vern Shiffley had practically memorized the Code of Virginia—at least the criminal portions of it. And if you asked him a question about criminal law that he didn't know, he wouldn't rest until he found the answer.

So as I ambled through Edgar's yard I dialed Vern's number, hoping he wouldn't still be out in the middle of the woods guarding the crime scene.

"What's up, Meg?" he said, by way of hello.

"Oh, good," I said. "You must be back in civilization."

"Nope," he said. "In Clay County, liaising with Sheriff Dingell. But at least my phone gets a signal here. What's up?"

"Would it be against the law for someone to spray insecticide on a beehive?" I asked. "Someone else's beehive, that is."

"Pretty sure it would be," he said. "It'd come under the Crimes Against Property section. If you give poison to any kind of livestock with the intent to harm or kill it, that's a class five felony. And I'm sure honeybees count as livestock. Owned ones, anyway."

"Ooh, a felony," I said. "They'd get hard time, then?"

"Well, a class five felony's what you call a wobbler. Sometimes it gets downgraded to a misdemeanor, depending on how the prosecutor decides to charge it, or maybe how the judge or jury see it. If it stays a felony, then one to ten years in the slammer. If they bump it down to misdemeanor, it's still up to twelve months in jail and a fine of up to twenty-five hundred dollars. You catch someone trying to mess with your beehive?"

"No, I think someone already messed with Edgar's beehives."

"Beehives? Plural?"

"Ten of them."

Vern whistled.

"The value of the livestock's one of the things that might keep it in felony territory," he said. "Ten working beehives? Complete with a full load of honey? A jury'd take that seriously. Especially in a heavily agricultural county like Caerphilly. He have any idea who did it?"

"When we find him, I'll ask him. Talk to you later."

I had reached the house by now. I let myself in the back door.

"Horace?"

"Down here," came a voice from the basement.

Chapter 14

I locked the back door again and went down the basement stairs. The room at the bottom of the stairs was set up as Edgar's office. Not nearly as minimal as the upstairs, but still neat, tidy, and well organized. Horace was sitting at an eight-foot-wide built-in counter that served as a desk.

"So what was so interesting about Edgar's beehives that you had to take one of them apart?" he asked.

"Did you go outside to search, or were you just watching me from the kitchen window?" I asked.

"Neither," he said. "I was watching you on his bee cams."

"Bee cams?"

"Take a look." He gestured at something on the desk.

I strode over to stand beside him. He pointed to two small flat-screen monitors, each showing a peaceful view of the ten beehives—although I could tell from the background scenery that the two cameras must be mounted at opposite ends of the row.

"Is that live-action only, or is he recording it?" I asked.

"Pretty sure he's recording it," Horace said. "And it looks like a fairly new setup. Did you see something out at the hives that would explain why he's started spying on his bees?"

"There aren't any bees," I said. "I think someone poisoned

them. The hives are totally clean, but they still reek of insecticide. So I bet Edgar set up the cameras so he can catch the culprit if they try it again."

"Why would they, if there aren't any bees there anymore?"

"They might not know that," I said. "At least not if the culprits are who I think they are. They may not realize they got all the bees. Or if they see any bees in their yard, they may jump to the conclusion that he's got new ones. I didn't realize the hives were empty until I got pretty close. They probably know even less about bees than I do. And they wouldn't have had to get very close if they did what I think they did—came at night and used those hardware-store spray cans of hornet killer to zap the bees. They could almost have done it from the other side of the stream."

"So maybe the better question is why Edgar set up the bee cams if his bees were already dead," Horace said.

"He's probably planning to replace them eventually," I said. "He could be getting ready to protect the new bees. Because if word gets around that he's got new bees, I bet they'll try to repeat their attack, and he'll catch them in the act."

"You keep saying they," he echoed. "I assume you're thinking one of the NIMBYs."

"Exactly," I said. "Although I have no idea which one. And I suspect neither did Edgar, or he wouldn't need these cameras."

"Or maybe he thinks he knows which one and is trying to get the goods on them," Horace suggested.

"True," I said. "He's probably thinking that even if there aren't any bees in his hives, there are other bees out there. And as soon as the culprit sees a stray bee in their yard—or a wasp or hornet; I bet they can't tell the difference—they'd be right back over with more bug killer, and he'll catch them in the act."

Horace nodded. He was frowning.

"You do realize this could give him a motive," he said.

"To kill Inman, you mean?"

He nodded.

"Theoretically," I said. "Not that I can see Edgar doing it."

"Not even if he lost his temper?"

"I can see him losing his temper and hauling off and punching Inman," I said. "But dragging him to the far end of the county and shooting him? That's not temper, it's premeditation."

"We don't know him that well," Horace said. "We need to look into it."

"Let's find him first," I said. "And make sure he's not a victim of the same person who killed Inman."

"Good point." Horace stood up. "I can't tell if he's storing the video locally or if he's got it set up to save it to the cloud somewhere. At least I can't tell without doing more snooping than I'm comfortable doing right now. I can't even tell for sure how long he saves the files—video eats up disk space like crazy, so most surveillance systems delete the older files. I should probably ask Kevin to check it out."

"Make sure Kevin doesn't jump the gun and do anything before the chief gets either warrants or Edgar's permission," I said.

"Yeah," he agreed. "We wouldn't want to contaminate usable evidence. So you see Edgar as a suspect?"

"His video could still be evidence, even if Edgar had nothing to do with the murder." I pointed to one of the monitors. "See that stone wall there? That's in Inman's backyard."

Horace blinked, and then pulled out his phone and began doing something on it. I peered over his shoulder. He was studying a GPS mapping program.

"You're right," he said. "Not that I doubted you, but I had no idea we were so close. It's a good ten miles by car, but only a few hundred yards on foot."

"Which doesn't make Edgar guilty," I pointed out.

"No," Horace said. "But try telling the NIMBYs that."

We stood there for a minute or two, staring at the two little monitors.

"Let's call Kevin," I said. "Let him know we might need him."

Horace nodded. I pulled out my phone, dialed Kevin, and put the phone on speaker.

To my surprise, Kevin answered immediately. Although his first words suggested why.

"Anything happening with the murder?"

Getting Kevin's attention could normally be challenging, since on top of his demanding job at Mutant Wizards he was also the co-host of *Virginia Crime Time,* an up-and-coming true-crime podcast. But these days, thanks to the podcast, his fascination with all things crime-related was almost equal to Dad's. Right now, that could be useful.

"Nothing much that I know of," I said. "You could help change that."

"Thought I already had. You got those coordinates for Edgar's last-known whereabouts, right?"

"Yes, and Horace and I are about to head out to look for him. But we decided to drop by his house first. We'd feel pretty silly traipsing through the woods looking for him if it turned out he was at home and just wasn't answering his phone because he wasn't in the mood for conversation."

"Word." Had Kevin picked this up from the twins, or was it the other way around? "You find him?"

"No, but we did find something interesting. We're over at his house right now."

"Hey, Kev," Horace said.

"Edgar seems to have set up video surveillance of his beehives," I went on.

"Actually I set it up for him."

Horace, who had been idly glancing around the office, came to attention.

"Excellent!" I said. "When? And why?"

"Nine days ago. Someone snuck into his yard and killed all his bees. He was hopping mad, and pretty sure he knew who did it, but he didn't have any proof—or any way to keep it from happening again if he replaced the bees. He was venting to Grandpa, who suggested he set up video surveillance, but since neither of them exactly knew how to do that they roped me in to get it done."

"Does that mean that you know how to get into wherever his video is stored?" I asked. "Of course, we don't want to jump the gun and do anything before the chief gives his okay, but once that happens, Horace will probably want to get access to it right away."

Horace was nodding.

"I have Dad's key to Edgar's house," I went on. "Should I drop it off with you, so you'll have it if the chief gives you the go-ahead?"

"I don't need to get into his house to look at the video." Kevin's tone suggested that he was exercising extraordinary patience in the face of my technical ignorance. "I set him up with cloud storage. Easiest and cheapest way to get the amount of storage he needs, plus it's protected in case the jerks who did it try again and realize they're on candid camera. And he emailed me to ask if I could help monitor the video, so pretty sure I already have his permission to look at it. Are you thinking his video is going to have anything to do with the murder?"

"I have no idea," I said. "But I bet Wally the Weird is one of Edgar's prime suspects for the bee massacre. And once word gets out, I bet the rest of the NIMBYs are going to think Edgar's the prime suspect for killing Wally. So who knows. The chief might want to look at it."

"Nine days," Horace muttered. "And what's this about the chief looking at it? I bet it's going to be me who does the looking. Nine days times two cameras . . . what's forty-eight times nine?" He looked gloomy.

"I heard that," Kevin said. "Did I happen to mention that the cameras are motion sensitive? So it's only about fifty hours, and it wouldn't even be that much if Edgar would prune some of the nearby vegetation. Most of the footage is just scenery with gently waving clover, but I've got a log of what few events have occurred since we started the surveillance."

Kevin seemed to be getting into this. And Horace perked up a bit.

"A log?" he echoed.

"Don't tell me you've watched the whole fifty hours of video," I said. Even if he did it in some kind of fast-forward mode, that would take time.

"Nah," he said. "That would be like watching paint dry. And Edgar didn't really want to do it, either, so I'm having my watchers do it."

"Watchers?"

"Josh and Jamie and some of their friends. They get twenty-five cents for each hour of video they check, with a bonus for each time they find something other than just the empty hives sitting there. Three days ago a couple of Edgar's goats got loose and spent the afternoon eating clover around the hives—I must have paid out twenty dollars in bonuses for all those goat sightings. They've spotted Edgar doing fence repairs and stuff a couple of times. I'll check the logs and see if there are any other human sightings."

Horace leaned a little closer to my phone.

"You still have the video from all nine days now," he said. "But how long's your data retention? It's not going to start writing over the earliest footage, is it?"

"No," Kevin said. "We haven't yet decided how long a retention period he wants, so I set it up to notify me when he's starting to run low on storage space. We're not even close yet, and if there's any possibility of useful evidence on it, I can keep it all for the time being. I'll bump the storage up to a petabyte if I have to."

"That's good," Horace said. "Do me a favor. Let the chief know about this."

"Can do," he said. "And you're welcome to come watch."

"Thanks," I said. "Right now we're going to go see if we can find Edgar."

"Anytime," he said. "Just say the word. The goat footage is actually kind of funny."

With that we hung up.

"What's a petabyte?" Horace asked.

"I was going to ask you," I said. "I get the general impression it's big."

Horace picked up his phone and began typing into it.

I turned back to the monitor. One of the cameras was centered on the beehives and showed only them, but the other was a little less perfectly aimed. It showed all the beehives, but it also took in the creek and a little bit of the closest edge of Inman's stone patios. If you adjusted the aim just a little—

"A petabyte is a thousand terabytes," Horace said. "So yeah, I guess it's big."

"It's like quadrillions and quintillions," I said. "So big they're kind of meaningless. Look!" I pointed to the left-hand monitor— the one with the broader view. "That's probably the chief now."

"I only see shoes," Horace said.

Technically he was right—all we could see at the moment was a pair of well-shined brogues.

"Pretty sure they're the chief's," I said.

Then the brogues stepped off Inman's patio and gradually all of their wearer came into view, starting with the legs and ending up with his whole body. It was the chief. He walked down the terraces that covered the sloping yard until he was standing on the bank of the stream, frowning as he stared across at Edgar's beehives.

"That's good," Horace said. "He's got Inman's house secured. No reason why we can't take off and look for Edgar."

He took a last look around the basement office, and then we went back upstairs. He poked around the front yard while I greeted the waiting Pomeranians and assured them that yes, I was delighted to see them again.

"I suppose we should search the pastures." Horace seemed unenthusiastic about the idea. We ended up driving out at about three miles an hour, with Horace scanning the left-hand side and me the right, stopping our vehicles to scamper out into the pastures for a more detailed search whenever we spotted a bit of dense shrubbery or other possible hiding place. Actually, I did most of the scampering, since the goats in the pastures on the left rather unnerved Horace and he wasn't convinced that the pastures on the right held only sheep.

Eventually we reached the road. Horace, who was in the lead, stopped, and I could see him doing something with his phone. Plugging in the coordinates Kevin had given us for Edgar's eagle photo, I assumed. I did the same, and we set off to see how near we could get to the spot.

We followed familiar roads for the first part of the trip—it was the same route I used when I went to visit my cousin Festus. Eventually we took a left fork instead of the right that would have led to Festus's place, and Horace slowed down, probably so he could pay more attention to the directions his GPS app was offering. Eventually we came to a turn that would take us onto a road that was little more than a dirt track through the under-brush. After a brief consultation, we decided to consolidate.

"If we can't find a place to turn around in there, it'll be easier to back up one vehicle," Horace said.

So I parked the Twinmobile and we moved the dogs from the crate to the back of his cruiser.

The dirt track was so narrow that tree branches often brushed against the door of his cruiser on one side or the other. Some-times both sides. After a mile or so on it, Horace and I both shouted "Bingo!" simultaneously.

We'd spotted Edgar's bright yellow truck.

Chapter 15

"A very un-mellow yellow," I said. "You think maybe Edgar's truck glows in the dark?"

"All he has to do is paint brown stripes on that thing and it would look just like a giant bumblebee," Horace said.

"Don't give him ideas. Wait—there's another truck there."

We both tensed, and Horace slowed his cruiser ever so slightly. Then Vern Shiffley stepped out from behind the two trucks and waved at us.

"Does he think we're going to get lost in the woods without him?" Horace sounded annoyed.

"He probably thinks we could use someone to watch our backs while we concentrate on the dogs," I said. "Since whoever shot Inman is still at large."

Horace nodded but didn't seem entirely placated.

"And he must have a reasonable amount of confidence in the Pomeranians," I added. "Or he'd have brought along his cousin Dagmar and her search-and-rescue Lab."

"That's true." The thought restored his good humor, and he greeted Vern with unforced cheerfulness.

"Theoretically, I just went off duty," Vern said. "But this expedition of yours sounded right interesting. Figured you wouldn't mind if I tagged along to see how it goes."

"Wait till you see the girls work." Horace opened the back door of his cruiser and the three Pomeranians leaped out to greet Vern and snuffle eagerly at his jeans, which probably smelled like his hunting dogs.

"And once we find Edgar, I can calm down all my cousins," Vern added. "They're pretty worried about him being missing."

"All your cousins?" I echoed. "Not just Sam?" I wondered why Edgar would be such a favorite with the Shiffley clan.

"Well, yeah, Sam's worried," he said. "Edgar's a good neighbor. But Mel and Janice are even more worried. He's pretty vital to that new business they're trying to start up."

"New business?" Horace had handed leads to Vern and me so we could each take charge of a dog—assuming we could get them to stand still long enough to attach the leads. Thank goodness I'd already put the working harnesses on them back at the house.

"They're making mead," Vern said. "Tasted the stuff when they went to Miz Cordelia's Renaissance Faire and took quite a liking to it."

"You said new business." I succeeded in attaching the leash to Watson's harness. "They're going to sell it, then, not just make it for family consumption?"

"They figure if they can get good enough at making it, they'll try to sell it," he said. "Once all the family taste testers agree that it's ready for the market."

"If they need any more taste testers, I'd be happy to volunteer," I said.

"I'll let them know," Vern said, with a chuckle.

"I didn't know Edgar was a mead expert." Horace had leashed Winnie and was watching Vern's attempts to wrangle Whatever.

"He's not," Vern said. "Mel and Janice can handle the mead-making part themselves. That's one thing about my family—if you ever need to know anything about brewing, fermenting, or distilling, we've got the expertise. But it takes a lot of honey to make mead and that stuff's expensive to buy. So they worked out a deal with Edgar. He sets up some of his hives on their farms and comes round every week to take care of them and pull out the honey when possible, and they reward him with a regular supply of mead."

"Sounds like a good deal," I said.

"Are we ready?" Horace was visibly impatient to get started.

"Got the little rascal." Vern raised one fist in a victory salute as he finally snapped the leash onto Whatever's collar. "Ready."

Horace put on a pair of gloves, as if he were about to start processing a crime scene. He took out a mason jar, opened it up, and pulled out a grungy-looking white sock.

"From Edgar's laundry hamper," he said as he held out the sock to Winnie—who buried her nose in it as if it held some rare and intoxicating perfume.

Watson whined and pulled at the lead, so I led him close enough that he could examine the sock. Vern brought Whatever over to join the fun.

The three dogs inhaled deeply and repeatedly, made whuffing noises, and occasionally exchanged glances as if silently discussing their perceptions.

"Whew," Vern said. "There's no accounting for taste, is there? I can smell that damned sock from here."

"I think they've got it," Horace said. He stuffed the sock back in the mason jar and sealed it up. He held the jar out to me. "Can you hang on to this?"

I took possession of the jar, checked to make sure the lid was screwed on tight, and stuck it in my tote.

"Okay, girls," Horace exclaimed. "Let's find Edgar! Go find! Go find!"

Winnie and Whatever barked and twirled in circles for a few

seconds—typical behavior for all of the Poms. Then they both suddenly grew still, lifted their heads in the air, and sniffed.

They had interestingly different styles of sniffing. Winnie stood in a graceful pose, one front paw curled and lifted, the opposite rear leg extended. She lifted her head a little higher each time she sniffed and looked for all the world as if she might levitate and float away with the next exciting whiff of scent. Whatever sat still, moving her head in a slow, sweeping circle, all the way to the left, then all the way to the right. Occasionally she'd sit up on her hind legs like a meerkat, as if more height would help her sniffing.

Watson just stood on his four sturdy little legs, looking around and occasionally taking a deep sniff and then whuffing it out as if disappointed.

Whatever continued to sample the air while Winnie tugged Horace over so she could sniff the ground beside the driver's side of Edgar's truck. Whatever pulled Vern over to do the same. Winnie uttered a small, businesslike bark and began bounding toward the woods. Whatever sniffed at the step of the truck, then turned to follow Winnie.

Watson had seemed less than excited by the sock. And while he'd drifted over to Edgar's truck after Winnie and Whatever, he seemed bored by its olfactory offerings. I took this as a reassuring confirmation that there had been no dead bodies in or around the truck.

He perked up a little when first Winnie and then Whatever took off into the woods. He didn't stop frequently the way they did, to inhale the air or snuffle the ground, but he trotted along behind them with enthusiasm, and waited patiently whenever they stopped to sniff.

"He's a born cadaver dog," Horace said during one of our stops, with a note of pride in his voice.

"This is the spot where Edgar took that eagle photo," Vern remarked a little while later. "Look—there's the nest."

That was a good sign, wasn't it? The girls had led us straight from Edgar's truck to the spot where he'd taken his last known photo.

Of course, who knew how far he'd traveled since taking that photo. We could have a long hike ahead of us.

"I can see one big advantage to these itty-bitty search dogs," Vern said during another of the dogs' pauses to sniff. "They don't pull your arm out when they're going. They try, but they're just not big enough."

"And they're easier to keep up with," Horace added. "Not that they're slow, but their little legs can only cover so much ground."

They were covering it quite fast enough to keep me hopping. I was glad for the periodic sniffing stops.

I felt a twinge of anxiety when Watson suddenly began barking. Vern and Horace looked worried, too, until we figured out that it was only a squirrel. Winnie and Whatever didn't even bother with the squirrel—they just kept surging ahead.

They were going faster now and stopping less often to sniff. Was that a good sign? Did it mean the trail was fresh and we were nearing our goal? Or just that they were working themselves into an overexcited state, as the Poms sometimes did?

Then both Whatever and Winnie began barking eagerly and pulling hard on their leads.

"I think they've found something," Horace called over his shoulder. Winnie had taken the lead, though Whatever was pulling hard to catch up.

And then we heard it.

"Over here! Over here!" someone shouted ahead of us.

We let the dogs drag us along at a run—well, a slow jog, since going too fast in the woods was perilous—and in a couple of minutes we spotted someone.

Edgar.

He was sitting with his back propped against a large tree. He waved one hand as we drew near. His left leg was drawn up with his elbow resting on it, and his right leg was outstretched and wrapped in bloody bandages that appeared to be made from the sleeves of his plaid shirt and part of his pants leg.

"Mighty glad to see you people," he said. "I was starting to get a little worried about how I was going to get out of here."

"Good girl!" Horace was saying to Winnie, as he handed her a treat.

"Good girl!" Vern echoed to Whatever as he gave her the treat Horace had tossed him.

I gave Watson a treat, too—maybe as a thank-you for not finding a dead body this time.

Vern handed Whatever's leash to me and went over to take a closer look at the bandages.

"You mind if we set the dogs loose so they can come over to see you?" Horace asked. "It's sort of part of their reward for finding you. But only if you're okay with it."

"As long as they steer clear of my leg, I'm fine with it," Edgar said. "And I like dogs. Especially dogs that have probably saved my fool life."

So Horace and I led the dogs until they were past Edgar's bandaged leg before dropping their leashes. Winnie and Whatever both crawled up onto Edgar's lap and began jumping up to lick his face, as if they knew he needed comfort. After a moment of sniffing the air, as if hoping to find something more to his taste, Watson joined them.

"What happened?" Vern asked.

"Rockslide," Edgar said. "Not here," he added, seeing Vern's glance around, puzzled, because there were no rocks in sight. "About a quarter of a mile that way there's a sort of gully. I was on one side of it, and I spotted a fox's den halfway up the other side, with some kits playing around the entrance. I was trying to get into a good spot for taking some shots of them, and like a fool I was watching them instead of my footing. I ended up at the bottom of the ravine with a broken leg."

"Are you sure it's broken?" Horace asked. "A really bad sprain—"

"If it was just a bad sprain I wouldn't be able to see the end of the bone poking out of my leg." Edgar sounded just a bit cranky, which was understandable, under the circumstances.

"You've traveled a quarter of a mile on it?" I was impressed.

"Dragging it, mostly," he said. "Getting out of the gully was the worst part. That and wondering if I'd last long enough to crawl back to civilization. You doing that for a reason, Vern?"

I turned to see that Vern had pulled out his pocketknife and was cutting an inch-thick branch off a nearby tree.

"Figured we could make a travois and haul you out of here." Vern noticed Horace's puzzled look and elaborated. "You know, one of those contraptions the Indians used to drag stuff around with. We get two long poles, we weave a bunch of vines and branches till it sort of looks like a stretcher, and we've got ourselves a travois. So look around for sturdy fallen branches. And vines to tie it all together."

As we gathered vines and branches and lashed together the travois, I decided it was a very good thing Vern had decided to join us. I might have thought of making a travois, but it would have taken me three times as long to make it.

When it was ready, Vern and Horace gently lifted Edgar onto it while I took charge of all three dogs. Edgar didn't make a sound during the process, but his face grew sweaty and visibly paler.

"Okay," Vern said. "Let's get this show on the road. Horace, let's you and I take turns pulling the travois. Whoever's not pulling follows along to ease it over any rough spots and make sure Edgar doesn't get whacked by any branches."

"I can help pull," I said. "I'm pretty strong." In fact, probably stronger than Horace, though I wasn't going to bring that up.

"I figure you are," Vern said. "But I don't think either Horace or I would be very good at doing three things at once, so you get to take point. Use your GPS to guide us back to where we parked, keep the dogs out of trouble, and check every so often to see if you can get a phone signal. Be nice if we could have an ambulance meet us at the road."

So I led the way, and at first I agreed that Vern hadn't given me the easy job. When we started out, the dogs pulled in all directions and wanted to stop and sniff everything. But after we'd been traveling for a few minutes, first Watson and then the rest of the pups seemed to grasp the idea that we were returning to the vehicles and began eagerly pulling in exactly the right direction. I still had to find paths around the various thickets, rocks, and fallen trees we came across, and the dogs were very impatient with the slow speed at which Horace and Vern were hauling the travois.

The only thing I didn't manage was getting a phone signal to call for an ambulance. So when we reached the vehicles, we carefully lifted Edgar up into the back of Vern's truck.

"At this point we might as well just take him on down to the ER." Vern handed me a couple of bottles of water. "Meg, why don't you ride in the back and keep an eye on our patient."

"I'll call in an update." Horace had loaded the dogs into the back of his cruiser and was already holding the receiver of his car radio. "Get Meg's dad to meet you at the hospital."

I settled in the bed of the truck beside Edgar and offered him one of the water bottles. He grabbed it and took a deep drink. Vern eased the car onto the road and set off very slowly, but I could tell even the minor jolts he couldn't avoid were hitting Edgar hard.

"Just let me know if you want peace and quiet," I said. "Or if you want me to talk and try to distract you."

"Let's see how distraction works for starters," he said. "I'd be curious to know what made you all come looking for me. And how you found me. Grateful as all get-out; don't get me wrong about that. But wondering what made you come looking for me all of a sudden. It's not like I don't slope off into the woods pretty regularly."

"You don't normally slope off without asking Dad or Sam Shiffley to keep an eye on your animals," I said.

"True," he said. "Although I didn't expect to be gone all that long this time. Was I hallucinating, or were those fluffy little lap dogs really leading you to me? They didn't trail me all the way from my house, did they?"

So I distracted him from the occasional jolts and bumps by telling him about how Kevin had determined his last known whereabouts so we'd have a good starting point, and how Horace was training the Pomeranians for scent work. I mentioned taking them out to find the Muddy Hollow graveyard, but veered away from mentioning finding Inman's body by giving him a blow-by-blow description of Dad and the bees. A good thing he'd broken a leg rather than a rib, given how hard he laughed.

"Good for James," he said. "Important to have respect for the bees, but also important not to fear them."

"By the way," I said. "Horace and I checked to make sure you weren't at your house before we came out here to look for you. We saw your surveillance system and heard from Kevin about why you have it. I was sorry to hear about your bees."

"Thanks," he said. "Really ticks me off. And I'm still trying to decide if it's safe to put out another hive of bees. On the one hand, I could really get the goods on whoever did it if they tried it again. But on the other hand, I'd be risking the lives of another hive of bees. Can't quite bring myself to do that. And I already almost got myself in trouble trying to figure out who did it."

My stomach tightened.

"Almost got yourself in trouble how?" I asked.

Chapter 16

"I figured whoever murdered my bees would want to get rid of the evidence," Edgar said. "Pretty sure they used cans of ordinary wasp-and-hornet spray—I recognized the smell. Spent considerable time cleaning up all the dead bees to keep as much of the stuff as possible out of the food chain. It's highly toxic to fish and aquatic insects, so not something you want to be spraying around near a stream. And not all that good for mammals, either. Anyway, I know you have to use a whole can of that stuff on a wasp's nest, so I figured they'd have a mess of empty spray cans that they wouldn't want to leave lying around. Happened on a Tuesday, and Thursday morning's trash pickup in Westlake. So I went over very early Thursday morning—about one a.m.— and checked their trash cans."

"Every trash can in Westlake?"

"No," he said. "Just the terrible trio—the Griswolds, the Brownlows, and Walter Inman. But I guess they were smarter than I thought. Didn't find any discarded cans of insecticide."

"Or maybe they were lazier than you thought and hadn't gotten around to discarding the used cans yet."

"Could be, but I wasn't about to try again. Almost got picked up for trespassing on my way out of the neighborhood. Fortunately,

Deputy Butler understands the law a little better than the West-lake crowd. No matter how much they wish they were a gated community and could keep out the riffraff like me, their streets are still public property."

"She didn't find it weird that you were strolling around West-lake in the middle of the night?"

"Not after I told her that I was doing a spotted lanternfly in-spection," he said. "That's an insect—"

"That we're supposed to kill on sight because it's an invasive species that can decimate crops," I finished. "Dad's very militant about them. Aida Butler didn't find it odd that you were doing a spotted lanternfly inspection in the middle of the night?"

"It's not as if it ever gets really dark over there, with all the security lights. And I explained to her what a hard time the Westlake residents give me when I try to do it in broad daylight." Edgar chuckled. "I even brought along a plastic bag with a dozen or so squashed lanternflies for verisimilitude."

No wonder Dad and Edgar got along so well. I could imagine Edgar creeping through Westlake with his bag of bugs. I won-dered if he dressed all in black for the expedition. Dad would have.

"Not that they ever listen to me anyway, those Westlakers," Edgar said. "I don't know how many times I told Walter Inman to stop serving banana daiquiris at his parties."

"You've got something against banana daiquiris?" I asked, wondering what this had to do with either bees or spotted lan-ternflies. "I prefer strawberry myself, but to each his own."

"I don't have anything against them," Edgar said. "Some people think bees might. There's a chemical, isoamyl acetate, that's a major component in both the smell of a banana and the pheromone that honeybees emit when they're alarmed and want to get other bees to attack."

"So bees will attack people who smell like bananas?" Why hadn't anyone warned us, now that we had a hive in the backyard—

the backyard in which we often ate picnic breakfasts during the summer? Bananas were a staple ingredient in Michael's popular homemade smoothies.

"Some say they will, and some say that's hogwash," Edgar said. "But if you were having as much trouble with your guests being stung by bees as Inman keeps claiming he has, don't you think you'd at least consider changing your menu to protect your guests?"

"Good point," I said.

"That reminds me," Edgar added, "about the only good thing about spending last night out there in the woods with my broken leg is that I had a lot of time to think. And I've come up with a plan. I haven't wanted to put any new bees out there unprotected. But what if I could get some folks to help with a bee stakeout? Maybe your dad or your grandfather could recruit some environmental-minded folks to help out. If we got enough people to each take a short shift we could do it. And Kevin's got the cameras set up so you can watch online, so all they'd have to do would be sit in front of their computers for an hour or two and sound the alarm if they saw anyone making a move on the bees."

"It might work," I said.

"Only problem is that we'd have to keep doing it until the bee killer attacked," Edgar said. "Could get boring. People would lose heart."

I nodded. And then an idea struck me.

"Not if you gave the bee killer a reason to act quickly," I said. "What if you started a rumor over in Westlake that your bees were going to swarm any day now, and they should keep their windows closed and stay indoors as much as possible."

Edgar's face lit up, then fell again.

"But the bees probably wouldn't swarm in that direction," he said. "They'd be more likely to head for the woods. And—"

"And you think the denizens of Westlake would know that?" I said. "They probably can't tell bees from hornets. If you tell them they're about to be invaded by half a million bees, that would drive them to action, wouldn't it? And before you tell me that a swarm from one of your hives wouldn't be anywhere near half a million bees, remember—they don't know that, either."

"I like the way you think. They'd fall for it. Yeah. It could work." His smile was a curious mixture of beatific and mischievous. "I can't wait to see Walter Inman's face when we catch him in the act."

My face fell. Edgar noticed.

"And if Wally the Weird is a friend of yours, I'm sorry," he said. "But if I had to put money on it, I'd bet he's the one who did it."

"He's no friend of mine," I said. "And I agree that he seems like a prime suspect. But there's no way you're going to catch him in the act of killing your bees."

"Give me one reason why not." Edgar's face was set in a stubborn scowl.

"Because someone killed him. Probably yesterday. So he may have committed the last bee massacre, but he's not going to be able to do it again."

Edgar's mouth fell open in astonishment and he didn't say anything for a good long minute.

A horn honked behind us. I glanced up to see Dad's car following us. He waved and gave me a thumbs-up.

Dad probably meant for me to reassure Edgar that he'd meet us in the ER. I glanced back at Edgar.

He looked sad.

"The poor sod," he muttered. Then he glanced up. "Oh, I know, that sounds rich coming from me, given all the times I've cursed him out. But as the poet said, 'any man's death diminishes me.' And now Inman will never have his bed curtain moment."

Okay, he'd lost me there.

"You know, in *A Christmas Carol*," he explained, seeing my puzzled look. "When Scrooge wakes up after seeing the last of the three spirits, and his bed curtains are still there—they haven't been taken down, curtain rings and all, and taken to the pawn shop."

I nodded. Now that he'd explained it, I knew exactly what he meant. Since Michael did a one-man dramatic reading of *A Christmas Carol* every holiday season, I not only knew the passage, I could probably have quoted it.

"Maybe it's foolish of me," Edgar went on. "But I keep hoping that somehow, something will get through to people like him and the rest of the Westlake people. I mean, can you imagine how much good they could do in the world if they used all their time and money and energy for some good cause? Climate change. Social justice. World peace. Hell, if they just devoted themselves to picking up litter and installing a dozen or so Little Free Libraries around town they'd do tons more good than they're doing now."

"Were you really optimistic about that happening?" I asked.

"No." He sighed. "But as long as he was alive, there was always a chance. Not anymore."

So he was mourning the Inman Who Might Have Been, not the real thing.

We were pulling up at the ER entrance now. Vern parked, put on his flashers, and ran inside. He dashed out again almost immediately, followed by three scrubs-clad figures with a stretcher, so I deduced that someone—probably Dad—had given them a heads-up to keep an eye out for our arrival. Before they even began loading Edgar onto the stretcher, Dad came running up.

As I watched them haul Edgar away on the stretcher, I realized how much the back of his head looked like Inman's—same salt-and-pepper hair in the same shaggy haircut. Had the chief considered the possibility that the killer had actually been after Edgar?

I followed them inside, but Edgar and Dad and the ER personnel almost immediately disappeared into the bowels of the hospital, leaving Vern and me standing by feeling useless.

"Well, he's in good hands," Vern said. "How about if I run you back to your SUV?"

On the way, I filled Vern in on what Horace and I had seen at Edgar's farm. Not that any of it seemed of earth-shattering significance to the murder case, but I figured the more the chief and his deputies knew about what was going on in Westlake and at Edgar's, the better equipped they'd be to solve the case.

"That bee-poisoning thing bothers me," Vern said. "Is the stuff they used something that could poison other critters?"

"It must be," I said. "Edgar mentioned that he made a point of cleaning up as many of the dead bees as he could find, so I assume it's something you don't want rippling up the food chain."

"It's the eagles that get the worst of it," Vern said. "Being apex predators and all. I'm fond of eagles. Edgar should have reported that someone had killed off his bees. We'd have had a lot better chance of catching the culprit back then, when all the evidence was fresh."

"And when it would have been the biggest crime in town," I added.

"That's so," he said. "Well, here you are."

I could see the Twinmobile in the distance. It occurred to me that we should have drafted someone else to drive Edgar's banana-yellow truck back. Ah, well. Vern would handle it.

"I'm sure you'll be glad to get back to whatever you were planning to do today," he went on. "You think of anything else you think might have something to do with the murder, I'm sure the chief would love to hear about it."

Was Vern deliberately warning me to stay out of the way while law enforcement handled the murder? He should know me by now.

Yes, and maybe that was why he'd said it.

He dropped me off by the Twinmobile, turned around, and waved before driving off. I pondered what I should do next. If the murder hadn't happened, I'd probably have had to spend the whole afternoon trying to calm down the Brownlows and the Griswolds. And Walter Inman. Trying, in vain, to make them see that just because they didn't like Edgar's bees didn't mean they had the right to make him get rid of them.

Now I only had two bee-hating NIMBYs to placate. At least until whoever inherited the Inman house either moved in or sold it. The thought gave me a brief twinge of something like joy. Followed, of course, by a wave of guilt. I wasn't exactly glad Inman was dead. I'd even given up wishing he'd grow tired of Caerphilly and leave town, because I'd come to a pessimistic conclusion. The odds were that anyone who was both able to buy a house in Westlake and willing to live in a place that pretentious and overly manicured . . . probably wouldn't be much of an improvement on Wally the Weird.

I got behind the wheel, but before starting the engine, I put in a call to Cordelia. No answer. So I texted her to say that I was heading back to the house, and to let me know if she was doing anything interesting and wanted me to join her.

Then I glanced into the back seat, where all the issues of *Sweet Tea and Sassafras* were hiding under the picnic blanket. I didn't want to irritate the chief by interfering with his murder investigation. But maybe I could distract myself by fulfilling Cordelia's request that I find out more about the magazine. While waiting to hear from her, I'd go home and look at the library's issues.

Back at the house, I parked in my usual spot, then fetched the metal garden cart we used for hauling big loads of groceries and other heavy cargo to the house or the barn. I loaded the stash of *Sweet Tea and Sassafras* issues into it—did the intern really give me that many, or had they been breeding while my back was turned? I threw the picnic blanket over them, dragged them back to my office at the far end of the barn, and liberated a copier paper box to hide them in. Actually, it took two copier paper boxes.

While boxing them up I also sorted the magazines into chronological order. So it was easy to leaf through them, starting with the most recent issue and then moving back in time.

Although opening even one issue felt like going back in time. To the 1950s.

A lot of decorating articles, usually featuring a stiffly posed photo of the lady of the house pretending to arrange flowers or pour tea, and maybe another of her solemnly conferring with the decorator who'd designed the room. If I'd been looking to hire a decorator, I'd have put all of these people on my "hell, no" list. About half of the articles featured before and after pictures, and if they'd given me a vote on these I'd have been Team Before all the way. Some of these places would have made Versailles look subtle by comparison. I mentally took back every complaint I'd ever made about Mother's decorating. Compared to this lot, she was marvelously restrained. Understated. Almost minimalist.

A lot of articles on debutantes and cotillions. Charity galas. Banquets to honor women's service to various civic and charitable organizations. All perfectly fine things to be doing and writing about, of course. But the magazine seemed to have carved out a singularly narrow niche for itself. Narrow and, for my taste, rather bland.

And yes, each issue had at least one feature on a prominent woman. None of them were women who seemed anything like Cordelia.

In fact—holy cow! One of the women they'd profiled a year and a half ago was Mavis Anstruther.

A profile rather than an article about her decor, but the accompanying photos did show enough of her house to prove that yes, at least as of a year and a half ago, the rumor was correct—her sofa did, indeed, sport two needlepoint pillows featuring the Confederate flag. Not exactly someone I wanted to see touted as a leading citizen of Caerphilly.

And I took the time to read the article. What a crock! I started off laughing at how pretentious and self-absorbed she was, but by the time I finished the article, I was furious. According to the article she had transformed her garden into a lush paradise through her own expertise and hard work. Nonsense. She'd hired a pricy Richmond landscaping company and had them install not only shrubs and bulbs but a pair of full-grown trees. But at least she'd bought and paid for her landscaping. Elsewhere in the article she also claimed responsibility for half a dozen accomplishments that actually belonged to other people. She had not single-handedly revitalized the Caerphilly Garden Club—Mother had. She hadn't founded the Ladies Interfaith Council—the credit for that went to Robyn Smith, the rector of Trinity Episcopal, and Mrs. Wilson, the wife of the pastor of the New Life Baptist Church. Donating her copies of *Sweet Tea and Sassafras* had probably been the sum total of her "generous and untiring support" of the Caerphilly Library. I'd never seen her at the library book sales or bake sales, as either a volunteer or a shopper—and I would have, if she was that tireless. The last time I'd missed helping with any of these events was the year I'd been pregnant with the boys. The various events and festivals, like Christmas in Caerphilly and the Un-Fair, that had made Caerphilly such a popular tourist destination were all Randall Shiffley's brainchildren, not hers—and executed with a lot of work from a whole lot of residents—especially me. I hadn't once seen her helping out at the Caerphilly Women's Shelter. As far as I could recall, her sole contribution to any of these enterprises was to protest that they would cost too much, raise picayune objections about how they were being organized, and predict that they'd be complete failures.

"This whole thing is a tissue of lies," I muttered. Had anyone at *Sweet Tea and Sassafras* ever heard of fact-checking? Maybe whatever idiot had written the article might have been taken in by Mrs. Anstruther's blatant falsehoods, but—

I flipped back to the first page to check the article's byline: Britni Colleton.

Chapter 17

Okay, just because Britni was an idiot didn't mean she was going to write an equally obsequious and inaccurate article about Cordelia.

But what would she do when faced with a profile subject who did have genuine accomplishments . . . just not ones that would fit neatly into the *Sweet Tea and Sassafras* mold?

I had a bad feeling about this. Okay, compared with a murder it was a minor worry, but I'd done all the chief would allow me to do on the murder.

I kept on flipping through my stack of magazines. As I drew near the bottom of the pile it dawned on me that the magazine was only a little over four years old. Evidently Mavis Anstruther had been a charter subscriber and had given the library her entire collection.

I recognized a few names. The wife of a North Carolina politician who was now in disgrace for taking bribes a little more blatantly than usual, even in his historically corrupt city. A Northern Virginia decorator who'd done a room in the same designer showhouse as Mother a few years ago—a room so tacky and over the top that five years later its memory still made

Mother shudder and press a hand to her temple as if feeling the start of a migraine.

And Mrs. Brownlow.

They'd done her in their sixth issue, around the time she'd moved from Richmond to Caerphilly. And again it was Britni who'd done the article. After the laughable job she'd done with Mrs. Anstruther, I knew better than to take every word of the article as gospel. But there were probably a few things even Britni couldn't mangle. The Brownlows had lived in an elegant Queen Anne–style house in the historic Fan District of Richmond, Virginia. There was a full-page picture of it in the magazine. They blocked out the house number, but mentioned the street name, and it was a fairly distinctive house. A few minutes' work with Google Street View and I had the address. Another few minutes with Zillow and I learned that the Brownlows had sold it three years ago for very close to a million dollars. The financial management company from which Mr. Brownlow was now retired must have been fairly successful.

Curiously, the article didn't make out Mrs. Brownlow to be one of the city's movers and shakers. Maybe the magazine's circulation in Richmond was big enough that Britni didn't think she could get away with that. Apart from heading up the committee that was organizing a big charity ball that year—probably the reason they were profiling her—she wasn't claiming to be in charge of anything, which made a nice change from Mrs. Anstruther. The article named a couple of societies she belonged to. Several fancy restaurants where she and her husband enjoyed dining. Her favorite antique and clothing stores. How much she enjoyed the Virginia Opera and the many museums found throughout Richmond.

Kind of a snooze, actually. Mrs. Brownlow sounded like a fairly normal person—at least if your definition of normal involved not having any kind of job or career and living in a million-dollar house that featured a three-story Art Deco–style Otis elevator, a small conservatory, and a mint-julep sipping room, whatever that was. Then again, she also came off as sane and even pleasant. Britni certainly had a flair for fiction.

And I was still puzzled why *Sweet Tea and Sassafras* would want to profile Cordelia. Maybe my grandmother was right to be apprehensive.

I decided to enlist an expert. I picked up my phone and called Mother.

"Meg, dear," she said. "I was just thinking of calling you. Your father has been so embroiled in this morning's tragic events that he hasn't had a minute to talk."

Translation: Dad hadn't given her any juicy inside details about the murder.

"I can fill you in," I said. "So you'll know what we'll all need to deal with." I was pleased with how that last bit came out—almost made it sound as if we had a vital part to play in solving the crime. "And I have something I want to show you and get your help on—something that's both bulky and confidential. Any chance you could drop by our house anytime soon?"

"I'm at your house now," she replied. "I just brought your grandmother home. Are you—"

"In my office," I said.

In another five minutes, Mother was seated on my guest chair and trying very hard to pretend she wasn't staring critically at my office's decor. Or more accurately its lack of decor. The space looked like exactly what it was—a converted tack room at one end of a barn. She didn't have to remind me that she would be delighted to sketch up some decorating ideas, if I could just tell her what I wanted. So I didn't have to say, for the umpteenth time, that for right now I liked it the way it was.

"Poor Cordelia," she said. "She's had a trying afternoon. First she had to have tea with that reporter person—at least it was at the Frilled Pheasant, which must have been nice."

"Nice for you, maybe," I said. "You know how I feel about the place."

"Yes, dear," she said. "And curiously, I gather Cordelia's not a fan, either. And then that wretched Britni person came down with a migraine and didn't feel up to bringing your grandmother home, even though she was feeling the onset of a migraine herself, so I had to go and rescue her."

"Have you told Rose Noire that Cordelia has a migraine?" I hoped she hadn't. While Rose Noire's attentions to anyone who was suffering were well meant and sometimes surprisingly effective, they could also be very trying.

"No, let's leave her in peace. I don't think she's in need of any strenuous attention—just a bit of a rest. She's lying down now. And she didn't even feel up to telling me very many details about how you found the body together."

So I gave her the scoop on the morning's events—both finding Walter Inman's body and locating Edgar. Mother always made a highly satisfactory audience, interjecting comments like "No! He didn't!" or "Well done!" at all the right moments.

"Thank you, dear," she said when I had finished. "I'm sure your father will tell me all about it when he can—"

"But you want to know now," I said. "Besides, Dad will want to tell you all about the details you don't want to hear, like the autopsy and the forensic entomological details."

"I'm used to that," she said. "I just smile and think about passementerie. You said you needed my help. Is it something to do with the murder?"

"Probably not," I said. "But I might be wrong. What do you know about Mrs. Anstruther?"

For a moment she looked taken aback.

"Mavis Anstruther?" she asked.

"There's more than one Mrs. Anstruther in town?"

"No, thank goodness. What do you need to know about her?" Her tone suggested that she might also be wondering "And why do you even care?"

"*Sweet Tea and Sassafras* did a feature on her about eighteen months ago."

"Really." Mother sniffed slightly. "What could they possibly find worth writing about?"

"You'd be surprised." I handed her the relevant issue of the magazine.

I watched as she read. Her reaction was much the same as mine, but she was excellent at hiding it—only someone who knew her well would know how appalled she was.

"How very interesting," she murmured as she handed me back the magazine, holding it between her thumb and forefinger as if it were something damp and unwholesome. "Interesting" was her usual adjective for those occasions when she could think of nothing positive to say, but never had I heard her utter it with quite so much revulsion and scorn.

"Should we worry about the profile she's doing on Cordelia?" I asked. "Because I think Cordelia is. And after reading that profile of Mrs. Anstruther, it's obvious that Britni's not much for accuracy."

"No." Mother looked pained. "But it's not as if she'd need to invent anything to make your grandmother interesting."

"What if she does a profile on Cordelia that's equally inaccurate and completely unflattering?" I asked. "I can see that happening, if Cordelia's not the kind of interesting *Sweet Tea and Sassafras* likes. Because if you ask me, their judgment is highly suspect." I handed her the issue with the feature on the decorator she so disliked.

"Evidently," she said as she leafed through the article. "If they're choosing to showcase this pretentious nonsense."

"They should see what elegant decorating is really like," I said. "Let's see if we can talk Britni into doing a feature on your decorating business."

"Let's not," she said, with a slight shudder, as she continued to leaf through the magazine. "It's part of the decorator's mission to express the taste of the client, not her own, and I don't think I'd be very sympatico with the readers of *Sweet Tea and Sassafras*. And I'm beginning to wonder if letting them interview Cordelia is really a good idea." She looked up and looked sternly at me. "Cordelia's right. We need to find out more about the magazine and Ms. Colleton. See what you can find out. I'll do the same."

"Roger." Actually, I was hoping I could enlist Kevin's cyber-sleuthing skills to do the job. But an idea struck me. "Where do the Anstruthers live?"

"Westlake, of course. And it's only Mavis now. Virgil, her husband, died last year. Not exactly a shock—he was a good twenty-five years older than she was—over eighty, I think. Anyway, she has that huge, awkward-looking fake Spanish hacienda on Hawthorne Street. You'll know it when you see it."

Yes. In fact, I was pretty sure I remembered it. It was just around the corner from the Griswolds, the Brownlows, and Walter Inman, so lately I'd passed it often enough.

"I'm going to a Garden Club meeting," she said. "Mavis Anstruther doesn't usually bother to show up, but if she does, I'll see what I can find out about her experience with Britni."

"Thanks," I said. "If she's not at the meeting, I might be able to catch her at home. Her and Mrs. Brownlow. I'll keep you posted on anything I learn."

"Be careful," she said. "Mavis Anstruther and Connie Brownlow could very well consider Britni a friend. After all, she wrote positive articles about them."

"Don't worry," I said. "I'll be careful. Subtle, even. I can do subtle when I work at it," I added, seeing her expression.

"You'll do fine, dear." She was wearing her Joan of Arc expression. "And remember: We do not want that woman giving your grandmother any trouble."

She sailed out, looking as if she were planning to storm a castle rather than just interrogate a middle-aged snob. But she was as fond of Cordelia as I was. I thought, not for the first time, how lucky Mother had been, having Cordelia as her mother-in-law. Her only regret was that they hadn't met sooner, since it had only been a few years ago that we'd reconnected with the mother who, as a frightened teenager, had given Dad up for adoption at his birth.

In contrast, Michael's mother's best feature was her passionate addiction to traveling abroad, which meant she was never here often enough or long enough to wear out her welcome. Well, that and the fact that she did have pretty good taste in presents for her grandsons.

I headed back to the house. If I was going visiting in Westlake, maybe I should change into something other than the jeans and Caerphilly College t-shirt I'd worn for this morning's expedition to the woods.

In the kitchen, I found that Horace must have dropped off the Pomeranians. They were sitting in a circle at Rose Noire's feet, gazing up at her expectantly. No doubt they were hoping she'd need them to serve as guinea pigs for another experimental batch of all-natural dog treats. They were doomed to disappointment. She was preparing a tray. It already held a teacup, a teaspoon, a small sugar bowl, and a plate of assorted homemade cookies. She was lifting a boiling kettle and pouring water into a small teapot. Oh, dear.

"For Cordelia?" I asked.

"Yes," she said. "We were having a lovely time at Flugleman's, picking out the things we need for the hummingbirds, when that reporter dragged her away. I'm not at all sure I approve of that woman."

"Mother definitely doesn't," I said. "What do we need for the hummingbirds?"

"Well, a few more feeders, so we can space them far apart enough that the one bird won't see them all as his territory. And little guards to keep the bees from drinking the sugar water."

"You've got something against our bees?"

"Of course not! I've planted loads of flowers for them. And we could always put out some sugar water just for them. But we don't want them stealing the hummingbirds' nectar." With that she picked up the tray and glided out.

I was refilling my water bottle and wondering whether to pack a snack for the road—the homemade cookies were still warm and smelled divine—when Kevin appeared in the doorway that led to his computer-infested lair in the basement.

"Hey, Meg," he said. "Any chance you could do me a favor?"

Chapter 18

I refrained from reminding Kevin that on at least one recent occasion doing a favor for him had almost gotten me killed, when his podcast covered a so-called cold case that turned out to be a lot warmer than any of us imagined.

"A favor?" I said. "Possibly. What did you have in mind?"

"Can you go down to the hospital and see Edgar?" He slouched against the doorframe, suggesting that he thought it might take a while to persuade me. "I need to get the photos Edgar took while he was out in the woods."

"He can't just email them to you himself? Pretty sure there's good cell phone coverage all through the hospital." Not that I minded going down to the hospital—in fact, I'd like to check on Edgar. I could do it on my way to Westlake. But I was puzzled—doing things in person was never Kevin's style. Not even when he could delegate the in-person part to someone else.

"Normally he could," Kevin said. "But they've got him on a lot of painkillers and he's kind of having a problem remembering how. Plus it's not just the ones on his phone—he also had a digital camera with him. I want the photos from that, too. You could take your laptop down there and get a copy of them—you know how to do that, right?" A note of anxiety crept into his voice, as if he feared finding out that yet another family member was a technological nitwit.

"I can probably figure it out," I said. "And if I can't, I can always call you for instructions. Maybe even follow them, since I'm not currently on any interesting meds. Why the sudden interest in Edgar's photos?"

"I'm hoping I can use the time and location data in them to give him a solid alibi for the murder."

Now that was something I could get behind. Especially since Kevin was probably asking not just out of curiosity but in his role as official computer and data consultant to the Caerphilly police.

"In that case, I'm happy to do it," I said. "But are you sure it will do any good? I mean, he'd probably have stopped taking pictures when it got dark. Even at this time of year, he'd still have a good eight or nine hours to sneak over to the other side of the county and knock off Inman."

"He's big on photographing nocturnal creatures. Owls and possums and stuff. And he said he was having trouble sleeping, thanks to the pain from his broken leg, so he set up his low-light gear and took a lot of shots of the local night life to distract himself."

"That's lucky," I said. "Still, don't we also have to worry about whether Inman was killed before Edgar set out for the woods? Last time I heard, Dad was having trouble narrowing down the time of death."

"Well, there's some good news on that front." Kevin's face showed how pleased he was to have scooped me on any part of the murder case. I tried to keep my face from showing how pleased I was at getting information I might not otherwise hear. "We know Inman was alive at seven yesterday evening, because he had a massive argument with the Brownlows around then. And Edgar was already out in the woods by that time, taking that eagle picture at five fourteen, and he claims he broke his leg no more than an hour later. So as long as we can prove Edgar didn't come back from the woods at any time between seven p.m. and whatever time it was you guys found Inman's body, he's in the clear."

"And as long as the Brownlows are right about the date and time of the quarrel," I said. "What's to prevent them from changing their story when they find out it could alibi Edgar?"

"We don't have to rely on them." Kevin had that "gotcha" look. "We have the video from Inman's security system. Whole thing played out right in front of one of his security cameras."

"Awesome." A thought hit me. "How far back does Inman's video go?"

"It goes back to the night Edgar's beehives were destroyed, if that's what you're thinking," he said. "But if Inman did it, we can't prove it from his own security system. He only has one camera covering his backyard, and it's messed up."

"Of course it is," I said. "The one camera we really need to be working and it's on the blink."

"Actually, it's working," he said. "But I think it got knocked askew. You can't see any of his backyard—just bugs crawling all around in front of the lens."

"That's annoying," I said. "But the Griswolds and the Brownlows also have security systems. If you can get hold of their data, it might show something."

"I think the chief's already planning to," he said. "Want to bet they'll dig in their heels and try to fight it?"

"You know they will," I said. "Even if they're innocent themselves and know there's evidence there that could convict the actual killer. But he'll probably get it eventually. It'd be nice if he could get video back as far as when Edgar's hives were destroyed."

"Might be doable if there was any chance the destruction of the hives was somehow related to the murder."

"It could be," I said. "The NIMBYs are sure to claim Edgar

killed Inman in retaliation. Unless your photo idea exonerates him."

"Yeah. Let me know when you get back with the photos," he said. "I'll be here dealing with your rogue hummingbird."

"Dealing with him? How?" I suddenly felt very anxious about the tiny bully. "Okay, he's picking on all the other hummers, but he's just following his instincts. You have to admire something so small and yet so feisty. And besides—"

"Chill," he said. "Nothing horrible. No *Archilocus whateverus* will be harmed in the process. Here—watch."

He tapped on his phone, then held it up for me to look at. I saw a picture of the hummingbird feeder. As I watched, a hummer approached and the phone made a soft tinkling noise.

"Motion detection," he said.

We watched the tiny bird hover and feed. Then it darted away.

"And if your bully bird tries to cause trouble, you do this."

He tapped something on the phone and a jet of water appeared in the picture. Kevin did something else on his phone screen and the water jet moved in an arc.

"I've got better controls on the computer," he said. "I can zap him pretty consistently. Only when he goes after the other birds, of course—not when he feeds."

"So you're becoming a full-time hummingbird enforcer?" I asked. "Have you broken the news to Rob?" Kevin was a senior staffer at Mutant Wizards, my brother's software and computer game company, and probably had a few reasonably important projects on his plate.

"No," he said. "But I seem to recall that intermittent reinforcement is pretty effective. And I figure I can enlist a few other people to help. We can worry about that later. Oh, by the way, Edgar's in room two thirteen. And take this."

He handed me a small, zippered cloth-and-mesh case. I opened it and peered in. I saw a flash drive and a tangle of cords, cables, and small electronic gadgets.

"All the stuff you might need for getting the photos," he explained, before turning and heading back downstairs.

"Just answer the phone when I call to get you to explain it all to me," I called after him.

"Right."

I zipped up the case and stowed it in my tote. Then I grabbed a handful of cookies and went back to the barn. In addition to collecting my laptop, I located the copies of *Sweet Tea and Sassafras* with the articles about Mrs. Anstruther and Mrs. Brownlow and stuck them in my tote. I might not have the chance to tackle either of them today, but it didn't hurt to have the issues available.

When I stepped out of the barn, I saw that Kevin and the hummingbird were doing battle. An even smaller and differently colored hummingbird was sipping at the feeder while Kevin fended off the bully bird with short, well-aimed bursts of water. I was relieved to see that it didn't seem to hurt the hummer.

"I hope you don't have any big deadlines in the next few days," I muttered to the invisible Kevin.

Then I hopped into the Twinmobile and took off for town. I was halfway there before I remembered that I was still wearing the jeans and t-shirt I'd been hiking around the woods in.

Ah, well. By now the Westlakers probably knew better than to expect formality from me.

I felt the all-too-familiar reaction when I pulled into the hospital parking lot, a half-unconscious blend of anxiety and adrenaline. I had to remind myself that I was only here as a spectator—not a patient or family member of a patient. Between having two active and adventurous sons and the fact that Dad was militant about getting even the mildest of his family's injuries thoroughly diagnosed and treated, I'd spent a lot of time here at the hospital. I'd even once foiled a murder on the premises.

As I was walking to the front door, my phone dinged. A text from Kevin.

"Chief Burke meeting you there to help with photo collection."

Since the chief was no more tech-savvy than I was, I wondered what sort of help he was expected to provide. Probably supervision. Preserving the chain of custody in case they turned out to be evidence.

I stopped at the reception desk to get a visitor's badge and took the elevator up to the second floor. Room 213 was on the better side of the corridor, where the rooms had a view of a grassy lawn fringed with trees rather than the parking lot. The door was open, so I knocked on the frame and called out, "Okay to come in?"

"Of course!" Edgar called.

"Meg! Perfect!" Dad exclaimed.

I strolled in, hoping I wasn't interrupting some medical procedure or consultation. Edgar was sitting up in bed, looking a lot better than he had the last time I'd seen him. He had a pair of binoculars hanging by their strap around his neck, so I assumed he'd been enjoying the view. A young man with the tall, lean build and cheerful long-jawed face of a Shiffley was occupying the guest chair, and Dad was standing by the head of Edgar's bed with his stethoscope around his neck and a broad smile on his face.

"Just the person we need!" Dad exclaimed.

Not a medical consultation, then.

"Meg, this is my next-door neighbor, Sam Shiffley," Edgar said.

Sam and I exchanged nods and smiles.

"He and your dad and I have been figuring out the details on how we're going to trap the wretch who killed all those bees of mine," Edgar went on.

"Edgar has a bunch of hives out at my cousin Mel's," Sam

said. "Your dad and I are going to move one of the hives into Edgar's yard tonight."

"And your grandfather's rounding up some of the Blake's Brigade members to keep watch through the cameras," Dad said. "That's all the volunteers who help out when he goes on an expedition to save an endangered species or bust up a dog-fighting ring or something like that," he added, turning to Sam.

"And we can probably recruit a few of our fellow SPOOR members," Edgar said.

If I'd thought about it, I could have predicted that Edgar would belong to Stop Poisoning Our Owls and Raptors, a local environmental group.

"We're going to make sure we have at least two watchers in every time period." Sam held up a spiral notebook, so I deduced he was acting as scribe and taking down the schedule.

"Kevin's going over sometime today to do a few enhancements to the security system," Dad said. "And a few of us plan to hide in Edgar's house tonight, so we can be there to run out and intervene if it looks as if anyone's about to attack the bees."

"Make sure the police know what you're up to," I suggested. "So they can swoop in to arrest the culprits."

"Already thought of that," Sam said. "If my cousin Vern's off duty, he's going to sack out in my spare bedroom. And if he ends up pulling an extra shift because of the murder, he'll make sure everyone who's out on patrol knows what's happening."

"Sounds as if you have everything covered," I said. "As long as word doesn't get around to the Westlakers about what's happening."

"We've sworn everyone to secrecy," Dad exclaimed.

Which wouldn't prevent word from getting around town but would slow it down. And it wasn't as if the NIMBYs were very connected to the local grapevine.

"Fine, then," I said. "What do you need me for?"

"Edgar seemed to think you might be able to rile up the

Westlakers," Sam said. "Motivate whoever has evil designs on the bees to strike now."

"Because right now our volunteers are pretty fired up," Dad said. "But if they have to watch for days, even weeks, their enthusiasm is going to flag. They could drop out or get careless."

"Remember what you suggested when we were riding into town?" Edgar said. "You could go there and talk to them. Make 'em think I've got a hive full of angry bees ready to swarm."

"I can do that," I said. "But now that I've thought about it, I'm wondering if it's really a good idea. I've been spending a lot of time trying to convince the Westlakers that they're in no danger from the bees—is it really wise to undo all of that in one fell swoop?"

"Do you really think you've convinced a single one of them that the bees are perfectly harmless?" Edgar asked. "It'd be one thing if you'd actually managed that, and our plan would undo it. But as far as I can see, they haven't budged on the subject."

Sadly, he was right. Over the last several years, ever since Randall decided that I had an ever-so-slightly better track record on dealing with the Westlakers, I'd lost count of how many hours I'd spent on them. I fielded their complaints about bees, smelly livestock, slow farm vehicles blocking the road, how often the deputies patrolled their neighborhood, how noisy the trash collectors were, and how late their mail deliveries were—would they ever figure out that I had no power over the U.S. Postal Service? I met with them individually and in groups. I attended their HOA meetings as Randall's representative. And I wrote calm, polite, factual replies to every single one of the many letters they deluged us with. With the possible exception of the town and county attorney, there was no one in Caerphilly as sick and tired of reasoning with the Westlakers as I was.

"Good point," I said. "Then just let me notify the chief that I'm going to be talking to some of his potential witnesses."

"Suspects, if you ask me." Edgar frowned sternly.

"Well, yes," Dad said. "We have to consider them suspects. But they're not the only suspects. From what Sam and Edgar tell me, Mr. Inman was generally disliked in the neighborhood."

"On account of being a yard nazi," Sam said. "Got himself elected to the Westlake homeowner's council and spends—spent—all his free time making everybody miserable over every little thing he could catch them doing."

"And from what I've overheard, he was just the same when he lived up near Washington," Dad said. "He could have long-standing enemies we don't even know about yet."

Curious that Sam and Edgar knew so much about what was going on in Westlake. They probably kept their ears to the ground for their own protection. I had no doubt that Inman had made enemies wherever he went. But I suspected most of them would be happy to leave him alone once he was no longer a nosy, bossy neighbor. Hard to imagine he could have done something so awful that after several years they'd bother to come all the way down to Caerphilly to take their revenge. Still, good that the chief was investigating the possibility.

And just then a brisk knock on the doorframe announced that someone was arriving. The chief.

Chapter 19

"Quite the convention here." He nodded at us all. "But since Dr. Langslow is here, I assume he'd chase us out if Edgar wasn't up to company. How are you feeling, Edgar?"

"A lot better now that I'm out of the woods and had my leg seen to," Edgar said. "But I'm a little loopy, so if I say anything strange, just blame the pain meds Dr. Langslow's been giving me. You want to interview me, right?"

"If you're feeling up to it," the chief said. "But first I'm going to supervise Meg getting copies of all the photos in your camera and your phone, and then I'm going to take them both into evidence for the time being."

"My phone, too?" Edgar looked worried. "I know it sounds silly, but I think I'm going to feel pretty naked without that."

"We'll get you a burner phone." Dad's excited tone suggested that acquiring a burner phone was a long-felt wish. "Of course, I have no idea where one does that—I think it's mostly spies and criminals who do it." He looked at the chief as if hoping he could supply the information.

"Actually, Horace already foresaw that Edgar would not want to be left phoneless," the chief said. "He had me bring this along." He held up a rather old-fashioned-looking flip phone.

"Doesn't have many bells and whistles, but it will let you make a call if you need it."

"It won't take photos," Edgar mourned. "And it won't have Cornell's Merlin app. Or— But that's rude of me, complaining when Horace has been so thoughtful. Take mine away! Quick! I'm a rip-the-bandage guy!"

Edgar held out his phone with one hand, covering his eyes with the other. The chief took it. Dad handed me a digital camera.

"And you'll need the password." Edgar beckoned to the chief. "Come closer and I'll tell you."

The chief came close and bent down so his ear was right next to Edgar's mouth.

"*Strigidae*," Edgar hissed, loudly enough that we all heard him.

"Could you spell that?" the chief asked.

"S . . . um . . ." Edgar looked puzzled, and I remembered he was on heavy pain meds.

"S-T-R-I-G-I-D-A-E," Dad and I recited in unison. Sam wrote it down in his notebook, then tore out the page and handed it to the chief.

"Exactly," Edgar said. "And if you forget, just remember that it's the family of true owls."

"Great," I said. "Chief, let's find a quiet place to deal with these, so they can get on with planning the sting."

"The Sting!" Dad exclaimed. "Why didn't I think of that?"

"It's perfect," Edgar beamed. "The Sting!"

"Good name," Sam said, with a nod of approval.

"Let's call Dr. Blake and tell him!" Edgar suggested.

The chief and I left them to it.

"What is this sting operation they're planning?" he asked. "Should I worry?"

I explained about the plan to flush out the bee killer.

"But if you'd rather I steer clear of the NIMBYs today, just say the word and I'll tell them to postpone it," I added.

"No, it's fine with me," he said. "Frankly, I'd welcome anything that might distract the residents of Westlake from calling me repeatedly to complain that they're terrified of being murdered in their beds and asking why haven't I caught the killer yet. A couple of them seem to think I can afford to spare several of my deputies to patrol their neighborhood."

"Typical," I said.

"And maybe you actually will flush out whoever attacked Edgar's bees."

We found an empty room across the hall, and the chief watched with bemusement as I sorted through the electronic tools Kevin had provided until I found what I needed to hook up Edgar's camera to my laptop. He had an interesting collection of photos. Early on it was all birds, insects, small animals, and interesting plants—he seemed to have a fascination with picturesque fungi. Then a few distant pictures of the fox kits. Followed by a rather gory series of his bloody pants leg, with the end of his femur sticking out. A few shots documenting his harrowing crawl through the woods, presumably to the spot where we'd found him. And then the nighttime shots. A deer, gazing at him with curiosity. A possum, showing all of its many pointy little teeth. The moon, seen through an opening in the tree canopy. An owl that seemed to be contemplating whether Edgar was predator or prey. Then light returned, and Edgar seemed to be distracting himself from his pain by photographing every single object within camera range. The final photo in the bunch was of Horace, Vern, the Pomeranians, and me, arriving in his clearing. The Pomeranians' look of joy and triumph was classic. I was going to ask for a copy of that one.

I finished copying them all to a folder, unhooked the camera, and handed it to the chief. I managed to type in *Strigidae* accurately to unlock Edgar's phone and perform the same operation on it.

"Thank you," he said when I handed him the phone. "Tell

Kevin I'll be looking forward to his report on whether these support Edgar's alibi."

He left the room. I packed up Kevin's electronics toolkit and headed out. I stopped in the hall long enough to peer into the door of Edgar's room. There was a large whiteboard on one wall, presumably for doctors and nurses to use for medical purposes. Dad had drawn a large grid on it and was filling in names. Sam appeared to be copying down the chart. Edgar was staring at his loaner phone, clearly puzzled at how to operate it. The chief was standing at the foot of the bed, looking as if he was about to shoo Dad and Sam out.

"It's my destiny, you know," Edgar was saying. "Beekeeping, I mean. I even have the name. Bortnick's a Ukrainian name that means beekeeper."

"That's fabulous!" Dad exclaimed.

I decided to vamoose before they found something else for me to do. Besides, school was letting out, and I liked to be home when the boys arrived.

I arrived at home just as the carpool pulled up in front of our house to drop off Josh and Jamie. TJ Washington, Isaac's wife, was driving this week. Josh, Jamie, Adam Burke, and Isaac, Jr. erupted from the car and dashed off toward the backyard. TJ rolled down the window when she saw me.

"Thank you for taking Isaac's granddaddy out there," she said. "And taking such good care of him."

"I just hope the whole thing wasn't too tiring for him," I said.

"Gracious, no." She laughed. "I don't know which made him happier—finding that old cemetery or having a front-row seat for a murder investigation. Although . . ." She frowned, and she seemed to be trying to decide whether or not to say something else. "Is it true that Walter Inman was the victim?"

I nodded.

"Damn."

"You knew him?"

"Not hardly." She shook her head. "We don't exactly travel in the same social circles. But I knew *of* him. And I sure hope his murder doesn't cause problems for a lot of people who were just trying to protect their kids."

"From Walter Inman?"

"Yes." She glanced around as if to make sure none of the boys were within earshot. "Or Mr. Creepy Stalker Guy—that's what some of us have taken to calling him. The last couple of months he's been spotted several times following teenagers when they drove home at night. From the movies, from games at the high school—even from choir practice over at New Life Baptist."

"Definitely creepy," I said. "The chief knows, I assume."

"Yes, and he and his officers have been keeping an eye on the guy. But there's only so much the police can do. It's not as if it's illegal to drive on the public roads, and I gather the few times they stopped him he always had a plausible reason for being out. But it's going to be hard on the chief. He's going to have to investigate a whole lot of perfectly innocent people just because they complained about Mr. Creepy Stalker Guy."

She clenched her jaw slightly, and I wondered if she was thinking the same thing I was—that just maybe one of those worried parents wasn't perfectly innocent. What if one of them thought Inman had done something worse than just following their teenager around?

"Mostly kids from New Life Baptist?" I asked. Which, since the church was heavily African American, was a roundabout way of asking if Inman was an equal opportunity stalker or if he seemed to be targeting Black teens.

"That I know of," she said. "Isaac's kid sister was one of them. The chief would know for sure."

I nodded. I was still trying out the concept of Wally the Weird being Creepy Stalker Guy. It didn't seem at all implausible.

"Well, no use borrowing trouble," she said. "Is it okay if I leave Junior here for a while? He claims he and Josh need to work on a school project together."

"Fine by me," I said.

We said our goodbyes and TJ drove off. I strolled into the backyard to see what the boys were up to. Jamie and Adam were feeding treats to the llamas. Josh and Junior were hanging on the fence, presumably watching the beehive from afar.

What would I do if I caught someone like Wally the Weird following them around? Under normal circumstances, I'd have said I wasn't capable of murder. But if someone threatened one of the boys . . .

Probably a good thing I was leaving this to the chief.

I headed for the back door, but just as I was stepping inside my phone rang. The chief.

"What's up?" I said.

"I'm looking for Ms. Colleton," he said. "I wanted to interview her before she forgets what few details she noticed this morning. But she's not answering her phone, and neither is your grandmother—I thought perhaps they might be together."

"Last time I checked, Cordelia was still upstairs recovering from a Britni-induced migraine," I said as I strolled through the kitchen. "And Britni supposedly went back to the Inn to nurse a migraine of her own. That could account for both of their phones being off."

"Evidently Ms. Colleton made a more rapid recovery than your grandmother," the chief said. "According to the Inn's front desk, she drove off nearly an hour ago."

"The wretch," I muttered. "Hang on a second."

I walked through the house and out onto the front porch.

"No unfamiliar cars here," I said. "So mere Britni is loosed upon the world. If I run into her I can tell her you want to talk to her."

"If you would be so kind."

We signed off before I could give way to the impulse to ask if he thought Inman's stalking had anything to do with his murder.

I strolled into the kitchen. Rose Noire was there—and Cordelia.

"Feeling better?" I asked.

"Not appreciably," Cordelia said. "But it will make me feel a little better to know that my head isn't standing in the way of solving your hummingbird problem. As soon as Michael gets home, he's going to get the boys to help him install the new feeders. I wanted to give them a diagram of where they should go."

She pushed a piece of paper across the table toward me and slumped back in her seat. I studied the diagram for a few moments. It was clear, although her hand was obviously a bit shaky. And she looked deathly pale. I felt a sudden surge of murderous rage at Britni. She did this to Cordelia, and then abandoned her in the Frilled Pheasant.

"Looks fine to me," I said. "Let's get you back upstairs so you can rest."

Rose Noire and I made sure Cordelia was settled down in the darkened bedroom, with the blackout shades pulled down and an ice pack for her head. I nixed Rose Noire's suggestions of aromatherapy and soothing New Age music. Maybe they'd have helped, but Cordelia had specifically requested peace and quiet and darkness.

As we made our way quietly downstairs again, I found myself examining my rage at Britni. I'd jumped very quickly to the assumption that she'd only been pretending to have a migraine. Faking it so she'd have an excuse to shirk driving Cordelia home. For all I knew, she had been—and maybe still was—in genuine agony. Maybe she'd left the Inn to go into town in the hope of getting a prescription for migraine medicine filled before her head got even worse. And maybe Cordelia hadn't revealed that she was getting a migraine. She might have been in one of her stoic moods, not wanting to admit weakness to a relative stranger. A relative stranger who might broadcast it to the world. Why was I so quick to accuse Britni of thoughtless and dishonest behavior?

We had reached the front hall. Rose Noire was still standing, looking wistfully up the stairs, as if wishing she could think of something else she could do.

"You know what's the best thing we can do for Cordelia?" I said.

"What?" Her tone was eager.

"Keep everything quiet, and keep everyone away from her, no matter what," I said. "Especially Britni—the reporter who's doing the story on Cordelia. The migraine's probably her fault."

"Then I'll make sure she doesn't come anywhere near your grandmother." Rose Noire drew herself up in a passable imitation of what we called Mother's Joan of Arc pose.

"You've met her, right?" I asked. "What do you think of her?"

"Her aura, you mean?"

Actually, I wasn't at all sure I believed in auras, but I'd long ago realized that when Rose Noire described someone's aura, she was actually giving me a character sketch, and she was a better-than-average judge of character. So I nodded.

"I don't know yet," she said. "I can't get a good reading on her. She must be repressing her emotions very strongly—that can't be healthy. No wonder she has migraines, poor thing."

I nodded absently. Why did I find the idea that the annoying Britni might be deserving of sympathy so unwelcome? Maybe I really was doing her an injustice. I was seeing her as a stereotype—the spoiled and rather prissy city dweller, looking down her nose at much of Caerphilly. How much was I seeing the real Britni and how much was I transferring to her some of the annoyance I felt at the NIMBYs? How much of her appearance and behavior were the real Britni and how much were part of a role she was playing as the representative of *Sweet Tea and*

Sassafras? Maybe she behaved the way she did because that's what it took to work with the people she normally interviewed.

In fact, the more I thought about it, the more I could see her behavior the whole time she'd been here as a performance. And not a very original one. She'd been playing the sophisticated young urban professional woman with a demanding fast-track career. If she'd done it in Michael's Introduction to Acting class, he'd have told her to dig deeper. Probably rude to say something like that in real life—especially since she might be doing it out of anxiety and insecurity.

I made a silent vow to try a little harder to understand Britni. To give her the benefit of the doubt.

"She doesn't make herself very easy to like, though, does she?" Rose Noire said, with a sigh.

So maybe if trying harder to understand didn't work, it wouldn't be entirely my fault.

"Will you be here to keep an eye on the boys until Michael gets home?" I asked. "Randall asked me to placate the NIMBYs."

"And you want to get it over with instead of having it hanging over you," she said. "Don't worry. I'll hold down the fort."

So I grabbed my tote and headed for town.

Chapter 20

When I arrived at Westlake, I decided to start with Mrs. Anstruther. Not that I thought dealing with her would be any easier than dealing with the Griswolds or the Brownlows, but at least she wasn't up in arms about Edgar's bees, so I hadn't seen quite so much of her lately. I parked in front of her house and made sure my tote contained the right issue of *Sweet Tea and Sassafras*—the one with the article about her. Then I marched up her front walk.

It was slightly intimidating, thanks to the sheer blatantly overwhelming size of the place—like marching up to the portcullis of a castle. There was even the suggestion of a moat. Just before you got to her front porch the stone walk turned into a bridge for about ten feet so you could cross over a pond. Two enormous water lilies floated in the pond, one on each side of the bridge, and at least a dozen enormous white and pale gold koi loomed up to the water's surface on my left and right. No, make that two dozen, and most of them swimming in place and sticking their mouths out of the water, slowly opening and closing them as if silently begging for food. I'd have felt sorry for them if they hadn't all been so enormous that it was obvious they weren't starving.

There were spotlights positioned here and there to light up

the pond after dark, and I couldn't help thinking the koi would look pretty creepy doing their silent chorus at night.

The door opened before I had a chance to touch the doorbell. Not surprising, really. She probably had a security system, complete with cameras and motion detectors. I doubted if there were many houses in Westlake that didn't. Mrs. Anstruther stood, blinking as if dazzled by the late-afternoon sun. She was tall, only an inch or so shorter than my five foot ten. She looked a little different today. It took me a few moments to figure out why. This was the first time I'd seen her when she wasn't dressed to the nines, carefully coiffed, and heavily made-up. In jeans and a polo shirt she seemed—well, not exactly younger. She looked the fifty-something she was. But she didn't seem quite so unreachably on the other side of a vast generational chasm.

"What do *you* want?" Not the most gracious greeting I'd ever heard. Her words were slightly slurred, and she was holding a highball glass, half filled with ice cubes and a clear liquid. I wondered how intoxicated she was. A little bit might increase my chances of getting information out of her. Too much, and my visit would be both useless and unpleasant.

"Actually, I want your input about something," I said.

"Something connected with the murder?" she asked.

"Goodness!" I exclaimed. "I certainly hope not."

I just stood, smiling as innocently as I could manage. With luck she'd be curious enough to invite me in, if only for long enough to find out what I wanted her input on.

"Okay, tell me about it."

But instead of keeping me standing in the doorway, she turned and headed away from the door, leaving me to enter, close the door behind me, and follow.

The foyer was about the size of our living room, with a cathedral ceiling. All the blinds or curtains or whatever window coverings it contained were tightly drawn, and it was lit only with a small iron wall sconce, vaguely Spanish-looking, with amber glass and a few too many decorative metal curlicues. The sconce contained a single faux tea candle that flickered to suggest real flame, but only gave about as much illumination as a night light. Still, it was enough to keep me from running into anything as I crossed the stone flags of the foyer and followed Mrs. Anstruther into what I suspected was the living room, although it was hard to tell. The curtains were tightly drawn here, too, and the only light was from the flicker of a gas fire in the enormous baronial stone fireplace at the far end of the room. Mrs. Anstruther appeared to have vanished. I stood still and let my eyes adjust to the low light. Eventually I heard the clink of ice against glass and was able to locate Mrs. Anstruther, slumped in one of the three enormous black leather sofas grouped around the fire. I headed toward her, wondering if it would be rude to take out my iPhone and use the flashlight feature to find my way.

"Have a seat." She waved a hand vaguely toward the other two sofas. I took a seat on the middle one, on the end closest to hers.

"So spill," she said. "What is it you want my input on?"

I pulled the magazine out of my tote and held it up.

"This."

She peered but was clearly having trouble seeing it. So this time I didn't care if it was rude—I took out my phone and shone its little flashlight beam on the cover.

"That rag," she said.

"Ms. Ellie let me borrow a few of the back issues you've so generously donated to the library," I said as I pocketed my phone.

"I could stop my subscription now," she said. "I should have thought of that already."

"Stop your subscription? Why?"

"Let me see that."

She was on the end of the sofa farthest from me, so I stood, stepped closer, handed her the *Sweet Tea and Sassafras* issue, and sat down again. After some fumbling, she turned on a small, dim table lamp at her elbow, and peered down at the magazine.

After staring at the cover for a few seconds, she opened it to the pages with her article and leafed slowly through them. After a few minutes she lifted her head.

"What's she doing here?"

"She?" I echoed.

"I mean that nosy, greedy little bitch of a reporter. Britni." She tossed the magazine back toward me. It landed on the floor at my feet. The book lover in me wanted to pick it up and smooth its crumpled pages. I reminded myself that this was *Sweet Tea and Sassafras* and stayed my hand. And I deduced that Mrs. Anstruther, at least, was unlikely to tell Britni we were checking up on her.

"She says she wants to do an article about my grandmother," I said. "And—"

"Don't let her do it." She sat up straighter, shaking her head. "Make her go away."

"I take it your experience with her wasn't entirely positive," I said.

"You could say that." She slumped down again, laughing softly. "You could absolutely say that."

"What happened?" I said. "Give me a reason to get rid of her. If she's up to no good—"

"First of all, she'll twist whatever you say." She was staring straight ahead, her gaze unfocused. I hoped that meant she was remembering, not that she was about to pass out. "She got me at a weak moment—I was—" She shook her glass as if in explanation. "I told a few tall ones and she made them taller. I don't know. Maybe she wanted to embarrass me. Or maybe she was trying to make me sound important enough to suit their damned rag. She kept looking at me with this look like she was thinking 'is that all?' so I kept trying to come up with more stuff she'd like. Who knows?"

I nodded. So far this wasn't exactly earth-shattering.

"I was mortified when it came out," she went on. "I thought people would never let me hear the end of it. I mean, yeah, I'm definitely a contributor to the Garden Club, but I don't think I've been to more than two meetings of the Ladies Interfaith thing in my life. Turns out no one else in town reads the lousy rag."

"Lucky break."

"Yeah." She sipped thoughtfully from her glass. "But the other thing wasn't so lucky."

I waited.

"She overheard one of my arguments with Kimberly. My daughter."

I nodded. I knew Mrs. Anstruther had a daughter. I'd even met her once or twice. She didn't live in town and didn't seem to visit all that often.

"She was still in college then," Mrs. Anstruther said. "She had one of those home DNA tests done, and she didn't like what she saw. Didn't think some of the results sounded like they could be from either of us. She as good as accused me of cheating on Virgil. Wanted to get him and me both to spit in a test tube so she could prove it. I told her 'Fine, go ahead and do that if you want to get both of us disinherited. Because if your daddy finds out he's not your biological father, that's exactly what he'll do. You'll have to drop out of that fancy college of yours, because I sure won't be able to pay the tuition.'"

I couldn't think of anything to say. Maybe that was a good thing.

"And in case you were wondering, no," she went on. "I didn't cheat on my husband. I tricked him, yeah. Had his sperm tested, and he was shooting blanks. Didn't tell him that—he'd never have believed it anyway. Although you'd think after forty years of trying with four different wives he'd have started to wonder if maybe the problem was him, not us. So I had artificial insemination. With donor sperm. That I picked out of a catalog at the fertility clinic—I wouldn't know her biological father from Adam. Virgil was pleased as punch. Never doubted she was his own. Everything was going fine until Kimberly got this bee in her bonnet about tracing her ancestry—and that bitch Britni overhead us arguing about it."

"What did Britni do?"

"Milked me for as much money as she could get out of me," Mrs. Anstruther said. "Oh, she pretended it wasn't her. But I know it was her. And she knows I know it."

I realized my mouth was hanging open with astonishment. I'd been worried that Britni might embarrass Cordelia. Write a silly, embarrassing article about her, out of either actual malice or just plain incompetence. But this—

"She's a blackmailer?" I exclaimed.

"That's what they call it." Mrs. Anstruther took a healthy swig of her drink.

"Is she still blackmailing you?" I asked. "Because maybe the police could do something. Now that your husband's dead—"

"Now that my husband's dead, I already told her where to go," she said. "The last time she tried to tap me, I left a box just where she told me to leave it, but instead of cash I filled it with dog poop. And stuck in a note saying this was the last thing she'd be getting out of me. Of course, I'd rather not have the whole world know about the trick I played on my husband. But I've talked to my lawyers. There's nothing anybody can do about it now. As far as the law is concerned, my husband's name is on the birth certificate, he acknowledged her as his daughter for the whole twenty years she's been on this earth, and his will left everything to me. We're safe. There's nothing anybody can do."

I nodded slowly.

"And if a rumor about this gets around town, I'll know who to go after," she added, fixing me with a malevolent stare.

"The only person I plan on telling about this is my grandmother," I said. "Because I think she needs to know why she should tell Britni to get lost."

She nodded, shifted her gaze back to the gas fire, and sipped from her glass. I studied her. She looked different. Nicer? Less annoying would be more accurate. Maybe the soft, dim light had a flattering effect.

Or maybe it was just that she wasn't trying to be superior and intimidating.

"How did she contact you?" I asked.

"Letters. Typed, no signature. Usually mailed. Sometimes left in my mailbox without postage, or on the doormat. That was creepy, knowing she was in town. And she'd tell me how much money she wanted and where to take it. And order me not to have anyone watching the pickup, or she'd spill the beans."

I nodded. I wasn't a mystery fiction buff like Dad or a true-crime guru like Kevin, but even I could see how many clues her blackmailer had left. How easily the police could have caught the culprit if Mrs. Anstruther had gone to them. And while I was certainly ready to think ill of Britni, and the circumstances might be suspicious, Mrs. Anstruther didn't have ironclad proof of Britni's guilt. Someone else could have overheard the quarrel with her daughter. Maybe they'd had more than one quarrel. Or Britni could have gossiped. Good for Mrs. Anstruther that she'd broken free, but now the police might never catch the black-mailer.

"Was there a schedule for the payments?" I asked.

"No. A couple times a year. I figured she had several of us, and when she needed funds she'd hit whichever one of us she thought was ripe for tapping."

I nodded. I thought of asking her how much money she'd lost to the blackmailer, but the question might offend her. Westlak-ers were weird about money, fond of bragging about how expen-sive their possessions were, but apt to take offense if you asked them directly what something had cost. I decided maybe if I didn't ask, she'd eventually blurt it out.

"Do you know any of her other victims?" I asked instead.

"Of course not." Her tone was exasperated. "The whole point of paying blackmail is so no one finds out you've got anything to be blackmailed about. You don't exactly hunt down other victims and form a support group."

"Of course," I said. "What I meant was did you ever see anyone else featured in *Sweet Tea and Sassafras* and wonder if maybe she was a victim, too?"

"I never read the damned thing," she said. "Just seeing it come in the mail sets off my blood pressure. So I slap the sticker on it and dump it at the library as soon as possible."

"They profiled Mrs. Brownlow before they did you," I said. "About three years ago."

"Mrs. Brownlow?" I watched as her face gradually took on a look of shock and indignation. "Connie Brownlow?"

"Yes," I said. "It was written when she was still in Richmond, so I have no idea how accurate it was."

"That cow," she muttered. "I bet she's the one who sicced Britni on me."

She sat there for a minute or so, staring straight ahead and rattling the ice cubes in her glass.

"It had to be her," she muttered. "She's never forgiven me for voting against her in the HOA elections. And a couple of things she's said over the years . . . yeah. Britni had to be blackmailing her. Gotta figure out why. Could be useful."

I wondered if I should warn Mrs. Brownlow that Mrs. Anstruther had it in for her. It probably wouldn't surprise her. Given how ready Mrs. Anstruther was to think the worst of her neighbor, maybe they already disliked each other. That was one thing I'd figured out from the last few painful years of working with the NIMBYs: they were quick to close ranks against outsiders, but when left to themselves they were a quarrelsome lot, constantly scheming and conniving and betraying each other. It wouldn't surprise me at all if Mr. Inman's killer turned out to be one of his neighbors.

Anyplace else I'd even have wondered if maybe they'd all gotten together and pulled a *Murder on the Orient Express*–style operation. But it was hard to imagine the NIMBYs pulling off that much teamwork.

"Where is that thing?" Mrs. Anstruther said suddenly. But before I could ask what thing she was talking about, she lurched out of her corner of the sofa, grabbed the issue of *Sweet Tea and Sassafras,* and sprawled back on the cushions.

"Gonna cancel them," she muttered. "Like I should have done months ago."

She flipped through the magazine until she found whatever she was looking for. Presumably, the phone number for *Sweet Tea and Sassafras*'s office, since she picked up her phone and dialed—rather slowly, looking back and forth between it and the magazine half a dozen times. Then she threw the magazine down and leaned back in her seat with a look of imperious anticipation, like a Roman empress awaiting the beginning of a gladiatorial competition.

Her expression gradually morphed into rage, presumably because the magazine's editorial staff weren't picking up. She finally muttered a few bitter obscenities as she hung up.

"It's after five," I said. "They're probably closed for the night."

"Then they should turn on their voicemail for the convenience of customers."

"Even the ones who want to become ex-customers," I couldn't help adding.

"Yeah." She took a swallow from her glass and leaned back in her seat. "Remind me to cancel them. In case I forget, you know." She shook her glass as if to suggest why her memory might fail her.

Normally I might have snapped at her that I wasn't her personal assistant. But she'd been helpful, after a fashion. And I had, as the saying goes, taken against *Sweet Tea and Sassafras.* Anything to do them a disservice. So I took out my notebook, jotted down a note to remind her, and smiled.

"Was that all you came by for?" Mrs. Anstruther asked. "To open up old wounds?"

Chapter 21

I thought of assuring Mrs. Anstruther that I had no idea that the subject of *Sweet Tea and Sassafras* would upset her, but she probably wouldn't believe me. And after all, she was right—I did have another purpose.

"Actually, it's not why I came by at all," I said. "I just thought I'd mention it while I was here. I wanted to give you a heads-up about something."

"Go on," she said, waving her glass at me.

"You're deathly allergic to bees, right?" I asked.

"Not that I know of," she said.

"I could have sworn you told me that," I said. "At this year's flower show, when we found that bee in Mrs. Burke's entry in the centerpiece competition."

She frowned slightly and then shook her head as if to indicate that she couldn't remember the incident. Not surprising, since I was making it up as I went along.

"Oh dear," I said. "I was so sure it was you. Now I've got to figure out who else it would have been so I can warn them."

"Warn them about what?"

"Edgar Bortnick's bees."

"I thought someone killed them all," she said. "That was the rumor going around, anyway."

"Apparently they didn't get all the bees," I said. "Or maybe Edgar brought in new ones. All I know is that his bees are unsettled. Probably going to swarm anytime now, and with him in the hospital there won't really be anyone around to deal with it. I mean if you're allergic, even one bee sting would be a disaster, right? And half a million bees? I thought I'd warn you, so you could take cover until it's over with. But if it's not you that's allergic, I need to find out who is."

"If there're half a million bees headed this way, I'm taking cover anyway," she said. "When's this supposed to happen?"

"No idea," I said. "It could be anytime. And of course they could head the other way, out into the nearby farms. And you should be fine—that many bees all buzzing angrily—they'll make a horrible racket. You'll hear them coming. Just stay inside until you get word that it's all clear."

"I may never go outside again," she said. "Fresh air is overrated anyway. Can't you do anything about that crazy man and his bees?"

"Unfortunately not," I said. "Mr. Bortnick has a legal right to keep his bees. No matter how annoying Mrs. Brownlow finds them."

"Does she, now?" Mrs. Anstruther chuckled softly. "Well, if they're perfectly legal, she'll just have to learn to live with them, won't she? Fussy old cow."

Mrs. Anstruther's cheerful mood persisted as she showed me to the door, chuckling at random moments. Clearly I had discovered an important new tactic for use in my dealings with the NIMBYs. As long as I could convince them that whatever they were complaining about was even more annoying to their least favorite neighbors, I could quash a lot of the whining and complaining. I made a mental note to get Mother to help me figure out who currently hated whom.

By the time Mrs. Anstruther and I reached the front door, I was almost as cheerful as she was.

And a thought hit me.

"Have you tried showing Kimberly your medical records?"

"My medical records?" She frowned as if puzzled.

"From when you had the artificial insemination. Maybe that would convince her of what really happened."

"It was twenty years ago," she said. "And it's not like I wanted to keep around anything that would let Virgil find out."

"Understandable," I said. "But even if you didn't save them, whatever doctor you worked with might still have them. It's worth a try."

"It might be at that."

She was still visibly digesting the idea when she closed the door behind me.

I'd definitely check back to see if she had any success. Because if she didn't, I knew a lawyer and a private investigator who might be able to help.

I crossed the moat in the good mood that comes from doing someone a good turn. My mood fell a little when I remembered that I was planning to tackle at least two more NIMBYs while I was here.

And then there was Mrs. Anstruther's accusation that Britni was a blackmailer. I had no idea what to think about that. On the one hand, Cordelia seemed to find her suspicious. And I had to admit, I'd taken an almost instant dislike to Britni. Probably, I realized, because she reminded me of several of the mean girls who'd tried to make my high school days miserable. I didn't much like her, and I'd be just as happy if Cordelia backed out of being profiled. But a blackmailer?

I reminded myself that I only had Mrs. Anstruther's take on that. And like so many of the NIMBYs, she was prone to making up her mind about something—or someone—and ignoring contradictory evidence. I'd want more proof before I believed her story.

I'd warn Cordelia, just in case. Not that I could think of anything Britni could possibly blackmail her about. But she could help watch for signs that Britni—or anyone else—was targeting more vulnerable people. If a blackmailer was at large in Caerphilly, we needed to stop them.

I was tempted to just leave my car in front of Mrs. Anstruther's house and walk into the cul-de-sac where the Griswolds, the Brownlows, and Mr. Inman lived. But it might annoy Mrs. Anstruther, and I didn't want to use up whatever goodwill I'd acquired with her, so I got in, drove around the corner into the cul-de-sac, and parked in front of Walter Inman's house, right behind an old but well-maintained truck.

"Hey, Meg." Braden Shiffley was sitting in a camping chair in the meager shade of one of the two small trees in Walter Inman's front lawn. Westlake's original developer had bulldozed all the existing trees on his property, and Inman was one of the few residents who had gotten around to planting replacements. Although since he'd chosen two invasive Bradford pear trees, his life choices weren't all that much better than the developer's.

"Hey, Braden." I saw the young man beam when he realized that I knew his name. "I'm going to see if I can talk to Mrs. Griswold. Don't let the Westlakers ticket me for trespassing while I'm at it."

He chuckled and gave me a thumbs-up.

I strolled down the sidewalk and then up a brick walk to the Griswolds' house. Their lawn was immaculate, although the large pile of lumber in one corner wasn't exactly scenic. Presumably supplies for the privacy fence they were hoping to erect. Might now be able to erect, with Inman not around to complain.

They'd gone a little overboard with the olde worlde details. There was a crest over the front door, a little larger than a hubcap and brightly painted in red, black, and metallic gold. The Griswold coat of arms, presumably. It featured two red zigzag lines through the middle of a shield, and two greyhounds, one above and one below the lines. At least I assumed they were intended to be greyhounds. To fit them into the limited space available on the shield they'd been kind of smooshed down, so they looked more like dachshunds.

But yeah, probably greyhounds. The steps leading up to the front door were flanked by a pair of three-foot cast-iron greyhounds with large iron rings in their mouths, suggesting that they'd begun life somewhere else as hitching posts. Two more greyhounds were visible through the sidelights that flanked the ornate double front door—white porcelain greyhounds with fawn markings and bejeweled collars painted on.

I braced myself and rang the doorbell. Inside I could hear trumpets braying out a medieval fanfare.

Eventually the right-hand door opened and Mrs. Griswold stared out. She was a short, stout woman of around fifty who usually gave herself a crick in the neck trying to look down her nose at me.

"Yes?" She didn't look very welcoming. In fact, I wondered if I could master that tone of cold indifference. It would work wonders on door-to-door solicitors.

"Good afternoon," I said. "I came by to give you a heads-up on something."

"The bee situation." She stepped back and opened the door a little wider. I stepped in, and then stepped aside so she could close the door.

"Careful of the Lladró!" she snapped. I froze and looked around to see whatever it was she thought I was endangering. Seeing my puzzlement, she nodded toward the nearest of the porcelain greyhounds. I was still a good six feet from it, so it had never been in any real danger. But now I was on notice that it was a Lladró, and presumably rare and expensive.

"I assume you're dropping by to tell me that you've made no

progress in getting rid of Mr. Bortnick's bees." She crossed her arms and scowled at me. And evidently I wasn't going to be invited any farther than the front hall.

"No, actually I'm not even trying to get rid of his bees," I said. "He has a legal right to have them. But the good news is that I seem to have talked him out of taking legal action against anyone for harassment."

I beamed as if vastly proud of myself. My spur-of-the-moment improvisation seemed to take her aback. Her mouth fell open.

"Legal action?" she repeated.

"Oh, yes," I said. "The verbal harassment was bad enough, but now that someone has actually physically interfered with his bees, he's furious. And unfortunately, so are the bees. That's what I came to tell you about."

"Really." Clearly she wasn't happy about the direction of our conversation.

"Edgar's been injured—long story, but the problem is that he's not there to handle the bees. And thanks to someone trying to kill them with insecticide, they're unsettled."

I was rather pleased with that last bit, which would counter any rumor she'd heard that the bees were dead—and give me a chance to study her face when I mentioned the insecticide. Her slight frown didn't seem to indicate guilt.

"Edgar's afraid they're going to swarm," I went on. "Don't worry—if it happens, you'll hear them coming. Half a million bees will make enough noise that you can hear them quite a ways off, and they'll be moving slowly. Just stay inside."

I smiled blandly.

"But this is unacceptable!"

"I agree," I said. "But it's what happens when people who know nothing about bees try to fool around with them."

"This is all Walter Inman's fault," she said.

"How so?" I asked. "Was he the one interfering with the bees?"

"How should I know?" she asked. "But it's the way he operates.

Instead of reporting a problem and letting the proper authorities take care of it, he tries to fix it himself. And now it's got him killed, hasn't it?"

"How do you figure that?" I was bracing myself to hear her accuse Edgar, but she surprised me.

"I guess he picked the wrong person to follow, didn't he?" she said. "Thinks no one notices when he parks on some side road and then waits until one of our kids comes along so he can follow them and try to catch them doing something he thinks is illegal. And I bet he started doing it to other kids, too—college students, or maybe some of those redneck ruffians. And look what it got him—I heard the place where they found his body was a known drug market."

She snorted derisively. I found it interesting that someone from Westlake would know about the drug market part.

Also interesting that she assumed it was following people other than Westlake residents that had gotten Inman killed. It did suggest that he was an equal-opportunity stalker, of course, but I didn't share her assumption that being the child of Westlake owners was an automatic alibi for murder. I didn't think the chief would, either.

And I wondered if anyone had told the chief how far Inman had gone with his vigilante efforts. Because, yes, that would absolutely explain how he'd been killed in that particular stretch of woods.

"Of course, I'm very sorry about what happened to him," Mrs. Griswold said. Perhaps she'd suddenly realized how it looked to be badmouthing a murder victim. "But after he escalated from making threats to actually reporting Shane to the police—well, perhaps it's not a surprise that someone took exception to his actions."

Took exception to his actions? That might be the strangest euphemism for murder I'd ever heard. I was opening my mouth to ask her if she'd told Chief Burke about this, but then I thought better of it. Maybe she had. And if she hadn't, the chief might be able to use that fact to his advantage.

"That's interesting," I said. "I guess that's some small consolation, isn't it? That sad as everyone is about the loss of Mr. Inman, at least things will be a little more peaceful without all his . . . eccentricities."

"Was there something else?" Evidently Mrs. Griswold didn't want to get dragged into a discussion of how the neighborhood was reacting to the loss of Wally the Weird.

"No," I said. "That's all."

She reached over and pulled open one of the doors. I was being dismissed.

"Thank you for your time," I said as I walked out.

She didn't close the door until I'd reached the sidewalk. And then she slammed it.

Chapter 22

As I strolled down the sidewalk back to Inman's house, I pulled out my phone and dialed the chief. And I stopped when I was past the Griswolds' property line but still out of Braden's earshot.

"What's up?" he asked.

"I'm over in Westlake doing my part to set up The Sting," I said. "Heard something interesting from Mrs. Griswold."

"I'm all ears."

"She says Walter Inman has been tailing young people around the county, hoping to catch them doing something illegal, and that following the wrong person is how he ended up getting killed near a known drug market. Her words, by the way, about the known drug market."

A slight pause.

"Now that's interesting," he said finally. "For several reasons. Over the last couple of months, we've gotten complaints about Inman."

"TJ Washington told me about that," I said. "Of course, Mrs. Griswold could be jumping to conclusions. Assuming her spoiled darling getting caught with drugs was part of some vigilante anti-drug crusade Inman was running, instead of the accidental byproduct of his playing neighborhood watchman."

"And she also could be right," the chief said. "Several of my deputies have commented about running across Inman driving around in places where they were surprised to see him. But we'd put it down to his known eccentricity. I mean, we speculated that he was prowling around or even following young people in the hope of spotting things he could report to us or the college administration or whoever he thought might care."

"Wally the Weird being his nosy and annoying self," I said.

"Exactly. But we had no reason to suspect he was deliberately trying to catch people in the middle of a drug transaction. If he was, it's not surprising that something happened to him. Also rather interesting that Mrs. Griswold knows both the location of the drug mart and that Mr. Inman was killed there. I haven't officially released that information. Did you say anything to her that would give her a clue?"

"No," I said. "I had no idea what you were releasing about the murder, so I tried to avoid saying anything at all about it."

"Well done. I can use this information when I see the Griswolds this evening. And—sorry. Something just came up. I'll talk to you soon."

He hung up before I could tell him about Mrs. Anstruther's blackmail experience.

I hovered for a few moments of uncharacteristic indecision. It could wait—or could it? The chief was completely focused on Inman's murder, and if Mrs. Anstruther was right about who had been blackmailing her, it was hard to see how the two crimes could be related. But what if Mrs. Anstruther was wrong?

I decided to call him again after I'd talked to Mrs. Brownlow, whether or not she said anything about being blackmailed. With that decision made, I put my phone away and covered the rest of the ground to where Braden was still sitting in the meager shade of the Bradford pear. He'd know whether Mrs. Brownlow was home.

"How's it going?" I asked.

"Okay." It wasn't exactly a ringingly cheerful "Okay." His long, freckled face looked anxious. "Considering," he added finally.

"Considering what?" I said. "The neighbors? I suspect they haven't exactly been helpful or welcoming."

Relief flooded his face—the kid would never make much of a poker player. But he kept his words diplomatic.

"Well, I figure they have a good reason to be kind of upset," he said. "On account of their friend getting killed."

Maybe I was doing the Westlakers an injustice, but I wasn't sure Inman's death would cause much actual grief in Westlake. More likely they'd be worried about the crime's effect on property values. Or concerned that anyone who disliked Inman enough to kill him might not be all that fond of them, either.

"Don't let them unsettle you," I said.

"I just wish they'd stop watching me," he said.

"Watching you?" I glanced back and forth between the Brownlows' house and the Griswolds'. I didn't see any faces at the windows. In fact, most of the windows in both houses were completely closed off with curtains or blinds, as if the occupants were vampires who would shrivel if a single ray of sunlight struck them.

My brain began trying to recall if I'd ever actually seen the Brownlows and the Griswolds in sunlight. I reminded my brain that we had more practical things to do and focused back on Braden.

"How can you be sure they're watching?" I asked. "Quite possible that they are, but try not to let it bother you."

"It's the cameras." He gestured with his head toward the Brownlows' house. I glanced up and saw a tiny camera mounted under the eaves on a curved white pole mount.

"Part of their security system," I said.

"Yeah." He stood up. "But watch this. Let's go check on something in the backyard. And don't stare, but try to keep your eyes on the camera."

We strolled around the side of the house. I pretended to be enjoying the scenery. The stone terrace wasn't that bad. In fact, it might have been rather nice if there wasn't such an awful lot of it. Nothing cozy and homelike about it.

And while appreciating the terrace, I also kept the camera in sight. After a few steps, it began to swivel so it could track us through the side yard. A second camera halfway down the side of the house picked us up after a while, and eventually handed us off to a third camera perched under the eaves at the back corner.

"Wow." I perched on one of the stone walls that bordered the terrace. "That's one seriously expensive security system. They must really be paranoid."

"Yeah. Kind of creepy if you ask me. Less creepy if I stay put and the cameras don't move, but the chief said to check the backyard every hour or so. Still, getting watched through the camera's better than when they come out and talk to me."

"They've done that?"

"Oh, yes. Mrs. Brownlow, and both Griswolds. Separately."

"You shouldn't have to put up with that." I pondered whether there was anything I could say that would make the NIMBYs leave him alone.

"It's okay," he said, with a not-entirely-convincing air of unconcern. "I say 'sir' and 'ma'am' a lot and pretend I know even less than I do, and they get fed up and go back inside."

"Have you told the chief about the camera system?" I asked.

"I didn't want to bother him with complaints," he said.

"Sensible," I said. "And he probably knows about them anyway—they're not exactly inconspicuous."

He nodded.

"And he's probably already thought of the possibility that those security cameras might contain useful evidence."

Dawning comprehension spread over his face, and he glanced

up at the nearest Brownlow camera with something more like approval.

"But just in case he was too swamped to notice them, I'll let him know what you've said about the cameras." And if he was interested enough to call, I could mention the blackmail angle. I pulled out my phone and started a text to the chief. "And if it's something he's already noticed, he'll be annoyed at me, not you."

He nodded.

I glanced over at the Griswolds' house. The figure I'd seen earlier was still slumped in the Adirondack chair. From this angle I could see that it was a young man in faded sweatpants with sunglasses over his eyes and earbuds in his ears. Braden followed my glance.

"Hey, Shane," he called.

The figure didn't move. Braden shrugged.

"Guess he doesn't hear me."

"You know him?" I asked.

"From school. Not very well. At least, not anymore. We used to be on the track team together."

"What happened? Did he start hanging out with the wrong people?"

Braden thought about that for a minute.

"Not that I can see. It's more like he just stopped hanging out with anyone. He quit everything he was in. Sierra Club and Future Scientists Club and track team. I heard maybe his parents thought he should focus more on his classes. Who knows?"

I studied Shane for a few more minutes. Something about that forlorn figure bothered me. But there was nothing I could do about it just now.

"I always thought he was okay," Braden said, as if something I said suggested otherwise. Or possibly my facial expression. "The kind of kid who'd take spiders outside instead of squashing them."

I nodded. Then I focused back on what Braden and I had been talking about.

"Do the Griswolds have security cameras, too?" I asked.

"Yeah. Stationary ones. But from the look of them they have a pretty wide camera angle. And so does Mr. Inman. Stationary ones like the Griswolds."

I began typing my text.

"Braden S. has noticed that the Griswolds, the Brownlows, and Mr. Inman have security systems with multiple cameras," I said. "The neighbors' cameras are set up so they probably cover some of Mr. Inman's yard."

I didn't get an immediate response, so while I waited, I called Braden's attention to Edgar's beehives, which were clearly visible across the little stream.

"Yeah. Bees are cool." He smiled at the thought.

I was about to suggest that we return to his post in the front yard when the chief replied to my text.

"Thanks," he said. "Good observation. Could be useful."

I read both texts to Braden, who beamed with pleasure.

"I wonder if—" he began.

"Ms. Langslow!" a shrill, high-pitched voice behind me demanded.

I winced, then composed my face and turned around to see Mrs. Brownlow. She was of medium height, but thanks to her athletic build and good posture she looked taller. And at least a decade younger than her age, which had to be fifty-something. She was wearing tennis whites, as usual. I wasn't sure I'd ever seen her when she wasn't dressed for either tennis or golf.

"Good afternoon, Mrs. Brownlow," I said.

"*What* are you going to do about that *horrible* man and his dangerous insects!" she shrieked.

"Please calm down, Mrs. Brownlow," I said. Her voice was hard enough to take when she spoke normally. When she got

excited it rose an octave, doubled in volume, and became actually painful to the ear.

"How do you expect me to be calm when my very *life* could be
in danger!" she exclaimed. "I insist that the town *do* something
about that menace!"

She went on in much the same vein, in a voice more suitable
for addressing a large audience than a single person standing
only a few feet away. I'd have backed away, but that would look
as if I was backing down. I'd learned never to show a sign of
weakness when dealing with the NIMBYs. So I concentrated on
not wincing when her voice hit a particularly loud, high note,
and occasionally saying "Mrs. Brownlow," in the vain hope of
stemming the verbal tide.

And the sunlight didn't seem to bother her. Nice to know.

It only added to my growing irritation when I noticed that
Britni had suddenly appeared right behind Mrs. Brownlow.

"He killed poor Walter Inman with those evil bugs of his,"
Mrs. Brownlow proclaimed. "I'm not going to just stand around
until he comes for me."

Did she really think Inman had been killed by bees? Was the
chief keeping the cause of death a secret? Or had Mrs. Brownlow just not been paying attention?

Braden had backed away a good ten feet and was watching us
with his mouth hanging open.

Mrs. Brownlow finally reached the crescendo of her rant,
ending with:

"And just what are you going to do about this?"

She crossed her arms and stared at me with a look of vengeful
triumph on her face.

I lost it.

"Nothing," I said.

"I beg your pardon?" She was so surprised she couldn't quite
manage outrage.

"Absolutely nothing." I was polite, but firm.

"But—"

"The bees were here first," I said. "By the time you moved in here, Mr. Bortnick had been keeping bees on his property for at least a decade. If a bee-free environment was essential to your health and happiness, maybe you should have done a little more investigation before you bought your house. Beekeeping is legal in Caerphilly County. His land is zoned for agricultural use. You have absolutely no right to harass him for operating a business that is not only perfectly legal but beneficial to the surrounding farm community, and if you continue your attempts to browbeat me and other town and county officials in the attempt to get us to violate his rights, we will be seeking legal advice on how to protect ourselves and him."

She stood there for a few seconds, jaw hanging open with astonishment. Britni and Braden looked pretty shocked, too, although Braden's expression was starting to curl into a smile.

Mrs. Brownlow just stared at me for what seemed like a couple of centuries. Then she opened her mouth as if to reply—and screamed. She wrapped her arms around her head and threw herself onto the stone patio, still screaming.

Chapter 23

My first impulse was to rush over to Mrs. Brownlow to see if something was wrong with her. But I stifled the impulse. What if she was trying to pull something, like pretending I'd attacked her. If she tried that, I had witnesses. Braden. And while I didn't think much of Britni as a witness, she had taken out her phone at some point in Mrs. Brownlow's rant and appeared to be filming the excitement.

"It's after me! It's after me! Get it! Get it! Get it!" Mrs. Brownlow screamed.

"It"—not "she." Hmmm.

"What's after you?" I asked.

"The bee, the bee, the BEE!" she screamed.

I didn't see anything at first. Then I spotted it.

"That's not a bee," I said.

"Yes-it-is, yes-it-is, yes-it—"

"It's a hornet."

This provoked renewed screams from Mrs. Brownlow. Braden, on the other hand, drew near. No faint-of-heart watchdog he.

"A murder hornet?" He seemed to think that would be a rather cool discovery.

Even more vigorous screams from Mrs. Brownlow.

"I don't think so," I said. "Just a regular hornet."

Mrs. Brownlow didn't seem to find this much of an improvement. Her screams turned into wrenching sobs, and she curled up in a fetal position on the paving stones, occasionally muttering "get it, get it, get it" in a despairing tone.

"Probably coming from that nest." I pointed up at the eaves of Mr. Inman's house where the delicate-looking but enormous paper nest hung.

"Wow," Braden said. "That thing's bigger than a basketball."

Louder sobs from Mrs. Brownlow.

"Britni, can you help Mrs. Brownlow back to her house," I asked. "Braden, why don't you go along and see her safely inside. I'll watch Mr. Inman's house while you do that. Then when you get back, I'll go to Flugleman's to get a can of wasp-and-hornet spray so we can kill that nest."

"Okay," Braden said.

He and Britni managed to coax Mrs. Brownlow out of her fetal position and onto her feet, and then steer her across her deck to where we could see a sliding glass door still partly open. Surprisingly, it was Britni who was visibly suppressing impatience. Braden was all care and concern, as if helping panic-stricken entomophobes was a normal part of his day.

Ordinarily I'd have pitched in to help, but I really didn't want to have anything more to do with Mrs. Brownlow just then—and more to the point, I suspected she probably felt the same way about me. Probing to find out if she, too, had been blackmailed would have to wait for another day.

She did recover enough to spit out a final complaint.

"It's all his fault," she said, waving her arm wildly in the general direction of Edgar's farm. "This wouldn't be happening if he hadn't brought in those horrible insects of his!"

If she'd been calmer, I'd have tried to explain that Edgar's now deceased bees had absolutely nothing to do with Walter Inman's failure to notice that a completely unrelated species of insect was building the hornet equivalent of a McMansion under his eaves. I didn't think I'd have any luck getting that point across at the moment.

And besides, I seemed to have accomplished much the same results with her as the wild story about bees swarming had produced in Mrs. Anstruther and Mrs. Griswold: given her a sudden, desperate desire to rid the neighborhood of Edgar's bees.

So while Britni and Braden half led and half carried her inside her house, I inched a little closer to the hornets' nest and took a few pictures of it. Definitely a live nest, with dozens of its winged residents darting in and out. Then I looked around for some hornets that would sit still for a close-up. I found a few dining on spilled food near the built-in stone grill.

Then I texted the best of the photos to Dad, followed by a question.

"These aren't murder hornets—right?"

While I waited for his response, I strolled back around to the front yard and sat in Braden's chair.

I was still getting settled when Dad called.

"My goodness, what an enormous nest!" he exclaimed. "Especially for so early in the year. They build a new one each year, you know. But no, they're just ordinary bald-faced hornets. *Dolichovespula maculata*. They're black and white instead of black and yellow, like most wasps and hornets."

"So they're not a danger to anyone's beehives," I said. "I remember you mentioning that murder hornets sometimes ate bees."

"Oh, they do!" His voice shook slightly at the horror. "But bald-faced hornets are no danger to the bees. Still, we should probably do something about that nest, unless it's someplace pretty far from human habitation."

"It's in Westlake," I said. "On Mr. Inman's house."

"Oh, dear," he said. "Yes, we're probably going to have to deal with that. Before the Westlakers overreact."

"More than likely they'd call in an out-of-town exterminator who will poison every living thing within miles," I said. "Don't worry. I'm on it."

I was about to stick my phone back in my pocket when something occurred to me. I called Kevin.

"What now?" he asked. One of these years I'd work on teaching him proper phone etiquette.

"What kind of bugs were you seeing in Inman's security camera?"

"I don't know. Crawly ones. With wings. Is it important?"

I called up my closeup picture of the bald-faced hornets and texted it to him.

"Take a look at the photo I just sent you."

A pause.

"Could be. Let me pull up some of his video." Another pause. "Yeah, they could definitely be it. Why?"

"Then I think this is what's wrong with Mr. Inman's security camera." I texted him my best picture of the monster hornets' nest. "Any chance his camera's behind this?"

"That explains it," he said after a few moments. "You can actually see the end of the bracket that holds the camera in place. Nice to know what went wrong, but it doesn't really help the case."

"No, but I like solving even small mysteries. And it means after we zap the hornets' nest, his camera will be working again."

"Horse. Barn door."

It took me a second to decipher this typically laconic pronouncement.

"Yes," I said. "By restoring the camera now that Inman's murder has already happened, we are doing the equivalent of shutting the barn door now that the proverbial horse has escaped. But maybe it will help keep Inman's house secure until Horace can process it for evidence. Talk to you later."

We hung up and I relaxed. Braden still hadn't returned, and

I was more grateful than ever that I hadn't volunteered to take care of Mrs. Brownlow. I glanced at my phone when Braden finally came out of the Brownlows' front door. It had been a good twenty minutes. He strode down their front walk to the sidewalk and returned to Mr. Inman's yard.

"You don't have to get up," he said when I rose to return his chair.

"Pretty much have to if I'm going down to the feed store for hornet spray."

"Yeah. Of course, we're probably going to have to wait until dark to spray them," he said. "That's what my dad always says. Wait till they're all asleep."

"True," I said. "Much less chance of getting stung that way. Plus a much better chance of finding all the hornets at home. On a sunny spring afternoon like this, any number of them could have been outside doing whatever hornets do all day. Collecting food for their young. Dive-bombing the nearby humans. But they'll all be home and asleep by dark. And by that time, we can clear it with the chief. For all we know, Mr. Inman's house is part of his crime scene, and the nest is attached to the house."

"Mrs. Brownlow isn't going to be happy about waiting till dark."

"In the unlikely event that she even peeps outside, don't tell her we're waiting till dark. Tell her that we're busy making preparations for the complete extermination of the hornets, and she should stay inside till we give the all clear. And once I bring you the hornet spray, you can wave that around and look fierce."

"Okay." He chuckled slightly. "Just as long as I don't have to keep her company in the meantime. Half an hour ago she was yelling at me to get off Mr. Inman's lawn and stop bringing down the property values, and now she's all 'don't leave me alone!'"

"Well, she's still got Britni."

"That didn't seem to reassure her much."

Perhaps I was underestimating Mrs. Brownlow as a judge of character.

"One thing puzzles me," he went on. "Why didn't you just tell her Mr. Bortnick's hives were empty?"

"How do you know?" I asked.

"Well, you can see it," he said. "I mean, I can. Mr. Bortnick has a bunch of his hives over at my brother Mel's farm."

"Mel who's learning to make mead?"

"Yeah," he said. "So I kind of know what they're supposed to look like. There should be plenty of bees coming and going all the time. During the day, anyway. Maybe you wouldn't notice at a casual glance, but if you watch for a while, it's pretty obvious they're empty."

"Can you keep a secret?" I said. "And it's not my secret—it could be relevant to Chief Burke's investigation."

He nodded eagerly, so I told him about the massacre of Edgar's bees, and his idea of putting out a new hive and keeping watch to see if anyone attempted to sabotage it.

"Coo-*ul*," he said when I finished. "Count me in to help with the stakeout. A pity whoever hit the bees didn't use one of those cans on that humongous hornet nest."

"For all we know, he never even noticed it," I suggested. "He or she. Mr. Inman in particular has been complaining for weeks about Edgar's bees buzzing his guests and occasionally stinging them. What if it was the hornets all along?"

"I'm betting it was," he said. "Is it heartless to wish you could say 'I told you so' to a dead guy?"

"Just human."

"Yeah." A frown suddenly darkened his face. "What if he did notice the hornets' nest, and that gave him the idea for killing the bees? What if he was buying a can of hornet spray and thought 'while I'm at it, I might as well get a dozen cans and take care of those pesky bees.' I can see him doing that."

"Unfortunately, so can I," I said. "Well, hold down the fort. I'll be back as soon as I can with the hornet spray."

With the hornet spray, and maybe a clue to whoever had attacked Edgar's bees.

When I got to my car, I pulled out my phone to text the chief.

"Braden and I discovered a HUMONGOUS hornets' nest attached to Inman's house," I wrote. "Neighbors freaking out. Going to the feed store to get a can of hornet spray; will leave it
with Braden so it's there when needed."

That should do the trick.

I had started the car and was about to take off when I heard
the ding of a text. The chief.

"Sending Horace to photograph it in situ. Don't act until he
finishes. You won't want to approach it before dark anyway."

"Roger," I texted back.

As I was pulling away from the curb, I suddenly noticed something interesting—the Twinmobile and Braden's truck were the
only vehicles parked by the side of the road. The only vehicles in
sight. In addition to the Griswold, Inman, and Brownlow houses
there were two other huge houses on the cul-de-sac—though
they were a little farther from the edge of the development and
didn't overlook Edgar's farm. And all five had three- or even
four-car garages, so even if they had a normal amount of clutter
overflowing from the house, they'd still have room to park their
cars securely inside. I wondered if Westlake had a rule, or at
least an unwritten understanding that the residents would park
in their garages to make it easier to spot outsiders.

And where was Britni's car?

I found it just around the corner—at least I assumed it must
be Britni's. It had rental tags. And I had a hard time imagining
any self-respecting Westlake dweller driving anything as small
and cheap as a Chevrolet Spark. Even if they'd had to take it as
a courtesy car while their own luxury vehicle was in the shop,
surely they'd whisk it out of sight in the garage.

Why had Britni parked outside the cul-de-sac?

And what was she doing here in the first place? Visiting someone? Rubbernecking at the house of the murder victim? She hadn't seemed to show that much interest in the case, but maybe she had a better poker face than I thought. Maybe she had been sightseeing, sighing over the big homes in Westlake and wishing her latest interview subject lived in one of them. And then if she heard Mrs. Brownlow's bellowing and was curious to find out what was going on . . .

I'd figure it out later. And better yet, I'd brief the chief on it. For now, when I came to the next stop sign, I paused long enough to write down the address she was parked at—23 Hawthorne Street. I could look up who it belonged to.

Or maybe I wouldn't need to. I didn't know who lived in the hulking brick McMansion at 23 Hawthorne Street, but it was right next door to Mrs. Anstruther's fake hacienda. Maybe she was the reason for Britni's presence.

What if Britni had decided to test the waters and see if she could get Mrs. Anstruther to pay blackmail again? In Mrs. Anstruther's current mood, that could be interesting.

Then again, how could I be sure Mrs. Anstruther was right about Britni being her blackmailer? Just because it started happening about the time Britni did the profile on her didn't mean Britni was responsible. Mrs. Anstruther hadn't offered anything that sounded like solid evidence.

I'd worry about that later. I set my course for the feed store.

Chapter 24

Flugleman's Feed Store and Garden Center was one of my favorite places in town. Although it had expanded its wares to include goods popular with town and suburban dwellers, it still catered primarily to the needs of the county's farmers. So not only could I drop by to pick up things we needed for our livestock, like chicken feed or llama halters, I could almost always find someone there to give me expert advice on any agricultural problems we might be having. Sometimes a few too many someones, since the shop was a hangout for a number of old-timers with strong opinions on such important subjects as how long to season manure and how often to deworm chickens.

And it was also a great place to pick up gossip.

I selected a can of wasp-and-hornet spray after studying the labels of the two available brands for quite a long time. They had similar active ingredients and similarly dire health and environmental warnings. Should I wait and ask Dad, or perhaps Grandfather, if there was a less noxious way to get rid of a wasp's nest?

Next time. For now, we needed to be ready to deal with the hornets' nest hanging from the roof of Walter Inman's house before Mrs. Brownlow lost it completely. I penciled a task in my notebook to ask Grandfather about environmentally friendly wasp and hornet extermination. Then I picked out the spray with the longest range—twenty-seven feet instead of merely twenty.

I took my purchase up to the checkout counter, and exchanged greetings with Gertie Flugleman, the family matriarch. And it suddenly occurred to me that Flugleman's wasn't just the logical place to go in Caerphilly if you wanted a can of hornet spray. It was almost the only place.

"Weird question," I said to Gertie. "But has anyone come in during the last month or so and bought a whole lot of this stuff? Like ten or twelve cans?"

"Not that I know of," she said. "We never have more than half a dozen in stock. And why would anyone want that many? If you wanted to spray that much of any kind of chemical, you'd probably go for a pump sprayer—you know, one of those backpack style things where you mix up your chemicals from concentrate. But I can't imagine why anyone would want to do that with wasp spray—it's nasty stuff. Not something you can use around crops, so most farmers would be pretty careful with it. If they use it at all."

"This wouldn't be a farmer," I said. "Probably someone from Westlake."

"Oh, them," she said. "Yeah, I can see them spraying that stuff around like it's air freshener, but they wouldn't have bought it here. They hardly ever come in here, and when they do, you should see how hard they try not to touch anything."

She glanced around and shook her head as if she couldn't understand the Westlakers' squeamishness. I couldn't either, actually. Discriminating tourists found Flugleman's a wonderfully authentic piece of Americana, according to a recent article in *Travel + Leisure*. But authentic Americana probably wasn't something the Westlakers appreciated.

"Is there someplace else in town where they could get it?" I asked.

"I think maybe the drugstore might carry a can or two in season," Gertie said. "Not ten or twelve. But Westlakers don't shop there much, either. I figure they get most everything online."

"They would, wouldn't they?" So much for efforts to solve the mystery of the bee massacre. I paid for my hornet spray and we wished each other a good day.

"By the way," Gertie said, as I was tucking the spray can and receipt into my tote. "What's with that young cousin of yours?"

"Which young cousin?" I asked. "I have more than a couple, you know."

"The snooty one who's been following your grandmother around."

"You mean Britni? No cousin of mine."

"Glad to hear that." Gert shook her head. "She waltzed in here while your grandmother and Rose Noire were picking up some hummingbird feeders and dragged poor Ms. Cordelia off to have tea at the Frilled Pheasant. I figured she was a greedy young opportunist who wanted an expensive meal at your grandmother's expense."

"No, she's a . . . young reporter who's researching a story about Cordelia, and if she's greedy enough to stick her subject with the check instead of putting it on her expense account, I'll report her to her boss."

"Good. Should have known she was no kin of yours. No manners. See you!"

Actually, I could think of several cousins whose manners were probably as bad as Britni's. But Cordelia would have lectured them, not taken them for tea and crumpets.

Another customer had arrived at the counter, and Gertie turned to ring him up.

I returned to my car in a thoughtful mood. Thoughtful, and

a little guilty. I found myself wishing I'd been free to tag along with Cordelia and Rose Noire. I could have helped Cordelia steer Britni away from the Frilled Pheasant to someplace less snooty. Muriel's Diner. The Shack, a down-and-dirty barbecue joint run by several Shiffley cousins. A recent review of The Shack in the *Caerphilly Clarion* opined that "The decor may remind you of *Deliverance,* but you won't find better food this side of paradise."

Yes. If we didn't get rid of Britni—and I was rooting for that—we'd need to introduce her to the real Caerphilly. I'd put that on my to-do list. As soon as I'd taken care of the hornets and the NIMBYs. I was dreading the NIMBYs more. At least I could delegate the hornets to Braden. Or whoever was available come nightfall. Better yet, maybe I could recruit Dad to come over with his complete beekeeping outfit to root them out safely. He'd probably enjoy it—as long as he remembered that these were bald-faced hornets, not his gentle Italian bees, so he should keep his veil and gloves on. And before I started the engine, I pulled out my phone and called the chief.

"Yes, Meg?" he said.

"I've been butting in again," I said. "Not into the murder case—into the case of the destruction of Edgar's bees."

"I do wish he'd reported that when it happened." The chief sighed with exasperation. "It would have been a lot easier to investigate it ten days ago, when any possible evidence was still fresh."

"And when you didn't have a murder case on your hands. But one piece of evidence might still be findable." I related Gert's opinion that if one of the NIMBYs had poisoned Edgar's bees, they'd have bought the hornet spray online.

"Makes sense," he said. "I'll keep an eye out for that when we get Mr. Inman's financial records and access to his computer. Thanks."

He sounded hurried, so I didn't bring up the blackmail angle. After all, I hadn't talked to Mrs. Brownlow yet.

And anyway, it might be a good idea to get a little more information before I told him about it. If Mrs. Anstruther was right, both that Britni was her blackmailer and that she wasn't the only victim, the logical place to look for some of the other potential victims was in the back issues of *Sweet Tea and Sassafras.* If I could carve out a little time to leaf through them when I got home, I could give him a complete list of women they'd done features on. Unless there were others in Caerphilly, I doubted I'd know any of them—certainly not well enough to ask, "By the way, has a woman named Britni Colleton been blackmailing you?" But Mother might know some of them. She was active in the Garden Club, the Ladies Interfaith Council, and half a dozen other good causes for which she often attended state or regional meetings. She regularly did rooms in decorator show houses. Some of her haunts would also be theirs. And in the unlikely event that she didn't know a few of the women on the list, she was bound to know someone who knew them. Between the Hollingsworth clan and her vast network of antiques dealers, caterers, florists, tailors, cabinetmakers, and fellow decorators, she'd find a way.

So I stuck my phone back in my pocket and returned to Westlake. Horace's cruiser was parked behind Braden's pickup. I entrusted the hornet spray to Braden, with orders to hang on to it until the chief gave the orders to use it.

"Will do," he said. "And I'll pass along the word to Vern."

"Is he coming here to take over when you go off duty?" I asked.

"He's here already. And yeah, I guess you could say he's taking over. He's going to stay behind when Horace leaves and guard the place overnight. But don't tell anybody!"

"I won't." Having Vern in Inman's house was even better than having him at his cousin Sam's—just as close, and with a better view.

"I guess the chief has reason to suspect Mr. Inman's killer might come back to destroy some kind of evidence." Braden frowned and glanced at me as if hoping I'd offer enlightenment.

I nodded. Actually, I suspected the chief was stationing Vern there as backup in case someone tried to harm Edgar's bees. Or maybe Vern was doing it on his own. Either way, it definitely made me feel better about The Sting, knowing that if anything did happen, help would be just across the little plank bridge.

Just then Braden's cell phone rang.

"'Scuse me," he said, as he pulled it out of his pocket. "I should take this. Hello?"

He listened for a good minute or so, while I fidgeted. The modern world has yet to solve many of the etiquette problems surrounding cell phones, such as what to do when a person you were about to say goodbye to suddenly gets a phone call. Not to mention how to pretend you're not listening to that person's side of the conversation.

Fortunately, Braden's phone call was relatively short, and his side of it consisted of two "okays" and an "I understand." He was grinning when he hung up.

"Want to go watch the beekeepers do their thing?" He didn't wait for an answer but strode along the side of the house to the backyard.

The stonework in Inman's backyard included a large main patio area on the same level as the house, and then a series of smaller terraces and patios, joined by stone steps or, occasionally, shallow stone ramps to cover the part of his yard that sloped gently down to the stream. Braden leaned against the low wall that surrounded the patio, staring across at Edgar's farm. I joined him.

There was activity around the beehive at the far left end of the row. A pair of tall men in jeans and t-shirts were disassembling it and loading its assorted boxes and other components into a wheelbarrow. Nearby stood another batch of boxes—presumably the makings of a new, insecticide-free hive.

We watched as the workers set the new hive in place and then trundled off with the wheelbarrow full of old parts. Two men in beekeepers' suits took their place. One tall and skinny, the other short and round—rather like Jack Sprat and his wife.

"I think it's your dad and your grandfather," Braden said, pointing at them.

"Probably." I glanced around to see if any of the nearby NIMBYs were watching. The only one I saw was Shane, still slumped in the Adirondack chair. "Should we be calling attention to them? What if they want to be reasonably discreet about installing the new bees?"

"They don't," Braden said. "That was your dad who called just now. He said to do whatever I could to make sure everyone over here saw what they were doing."

The two beekeepers made short work of dumping the bees into their new home. Probably Grandfather's no-nonsense influence. But then they stood around for rather a long time, still in their protective gear, gazing at the hive and pointing first at it and then up at the growing swarm of bees circling around them and overhead. When they noticed us watching, they waved wildly at us and began making wild, dramatic, and completely incomprehensible gestures, as if trying to communicate some important fact about the hive.

"Do they want us to do something?" Braden looked puzzled and a little anxious. "Why doesn't your dad just call again?"

"I think they want us to make a fuss," I said. "Let's gesticulate back at them."

We began by waving and pointing, and escalated to making increasingly strange gestures. Grandfather and Dad seemed to realize what we were doing and did their best to increase their own weirdness factor. When Dad began doing his Weaseltide dance—a series of rapid hops, jumps, and twirls intended to imitate the war dance weasels performed to celebrate successfully stealing something or capturing a particularly choice bit of prey, Braden joined in with enthusiasm. After that fateful Earth Day when Dad had demonstrated the Weaseltide dance at Caerphilly

High School, the students had adopted it as part of their cheering routine at sports events, to the dismay of both opposing teams and the school administration.

"If that doesn't get their attention, I'm not sure what will." I seated myself on the low stone wall, took off my sunglasses, and pulled a tissue out of my purse to clean them with. By polishing them rather obsessively and then holding them up repeatedly to inspect the results, I managed to steal a look at both of the neighboring NIMBYs. At the Griswolds', Shane had finally moved. In fact, he was sitting up and using a pair of binoculars to stare at the activity across the stream. And someone else was presumably peering out of an upstairs window, since the curtains had been drawn slightly aside and twitched from time to time. I didn't see any opened curtains at the Brownlows', but at least two of their movable security cameras were aimed at Braden and me, while the rest were pointed straight back toward Edgar's farm.

"I think we've done our part," I said. "Anyone in Westlake who doesn't already know the bees are back will find out soon, I suppose."

"I don't know," Braden said. "I don't fancy these rich people spend a lot of time gossiping over the back fence."

"More likely they'll call each other to ask, 'have you seen what those horrible farmers are doing now!'" I said. "Nothing more we can do. Drop the hornet spray off with Horace and Vern when you get a chance. I'm going to go home and relax."

Though when I got home, relaxing wasn't first on the agenda. Apparently Dad had recruited Michael to join his overnight vigil in Edgar's house to keep watch in person over the beehive. And when Josh and Jamie had heard about the expedition, they'd begged to go along, pointing out that it was a Friday night and Michael had been promising them a camping trip for weeks. By the time I arrived back at the house, the in-person component of The Sting had ballooned into an overnight party for the boys and half a dozen of their friends.

Including Adam Burke, the chief's grandson, and a junior Shiffley. Reassuring—I had no doubt that Edgar's house and its environs would be closely watched all night.

I helped them pack—strange that the camp-in, as they were calling it, seemed to require even more gear than our last several outdoor camping trips. Rose Noire had assembled a large supply of provisions—as had the families of all the boys' friends. I briefly considered accepting their invitation to come along, just for the food.

"I think this should be a boys' night out," I said finally. "But if it's okay, I'll drop by for a visit sometime this evening."

"Remember to turn your headlights off when you get to Mr. Bortnick's driveway," Josh said.

"And no flashlights allowed!" Jamie added. "We don't want anyone to know we're there."

"If no flashlights are allowed, how are you going to find your way around?" I asked.

"There's a full moon tonight," Michael said. "And Kevin has provided some useful gear."

"Night-vision goggles!" Adam exclaimed from somewhere behind me. I turned and started slightly at the sight of the eight boys, all wearing night-vision goggles that made them look like oversized insects.

And oversized insects of a bewildering variety of species. Only two wore objects that I would definitely describe as goggles, like spectacles with weird robotic excrescences over each eye. Another two wore what looked to be aviator sunglasses made with glass or plastic in a sickly yellow-green hue that made me think of radiation or Kryptonite. The remaining bee watchers wore what seemed to be telescopes, either held in place with head straps or mounted on hard hats—but not one of the eight wore gear that was precisely identical to any other's.

"Kevin can probably lend you a set," Michael said.

That explained it. I looked forward to finding out if Kevin

was merely collecting a varied supply of night-vision equipment, or if he was taking an interest in improving it, in which case some or all of the gear the boys were wearing would turn out to be his own inventions.

After giving me a quick goodbye kiss, Michael led the noisy swarm of goggle-eyed insects out to the Twinmobile and Dad's car.

"I'll leave a pair of night-vision goggles on the kitchen table for you," Kevin said. "I might be napping when you take off."

"Napping?" I glanced at the hall clock. "I think if you go to sleep at seven in the evening it counts as going to bed really early."

"Not if you're planning to get up around midnight and keep watch," Kevin said. "I want to see how things go on the first night of The Sting. I installed a bunch more cameras over at Edgar's. Inside the house, too, in case you want to see what the boys are up to. I'll send you a link. I want to keep an eye on things. See if I need to make any adjustments to the cameras. Whether the low-light mode works well. That sort of thing."

He ambled back toward the kitchen, and I heard his quick footsteps disappearing into the basement.

Yeah, he probably did want to fine-tune his cameras. But I had the feeling he was just a little anxious—about the bees or the boys? Maybe both. It made me feel better, knowing he'd be keeping watch.

The house grew quiet. Rose Noire was sitting in the kitchen, sipping tea and reading a book. Presumably Cordelia was still napping. I decided to make my list of potential blackmail victims so I could call the chief.

"I'll be in my office for a while," I said.

Rose Noire nodded and returned to her book. I was strangely disappointed. Dad would have assumed I was going out to my office to do some kind of sleuthing and would have interrogated me fiercely. Wouldn't I have found that intensely annoying?

Then why was I disappointed that Rose Noire showed no interest in what I was up to?

She glanced up from her book.

"Something wrong?" she asked.

"No," I said. "Just thinking. Back soon."

Chapter 25

Out in the office, I opened up my laptop, grabbed the first issue of *Sweet Tea and Sassafras*, and began making my list of possible blackmail targets. I decided to include every woman who was profiled, whether or not Britni had written the article, plus anyone else featured or interviewed in any of Britni's other articles. Apparently she'd come on board for the third issue in their first year and did 90 percent of their monthly profile features. Occasionally she wrote a second article, usually about a decorating business, an antiques shop, a restaurant, or a bed-and-breakfast. Most of her subjects were in Virginia or the Carolinas, with an occasional foray into one of the other southern states. Clearly *Sweet Tea and Sassafras* had a long way to go to catch up with *Southern Living* or *Veranda* or whatever other publications it considered its competition.

When I'd finished, I called Mother, only to get her voicemail.

"Call me," I said. "It's about Britni."

Of course, Mother had strict rules about when she answered her cell phone. Me, I just turned it off during formal meals and while I was driving. Mother's list of activities incompatible with cell phone use was so long and complicated that she could always come up with a perfectly plausible reason to let any call she didn't feel like answering go to voicemail.

So I boxed up the magazines, printed out my list of possible blackmail targets, and emailed a copy to myself so I'd have it in my phone and could forward it to the chief once I'd told him about Mrs. Anstruther's accusations against Britni.

Although the more I leafed through the glossy pages of *Sweet Tea and Sassafras* the more I wondered if Mrs. Anstruther was accusing the right person. She'd said Britni had heard one of her quarrels with her daughter. Which meant she'd had more than one. Maybe she was right that Britni had heard one of them—although I'd have expected Mrs. Anstruther to be on her best behavior when Britni was around doing her profile. But wouldn't it be even more likely that a neighbor could have heard one of the quarrels? No one can be on their guard all the time, and the neighbors would be around a lot more than Britni. Including Walter Inman, who lived just around the corner from Mrs. Anstruther and was known for sneaking about to catch his neighbors in any kind of wrongdoing.

I suddenly remembered something Mrs. Griswold had said, about Inman escalating from threats to turning Shane in to the police. What if what she was calling threats were actually Inman putting out feelers to see if the Griswolds were vulnerable to blackmail?

I decided to run this theory by someone else to make sure it didn't sound too crazy, and then call the chief. Michael was busy with the boys. So I locked up my office and headed for the back door. Always possible that Mother would be here, doing her best to protect Cordelia from the annoying Britni.

I found Cordelia in the kitchen, making a pot of tea.

"How are you doing?" I asked.

"Much better. I feel like a wimp, fading like that."

"You had a strenuous morning," I said.

"It wasn't the strenuous morning that did me in." She was adding half a dozen cups, saucers, and teaspoons to the tray the teapot was sitting on. Evidently the house was no longer nearly empty. "It was having tea with Britni. She insisted on dragging me to that wretched place in town."

"The Frilled Pheasant?" I asked. "I heard you'd gone there."

"Yes." She shook her head. "Britni seemed to like it, but it's the sort of place that I always leave feeling hungrier than when I walk in. Not to mention being relieved if I manage to get away without breaking anything. I think they deliberately arrange the place to be full of fragile things in precarious spots so they can overcharge the customers for the breakage. And the place reeked of some kind of rather unpleasant potpourri. I think I had an allergic reaction to the stuff. I should send Rose Noire in to ask what it was so I can avoid it in future."

"Maybe you've developed an allergy to Britni," I said. "Why don't you just tell her you've changed your mind. That you're sorry for all her trouble, but you've decided you don't want anyone to profile you for *Sweet Tea and Sassafras*." I realized that if I shared what I'd learned from Mrs. Anstruther, I could almost certainly convince her to cancel the interview. I was about to do so when she went on.

"I've already regretted agreeing to the profile," she said. "And I think I would have told her to get lost already, except that now I'm mildly curious about what she's up to."

"Up to?" I echoed. "What do you mean?"

"It was while we were waiting for our bill at the Pestilent Pheasant," she said. "Britni started going on about how she hadn't found out any information about my wedding, and she wanted to interview me about that, and did I have any pictures. And I told her there wasn't much to tell, Andrew and I had gotten married at the courthouse, and if anyone took any pictures I had no idea where they'd be. And she said 'Oh, no, I meant your wedding with Dr. Blake.' And something about her tone made me think she wasn't the least bit surprised when I told her we'd never been married."

"Interesting," I said. "And not in Mother's sense of the word."

"She must not have talked to your father," Cordelia said.

A good point. If Britni had talked to Dad, he would have told her about how he'd been found as an infant in the mystery section of Charlottesville's public library, and then reunited with his biological parents decades later. Neither Cordelia nor Grandfather seemed to find this topic in any way embarrassing, and as long as Dad glossed over the fact that these days they couldn't stand each other, it made a romantic and heartwarming story.

"She pretended to be sooo sorry to have brought up what she knew must be a sensitive subject," Cordelia went on. "And I told her it wasn't a problem. And then she kept going on about how she supposed I wouldn't want her readers to know about that, and she should probably avoid bringing it up, and I told her she could suit herself. That I didn't care one way or another, but if she thought it would give her readers the vapors she could leave it out."

"And how did she react to that?"

"Seemed a little taken aback. Complained that she had another migraine coming on and went back to the Inn to lie down."

I mentally apologized to Mrs. Anstruther. Maybe she'd been right about Britni being a blackmailer.

"She's dropping by a little later tonight, more's the pity," Cordelia went on. "I was rather hoping she'd gone off to regroup before retreating. Notify her editor that their profile subject has turned out to be a scarlet woman and they'd have to find a new subject ASAP."

"Actually," I said, "it's possible that she's gone off to sulk because she won't be able to blackmail you."

"She was probably just being catty," Cordelia said. "Annoying as she is, I can't quite see her as a blackmailer. Unless you know something I don't." Her tone of voice suggested that if I did, it would give her a perfect excuse for telling Britni to get lost.

"I just talked to someone who thinks she is," I said. "Although she didn't exactly have anything that resembled evidence."

I gave her the gist of my conversation with Mrs. Anstruther.

"A pity she didn't go to the authorities," Cordelia said. "Once her husband was dead and she no longer had to worry about getting disinherited."

"I think she still wanted to avoid the embarrassment," I said.

"True," she said. "But that left a dangerous blackmailer free to harm others."

"Yes, but we don't know if it's Britni." Why was I suddenly so eager to defend Britni? Guilt, probably. Just because I didn't like her didn't mean she was a blackmailer. Mrs. Anstruther could be jumping to conclusions.

"We don't know," Cordelia said. "But we can try to find out. Britni called half an hour ago to say she was coming over. Maybe I should string her along a little. Show a little eagerness to have the circumstances of your father's birth suppressed—at least until we can consult the chief about whether we can work with him to set up a sting."

Was it the return of the bees that made everyone so prone to using that term?

"Although I hate to bother him right now," Cordelia went on. "When he's in those critical first hours of a murder investigation."

"How about if I tell him about it?" I suggested. "Find a time when he's less busy and ask what we should do?"

"Good idea," she said. "I'm going to take this tea into your living room—your mother's here. She came over as soon as I told her Britni was returning, and she brought along several ladies from the Garden Club for moral support. With luck we can natter on about herbaceous borders and milky spore disease until Britni gets bored and leaves."

"Good," I said. "I'll join you when I've finished talking to the chief."

She nodded and picked up the tray.

"Then again, you could just tell her you've changed your mind about the profile," I suggested.

"But then we'd never find out if she's the blackmailer," Cordelia said. "Frankly, that's a lot more interesting than being profiled." She strode out of the kitchen with something more like her usual brisk, efficient manner.

I took out my phone and dialed the chief.

"Good evening, Meg," he said. "And in case you're worried, we're keeping in close touch with Michael over at Edgar Bortnick's farm."

"Good," I said. "Hope it's not too much of a pain, doing that on top of your murder investigation. And if you're busy, feel free to tell me to call back later. I hate to bother you about something that has nothing to do with the murder, but it could be a crime and—"

"Right now I'm playing a waiting game on the murder," he said. "Waiting for reports from the crime lab in Richmond, and from the police department in Loudoun County, where Mr. Inman used to live. I still haven't had callbacks from either of Inman's two children, which means I can't yet release his name to the press, and I know that's driving Fred crazy down at the *Clarion*. Oh, and waiting for a decision from Judge Shiffley on whether I can go after his neighbors' phone records and security systems now or whether I need to bring her more probable cause. And I forget what else. Besides, how do you know your sting operation out at Edgar's farm has nothing to do with the murder? For all we know the bees could have been the motive, remember. Tell me about whatever new crime you've discovered."

"Okay," I said. "You know Britni, the reporter who's doing a story on my grandmother?

"Singularly unobservant young woman," he said. "If I didn't

have four witnesses to confirm that she actually was out there at my crime scene, I'd think she was someplace else when you found the body. What about her?"

"She might be a blackmailer."

"Now that's interesting," he said. "What makes you think that?"

"I don't, necessarily," I said. "But Mrs. Anstruther does." I reported on my visit to Mrs. Anstruther and my conversation with Cordelia.

"Interesting." He seemed lost in thought for a bit.

"Of course, she has no proof," I pointed out. "If you ask me, there's someone else who's at least as good a suspect for the blackmail as Britni. Walter Inman. And if he was doing it, wouldn't that be a perfect motive for someone to murder him?"

"Yes," the chief said. "Although actually we don't have any shortage of motives for someone to kill him. A pity Mrs. Anstruther didn't seek our help. Whoever was blackmailing her—because I agree with your point that she doesn't have any proof it was Ms. Colleton—they were doing it very old-school. Leaving boxes of cash in a designated spot and ordering your victim not to involve the police? All you need is one person who feels more anger about being blackmailed than fear of exposure, and you've got the perpetrator dead to rights."

"Should Cordelia string her along?" I asked. "So you can get her for blackmail?"

"Well, first of all, the Virginia code doesn't have a law against blackmail," he said.

"That stinks," I said.

"It's all lumped under extortion," he continued. "Vern could do it better, but if memory serves, the statute says that anyone who threatens injury to the character, person, or property of someone else and by doing so extorts money, property, or pecuniary benefit is guilty of extortion."

"Well, that works," I said.

"Yes. But it can be a hard crime to prosecute. The way the statute's written, you pretty much have to catch them in possession of the proceeds, or they can claim they didn't mean it, they were just joking. Nonsense like that."

"If the blackmailer's method of collecting is to have people leave boxes of money around, that shouldn't be too hard."

"No," he said. "But if Britni's the blackmailer, then your grandmother already told her to publish and be damned. She might be a little suspicious if Ms. Cordelia comes back and pretends to be daunted."

"True," I said. "But what if it's not Cordelia who begs her to keep the secret. What if it's me? I could go to her and say 'maybe my grandmother doesn't care if the whole world knows her secret, but I do. I don't want my family disgraced.' Or better yet, Mother. She could pull it off brilliantly."

"I'm sure either of you could." I could hear amusement in his voice. "But remember, if she's a blackmailer, she could be dangerous. It would be wiser to see if we could get information from Mrs. Anstruther and see what we can do with that."

"Oh, you're no fun," I said. "I'll see if I can persuade her to talk to you. What if we could find other victims? I can send you a list of the other women Britni has interviewed for *Sweet Tea and Sassafras*."

"That would be very helpful," he said. "I probably couldn't do much on it immediately—"

"Not until you catch Inman's killer," I said. "No rush—if it's actually happening, it's been going on for years."

"Get that list together and I'll see what I can do with it."

I thought of telling him I already had the list, but I didn't want him to feel I was pressuring him. He had enough to do with the murder investigation. I'd send it a little after we hung up.

And it also occurred to me that of course he couldn't say "yes, go ahead and see if you can catch Britni trying to blackmail your grandmother." We'd be acting as agents of the police, and there were rules about that. It might even count as entrapment. But if we went ahead and did it anyway . . .

We signed off, and I headed out to the living room to greet Mother's guests. Technically also my guests. Three of Mother's Garden Club cronies were sitting near the fireplace with Cordelia and Rose Noire, all of them sipping tea or lemonade and chatting with great enthusiasm about espaliers and lespedeza. I had only the vaguest idea what espaliers were and couldn't remember offhand whether lespedeza was a desirable plant, a dangerous invasive species, or a plant disease that I should be worrying about, so I focused on asking the visitors about their families and looking to see if their teacups and lemonade glasses needed filling.

"And here's Britni!" Mother appeared in the archway that led to the hall, trilling her words in a tone that struck me as just a little too bright and cheerful. "She's profiling Cordelia for *Sweet Tea and Sassafras* magazine. Such an *interesting* publication, don't you think?"

All three visiting ladies were cronies of Mother's who knew that she never used "interesting" as a compliment. All three came to attention, no doubt hoping that they were about to witness some form of verbal jujitsu.

"Meg, why don't you bring Britni some lemonade?" Mother suggested. "Unless you'd prefer tea," she added, turning to favor Britni with the full power of her gracious hostess persona.

"Lemonade's fine," Britni said.

From her surly expression, I suspected she considered lemonade the lesser of two evils rather than fine. Telling her that Rose Noire had made it fresh from sustainably grown lemons and organic, fair-trade, non-GMO sugar probably wouldn't make her like it any better. I headed for the kitchen. One of the Garden Club ladies stood up—Mrs. Vetrano, whom I knew better than the other two because one of her grandsons played baseball with the boys.

"I'll help Meg," she announced, and followed me out to the kitchen.

"What is this *Sweet Tea and Sassafras* thing?" she asked when the door to the hall was shut and she was sure Britni couldn't hear. "I gather your mother doesn't quite approve of it. I hate it when everyone else is up on the latest trends and I'm clueless."

"Don't worry," I said. "It is not and probably never will be a trend. Take a look."

I fished out one of the issues I'd been carrying in my tote and handed it over. She flipped through it while I tossed ice cubes in a glass and poured lemonade over them.

"If a publication's going to rely this heavily on pictures, it should at least hire competent photographers," she observed as she handed the issue back to me. "Is this young lady they sent nice?"

My first impulse was to say "No, not in the least." But was that true? Fair? Not really. I paused for a moment to think of an answer that was accurate and yet not unkind.

"If it's taking you that long to come up with your answer, then I expect it's no," Mrs. Vetrano said, with a chuckle.

"I wouldn't say she's not nice," I replied. "But—full disclosure—for some reason she's rubbed me the wrong way since the minute I met her, so I'm probably not the best person to give an accurate answer. She's profoundly out of her element here in Caerphilly, and nobody's ever at their best in that situation. And she's very young and very driven to get her story for the magazine, and I think that makes her a little . . . insensitive to what Cordelia wants. But she could be a perfectly nice person making a bad impression because she's stuck in a difficult and uncongenial situation."

"That's fair," she said. "And very kind of you."

I thought so myself. Fair, but not so rosy that I'd look like an idiot if later we found out for sure she was a blackmailer.

"So we'll give her a chance," Mrs. Vetrano said.

"Yes," I replied. "And you can also help us keep her from annoying Cordelia for however long she stays here. Which might not be that long—I think Cordelia's regretting that she ever agreed to be profiled." Actually, I suspected she was starting to enjoy it, now that we were angling to trap a blackmailer—but I couldn't exactly say that to Mrs. Vetrano.

"That's good. Let's take a pitcher out to the party while we're at it."

So we strolled back with her carrying Britni's glass while I brought along a fresh pitcher of lemonade. I was already calculating how long I had to stick around to keep my reputation as a polite hostess. Not because I minded the Garden Club ladies. But Britni . . .

Chapter 26

Back in the living room I noticed that Mother and Cordelia had retreated to two chairs in a corner and appeared to be having a quiet conversation. But they kept glancing over at Britni, with an occasional side glance at me. Then Mother caught my eye and nodded slightly in Britni's direction. I deduced that they were going to attempt to lay their trap to see if Britni was a blackmailer. Convince her that however philosophical Cordelia was about Dad's out-of-wedlock birth, Mother didn't want it noised about. And they wanted my help.

With a sigh, I grabbed a glass of lemonade for myself and drifted through the room until I ended up beside the sofa where Britni was sitting. She was ignoring the garden talk, which had moved on to the virtues of neem oil. She was leafing through one of the family photo albums. And not enjoying it, from the glum expression on her face. Maybe she wasn't finding anything sufficiently embarrassing to serve her nefarious purposes. Assuming she actually had nefarious purposes. I reminded myself that I could be maligning her.

Mother beamed at me briefly, and then went back to what seemed to be an absorbing conversation with Cordelia. I wasn't sure what Mother was planning, and wished she'd clue me in. I always make a better co-conspirator when I have some inkling of what the plot is.

Britni glanced up at me and nodded slightly.

"Did you manage to connect with Chief Burke?" I asked, taking a seat beside her. "I know he wanted to get your interview over with."

"So annoying," she said. "I wasn't even in town when it happened, and just because I was nearby when you found that dead body doesn't mean I know anything about it."

"I'm sure he knows all of that," I said. "When the case goes to trial, the chief has to be able to say that he interviewed all the potential witnesses as soon as possible after the body was found, or the defense will try to use that to show that he didn't do a thorough investigation."

She made a noncommittal noise.

"And isn't it nice to have gotten it over with." I winced when I heard how my words came out. Rather like the tone of hearty false cheer a relative unaccustomed to dealing with children would use in a misguided attempt to talk the boys into something they didn't want to do. What was it about Britni that made me want to speak to her as if she was a child? A particularly wayward one, and maybe even not too bright. Clearly I needed to work on my attitude.

"Whatever," she said.

Just then something caught my eye. The conversation between Mother and Cordelia had grown more animated. And from the look of it, slightly heated. Mother appeared to be taking Cordelia to task about something—scolding her, and rather sternly. Cordelia appeared to be snapping back, defensively.

Britni, hunched over the album, was missing all their efforts.

"Oh, dear," I said. "I wonder if I should intervene."

"Intervene?" Britni looked up eagerly. "What's wrong?

"Mother and Cordelia," I said. "They seem to be arguing about something. Which is odd—normally they get along great."

"Isn't that kind of unusual," Britni said. "To get along well with your mother-in-law?"

Mother and Cordelia, realizing that Britni had missed their earlier efforts, took it from the top. I watched the pantomime play out. Something Cordelia said had upset Mother. Made her just a bit angry. A disagreement followed—not exactly a quarrel, but an exchange of slightly testy words. And then Mother's face softened, and she patted Cordelia's hand in a reassuring manner, as if to say, "Don't worry—I'll take care of it." Accompanied by a quick, meaningful glance in Britni's direction.

I could see from her face that Britni bought it. Hell, I knew what they were doing and I almost bought it. Would Mother follow up immediately with her plea to Britni not to air the family's dirty laundry? Or would she wait awhile, allowing time for Britni's curiosity to grow? Better yet, allowing time for Kevin to set up some of his electronic gadgets so we could document any incriminating statements Britni might make.

And then the power went out.

"What happened?" Britni sounded anxious—almost fearful.

The rest of the company, all either Caerphilly natives or longtime residents, seemed to take this in their stride.

"Just a power outage," Cordelia said. "Nothing to worry about."

"What should we do?" Britni sounded at the edge of panic. "Isn't there something we can do? Shouldn't we be reporting it?"

I felt a sudden surge of pity for her. A novel sensation. But she was so completely out of her element here in Caerphilly to begin with, and was probably already a little worried about how she could possibly fit Cordelia into an article that would meet the expectations of her editor and her magazine's readers. And then we had dragged her out into what she probably perceived as the trackless primeval forest and made her the unwilling witness to the discovery of a murdered body. I had the feeling it wouldn't take much to send her over the edge completely, and I hoped the power outage wouldn't be the last straw.

"Happens all the time this far from town." I kept my tone cheerful and upbeat. "A lot of times it just flickers off for a little bit and then comes right back on again."

"But what if it doesn't?"

"First we put some light on the subject." Using my phone's flashlight app to avoid tripping over anything, I walked over to a carved wooden chest that stood under one of the front windows and lifted the lid. Inside, neatly arranged, were half a dozen LED lanterns, at least a dozen flashlights, and a wicker basket full of headlamps—small LED lights attached to elastic straps. I donned a headlamp, turned it on, and carried two lanterns over to set them on the coffee table. Mother and Cordelia returned to the sofas. Rose Noire darted over to the chest, picked up the wicker basket, and began making the rounds, offering each visitor her choice of headlamps.

Surely the fact that we had such a lot of supplies for dealing with power outages—and had stored them so conveniently at hand—would reassure Britni that this was an ordinary and unthreatening occurrence.

"But how long will it last?" she asked.

"No idea," I said. "But I'll go and find out."

The rest of the group were doing a postmortem on the Garden Club's spring seed swap, but Britni was sitting on the edge of her seat, as if she thought she'd have to flee at any second. Her eyes followed me out of the living room. I arrived in the kitchen just as Kevin emerged from the basement, wearing a headlamp and carrying a laptop case.

"Any news on what took out the power?" I knew that Kevin, whose entire life revolved around electronics and cyberspace, would already have called in the outage and learned everything he could about its cause and the prognosis.

"Tourist in an SUV took out a couple of light poles just beyond the Washingtons' driveway," he said.

"An accident, then. And only local." Was I the only one who

had immediately wondered if someone had sabotaged the power countywide, to open the way for an unobserved attack on Edgar's bees? Probably. "The power's still on out at Edgar's farm?"

"Right," he said. "And in town, of course, so I'm going to head there. Work in my office. I can keep watch over the hives from there. I want to make sure everything's working smoothly this first night. I'll probably head back as soon as the power's on again."

"Did they give you any idea when that would be happening?"

"They don't know yet. Shouldn't take too long. No mystery what happened, so it just depends on how soon Dominion Power sends out its repair crew."

And also whether Horace would need to do a full accident scene investigation. And we both knew that an outage affecting a mere dozen households would be low on the power company's priority list. I hoped it was a quiet night elsewhere in Central Virginia.

Kevin turned back toward the stairs and whistled. Widget, his Pomeranian, came bounding up out of the basement. After the usual short game of catch-me-if-you-can, the pup allowed Kevin to attach the leash and they headed for the hall. I followed them, returning to the living room so I could report what Kevin had learned.

Everyone except Britni took the news philosophically.

"I was going to type up my notes from the day," she said. "I'm really going to get behind."

"Don't mind us, then," Mother said. "Meg, why don't you take her to the library so she can work in peace and quiet."

"Sure." I stood and turned to show Britni the way.

"But my laptop's out of power. I need to plug it in."

Typical, I thought. And realized I had picked up one of Kevin's prejudices. He was always railing against careless people who waited until their batteries were dead or very nearly so before thinking about recharging. I could see his point.

"You could go back to the Inn—I'm sure they've got power there." Cordelia didn't quite manage to sound as if Britni's departure would distress her, but she made a valiant effort.

"But I was going to work here. What if I need to ask you questions about something?"

The sympathy I'd been starting to feel for Britni was fast vanishing.

"I have it," I said. "Back in a couple of minutes."

"Why don't they have one of those thingies people use when their power goes out?" I heard Britni ask as I was leaving the room.

"A generator?" Cordelia asked. "I suppose they could."

"But they can be so noisy and smelly," Mother said. I couldn't see, but suspected she was visibly repressing a shudder.

"And sometimes dangerous," Cordelia added.

"I think Meg and Michael prefer to go with the flow," Rose Noire announced. "And accept, if the power goes out, that maybe the universe is telling them it's time to take a break and just breathe."

Actually, that was Rose Noire's view of power outages. Michael and I knew that, though frequent, they were rarely long, and also that a generator would spoil the boys' enjoyment of them as adventures.

I went down the long hallway to the library and grabbed an object I knew was there—a Royal typewriter from the 1930s. We'd acquired it as a prop a few years ago when Michael had directed a production of *The Front Page*. We kept it on the library shelves as a decoration, but it was in perfect working order—Kevin seemed to consider it an honorary computer and subjected it to the same regular inspection and maintenance he gave to all our electronics.

Then I dropped by Michael's office, which was next to the library, and grabbed a wad of printer paper.

Back in the living room I set the typewriter and the paper on the coffee table.

"Voilà," I said. "You can type up your notes on this. No power needed."

Britni eyed the antique typewriter as if she half expected it to explode.

But after I showed her how to insert the paper and typed a slow but accurate rendition of "The quick brown fox jumped over the lazy dogs," she seemed to resign herself.

"I suppose it's better than nothing," she said. "What's this about a quick brown fox?"

"It's a pangram," I said. "A sentence that includes all the letters of the alphabet. You use it to test keyboards or demonstrate typefaces."

"I never use the quick brown fox one," Cordelia said, in a tone of mock disapproval. "I prefer 'The five boxing wizards jump quickly.' It's shorter, too."

"Sphinx of black quartz, judge my vow," Mother intoned dramatically.

"How vexingly quick daft zebras jump!" Rose Noire suggested.

"Amazingly few discotheques provide jukeboxes," Cordelia added.

I couldn't see Britni's face all that well—she was bent over the typewriter and frowning. But I sensed she wasn't enjoying the family pangram hobby.

"Let's give Britni some peace and quiet to work on her notes," I suggested.

Britni picked up the typewriter, then let out a gasp of surprise at how heavy it was and almost dropped it. I managed to catch it before it crashed onto the coffee table.

"I was going to take it over there." She pointed to a corner where a small table and chair made a better place for using the typewriter.

I helped her carry it over and set up one of the LED lanterns so she could see what she was doing. And then I returned to the group around the fireplace, leaving her to her work.

Although it took her a while to settle down to it. She kept glancing over at us with what seemed like a surly, resentful expression. Did she think we'd deliberately zapped the power just to inconvenience her? Or perhaps she suspected us of having a concealed generator on the premises, one that we were deliberately not using for the sole purpose of making her life difficult. I thought of shifting so I didn't have to see her martyred facial expressions and exasperated eye rolls, but I'd still be able to hear the occasional heavy sigh.

She's out of her element, I reminded myself. In a strange place, among people she doesn't know or understand. People she probably suspects don't actually like her all that much. I should cut her some slack.

Then again, maybe she was just a drama queen who was sulking because no one was giving her the attention she seemed to crave. Either way, I figured we should leave her alone to type up her wretched notes.

And I had other things to do.

"I promised Michael and the boys I'd drop by to see them before bedtime," I said. "Camping trip in a friend's backyard," I added for Britni's sake, since she wasn't in on the secret of The Sting. "Anyone need a ride back to town?"

No, everyone was fine. With the possible exception of Britni, but she had her own car and could leave anytime she felt like it.

So I grabbed my tote and the keys to my car and headed for town.

Chapter 27

On my way to town I passed the cause of our power outage. The tourist's SUV was still in the deep drainage ditch that bordered the Washingtons' farm, but Osgood Shiffley was there with his tow truck, preparing to drag it out. Horace was there, but he was only holding his crime-scene camera, not taking photos, which probably meant he'd finished whatever forensic work the accident required. And Aida was administering a field sobriety test to the SUV's driver.

As soon as I passed the accident scene I could see lights—first scattered lights from the farms I passed, and then more and more lights as I reached the outskirts of town. I followed a route that kept me as far as possible from the heart of town, which could be thick with tourists this time of year, and eventually headed out into the country again.

I turned in to Edgar's driveway and, remembering the boys' warnings, turned off my headlights. As Michael had predicted, the moon was nearly full, so there was some light to see by—but still, it wasn't daylight. I slowed my car to a crawl so I'd have at least some chance of stopping before I ran into anything else that might be prowling the lane—an insomniac sheep for instance.

Or a night-prowling goat. Or a car that might be leaving with its headlights also dark.

As I crept along I glanced to the right and left, looking for Edgar's goats and sheep, but didn't spot any. Maybe they preferred to sleep in places where they wouldn't be disturbed by passersby.

I reached Edgar's front yard without running into anything and parked near the other vehicles—in addition to the Twinmobile and Dad's car, I spotted several trucks. My eyes had gotten pretty well adapted to the dark, so I decided to see how I did without Kevin's night-vision goggles. I walked up to the front door—which opened just as I drew near. I could barely make out the two figures in the front hall.

"We saw you coming," Josh said in a near whisper. He was wearing the robot spectacle style of goggles. Adam Burke, at his side, had the Kryptonite-green sunglasses style.

"Better put your goggles on," Adam added, almost inaudibly. "It's pretty dark in here."

So I pulled my robot-style goggles out of my tote and put them on. Suddenly the whole world was bright green. I could easily see to follow the boys down the hallway.

"We're all staying in the basement as much as possible," Josh said over his shoulder.

"It's got no windows, so we can have lights on and make as much noise as we like."

Considering how many boys must have been lurking somewhere in the house, it was remarkably quiet.

"Entering the decompression zone!" Adam said.

Josh opened the basement door. Sound welled up—a muted mix of conversation, music, a variety of electronic noises, and the unmistakable sound of Ping-Pong balls bouncing and being hit.

The boys waved me in. Even with the goggles the stairway was still relatively dark, although I could see glaringly bright slivers of green light at the bottom, where someone had hung a curtain to turn the stairs into a buffer zone for light and noise. I descended, slowly and carefully. The boys followed and shut the door behind me.

"Exit secure!" Josh said, in a normal tone of voice.

"You are now free to move about the basement," Adam said, as he flicked a switch to turn on the light over the stairs.

The additional light made the glowing green world I could see through my goggles uncomfortably bright, so I pulled them off as I took the last few steps, pulled the curtain aside, and walked out into the basement—which was now revealed as a fair approximation of a pre-adolescent boy's idea of paradise.

And a very noisy one at that. A large TV screen on one wall was showing a Japanese monster movie, with Godzilla or one of his ilk noisily destroying a generic city while Dad and two of the boys sat in folding camp chairs, watching and munching popcorn. I hadn't noticed the Ping-Pong table in my earlier visit to the basement—perhaps it had been folded up and stored out of sight. Michael and another of the boys were now hard at play on it. Another boy was zapping enemy starships in a video game at Edgar's desk, with a friend looking over his shoulder—either to cheer him on or to stake a claim to the next turn. Horace and Jamie were seated companionably nearby in two more camp chairs, staring at the bank of bee-cam monitors—evidently there were now eight bee cams. No, seven bee cams and an Edgar cam—the bottom right monitor showed Edgar, sitting up in his hospital bed, eating food that was almost certainly not standard hospital fare—buffalo wings, popcorn, and pizza. Perhaps the Sting party had dropped off some of their provisions on the way here—but if so, they hadn't made much of a dent in the bounty the families had provided. Every horizontal space in the room boasted at least one pizza box, chip bag, fried chicken platter, or tin of homemade cookies, along with a scattering of soda cans, energy drink bottles, and milk cartons.

And there were dogs scattered about the room—at least five of the Pomeranians were sleeping in laps, crouching under bits of furniture, or chewing things they probably shouldn't be chewing. Tinkerbell, Rob's Irish Wolfhound, seemed to be a Godzilla fan. And Spike, aka the Small Evil One, was sitting on Edgar's desk, staring intently at the bee-cam screens. He took his eyes off them only occasionally to cast scornful glances at the other nearby dogs, as if silently chastising them for not focusing on the real purpose of the gathering.

On screen, Edgar was holding an iPad on which he was watching something—a miniature view of the basement scene around me.

"Hi, Meg!" he called, lifting his diet root beer in salute.

I waved back.

"It's been quiet so far," Horace said, gesturing at the wall of bee cams. Evidently he was referring to the hives. The basement was anything but quiet. Edgar's house must have excellent insulation.

I was opening my mouth to suggest that they were all having so much fun that they might not notice someone sneaking over to fiddle with the hives. And then I shut my mouth firmly with the words unsaid. After all, Kevin was recruiting remote volunteers to do the bulk of the watching. If one of them spotted a threat to the hives, did I want the boys and their friends swarming out of the basement to tackle the intruder? Hell, no. I wanted them to stay safe and sound in the cellar, bearing witness, while one or two of the adults went out to deal with the situation. Preferably Horace, who was still in uniform—backed up by Vern from across the stream—while Michael and Dad kept the boys busy scanning the monitors.

"Look!" Jamie was sitting up straight and pointing to one of the screens. Everyone suddenly abandoned Ping-Pong, Godzilla, and invading starships to crowd around the bank of monitors.

We could see a speck in the corner of one of the monitors.

Horace quietly stood up and moved closer to the curtain at the foot of the stairway, his eyes still on the screens.

"Motion detected on camera three," Josh said into a microphone on the desk.

We all watched in breathless silence as the speck grew larger, began to show up on at least one of the other monitors, and was revealed as—

"A fox!" several of the boys breathed, as if speaking too loudly would scare away the visitor.

Murmurs of "cool!" and "awesome!" and "right on!" went around the room.

"A young fox, by the look of it," Dad said. "And very sleek and healthy."

"*Vulpes vulpes*," I said, since Grandfather wasn't there to do the honors, and this was a Latin name I happened to know.

We watched as the fox slowly trotted through the clover, raising his head occasionally to sniff the air in much the same way as the Pomeranians had when doing their scent work. When he came to the tenth hive—the newly occupied one—he stopped and sniffed intently at it and the area around it for a minute or so. One of Kevin's cameras gave an excellent view of the tenth hive, close-up and so sharp that we could see the fox's black whiskers twitching as he sniffed.

"Do foxes eat bees?" one of the boys asked in an anxious tone.

"No," Dad said. "He might be reacting to the smell of humans. It was only a few hours ago that Dr. Blake and I were out there setting up the hive. He can definitely still pick up our scent."

We all watched with rapt attention. The fox finished his study of the hive and looked around, ears pricked forward and then swiveling around, as if sampling the surrounding sounds to help him decide where to go. Then he turned and trotted briskly away in the direction of Westlake. Scorning the plank bridge, he crossed the stream with one agile leap and continued up the hill, passing between Walter Inman's house and the Brownlows' and disappearing over the top.

"I hope none of them spot him." Horace sounded worried. "Or Debbie Ann will be swamped with calls from people claiming he's rabid and demanding that we come out and shoot him."

"Why would anyone want to shoot something as cool as that?" one boy asked.

"City folk," the young Shiffley said. "Scared of anything bigger than a chipmunk."

"None of them bother to secure their garbage cans properly," Horace said. "That's a big part of the problem. They're lucky it's mostly foxes and raccoons showing up to raid them. Could easily be bears."

Meanwhile I was studying the new expanded array of hive cams. Some of them didn't even show the hives. One gave a close-up of the plank bridge, and two others gave excellent coverage of the three NIMBYs' backyards. Which made sense, given the probability that any threat to the bees would come from that direction.

A couple of the boys lingered briefly in front of the monitors, as if hoping the fox would return. But eventually, except for Horace and Jamie, the basement's denizens went back to their entertainment.

I stayed long enough to sample a few of the goodies—some of Minerva Burke's ham biscuits, TJ Washington's buffalo wings, and Rose Noire's chocolate chip cookies. But it was definitely boys' night out here in Edgar's combination office and game room. When I'd finished my snack, I said goodnight to Michael and the twins, located my night-vision goggles, and headed for the stairs.

Josh, self-appointed keeper of the gate, escorted me out, making sure the light over the stairs was out before I opened the door to leave. But I assured him that I could find my way unaided to the car, and he returned to the basement.

Instead of heading outside, though, I took off my goggles and waited until my eyes had adjusted. While I was waiting I checked to see if I had a good cell phone signal, and sent the chief my list of women Britni had profiled. Then I went into the kitchen and stood in front of the bay window. I was curious to know what kind of view Edgar had had before Kevin had installed the cameras—of his hives and of his three nearest Westlake neighbors.

And he couldn't have seen much of the hives. Even using the binoculars he'd left lying on the table, I could catch a clear view of only one of them, plus partial views of two others. He might not even have seen the attack on his beehives unless he'd been out in his yard at the time.

He had a slightly better view of the three NIMBY McMansions, since they were at the top of the hill that sloped up on the far side of the stream.

The Brownlow and Inman houses were dark. I wondered if Vern was lurking in Inman's house, and if Kevin had furnished him with night-vision goggles for his vigil. The Griswolds' house had only one low light on in an upstairs window.

And a human figure sitting in one of their deck chairs.

Chapter 28

I snagged one of Edgar's kitchen chairs and sat down to take a longer look at the lurker.

He—or she—was in the shadow cast by one of the pergolas, so I couldn't get a clear view. Why would someone be sitting there in the dark? I could think of any number of things a person might be doing, but I had a hard time imagining Mr. or Mrs. Griswold doing any of them. Stargazing? Owl watching? Listening to the frogs, crickets, and whatever else composed the music of the night? Out of character. Listening to music or an audiobook through earbuds? More plausible—especially if the lurker was Shane—but why do it outside, risking mosquito bites and possibly having to smell the nearby farms?

I'd been studying the shadowy figure for several minutes when I detected a small reddish spot of light. The lurker was smoking a cigarette.

I pulled out my phone and called Vern Shiffley.

"Something up, Meg?" His voice was wary.

"You still over at Wally the Weird's place?"

"Eyes glued to the beehives. Why?"

"Does Mrs. Griswold forbid her husband to smoke in the house?"

A short pause, then he chuckled.

"Out the deck, you mean? It's the kid. Shane. Not sure if she makes him do it outside or if he thinks he's putting one over on her, sneaking out to light up."

"So a member of the household, not an audacious burglar."

"Yup. Just a kid who thinks he's invulnerable. And is probably pretty bored, being stuck at home since he lost his license."

"DUI?"

"Number two. Another one and he'll do prison time."

"Maybe he'll learn his lesson and stop at two."

"And maybe my cousin Sam's porkers will grow wings and flap over here to keep me company."

I had to smile at the vision of the enormous Red Wattle and Gloucester Old Spot pigs becoming airborne. Then a sobering thought hit me.

"Did Walter Inman help bring about one of those DUIs?"

Vern was silent for what seemed like a long time.

"Both of them, at least the way they tell it," he said finally. "The kid and his parents, that is. Me, I'd blame the kid himself, plus whoever sold him the alcohol, but I doubt they see it that way. And yes, you could say that gives them a motive for killing Inman. A pretty stupid one, if you ask me. We'd have pulled Shane over again sooner or later, even if Inman hadn't started his whole vigilante thing. But I can see how it could happen. Spur of the moment, like if one of them confronted him, argued with him, and completely lost his temper. Or her temper."

I nodded—not that Vern could see me. Shane was the Griswolds' only child. I could, after a fashion, understand their anger at Inman. They'd blame him for Shane's current troubles. Although it would be hard to argue that Inman had done anything really wrong. Handled the situation badly, maybe, and maybe even acted more out of self-righteousness or spite than any real respect for law and order. But Shane wouldn't have gotten in trouble if he hadn't had alcohol in his system and drugs in his car. Or, for that matter, if he hadn't tried to run away.

The Griswolds wouldn't see it that way, of course. I knew how angry Michael or I would be if we thought someone was endangering our boys. But I was reasonably sure if they ever got up to anything even half as serious as driving drunk or taking drugs, neither Michael nor I would take it out on someone who did what Inman had, no matter what his motive was. I didn't feel the same assurance about the Griswolds.

"I feel bad for the chief," I said aloud. "Yet another bunch of people with a grudge against Inman."

"Yeah, pretty soon we'll have enough suspects to field a regiment," he said. "The chief will sort it out."

Nice that he had confidence in his boss. I did, too, but I knew that even the best investigator sometimes came up against a criminal who was smart enough—or lucky enough—to get away with murder.

I was about to sign off when I spotted something.

"Headlights entering the cul-de-sac," I said.

"Yup," Vern said. "Going into one of the front rooms to see who it is."

"Maybe it's the Brownlows coming home."

"Car's too small. And it's stopping in front of the house, not pulling into the garage. Looks like that reporter friend of your grandmother's."

"Britni?" I snorted. "I wouldn't call her a friend. And for that matter, she's not much of a reporter."

"She does have a knack for rubbing people the wrong way, doesn't she? I can't get a good view on account of the shrubbery, but I'm pretty sure she's ringing the doorbell. I doubt she'll get an answer. Mrs. Brownlow took off this afternoon a little while after you left and hasn't been seen since. And I gather the husband's out of town."

"Out of town for long enough to give him an alibi for Inman's murder?"

"No idea yet. Chief hasn't talked to him. Doesn't answer his cell phone, and all Mrs. Brownlow will say is that the next time she talks to him she'll be sure to tell him the chief wants to interview him."

"That's weird," I said. "Almost as if she hasn't talked to him herself."

"Sounds like. So I figure the chief will be pretty pleased when he finally gets to talk to Harry Brownlow."

I suppressed the impulse to ask "When—or if?" My mind conjured up all kinds of melodramatic possibilities. Mr. Brownlow hiding in the basement of their house, hoping to avoid talking to the chief until some other suspect had been arrested for the murder. Mr. Brownlow on a flight to some country that didn't have an extradition treaty with the US. Mr. Brownlow lying dead in some other part of the woods, after a fight in which he and Inman had killed each other off like the Kilkenny cats. Should we have let the Pomeranians spend a little more time searching? Or brought in Dagmar Shiffley and her fully trained German shepherd cadaver dog? But the chief—and Randall—would already have thought of all these possibilities, so I didn't voice them.

"Frustrating, though," I said instead. "Just having to wait for him to show up."

"Well, we can do a little more than wait." His voice held a note of satisfaction. "Chief's got a statewide BOLO out on his car. No sightings so far, but one way or another, he'll turn up. Looks like Ms. Britni got tired of waiting. Heading back to her car."

A few seconds later, the headlights reappeared, and then gradually disappeared as Britni drove out of the cul-de-sac.

"A pity," I said. "If she's over here visiting the Brownlows, she's not driving Cordelia crazy. I hope she goes to her hotel, not back to the house."

"And just why would she be visiting the Brownlows to begin with?" Vern asked. "That's a little weird, if you ask me. Think maybe she's trying to get a scoop about the murder?"

"She hasn't seemed all that interested in it," I said. "I don't think her magazine covers anything as déclassé as murder. A few years ago she wrote a feature about Mrs. Brownlow for her magazine. Pretty sure that's how she knows them. Mrs. Brownlow, anyway."

"A feature." Vern sounded interested. "I'd like to see that. Maybe it could give us some useful information on the Brownlows."

"I doubt it," I said. "Not much to it, except that they lived in a nice neighborhood in Richmond and she did a lot of volunteer work. Including organizing a big charity ball the year they did the feature. And belonged to a country club. I can't remember which one."

"The name wouldn't mean a thing to me even if you did remember it. Different worlds."

"You can say that again," I said. "Hope you have either a pleasant, uneventful vigil or a productive one."

"I'm hoping for both," he said. "That'd be optimal—the bee killer shows up in the next hour or so, and we can all sleep soundly the rest of the night."

"Except for whoever has to take the bee killer down to the station and book him," I said.

"Or her," he prompted me. "And you're right, but that would be worth losing a little sleep over."

We wished each other good night and hung up.

I made my way back to my car and headed home.

As I drove, I realized how very tired I was. It felt as if several days had gone by since we'd found Inman's body, instead of a single very hectic day.

The house was dark when I got home, but the several outdoor fixtures that lit up the front walk and the porch were on, signaling that the power was back on. I made my usual rounds, checking to make sure all the windows and outside doors were locked. Normally I left that to Michael—and normally I wouldn't have worried quite so much. But the dogs, who would usually have given a noisy warning of any potential intruder, were all down at Edgar's. And whoever had killed Walter Inman was still at large.

But not for long, I told myself as I drifted off to sleep. Maybe I'd even wake up to the news that the chief had arrested the culprit.

Chapter 29

I woke up feeling slightly groggy, and I could tell from the way the light slanted into the bedroom that I'd overslept. But wait— according to our digital bedside clock, it was Saturday. If there's nothing you have to get up for, it's not oversleeping—it's sleeping in. Self-care. A weekend luxury. Michael wasn't there, which was a minus, of course. But that was probably because he'd gotten up early to do something with the boys. Something that had probably made it possible for me to sleep in. I'd remember just what when I was a little more awake.

Still, I had the nagging feeling that there was something I should be doing. Or thinking about. Or at least feeling guilty that I wasn't doing or thinking about it. I turned over, intending to grab my notebook from the bedside table where I normally put it. Anything urgent would be in my notebook. My eyes fell on the stack of books that also occupied the bedside table.

The Beekeeper's Bible. The Backyard Beekeeper. The Beekeeper's Handbook. Beekeeping for Dummies. Natural Beekeeping. The Secret Life of Bees. The Mind of a Bee. Honey and Venom: Confessions of an Urban Beekeeper. Bee People and the Bugs They Love. Show Me the Honey. The Sting of the Wild. Most of them looked fascinating.

One or two of them actually had bookmarks in them, which meant that either Michael or I had at least started reading them.

The bees. The sight of the books brought the recollection of yesterday's events flooding back into my brain.

Instead of grabbing my notebook, I picked up my phone and clicked on the link Kevin had given me to a page where I could view the video feed from all of his hive cams. Everything seemed quiet in Edgar's backyard. And in what I could see of the Westlakers' backyards. Bees were buzzing in and out of the replacement hive. Small boys were not buzzing in and out of any of the camera feeds.

Of course, for all I knew an entire army of Westlakers wielding spray cans could have invaded Edgar's backyard while I slept. I sat up and texted Michael.

"How's it going? Did you have a quiet night?"

He replied almost immediately.

"Outside, yes. Inside—don't ask. But everyone survived. All still speaking to each other. Unanimously approved going to the Shack for a barbecue lunch."

I breathed a relieved sigh.

"Should there be leftovers . . ." I texted.

"There won't be, so we'll bring you your own order. See you at the game!"

Of course—it was Saturday, so the boys had a baseball game. I checked my calendar. Their game wasn't till four. I had plenty of time.

I wasn't quite ready to give up the guilty pleasure of staying abed, so I rearranged my pillows to let me sit more comfortably while I caught up on what had been happening in the world while I was asleep. The *Caerphilly Clarion*'s website didn't show any breaking news. I had, as usual, a daunting number of emails, but most of them were junk and none required immediate action.

Maybe—just maybe—I could sneak in a little bit of the hammock time I'd been planning for yesterday. For some reason, I'd spent part of the winter daydreaming about hammock time. And not just daydreaming—I'd actually taken concrete steps to make hammock time even more enjoyable. The old rope mesh hammock was gone. I'd hated the way it dug into my body when I was lying in it, leaving crisscross indentations when I crawled out—not to mention the fact that the resident and visiting Pomeranians got a kick out of sneaking up and playfully nipping any exposed bits of me that bulged out between the ropes. No chance of that with the new cloth hammock.

And in anticipation of my eagerly awaited summer relaxation I'd spent some time at my anvil to make myself a little wrought iron stand to go by the hammock—the perfect place to set a glass holding some of Michael's latest batch of Arnold Palmers. The stand was also large enough to hold a few books. Maybe I'd make more progress in my bee books if I took them out to read while lounging in the hammock.

Of course, before making any plans, I should probably make sure I didn't have anything else on my plate. I fired off a couple of quick emails. Then checked to see if anyone had left me any voicemails.

I had two. The first was from Mother, telling me that she and Cordelia would be spending the morning together and would meet us at the game. Her last sentence delighted me.

"And if you see Britni, tell her we're *so* sorry we missed her, and we hope to catch up with her later."

Much later if Mother had her way. I was still smiling when I began playing the second message, but just hearing my caller's voice turned my expression into a scowl.

"Ms. Langslow, this is Constance Brownlow. I would like to ask you to do me the courtesy of responding to my request that you come and see me. We really need to discuss the insect situation."

"No, we really don't," I muttered. She was almost certainly referring to Edgar's bees, and I rather thought I'd given her chapter and verse on that situation Friday afternoon.

But that was just before she'd spotted the wasp and had hysterics, so maybe she hadn't taken it all in. Or maybe, as so often happened with the NIMBYs, she intended to ignore what I'd said and repeat her demands with increasing belligerence several more times before giving up. Or several dozen more times. It was like dealing with toddlers.

Ordinarily, I might have procrastinated about getting back to Mrs. Brownlow. But this morning I was curiously eager to confront her. For one thing, I hadn't found the opportunity yesterday to make her aware of the return of Edgar's bees. If she or her husband were responsible for the earlier bee killings, their lack of knowledge could explain the quiet night the watchers had enjoyed. And for another thing, she'd have to invite me inside if she wanted to converse about the "insect situation." Maybe I'd spot Mr. Brownlow lurking somewhere in their house—or at least get her to divulge a clue to his whereabouts.

And mainly, I realized, I was fed up with the Westlakers' antics. Randall seemed to think I was better at dealing with them. Maybe he was wrong. Maybe I was only bad at making them believe my "no" meant "no." And good at letting them waste my time and their own. Maybe I needed to be firmer with them.

Worth a try. So once I made sure I didn't have any other urgent messages or requests lurking in my computer, I threw on my clothes and went downstairs to grab a late breakfast.

Actually, I decided to call it an early lunch, since enough food had made its way back from Edgar's to feed the entire family several times over. I stuck a slice of pizza in the microwave and began to graze through a largely untouched tray of raw veggies with assorted dips. Then something caught my eye—something out in the yard—and I went to the window over the sink to get a better look.

The entire backyard was filled with hummingbird feeders. Okay, maybe it was only a dozen of them, but each bright red tube was thronged with hummingbirds, darting around them or back and forth from feeder to feeder. If the bully bird was among them, he was probably having a nervous breakdown, trying to protect so many food sources from so many rivals. And each of the feeders was surrounded by sparkling jets of water, catching the sunshine as they spurted, soared, died down, and then rose up again. They didn't seem to be zapping any of the birds, though. It almost looked as if the birds and whoever was at the controls of the zappers were celebrating together, performing an intricate aerial ballet of wing and water. As good as the Bellagio casino's water show, if you asked me.

Was it horribly pedestrian of me that even as I was admiring the beauty of the scene before me, I was also trying to calculate what it was going to do to our next water bill?

Just then the microwave dinged. I turned to collect my pizza. As I did, Kevin emerged from the basement, wearing what I always thought of as his Hopeful Roach expression.

"Just leftover pizza," I said.

"Not a bad breakfast choice," he replied.

"I'll nuke you a slice," I said, claiming the already-heated one before he could. "If you're up here, who's squirting around all that water?"

"The boys. They're really keen on learning to use the zappers. They worry about the praying mantises, you know, and this could be a good way to foil them."

I sighed as I stuck several slices of pizza in the microwave. Last year the boys had learned, from Grandfather, that large praying mantises were capable of catching hummingbirds and dining on their brains. The boys had spent way too much of their summer lurking around last year's single hummingbird feeder, ready to catch and relocate any mantises that were trying to prey on the birds.

"I was hoping they'd forgotten about that," I said.

"Not likely, with Great going on about his project to create biological controls to wipe out the mantises." Kevin frowned. "Should he be taking sides like that? I mean, normally he likes predators, right? Shouldn't he be letting nature take its course? Letting a few hummingbirds die for the good of the ecosystem and all that?"

"Normally he wouldn't take sides," I said. "But the native praying mantises aren't usually large enough to take down a hummingbird. It's the non-native mantises that get big enough to go after the hummers. And you know how fierce he is about alien invasive species."

"That explains it, then," he said.

The microwave dinged.

"It also explains why coming up with biological controls is going to be so difficult," I said. "Because he needs to come up with something that only affects the Chinese and European mantises, not our useful native ones."

"Yeah," he said, claiming his pizza. "But if anyone can do it, Great can."

With that he disappeared into the basement again.

I finished my buffet breakfast and then took off to tackle Mrs. Brownlow.

There were no other vehicles parked in the cul-de-sac. I wondered if Vern was still staking out Inman's house.

I strolled up the sidewalk to the Brownlows' house. It was rather bland compared with a lot of the houses in Westlake. No moats or koi, no rampant greyhounds, no three-story white pillars. It was just a honking big house with all the typical Colonial-style touches. An exterior of mixed brick and siding. A rigidly symmetrical design, the door in the center of the main part of the house and the same number of windows on either side of it, on both the first and second stories. Muted Williamsburg colors. Shutters that almost looked as if they were functional. A row of dormers giving light to the rooms in the third story.

Mrs. Brownlow's article in *Sweet Tea and Sassafras* had been on the bland side, too. And come to think of it, if I had to pick which of the NIMBYs was the least annoying, it would be the Brownlows. They rarely complained about anything that Walter Inman or the Griswolds hadn't already tackled me about. And while they certainly weren't easy to discourage, they somehow lacked the impressive relentlessness of the others. Dealing with the Griswolds or Walter Inman was like battling the Terminator. Dealing with the Brownlows was just time-consuming and tiresome.

So how had this very bland woman managed to do something worth blackmailing her about?

She probably hadn't. My only reason for suspecting her was that Britni had also profiled her in *Sweet Tea and Sassafras*. A connection that would be pretty meaningless if Mavis Anstruther was wrong about Britni being the blackmailer. And the more I thought about it, the more I suspected Mrs. Anstruther was wrong. Britni had embarrassed her by writing an article full of drunken boasts. Shortly after that, someone had blackmailed her. As Dad was fond of saying, correlation wasn't causation. Just because the blackmail had started shortly after she met Britni didn't mean Britni was the blackmailer.

By the time I reached the front door, I was feeling almost fond of the Brownlows. So I gave in to an impulse to be helpful. I spotted something sticking out from under the doormat—something that looked like the corner of a white envelope, very noticeable against the red brick of the stoop and the black rubber of the mat. I was stooping to pick it up when—

"What are you doing?"

Mrs. Brownlow had opened the door and was looking down at me. I stood up again without touching the envelope.

"It looks as if someone left something under your doormat," I said, pointing to the little white corner. "Either that or whatever you were hiding under the doormat is trying to sneak out. Do you want me to pick it up or tuck it back under?"

"Did you put it there?" She looked shaken. Angry and fearful at the same time.

"No," I said. "I just spotted it." She continued to stare at me. "If you don't believe me, check your security system."

"I can't," she said. "It's acting up. I packed it up for Harry to send to the repair shop when he's home again."

"Then ask the people across the street," I said. "I'm sure they have security cameras, too. I just got here, envelope-free." Maybe I should rethink that bit about the Brownlows being less annoying.

She looked at me for a few more seconds—although it felt longer. Then she nodded and bent down to pick up the envelope. Her fingers were shaking as she tore it open and pulled out a single sheet of paper.

"Oh, God, no!" she gasped. Then she dropped both paper and envelope and ran back into the house.

I used the corner of my shirt to pick them up. I put the envelope on the antique chest that served as the hall table and turned to the single eight-and-a-half-by-eleven sheet of white paper it had contained. It read: "$10,000. SMALL BILLS. THE USUAL PLACE. MIDNIGHT TONIGHT."

I studied it. The paper was unremarkable—ordinary printer/copier paper. The message was typed in all caps—in Courier, or a similar typeface. Very retro—a few of the letters even had the sort of small irregularities you used to see in old-fashioned typed letters.

I set it on the hall table, too, and took a picture of it with my phone. Then I texted the picture to the chief, followed by the words. "At Mrs. Brownlow's."

I was turning to see where Mrs. Brownlow had gone when I saw his reply.

"Thanks. Is she there?"

"Yes," I typed.

"Try to keep her there."

I could hear Mrs. Brownlow's sobbing from somewhere in the house. I followed the sound down a hallway to what I would have called the family room—although having been through the house last year during the Caerphilly House and Garden Tour, I knew the Brownlows referred to it as the Great Room. I wouldn't have called it great, but by Westlake standards it was relatively unpretentious. Almost cozy. You got the feeling real people actually spent time there.

Mrs. Brownlow had flung herself onto one of the sofas with her head buried in a pile of pillows, sobbing uncontrollably.

"What's wrong?" I asked.

She ignored me and continued to sob.

I wasn't sure what to do. It didn't look as if I'd have much trouble keeping her here until the chief's arrival. But I felt awkward just sitting there watching her. And yet I wasn't sure what kind of comfort she needed, or if she'd even want it from me. Still, I needed to do something.

The Great Room was divided from the enormous kitchen only by a marble-topped counter that was piled high with dirty dishes and food containers. I hiked over to the sink, which was similarly cluttered. Clearly the fashionable open kitchen plan wasn't optimal for the Brownlows' housekeeping style. Then again, maybe recent events had thrown them off their game. I found a clean glass and filled it with cold water. On my way back to Mrs. Brownlow, I passed by a short hallway. Glancing down it, I saw an open door that led to the garage. And there were two cars there. I had no idea what make and model they were—to the boys' intense disgust, I was completely useless at car identification. A pair of matching black sedans—large, luxurious looking, and gleaming in a way that suggested they had been not only washed recently but also waxed and buffed. Matching his and hers land yachts.

Was one of them Mr. Brownlow's? Or did they have more than a car each? If Mr. Brownlow might be home, maybe I should watch my back.

I returned to Mrs. Brownlow and handed her the glass.

"Here you are." I'd unconsciously fallen into the tone I'd used on the twins when they were toddlers and grew cranky rather easily. "Sit up and drink this. You don't want to make yourself sick."

Logically, of course, it was hard to see how drinking a glass of water would keep her from making herself sick, but she'd have to stop crying to drink it, so at least maybe she could avoid getting a post-crying headache.

And it seemed to work. She sat up, grasped the glass as if it contained a lifesaving elixir, and began taking small gulps. She was still sobbing, but softly, rather than hysterically.

"I thought it was over," she said.

Chapter 30

I didn't like the sound of that.

"Thought what was over?" I asked.

"I thought he was dead and couldn't bother us anymore," she said. "And now this."

"Who?" I asked.

"Walter Inman!" She spat out his name as if being forced to utter an obscenity. "That horrible, horrible man."

"He was blackmailing you?" I asked.

"Well, duh," she said. "What did that letter look like—a friendly bread-and-butter note?"

"No, it looked like a blackmail demand," I said. "But how do you know it was Inman—it wasn't signed."

"No, but he wouldn't, would he?" she said. "Because that would be evidence—not that we would have wanted to use it. But he was always prodding us. Reminding us. And in public, too. At a party, he'd come up and say something like 'So, what made you decide to leave Richmond, anyway?' And in that loud, grating voice of his, so everyone could hear."

I nodded. I'd noticed Inman's overloud voice. Was it a deliberate feature of his overbearing personality, or just a sign that his hearing was starting to go?

"And besides, I saw him once. Out there."

"Out where."

"Out where he had us leave the ransom."

"Out where he was killed?"

"Good heavens, no." She clearly found that idea both annoying and idiotic. "What would I be doing out in the middle of the woods? Behind the library, right beneath the book drop. A clever place, I suppose—it's out of sight, thanks to all those trees and bushes on the library grounds, and people don't go there very often, but they still have a good reason for being there."

Very clever. I wondered how Ms. Ellie would feel when she learned a blackmailer was using her library. Assuming that at some point the chief would be okay with her finding out.

"And you saw Mr. Inman there."

"Yes," she said. "I was actually returning a book, and I saw the little package sitting there beneath the book drop. I knew exactly what it was, of course. And it meant someone else in Caerphilly was getting blackmailed. So I parked my car where no one could see it and crept back and hid in the bushes and waited to see who came by to pick it up. Walter Inman."

I wondered, briefly, if Mrs. Anstruther would be happy to know that her blackmailer was no longer among the living or annoyed that she'd gotten his identity wrong. And felt a pang of regret that our elaborate scheme for apprehending Britni wasn't going to be needed.

"And just why did you decide to leave Richmond?" I asked. She probably wouldn't tell, but no harm asking.

"We had to go somewhere where they didn't know what Harry had done," she said. "It will all come out now, won't it? You'll go snooping around to see what dirt you can find."

"I don't know about it all coming out," I said. "Not to the general public, at least. Chief Burke will find it out as a part of his murder investigation. In fact, he probably already knows. He'd have started looking into everyone's background, to see who might have a motive for murdering Inman. What's he going to find when he looks into yours?"

"He won't find anything about me," she said. "But he'll find out that Harry had to resign under a cloud. He did some things that weren't technically legal—not to benefit himself, but to protect the firm. But when the higher-ups found out they threw him under the bus. And he didn't even try to fight it. It was all stupid. No one got hurt. Just stupid."

I couldn't tell if she was angrier with her husband or the firm that had fired him. She probably didn't know herself.

"Was that what you and your husband were arguing with Inman about Tuesday night?" I asked. "His blackmailing you?"

"What? No." She shook her head. "Harry didn't know about the blackmail. I didn't dare tell him—he'd have done something drastic. No, Inman wanted us to sign a complaint form against the Griswolds. To make them move all the lumber they have piled up in their yard. And everyone knows perfectly well why the lumber is still there—because he's doing everything he can to stop them from building a fence. A perfectly ordinary fence that will keep them from having to look at him. We didn't want to sign his complaint—we might want to build a fence ourselves. But he kept nagging and nagging until he actually nagged Harry into a heart attack."

"A heart attack?" And she only just now thought to mention it? "Is he okay?"

"No, he's not okay," she snapped. "He's still in the hospital."

My first reaction was that if Michael had had a heart attack, there was no way I'd have left the hospital. But then I reminded myself that maybe it had only been a minor attack and Mr. Brownlow was much better. Maybe it hadn't been a heart attack but an anxiety attack, brought on by Inman harassing them. Maybe he'd faked a heart attack to end the conversation with Inman. Understandable.

Maybe the hospital staff had decided her husband would be

fine and had seen what a state she was in and ordered her to go home and get some rest. Maybe they'd even decided her absence would speed his recovery. And the Caerphilly hospital was only ten minutes away, if she needed to go back.

But she was certainly upset. Had I been interrogating a woman on the verge of collapse?

And the chief was probably on his way to interrogate her some more.

Probably a good thing. Because from the sound of it, I just might be interrogating Inman's killer. She certainly had motive.

I wondered why the news about Mr. Brownlow hadn't gotten out. I'd call Dad once I left here—which I hoped would be soon. Dad would know what had happened and how Mr. Brownlow was doing—would know or could find out. HIPAA rules notwithstanding, nothing went on at Caerphilly General Hospital that he didn't know about. Or couldn't find out about.

"I was so sure it was him," Mrs. Brownlow said. "It had to be him. Definitely. But what if he had a partner? Someone who didn't know he was dead and delivered the note anyway?"

"It's possible," I said. It struck me that if someone was in cahoots with Inman on the blackmailing scheme, they might be a very good suspect for his murder. It would get rid of someone who could testify against them and double their share of the loot.

But something else occurred to me.

"I can think of a simpler solution," I said. "When was the last time you came into the house through the front door?"

She looked up at me, puzzled.

"Don't you usually come and go by car? Through the garage? And when you came out to talk to me yesterday, you used the back door."

"The terrace door." Her tone suggested that back doors were utterly déclassé and ought not to be mentioned in polite company. "You're right. Sometimes I go days without using the front door."

"There you are," I said. "He could have left it anytime. Maybe that's why he came over Thursday night—to drop off the letter. And only pretended he wanted you to sign his petition."

"I hope you're right," she said, with a fervor that was slightly unsettling.

Just then the doorbell rang. Relief flooded me.

"Would you like me to answer that?" I asked.

"Just chase them away, whoever it is," she said. "I'd really like some time alone."

Which was probably a hint to me. I'd let her think I'd be taking it.

"Of course," I murmured.

I went back to the front door and opened it. Chief Burke.

"May I come in?"

"I'm under orders to chase away whoever it is," I said. "Orders I think you can override. Take a look."

I pointed to the hall table. The chief pulled a pair of gloves out of his pocket and put them on while studying the letter. Then he pulled two brown paper evidence bags out of the same pocket and slipped the letter and the envelope into them.

"Did you handle these?" he asked.

"Only like this." I demonstrated my technique, with thumb and forefinger wrapped in the tail of my t-shirt. "She did, but only just barely."

He nodded.

"By the way, I think Mr. Brownlow's car is in the garage. She claims he's in the hospital with a heart attack."

"Yes, she finally mentioned that when I interviewed her an hour or so ago. Annoying—she could have told me a little sooner and saved me from having to put out a BOLO on his car. Where is she?"

"This way."

I led him back to the Great Room. Mrs. Brownlow was try-ing to blow her nose on a tissue that looked as if it had already served that purpose more than once. I fished into my tote and handed her the travel tissue pack I always carried.

"I'd like to talk to you about the blackmail letter you received," the chief said.

She focused on blowing her nose with a new tissue from my pack.

"I'll get out of your way," I said.

I went back out to the front hall. As I was about to open the door, I focused on something that I'd seen only out of the corner of my eye. A box, sitting on the far end of the hall table. Larger than a shoebox, though not as large as a copier paper box. And it was addressed to a home security firm in Richmond.

Mrs. Brownlow had said the security system was acting up. That she'd packed it up for her husband to send in for repairs. What if that was just a ploy to get the security system out of the chief's reach?

I pulled out my phone and took a picture of the address label. Maybe the chief could retrieve it from the company in Richmond. Though it would be better if it never left here.

I could tell the chief about it. Maybe he could shame her into letting him have it. I walked back down the hall that led to the Great Room. But when I got close I heard the chief's voice.

"No, according to the staff at the hospital you weren't there all night. You left around ten fifteen and didn't return until around nine this morning."

"I went home to rest," she said.

"Not according to the video from Mr. Inman's security system. That doesn't show you returning until nearly three a.m."

"I went to the driving range first."

"The driving range? The one out by the Inn?"

"Yes. I find it very relaxing, just hitting balls. If I'm upset or angry, I just go out there and hit balls until I feel better."

"They close the range at eleven," he said.

"I climbed the fence," she said. "I've done it before."

"Was there anyone else there?"

"No," she said. "And the Inn staff may not even have noticed I was there. There's a little hill between the driving range and the Inn—I think they put the range on the other side of the hill deliberately, so the guests won't be disturbed by people golfing very early or very late. Sometimes I turn the lights on, and they don't even notice. But there was a full moon last night, and I didn't even have to."

Silence fell. I could imagine what was happening. The chief would be looking at her with the gentle, thoughtful look that had more than once inspired someone to blurt out a confession. Mrs. Brownlow—would she be squirming with guilt or defiant, angry at having her word questioned?

And then I reminded myself that I was eavesdropping. I made my way quietly back to the hall and stared at the package.

I could take it away, pretending that I was going to be helpful and mail it for her. Probably not very plausible.

It suddenly occurred to me that what I'd been thinking of as the hall table was, after all, a chest. I took everything off its top—everything meant only the package, a vase of flowers, and a set of keys. The top lifted up. The inside was dusty and nearly empty. A faded dog leash and a battered folding umbrella lay on the bottom. I tucked the package containing the security system inside and replaced the vase and keys. Maybe Mrs. Brownlow wouldn't even notice it was gone. Maybe she'd be too distracted to remember its existence. Inside a chest that was obviously rarely opened wasn't the first place she'd look for it. And I could tell the chief where I'd hidden it—preferably after he'd gotten whatever paperwork he needed to seize it.

Then I quietly let myself out of the house.

When I got back to the car, I called Dad.

"Is everything a go for tonight?" he said. "For The Sting? You've primed Mrs. Brownlow?"

"Not really," I said. "I didn't get a chance. Did you know Mr. Brownlow was in the hospital?"

"No, I didn't. What happened? And when?"

"Apparently he either had or thought he was having a heart attack Friday night after their argument with Inman. And is doing well, but still hospitalized."

"Oh, dear," Dad said. "I'd have thought someone would have told me. I'll check on it immediately."

We signed off. I tried to think of something else useful I could do and drew a blank. Well, except for telling the chief about the package I'd hidden. And maybe it would be a good idea to do that in person, instead of texting him or interrupting him with a call.

I felt conspicuous, sitting there in my car in front of the Brownlows' house. So I got out and strode purposefully down the sidewalk to Inman's house, and then made my way along the side of his house to the vast stone acreage of his backyard.

I stood for a few minutes gazing over at Edgar's place. Nothing much to see. If any of the watchers were still there, they were keeping out of sight. I thought I could detect bees coming and going from the hive, but it was a little hard to tell at this distance.

While I was still gazing, my phone rang. Dad.

"Mr. Brownlow isn't here at the hospital."

"Maybe they discharged him already?"

"They never admitted him."

Interesting.

"Who told you he was here?" Dad asked.

"Mrs. Brownlow," I said. "And before I left her house I overheard her telling the chief the same story, so he'll get to the bottom of it."

"Very suspicious, if you ask me." Dad's enthusiastic tone suggested that by reporting this very suspicious happening I'd made his entire day. "I'll look into it."

We signed off. I glanced back at Edgar's, but my gazing mood was gone. I'd killed a little time. Maybe I should see if the chief was still inside the Brownlows' house.

But when I turned around I saw that someone else was watching the beehives. Shane Griswold.

Chapter 31

I studied Shane for a minute or so—it didn't feel awkward, since he seemed oblivious to my presence. He was on a stretch of deck halfway down the sloping back lawn, sitting in one of the Adirondack chairs. He was pale and weedy looking, with a long, discontented face. A cigarette was burning in an ashtray by his feet while he stared through binoculars at Edgar's place. At the occupied beehive.

Instead of heading straight back the way I'd come, I veered right and picked my way along the stone paths and stairs until I was as close as I could get to him without stepping off the terrace onto the neutral zone between the two yards.

Shane didn't seem to notice my arrival.

"See anything interesting?" I asked.

He started violently, dropping the binoculars, which bounced off the arm of the chair and would have fallen to the deck if not for the strap around his neck. He reached down as if his first impulse was to hide the ashtray, and then gave it up. Because he realized I'd already seen it? Or because he didn't care if I saw it?

"The bees are back," he said. "Only in one hive, though."

"It might take Edgar a while to fill the other hives," I said. "He'll either have to buy nine more batches of bees or find nine swarms. And I think he's a little wary of filling all the hives until he's sure they won't get attacked again."

"He doesn't have to worry about that," Shane said. "Now that Wally the Weird is gone."

Curious that Shane knew Inman's local nickname. I was careful not to use it around Westlakers. But Shane probably had more contact with locals than his parents.

"You think Mr. Inman was the one who destroyed Edgar's bees?" I asked.

"I know he was." Shane glanced up at me, then groped for his binoculars and held them at the ready, as if about to return to staring at the hive through them. "I saw him do it. I was out here getting some air." He glanced down at the ashtray and shrugged. "And ruining my lungs, as my parents keep telling me. I saw him."

"Why didn't you stop him?"

"No time. He was already on the next-to-last hive when I saw him. And I didn't figure out what he was doing until he was doing the last hive." He raised the binoculars to his eyes.

"You're sure it was him?"

"I watched him come back over the plank bridge and go into his house. Carrying a shopping bag full of empty spray cans." He sounded more comfortable now that he could shield his face with the binoculars.

"You could see the empty spray cans?"

"It was a quiet night. I could hear them clinking together."

His eyes were hidden by the binoculars, and what I could see of his face was expressionless. And he was obviously trying to keep his voice calm and neutral, but just a hint of emotion leaked past his control. Anger.

"You could have reported it."

He lowered the binoculars to look at me as if astonished at my stupidity.

"Oh, yeah," he said. "Like, who are you going to believe, the president of the HOA or the neighborhood cokehead? And like I wanted to give him another reason to go after me. He'd just have lied, said I was only trying to make trouble for him, and then gone after me some other way."

"You could report it now."

"What's the use? He's dead. He won't do it again."

His tone gave me pause. There was a note of . . . satisfaction? Or was it triumph?

"Edgar might feel a little better, knowing the person who killed his bees can't do it again," I said.

"No guarantee some other jerk out here won't do the same thing."

He had a point there.

"Doesn't he realize that pesticide residue might kill his new bees?" Shane asked.

It took me a second to realize he was talking about Edgar.

"He knows that," I said. "It's a new hive. Not brand new, of course. One of his hives that used to be someplace else. New to this location."

"That's good." He nodded and returned to gazing through his binoculars.

It occurred to me that if Mrs. Brownlow hadn't suddenly made herself such an object of suspicion, I might even now be assessing Shane's potential as a suspect. He was clearly not a fan of Inman. And maybe I shouldn't be so quick to assume that Mrs. Brownlow was guilty. I studied Shane out of the corner of my eye.

"What's up with Mrs. Brownlow, anyway?" he asked.

Was the kid a mind reader?

"What do you mean by 'up with her'?"

"Like, why were you visiting her? I know it wasn't a social call." I could hear the eye roll in his voice.

"She spotted a hornet and freaked out yesterday," I said. "I came by to make sure someone had taken care of the nest, and then reassure her that they were gone."

"Nest's dead," he said. "Some guy came out last night and sprayed a whole can of poison into it. But he was smart enough to leave it in place, so they'd all have time to die off. You could probably take it down now. But you might want to wait on talking to Mrs. Brownlow about it until the nest is actually gone. She'll probably freak out again if she sees it."

"Good point," I said.

"She's basically an idiot," he said. "Sorry. I know that's a rude thing to say, but she is. See her hummingbird feeder?"

I turned and peered across Inman's vast expanse of stone to the Brownlows' yard. Yes, there was a highly ornate copper-and-brass hummingbird feeder hanging from a pole in the middle of a section of deck. It was full of bright red liquid.

"Doesn't look as if she's getting much traffic today," I said.

"She never does," he said. "And never will. That's not sugar water—just water with a lot of red food coloring added."

"She doesn't realize you have to add sugar to attract the hummers?"

"She doesn't realize that it could make the birds sick or even kill them if you let the sugar solution go bad." He was frowning angrily. "You know, like having bacteria grow in it, which happens when it's been out there for a while. She wasn't getting a whole lot of birds when she first put the feeder out—it takes them time to find their way, you know. And she let the sugar water go bad. I told her a couple of times how dangerous it was, and it was like she didn't even care. So I snuck out one night, cleaned it out, and put in the sugar-free red water. That was like three weeks ago. The hummingbirds haven't taken a drop, but she hasn't even noticed. I figure she's not that interested in hummingbirds anyway. She just likes having the cool feeder to decorate her deck."

"While you're sneaking over and messing with her feeder, why not put the sugar solution in it?" I asked. "And sneak out as needed to clean it."

"I thought of that," he said. "It'd be kind of cool to see the hummers. My parents won't let me put up a feeder. Not even a regular old feeder with birdseed. I suggested it a couple of times, but my mom is convinced we'd come down with bird flu or something if we did. So yeah, I could fill the Brownlows' hummingbird feeder. But what if my parents carry out their threats and send me away to a military academy and there's no one to clean it out if it goes bad?"

I was starting to hope Shane Griswold didn't turn out to be the killer. He was a lot more congenial than anyone else I'd ever talked to in Westlake. Maybe the coke found in his car was just another stupid form of adolescent rebellion. Or a plant, designed to discredit one of the few people in the neighborhood who seemed to have any interest in the natural world. Okay, that was maybe a little melodramatic, but still, in spite of his surly air, I was starting to like Shane.

"Does it make sense to feel guilty about something you didn't even do?" he asked.

"Like what?" I asked, not sure where this was going.

"I was going to play a prank on Wally the Weird," he said. "I was going to get a bunch of drones—you know, male bees—and turn them loose during one of his parties. Watch all his guests freak out and spill their daiquiris."

"Bad idea," I said. "What if some of them got stung?"

"Like I said, I was going to use *drones*." He sounded impatient at my cluelessness. "They don't even *have* stingers. So if anyone claimed they got stung, you'd know they were either lying or imagining it."

"I didn't know that," I said. "Still, a good thing you gave up that idea. People would have panicked and maybe hurt themselves."

"Yeah, I guess so." He shrugged. "And anyway, I couldn't find any place that sells just drones. But I feel kind of bad that I would have done it to Mr. Inman if I could have."

I was trying to figure out exactly what to say to that when

something distracted me. I heard a car in the cul-de-sac. And partly because there wasn't a lot of traffic here, and even more because I have always been terminally nosy, I turned to see who was approaching—the houses were far enough apart that it was easy to see the street, especially from my position at the edge of Inman's yard.

A police car.

"Well, that's interesting." I headed for Inman's front yard. I was a little surprised that Shane heaved himself out of his chair and followed. We stood a few yards apart, each on our own side of the Inman/Griswold property line, and watched as Aida Butler got out of her cruiser, strode up the Brownlows' front walk, and rang the doorbell.

"Weird," Shane said. "What do you suppose that's all about?"

I stifled the urge to share what I knew. What I suspected. If I was right, the news would get out sooner or later.

Someone answered the door—from where we were we couldn't see who—and Aida went inside.

Another car appeared in the cul-de-sac. This time it was Horace who hopped out, hurried up the walk, and went inside. He was carrying his crime scene case.

"Isn't that the CSI dude?" Shane said.

"It is." I made a mental note to see how Horace liked being called "the CSI dude."

"Awesome."

A few minutes later, Aida and the chief emerged, escorting Mrs. Brownlow between them. They guided her into the back seat of Aida's cruiser. Then Aida drove off, followed by the chief in his sedan.

"Whoa," Shane said. "You think maybe they're arresting her for the murder?"

"Your guess is as good as mine," I said. "I'm going to go see what I can find out."

"If—" he began. Then he stopped.

"If what?" I asked.

"Never mind." His face went back to its usual surly expression, and he turned to resume staring at the Brownlows' house.

"You know," I said. "If you decide to fill Mrs. Brownlow's hummingbird feeder, you could always find a backup to take care of it in case your parents actually do pack you off to a military school."

"Like who?"

"Well, me, for instance," I said. "I can't promise to fill it myself, but I know plenty of people I could recruit to do it. People who are crazy enough about hummingbirds to sneak over here in the middle of the night and do it. Especially if they think it will annoy some of the neighbors."

"Yeah." He brightened up.

"Let me have your cell phone number, then," I said. "Because I have that program on my phone that blocks calls from numbers that aren't in my contact list. And then you could text me if you're prevented from tending the feeders."

We exchanged numbers, in what felt like a small ritual to seal the deal. I returned to my car and took off.

As I left the cul-de-sac, I glanced up and saw him standing in his front yard, gazing wistfully up at the sky, where a small flock of birds was passing.

"Please don't let him be the killer," I muttered.

Chapter 32

As soon as I was outside the boundaries of Westlake, I pulled my car over to the side of the road and called Horace.

"Kind of busy right now," he said. Maybe he was the source of Kevin's abysmal telephone manners.

"I know," I said. "I saw them arresting Mrs. Brownlow. At least I assume that's what they were doing." Horace didn't say anything, and I was pretty sure if they were merely taking her down for questioning, he'd have corrected my assumption. "While you're searching their house—does the chief have approval from Judge Shiffley to confiscate their security system?"

"We should have it soon, but it'll be too late," he said. "They've done something with it—it's not here. Not the main console, anyway, which is the part that stores the data."

"They were planning to send it back to the security company that installed it," I said. "I thought maybe that was a bad idea, so I stuck it inside that big chest in the hall."

"Hang on a sec. Yeah, here it is. Thanks. I'll plan on finding that again as soon as the warrant comes through. Good to get our hands on it before she comes back."

"Comes back? I thought the chief just arrested her."

"Sooner or later she'll make bail," he said. "Hard to convince anyone she's a flight risk with her husband in the ICU recovering from an attack of angina."

"If Mr. Brownlow is in the ICU, how come Dad knows nothing about it?" I asked.

"Because for some stupid reason she drove him down to Richmond," Horace said. "She's lucky it wasn't a full-blown myocardial infarction. I mean, VCU's a great hospital, but we've got some damned fine doctors here, too. If I ever keel over clutching my chest, I want a quick trip to Caerphilly Hospital, not a leisurely detour to Richmond."

"Your preferences have been duly noted," I said. "I'll let you get back to your search."

After ending the call, I sat for a moment, thinking. Were the Brownlows really that dismissive of the medical care they could get in Caerphilly that they'd risk the hour-long trip to Richmond? Or was there some more sinister reason for their seemingly reckless choice?

A rhetorical question that would be a lot easier to answer if I could actually think of a single sinister reason. About the only one that came to mind was the notion that if Mrs. Brownlow actually was the killer, maybe she was trying to bump off her husband, since he was the only living witness to her crime. If that was the case he'd foiled her by surviving.

So I texted Dad.

"Mr. Brownlow went to VCU, not Caerphilly."

And then, after a few moments of thought, I also texted Shane.

"Mrs. Brownlow definitely arrested."

Then I started up my car and headed for home. For the entire length of the drive, Dad was furiously texting me, asking if I knew how Mr. Brownlow was, and why had he gone to VCU, and what kind of idiots were they, anyway.

In the middle of Dad's furious rants about the importance of prompt treatment for cardiac events and the narrow-mindedness of people who looked down on the Caerphilly hospital was a single text from Shane.

"Thx."

"Don't be the killer," I said to my phone, in a stern voice.

By the time I got home, I had only a short time to get ready for the boys' game. So I wasn't thrilled to find Britni sitting in our living room with a sulky scowl on her face.

"How am I supposed to do a profile on your grandmother if she keeps dodging me?" she demanded. "Is she coming back anytime soon?"

"Probably not until after Josh and Jamie's baseball game," I said. "But that might be an interesting place to continue interviewing her. She played baseball herself, you know. In the All-American Girls Professional Baseball League."

"Baseball?" Her tone combined astonishment, outrage, and scorn. Clearly not a fan of America's favorite pastime. "No thanks. Can someone let me know when she's back?"

"Where will you be?" I had the sneaking feeling she was thinking of staying here, and the idea of leaving her alone at the house suddenly bothered me. Not that we had any deep, dark secrets lying around for her to pry into. Given how often we had visitors, including a steady stream of relatives as houseguests, Michael and I had long since gotten into the habit of keeping anything we didn't want the world to see locked up in his office or in mine. And even though it seemed as if Mrs. Anstruther was wrong and Britni wasn't the blackmailer, she was still nosy. The thought of Britni roaming the house, poking and prying, repelled me.

She sighed and looked around as if suddenly becoming aware of her surroundings. And finding them inhospitable.

"I'll be over at the Inn." Her tone suggested that the prospect was profoundly inconvenient.

Maybe she was hoping I'd tell her she was welcome to stay here.

But she wasn't. I waited until she'd slouched out the front door, then locked it behind her.

"Good riddance," I muttered, as I hurried to get ready for my departure.

The cranky mood Britni had provoked disappeared as soon as I reached the ball field. It was a perfect afternoon for baseball. Warm enough that the spectators didn't need coats, but not so warm that we worried about the players becoming ill from over-exertion in the heat. I wasn't scheduled to help run the Snack Shack, so I could relax with family and friends. The Meerkats, the boys' team, beat their archrivals, the Iguanas, with a score of 5–4. After a brief victory celebration—including a rendition of the Weaseltide dance in which both teams participated—most of the boys took to the bleachers, still in uniform, to watch the Mole Rats play the Yetis. Many of the Meerkat and Iguana parents stayed on to socialize with their friends among the Mole Rat and Yeti fans.

Cordelia, in particular, appeared to be having a wonderful time.

"I just texted Britni," she said. "To tell her that after the game, your mother and I are going to a meeting of St. Clotilda's Guild, and that she'd be welcome to join us." The Guild was Trinity Episcopal's main organization for women who wanted to get in-volved in a variety of good works. Though if they explained it to Britni that way, she'd probably assume it would be a snooze fest. It was actually a lively and entertaining group who knew how to have a lot of fun while working together on a project you'd be proud of afterward. The modern equivalent of an old-fashioned barn raising. But . . .

"Is she coming?" I asked.

"Probably not." Cordelia pulled out her phone and glanced at it. "She hasn't bothered to answer yet, although I can tell she's read it. Maybe she doesn't realize we dinosaurs know about things like that. With any luck, she won't get back to me until tomorrow morning, and by then I think I'll have plenty of ammo for telling her that clearly she doesn't seem to be paying any attention to most of the things I'm interested in, so perhaps we should just cancel the profile."

"You could actually have just told her that yesterday," I pointed out. "It was already pretty obvious."

"But then she could just have gone back to her editor and said I was temperamental and uncooperative," she said. "But today she turned down an invitation to go with your mother and me to the Garden Club's weeding bee."

"Weeding bee?"

"Where you go and weed for a member who's temporarily laid up," she explained. "A lady who just had a hip replacement, and another who broke her foot and can't yet put any weight on it. You should see what a difference we made."

"Mother was actually weeding?"

"She's very good at weed identification," Cordelia said.

I deduced that the answer was no.

"Which is especially important if you're working on a yard with a lot of native plants," Cordelia added. "She has a very useful plant identification app on her phone. And Britni turned down the invitation to watch baseball with us," she went on. "So if she turns up her nose at St. Clotilda, I'll have visible proof that *I'm* trying. She's the one who's slacking off."

"Then I hope for all our sakes that she bails on St. Clotilda, too," I said.

"Yes. By the way, what's Chief Burke doing here?" She pointed to a herd of folding chairs just outside the third-base line.

"His grandson Adam is on the boys' team."

"Yes, I know—shaping up to be a very nice little infielder. But isn't the chief rather busy with his murder case?"

She had a good point. Not that the chief wouldn't do everything he could to make Adam's game, even if the case were going badly. But the calm, relaxed, almost cheerful look on his face spoke volumes.

"Don't spread it around yet," I said. "But he may have had a break in the case." I gave her the highlights of my visit with Mrs. Brownlow.

"So his being here is probably a good sign, then," she said. "He's not just putting on a good front to reassure the public."

I nodded. But now I was curious. I looked around until I spotted Aida Butler. One of her nephews, only a little younger than the boys, played on the Yetis. I worked my way over to where she was sitting.

"Glad to see you," I said. And, after glancing around to make sure none of the town's worst gossips were in earshot, I added, more softly, "Gladder than usual, since I assume seeing you here means the case is going well."

"And I hear you're partly to thank for that," she said, keeping her own voice low. "Last I heard they were still waiting for Mrs. Brownlow's attorney to get here. From Richmond."

"Of course," I said. "Heaven forbid that she use a mere Caerphilly attorney. And the chief is really sure she's the one? I mean, she looked suspicious to me, but—"

"Keep this to yourself." She looked around, then leaned closer. "The blackmail note you found was enough for Judge Shiffley to issue a search warrant. And Horace found two spent shell casings in her garbage can. He's sending them down to the Crime Lab for confirmation, but he's pretty sure they're going to match the bullet that killed Inman."

"That's great!" I said. "Only . . . which garbage can? One of her inside ones, or the big one that sits outside where anyone who comes by could toss something into?"

"The big one," she said. "But it's not like it spends that much time outside. You know Westlake. HOA rule is that you can't leave your garbage can outside except the night before and morning of pickup. Rest of the time you have to keep it either inside or behind some kind of fence or privacy screen so nobody has to look at it. Brownlows keep theirs in the garage the rest of the time. It's been sitting in there since around nine a.m. Thursday morning. Well before the murder."

"That's good, then."

"And who knows what other evidence we'll find now that we're focused on her," Aida said. "Pretty sure there will be more. She's probably busy trying to use her trip down to the hospital in Richmond as an alibi—baloney! Hospital staff say she bailed not long after she got there—as soon as the doctors said her husband wasn't actually a goner. We've got her on the hospital security cameras driving out at around ten p.m."

I wondered if she already knew about Mrs. Brownlow's illicit visit to the golf course. Probably better to let the chief share that news.

"Vern's betting her attorney will tell her to plead some kind of temporary insanity," Aida went on. "Like maybe she went after Inman while still out of her gourd with worry over her husband. Won't work, but they'll try."

"A jury might be sympathetic if it comes out that Inman was a blackmailer," I said.

"For that matter, the chief and the district attorney might be sympathetic if she helps us get more information on that side of the case. Like giving us details on when and how much she paid Inman, so we can match that to his financial records. But I hear her attorney's a sharp cookie. He'll probably convince her to do that. And with luck we'll hear from a few more blackmail victims once word gets out that Inman's dead. So relax. Enjoy the ball game."

"Go Yetis!" I said.

"I heard that!" said another nearby friend—whose kid was a Mole Rat.

"Go Mole Rats, too," I said. "Just as long as they're not playing the Meerkats."

But as I strolled away, I began to worry a little. Would finding the shell casings be all that decisive? Mrs. Brownlow's sharp attorney could argue that they could easily have left their garage door open a little too long, creating an opportunity when the real killer came by looking for someplace to ditch the incriminating shell casings. Or the attorney could argue that the killer might be a neighbor to whom she'd given the garage code. I could think of at least two friends who had given me their garage codes for when they were out of town—it was easier than handing off a key if all they wanted me to do was check once a day and haul in any packages left on their doorsteps.

And maybe the attorney would have a good point. Mrs. Brownlow certainly looked like the prime suspect—but was she the only one? Someone could easily have figured out the Brownlows' garage code just by watching. They seemed to spend a lot of time watching each other there in Westlake. The security systems. HOA representatives patrolling the neighborhood to make sure no one was leaving out garbage cans after 9:00 a.m., letting their grass grow half an inch too long, or painting their garage door in a color that wasn't on the official list of permitted hues. It wouldn't be hard for someone to steal a garage code.

Someone like Shane Griswold, for example. His neighbors—especially the childless ones—were always complaining about the amount of time he spent just hanging around. And they could only have seen him hanging around if he was doing it outdoors, and mainly in the front yard.

Why was I so bent on finding reasons to suspect Shane Griswold?

Probably because I was really hoping it wasn't him.

The lights at the ball field were on by the time the Yetis vanquished the Mole Rats in a hard-fought game. Various parties of players and parents went off to celebrate or commiserate. Dad and Michael loaded the boys' baseball gear into my car, then collected the participants for tonight's version of the bee watch party. I was ready for some quiet time.

When I got home, I walked in, closed the door behind me, and took one of the deep, calming breaths Rose Noire was always recommending. It had been a long day. A very long two days.

But the house was dark and quiet. Delightfully quiet. Probably not entirely empty, but at least for the moment, I'd settle for mostly empty. Rose Noire and Cordelia wouldn't be home from the St. Clotilda's meeting until late. Kevin might be holed up in his basement—no, wait. It was Saturday, his Dungeons & Dragons night. He wouldn't be home until well after midnight. And Rob and Delaney had taken off this morning for a quick visit to her mother in California, and for once we didn't have a single member of the vast Hollingsworth clan staying with us. Even the dogs wouldn't be around, since the boys had taken them all to Edgar's again.

I'd have the house to myself for the next few hours. This didn't happen very often. I could read a book in peace and quiet. Watch a movie. Take a long, hot soaking bath. All of the above in turn.

But I felt restless. I wanted to be in the mood for bath, book, and movie, but I was still fretting. Which was silly—the chief had almost certainly caught Inman's killer. And if Mrs. Brownlow was right, Inman had been the blackmailer, so that menace was gone, too. And good riddance, if Mrs. Brownlow's violent reaction to the blackmail note had been typical of how his victims had been affected.

I realized that was what was preying on my mind—Mrs. Brownlow's reaction to seeing the blackmail note. Her hysterics. I still couldn't tell if they were genuine or if she was exaggerating for effect. Ordinarily, she was the calmest and most matter-of-fact of the NIMBYs, so her panicked reaction to the note—and for that matter, her earlier terror at the presence of the wasp—seemed out of character.

But maybe bugs and blackmailers were her Achilles' heels.

At first I'd assumed it was the blackmail note itself that made her lose it. Then, when she revealed that it was Inman who had been blackmailing her, I'd felt puzzled.

Was she distraught because the presence of the note appeared to show that Inman wasn't the blackmailer? Pretty upsetting if she thought his death had ended the blackmailing and it then looked as if he hadn't done it after all. And even more upsetting if she'd thought she'd done away with her tormentor, only to find she'd killed the wrong person.

But she knew he was the blackmailer—she'd watched him pick up a package from the very spot where she'd left her own packages of money. And she knew he was dead, and the note was no longer a threat.

She was overstressed. That probably accounted for it. Overstressed and not thinking clearly. And maybe, like me, she'd seen one too many scary movies where the implacable monster just keeps on coming, no matter how hard you try to stop him. Like Rasputin. The Terminator. Or Spike, the Small Evil One, doing battle with our poor mail carrier.

Inman didn't strike me as very plausible in the role of inexorable monster. But he hadn't been ruining my life.

"Let it go," I said. "The chief will sort it all out."

I shoved it all out of my mind and stepped into the living room. I glanced around. Spotless. Rose Noire and Mother had seen to that. The only thing at all out of place was the antique typewriter, which technically belonged in the library.

Although it looked very nice where it was, sitting there on the small table in all its gleaming retro glory. Maybe I'd leave it there for a while.

The typewriter.

Something stirred in my tired brain.

I crossed the room and looked down at it. Then I fed a sheet of paper into it, engaged the shift lock key, and leaned over to type a few lines in all caps—slowly, because it required a lot more pressure than a computer keyboard.

THE QUICK BROWN FOX JUMPED OVER THE LAZY DOGS.

THE FIVE BOXING WIZARDS JUMP QUICKLY.

SPHINX OF BLACK QUARTZ, JUDGE MY VOW.

What were some of the others? I couldn't remember offhand. But I didn't need them.

I opened up my phone and looked at the picture I'd taken of the blackmail note I'd found peeking out from under the Brownlows' doormat. Same font. And the same little telltale irregularities on some of the letters—a slight break in the crossbar of the capital H. A slight shortening of the upright of the capital T.

The blackmail note hadn't been typed in a retro font. Someone had typed it on our antique typewriter. Which hadn't left our library for days until I'd brought it out here for Britni to type on. Mrs. Brownlow was mistaken. Walter Inman wasn't the blackmailer—Britni was. Mrs. Anstruther been right after all.

I straightened up and closed the picture of the ransom note. I needed to call the chief and—

Something metallic pressed against the back of my neck.

"I knew you were trouble." Britni. "Put your phone down. Now!"

Chapter 33

Britni poked me with what I figured must be the barrel of her gun.

I started to put the phone into my pocket, but she struck my hand, knocking it to the floor.

"I said *down*." She emphasized the word with another prod from the gun. "Follow orders or I'll just kill you and get it over with."

"Aren't you overreacting a bit?" I said. "I guess you've figured out that I suspect you of being a blackmailer. But the only evidence I've got is the typewriter. Get rid of that and I won't have a thing on you. It's not as if any of your victims are going to speak up."

I felt an absurd pang of guilt at throwing the poor little typewriter under the bus to save myself. It didn't seem resentful. It just sat there, gleaming softly.

"Yeah, right. Pick it up."

"What are you going to do with it?" I asked—but I picked up the typewriter. No sense provoking her.

"Make it disappear. Now move. Out the front door."

I moved slowly, partly because the typewriter was heavy, and bulky enough to be awkward, but partly because I figured the more I could dawdle and put off whatever nasty plans she had in mind for me, the better off I'd be. With luck someone would show up while we were parading through the yard. The moon was only a day past full in a cloudless sky, so we were easy to see.

With brusque commands and occasional jabs from the gun, she directed me down the front walk and then to the left. My car was parked in the closest of the gravel spaces. I figured she was aiming for that, since her little rental Chevrolet Spark was nowhere in sight. But instead she guided me down the driveway to the overflow parking area beside the barn. There, hidden from sight behind our llama trailer, was a sleek black sedan. The sort of car designed to impress people who could tell one brand of car from another. Its charms were lost on someone like me, who relied on a familiar set of dings and dents to recognize my own aging Toyota in a parking lot. Probably a Mercedes-Benz, if I was remembering what their logo looked like. But I wouldn't have put money on that.

"I guess you exchanged your rental car," I said.

"Put it in the trunk," Britni ordered.

Evidently she was holding the remote. The black car's trunk sprang open an inch or so. I walked up to the back of the car and shifted the typewriter so I could hold it in one hand, balanced on my knee. I reached down to open the trunk all the way—and was so startled that I almost dropped the typewriter.

There was someone in the trunk.

Mrs. Brownlow. She was bound and gagged, but alive. And awake. Her eyes were bulging, and she wriggled and made grunting noises when she saw me.

"I said put it in the trunk," Britni ordered.

"Sorry," I said to Mrs. Brownlow. "She has a gun."

Actually, Mrs. Brownlow probably already knew that. I had the feeling the gun had played a part in whatever chain of circumstances had led to Mrs. Brownlow being tied up in the trunk of what I gathered was her own car. And then I realized maybe blackmail and kidnapping weren't the only crimes Britni had committed.

I found a space to wedge in the typewriter so it wasn't on top of any part of Mrs. Brownlow—although the knob you used to advance the paper was rather sticking into her ribs, no matter how I shifted it.

"Hurry up," Britni ordered. "You're driving."

So I climbed into the driver's seat. Britni took the back seat. When I looked in the rearview mirror I could see her behind me, leaning forward to keep the gun close to the back of my neck, its barrel poking through the space between the car seat and the headrest.

"I'm surprised to see Mrs. Brownlow out of jail," I said.

"They let her out on bail, of course," Britni said. "They always do with rich people. And I guess they figured she wasn't really much of a danger to anyone." She giggled. "Guess this time they were right, weren't they? Now start the car and drive."

"Okay," I said. "Where are we going?"

"Westlake," she said. "Back to Mrs. Brownlow's house. She'll like that, don't you think?"

No, actually I didn't think she would. But I just concentrated on turning the big car around and piloting it back to the road.

"So just what are you planning to do?" I asked.

"Shut up and drive," she said.

"Come on," I said. "At least tell me how Mrs. Brownlow ended up hogtied in her own trunk."

In the mirror I could see Britni simper, as if very pleased with herself.

"I was waiting for her when she got home."

"And she let you in?"

"I let myself in. These rich people—they spend tons of money installing security systems, and then get careless about using them. I figured out their security code when I was profiling her back in Richmond, and of course they used the same code here. The month and day of Mrs. Brownlow's birthday."

Of course.

"But what are you going to do with her?" I persisted. "And why do you need my help to do it?"

I had an idea, of course. But I thought it was a good idea to keep her talking.

"I figure I can kill two birds with one stone," Britni said. "Actually, two nuisances with one gun. If the chief shows up at the Brownlows' house in the morning and finds she killed you and then shot herself, all with the same gun that killed Walter Inman, that'll close the case."

"Why me?" I asked.

"Duh. Because you figured out it was me who killed Inman," Britni said. "And were probably going to tell the police as soon as you finished taunting me about it."

"Actually, I hadn't figured it out at all," I said. "I didn't even really believe you were a blackmailer—there wasn't any evidence. I had no clue you were a killer."

"Yeah, right." She laughed. "You were probably going to figure it out. Your father was bragging about how you're a brilliant amateur detective. Nothing but a first-class neighborhood snoop if you ask me, but I figured I should keep my eye on you. And anyway, you know now, so I've got to off you."

"Tell me why, then," I said.

"Because I don't want you turning me in." She sounded exasperated by my apparent cluelessness.

"No," I said. "I meant why did you do it? For starters, why were you blackmailing people?"

"Do you have any idea how little *Sweet Tea and Sassafras* pays me?" she snapped. "No way I can live on that. And every time I asked for a raise, they'd whine about how tight things were, how close they were to having to close the magazine down."

"You could have left and found another job," I suggested.

"Don't think I wasn't trying," she said. "But with nothing but a lame joke like *Sweet Tea and Sassafras* in my résumé, it just wasn't happening. And meanwhile I'd maxed out my credit cards and was getting threatening letters from my landlord and the power company and the Lexus dealer. I was about to go under when I overheard the Brownlows talking and found out how he'd stolen thousands of dollars from the company he worked for and they were just going to let him get away with it so people wouldn't find out how incompetent they were."

"So you decided to blackmail him."

"Her, actually. He might have said, who cares, but I knew she'd do anything to cover it all up."

"And why did you kill Inman?"

"Because he was onto me, too." Her face took on a sullen, petulant look. "First he stole a box of my money. Then he hid and watched me come and look for it and followed me around until he figured out what was going on. He threatened to turn me in unless I cut him in on the action. He tried to blackmail *me*."

"Of course," I said. "The library."

Nice to know I hadn't been completely wrong in suspecting Inman of being the blackmailer. Had he found the package of money and jumped to the conclusion that it was part of a drug deal? That would explain why he'd become convinced that the library was infested with drug dealers. And if he'd kept the money, it also explained why he didn't share his suspicions with the chief. Or had he become suspicious of the library for some other reason and discovered the money package as part of his stakeouts? Either way, he'd eventually run into Britni.

"Yeah, he figured out I was having people leave the money just under the book drop. I had to get rid of him."

"How did you get him out there in the woods?" I asked.

"Now that was pretty slick." She smiled at the memory. "I told him if he wanted a share of the money he should at least do a share of the work. And I pretended I was going to hide someplace and take pictures of a respectable citizen buying nose candy, and did he want to come along. I was going to lead him to someplace in town that would be deserted in the middle of the night, like the high school athletic fields or the grounds of one of those big old churches. But he piped up and said he knew where the drug deals happened and started describing this place out in the middle of the woods. Sounded like a nice, private place to deal with him. So he rode out there with me, telling me all the turns. Wasn't too hard to lure him out into the woods. Then I shot him, and dragged him into some bushes, and left."

The odds were good someone from Clay County had spotted them coming—and her leaving solo. And they'd have figured out by now that they were witnesses in a murder case. But the someone would probably be a drug dealer who wouldn't want to admit being there—or even if they weren't, fat chance of them coming forward to help Chief Burke.

"You must have gotten a shock when we dragged you out to that very place the next morning," I said.

"Yeah, that was no fun," she replied. "Took a while to figure out it was all a big coincidence."

"And then you used your knowledge of the Brownlows' security codes to put the spent cartridges in their trash can," I said.

"Actually, I didn't need to," she said. "I managed to do it when she had hysterics about seeing a bee and you had me and that hick kid help her back inside."

"And then you came back that night and stuck the latest blackmail letter under her doormat." With Vern and me both watching.

"I figured maybe I could get one last haul before they sent her to prison," Britni said. "Doesn't look promising, though. You sicced the chief on her a lot sooner than I expected. Turn that way."

She pointed to a side street. We had reached the outskirts of town, and she was steering me along exactly the route I'd have used if I wanted to get to Westlake with as little chance as possible to be spotted on the way. I cursed inwardly but kept my expression calm and neutral.

The roundabout route we were taking had one advantage: it

was slow. Maybe it would give me enough time to think of a way to get out of my predicament.

But it was hard to think of a plan that could get around the fact that Britni was holding the gun an inch or two from my brain. A couple of times I almost resolved to do something to distract her and just leap out of the car and take my chances—but then I remembered Mrs. Brownlow, lying in the trunk, helpless and terrified. Any plan I came up with had to include her. She might be an annoying NIMBY, but she wasn't a killer. I couldn't abandon her to whatever retaliation Britni would inflict if I escaped.

"What really puzzles me is how you convinced the Riverton police you had an alibi," I said. "How'd you manage to pull that off? Did you bribe Mrs. McWhatsit, the landlady at your bed-and-breakfast? From what I heard, she claimed she was nursing you through your migraine all night."

"Didn't need to bribe her," she said. "Once I'd convinced the old bat that I had a migraine and was too sick to move, she pretty much left me alone. Spent the whole evening tiptoeing around the house and shushing her cats. And she was out like a light by nine, and snoring like crazy. I locked the door to my room and snuck out the window. Made sure to look wan and sickly over breakfast. She never suspected a thing."

I wondered if she was hoping to pull the same stunt with the Inn. I didn't think much of her chances. The Inn had at least as many security cameras as Westlake. And unless she'd left her cell phone behind when she came to kidnap me, a search of its history would definitely show she'd strayed pretty far from the Inn. For that matter, I didn't expect her alibi from the B and B owner would have stood the chief's scrutiny for long, and I couldn't imagine her leaving her cell phone behind when she set out to the far end of the county with Inman.

But that was assuming the chief found any reason to check her cell phone records. And even if he did, that wouldn't do me much good if Britni had already done me in. I needed to find out a way to turn the tables on her now, so the chief wouldn't need cell phone records to know she'd snuck out of the Inn.

All too soon we were driving through the pretentious brick pillars that marked the entrance to Westlake. Not good news. I could see nothing but empty green lawns and closed garage doors. And even if a Westlaker did happen to be outside, what were the odds they'd notice anything amiss, much less come to my rescue?

It was small comfort to know that every house we passed probably had a security camera recording our stately progress through the neighborhood. Even if some of the cameras' owners monitored them vigilantly, all they'd see was Mrs. Brownlow's car following its normal route to the cul-de-sac. Even if something looked off to them, what were the odds that they'd report anything that didn't seem to threaten their property? They'd probably drag their heels even if the chief tried to subpoena their saved video files.

The cul-de-sac was quiet. No visible cars. Only a few lights in the Griswolds' and the Brownlows' houses. As we approached the Brownlows' driveway, the double garage door began opening, revealing their other car parked inside.

I slowed almost to a standstill as I pulled into the driveway.

"Don't stop here," Britni snapped. "Drive inside."

"That's what I'm doing," I said. "But I'm taking it slow, since I assume you'd rather I didn't run into anything while doing so. We don't have a garage, remember, and I'm driving a strange car that's much bigger than mine."

"Just do it," she ordered.

I was having a moment of panic. What if she decided to shoot me the second the garage door shut behind us? That seemed like the most logical time to strike. Shouldn't I do something to distract her?

"It'll be interesting to see how you plan to get the forensics right," I improvised.

"What do you mean?" She seemed to find my remark unsettling. Good.

I shrugged.

I pulled into Mrs. Brownlow's garage space, my eyes on the rearview mirror. Britni seemed more focused on the garage door than on me. She used the remote to shut it behind us and exhaled in relief when it was all the way down.

"Get out slowly," she said.

Relieved, I followed her order. She got out, too, carefully maneuvering to keep me covered while making sure she wasn't within easy grabbing distance.

I heard the small noise of the trunk opening.

"Get Mrs. Brownlow out of there," she said. "And carry her into the house."

"Carry her?" Mrs. Brownlow wasn't exactly petite. "Wouldn't it make more sense to untie her feet and let her get in under her own steam? You could leave her hands tied."

"No," Britni said. "She's completely unreliable. I don't want her running around loose, even with her hands tied. Just do it."

And I was reliable enough to be trusted to cooperate with someone who wanted to kill me? Not a reassuring thought.

Mrs. Brownlow writhed and struggled, making it remarkably difficult to get her out of the trunk. I couldn't decide whether this was a good thing, because it was distracting Britni, or a bad thing, because it was making her impatient. But I finally managed to get Mrs. Brownlow out and sling her over my shoulders in a sort of modified fireman's carry.

There were three steps up to the door from the garage to the house. Mrs. Brownlow revved up her wriggling as I was climbing them.

"Make her stop that," Britni ordered.

"I'd love to," I said.

As I reached for the doorknob, Mrs. Brownlow tried to

head-butt me. I staggered slightly, then pulled the door open. I had to turn sideways to get into the door.

And I decided now was my chance.

I heaved Mrs. Brownlow off my shoulders and down onto Britni. With any luck Britni would break Mrs. Brownlow's fall. I took off running into the house.

I heard a shot, and a scream from Britni. At least I hoped it was Britni. I'd feel guilty if she'd shot Mrs. Brownlow. I was counting on Britni being too focused on trying to stop me to worry about Mrs. Brownlow, who was still securely tied up.

I raced toward the back of the house. I found a sliding glass door leading out onto the deck, unlocked it, and slammed it open, leaping out onto the deck just as Britni emerged from the garage.

As I sprinted across the deck, dodging patio furniture and pergolas, I heard another shot from behind me, and the sound of shattering glass.

Two shots. If this were an action movie or TV show, I would know exactly how many bullets Britni's gun held and would be counting her shots. But I suspected modern handguns held more bullets than the six that would fit into an old-fashioned revolver. So I kept running.

I was hoping Vern was still hidden in Inman's house, staking out the neighborhood. But I couldn't count on that. Still, if I could make it across the plank bridge to Edgar's backyard, at least whatever Britni did would be on camera. Someone would be watching. They'd send help.

But Michael and the boys would be watching. If Britni killed me on camera, they'd see it. And what if they came swarming out of Edgar's house and put themselves in danger?

The thought broke my concentration, and I tripped going down one of the many sets of steps between deck levels. In a feat of athleticism I could never have pulled off in cold blood, instead of going splat on the deck, I managed to roll, regain my feet, and keep running. But I'd lost precious time.

"Stop it!" I heard Britni say behind me. But not loudly—almost under her breath, as if she were also aware of the possibility of being heard—and seen—out here in the open air.

Just then a figure came leaping over the nearby planters like an Olympic hurdler. I looked back and saw Shane, aiming a flying tackle at Britni.

"Keep going!" he shouted. "I'll try to stop her."

Britni dodged the full impact of his tackle, so he only managed to grab her by the ankle. She launched a couple of vicious kicks to his face, but for some reason she didn't try to shoot him. Maybe because she was too focused on me. I decided the best thing I could do for Shane was to keep Britni chasing after me, so I put my head down and focused on covering ground.

Twice she fired off shots as we raced down toward the stream. I could hear her panting hoarsely. I was panting, too—but not as badly. She might be at least a decade younger than me, but she was out of shape. I could outrun her.

But I couldn't outrun a bullet.

I thundered across the plank bridge and began running up the slight incline into Edgar's yard. I made for one of the beehives—not the one on the end, which had live bees in it, but the next one over. Maybe I could take cover behind the beehives.

Britni was over the bridge now and heading my way.

Taking cover behind the beehives would be a lot more effective if I had some way of keeping her from simply running up and shooting me. What if—

"Police! Freeze!"

A bank of floodlights lit up, illuminating the whole area around the beehives. Britni didn't quite freeze, but she slowed to a walk and threw her left hand across her face to ward off the glare.

"Ms. Colleton. This is the police. Put down your gun and put your hands in the air."

But it wasn't the police. I recognized Kevin's voice. Evidently he'd installed floodlights and loudspeakers in addition to cameras.

Britni fired a couple of wild shots in the direction of the voice. She managed to hit one of the floodlights, which went dark with a tinkle of broken glass.

"I repeat: put down your gun and put your hands in the air."

I heard a yapping noise coming from the house. No! Someone must have released the Poms. I was torn between keeping my eyes on Britni and running toward the house to catch the dogs before they ran into danger.

"Put down the gun," the voice repeated.

Just then a dark shape leaped onto Britni, knocking her down. She screamed and fired off several more wild shots. Then she fell silent.

I peered around the hive I was hiding behind. Britni was lying flat on her back, looking up wild-eyed at Tinkerbell, who was crouching on Britni's chest and staring down at her face with silent menace. I wasn't even sure Britni noticed that Spike had sunk his sharp little teeth into the hand that had given up its grip on the gun.

"Meg? Are you okay?" Kevin asked, in his normal tone.

"I'm fine," I said. "Tell everyone to stay inside."

"Vern already told them that. He and Horace are on their way."

I saw two figures running down from the house, a little hampered by the pack of Pomeranians running along with them. When they arrived, Horace took possession of Britni's gun while Vern handcuffed her and Mirandized her.

The Pomeranians alternated between barking furiously at Britni and turning their backs so they could kick dirt on her. Spike and Tink didn't move a muscle.

"Meg," Vern said. "You think you could call the dogs off so we can take Ms. Colleton down to the jail now?"

Chapter 34

"So the Brownlows are leaving," Michael said.

"I guess the rumors were true," I replied.

We had been over at Edgar's, helping him with some of the outdoor chores he couldn't manage until his broken leg healed. But when we glanced across the stream and saw a moving company's truck pull up in the cul-de-sac, we decided to stroll over and check it out. By the time we got there, Dad was already on the sidewalk in front of the Brownlows' house, kibitzing.

"The movers won't reveal where they're going," Dad said. "I suppose the company has rules against that."

"They may not know yet themselves," I said. "Either the movers or the Brownlows."

"Exactly," Michael agreed. "That looks like one of those moving pods, the kind you can use for storage if you have a gap between your old and new homes. Could be the movers are just going to take it back to a warehouse and have no idea what its ultimate destination is."

I felt sorry for Mrs. Brownlow. Her house wasn't to my taste, but she was proud of it and had worked hard on decorating it. I remembered seeing her during last year's House and Garden

Tour, her face tired but triumphant at seeing so many people admire the results.

"Are they going back to Richmond, do you think?" Dad asked.

"I doubt it," I said. "According to what I heard, Mrs. Brownlow doesn't ever want to go back to Richmond. Everyone there knows about whatever financial chicanery her husband committed, and some of them lost money as a result. She's decided Caerphilly wasn't far enough away to shake the past. She's considering either Florida or California. The betting is that she'll put everything in storage and move into one of those extended-stay hotels until she decides."

"And until her husband is well enough to travel, I suppose." Dad nodded sagely.

"The jury's out on whether he's going with her," I said. "She blames him for everything. If he hadn't been a crook, she wouldn't have been vulnerable to blackmail, and Britni wouldn't almost have killed her. Everything that happened over the last few days kind of turned into the last straw."

"Where is all this coming from?" Michael asked. "You suddenly seem to be plugged into the grapevine here in Westlake."

"It's Mrs. Anstruther," I said. "She's suddenly very friendly. I guess maybe she's grateful for the part I played in bringing Britni to justice. Anyway, according to her, the Westlakers are worrying about having two houses for sale at the same time."

"As well they might," Dad said. "What if someone sane moved in?"

"According to Vern, Jeanine Shiffley may have found a family that wants to buy the Inman house," Michael reported.

"Nice for Wally the Weird's kids, I suppose," I said. "And nice for Jeanine, given how large a commission I assume she'll be earning on the deal." I liked Jeanine, Vern and Randall's real estate agent cousin. It wasn't her fault that the buyers she found for houses in Westlake invariably turned out to be NIMBYs. "But what are the chances that anyone who buys the place will be an improvement over Inman?"

"A pretty good chance, in this case," Michael said. "The potential buyers are the incoming chair of the college biology department and her writer husband. They originally loved the idea of living out in the country, with a big old house and yard— even a farm—but they figured out that for a variety of reasons it's not practical at this point in their lives. She wants to be close enough to bike to the college, and they like the idea of biking or walking to do their shopping and such. And they need a big place because they have a dozen kids—most of them adopted from a variety of ethnic backgrounds. And several of the kids have special needs, so the fact that the Inman house has an elevator and a generator and was built to be wheelchair accessible is a big plus."

"Wonderful!" Dad exclaimed.

"They sound almost too good to be true," I said.

"That was my first reaction," Michael said. "But everyone who knows them thinks highly of them. Good people. The only drawback—the thing that almost killed the deal—was when they saw that stone wasteland Inman made of his backyard. The husband's a gardening expert. Writes books about sustainable, environmentally sensitive landscaping with native plants. He wants a yard he can turn into a kid-friendly, wildlife-friendly, pollinator-friendly paradise."

"Almost killed the deal?" I echoed. "You mean they're buying it anyway? What are they going to do—have all the stone ripped out? That will cost a fortune."

"It would if they had to pay to have it done," Michael said. "Jeanine talked to Randall, and Randall made the buyers an offer. If they'd donate all the stone to the town, he'd have his construction company rip it out for free and regrade the yard. Evidently it's exactly the kind of stone Randall has been wanting to get to make fancy new paths for the town square, but the cost of buying it new would be astronomical."

"They should take pictures along the way," I said. "And the husband could write a book about turning a stone wasteland into a lush garden."

"I like that idea," he said. "If he hasn't thought of it, I'll suggest it. And we should definitely introduce them to Edgar. They both went into raptures when they saw his beehives."

"They're not going to be popular with the rest of the Westlakers," I noted.

"I think once they meet their neighbors, they're going to enjoy being gadflies." Michael grinned at the thought.

"This is great news," Dad said. "And if you think the Westlakers are going to hate the new occupants of the Inman house, wait till they hear what might be happening next door at the Brownlows'."

"What could they possibly hate more than environmental activists with a rainbow family of a dozen kids who plan to replace that flawless turf lawn with wildflowers?" I asked.

"Your grandfather's considering buying the place." Dad beamed.

"Grandfather?" I wondered if he was joking. "Okay, obviously he can afford it, in spite of all the money he donates to environmental causes. But why in the world would he want to live in Westlake?"

"He doesn't," Dad said. "But he's looking into whether he can turn it into a group house for some of his employees and interns."

"Seriously?" I couldn't help grinning at the thought of a group of Grandfather's young, diverse, and slightly scruffy staff members taking up residence in Westlake.

"He's got your cousin Festus making sure there aren't any obstacles in the zoning ordinances or HOA rules," Dad said. "And the odds are good—Festus thinks the HOA rules were probably a quickie cut-and-paste job by the developer, and they don't seem to include anything that could interfere with your grandfather renting out rooms to as many people as he likes. There he is." Dad dashed off to where Grandfather was striding across the cul-de-sac.

"I want to be a fly on the wall when the Westlake Homeowners Association finds out about this," I said. "And the Griswolds will go ballistic."

"Maybe not," Michael said. "Your father and grandfather seem to have found a way to charm them."

He pointed over to the Griswolds' front yard. All three Griswolds were there, talking to Dad and Grandfather.

Correction: Grandfather was talking to Shane Griswold. Lecturing him, and rather sternly. Dad and Shane's parents were listening, their faces all smiles. Shane wasn't smiling, but he'd lost the supercilious sneer that had so often marred his otherwise pleasant face.

I strolled over to see what was up.

"Morning, Meg," Grandfather said when I drew near. "Meet my new intern."

Shane actually grinned.

"Shane's attorney convinced Judge Shiffley to sentence him to probation with community service," Mr. Griswold explained.

"On account of it being my first offense," Shane said. "Well, first time they caught me," he added, with what I decided was commendable candor. I was glad I'd talked Festus into representing Shane.

"And he's going to do his community service out at the zoo," Grandfather added.

"I like animals," Shane said. "I think it would be cool to be a vet or something." He glanced over at his parents as he said it, a slightly anxious look on his face, and I suspected that his parents hadn't previously been very supportive of this career idea.

"Of course, he'll have to start at the bottom," Grandfather said. "Junior assistant in the Reptile Pavilion."

"I like reptiles." The look of bliss on Shane's face suggested that yes, he really did like reptiles. Nice that someone did—I could take or leave them myself.

"We'll see how you feel when you've been cleaning up after them for a few months," Grandfather said.

"And it will look good on his college applications, won't it?" Mr. Griswold said.

"Oh, yes," Dad replied. "As long as he works hard and gets good evaluations, it will look great on his college applications."

"Get him into any veterinary school in the country, as long as his grades are halfway decent," Grandfather added. "Or you could consider wildlife management. Lots of fascinating work to be done there. Good application fodder for any career, especially in the biological sciences. Which reminds me—have you met your soon-to-be neighbor yet? The new college biology chair?"

"Only briefly." Mrs. Griswold's pained look probably suggested that even a brief meeting had made her aware of how far from the typical Westlake mold her new neighbor was going to be.

"Excellent decision on the part of the college trustees," Grandfather said. "First-class scholar—but not afraid to get her hands dirty in the field. You should get to know her. She could be another good mentor for Shane here. Now, Shane, what do you say we take you over to the zoo and introduce you to some of the iguanas and pythons?"

Shane's face lit up with pleasure, and he strolled along with Grandfather to Dad's car. His parents stood at the end of the driveway, their faces a mixture of pride and anxiety.

I rejoined Michael.

"You're right," I said. "I don't think the Griswolds will be that much of a problem. There will still be plenty of troublemakers here in Westlake, though."

"Makes life interesting," he said.

And speaking of troublemakers, I had noticed Mrs. Anstruther lurking nearby. Although she was trying to look as if the work of the movers fascinated her, I suspected she wanted to talk to me. I still wasn't sure why she'd mellowed so much toward me. I only hoped it lasted. She had a frown on her face. But only an annoyed sort of frown—not the thunderous wrath-of-God frown I knew she was capable of.

I suppressed a sigh. And remembered Edgar saying he was a rip-the-bandage kind of person. Most of the time I was, too. It wasn't as if Inman's death and the Brownlows' departure would make a serious dent in the supply of NIMBYs in Westlake. I decided that whatever Mrs. Anstruther was annoyed about, I might as well listen to her and get it over with.

So I strode deliberately over to where she was standing.

"Morning," I said. I generally omitted the customary "good" when speaking with Westlakers. It seemed to provoke them into more strenuous complaints.

"Morning." She seemed slightly flustered. Perhaps because I'd approached her directly instead of attempting evasive maneuvers. She could no longer fuel her righteous indignation with the thought that I was trying to ignore her.

"Are the Brownlows actually leaving?" she asked abruptly.

Weren't the movers enough proof?

"According to Jeanine Shiffley, they've put their house on the market," I said. "And as you see." I gestured at the movers, who were struggling with one of the biggest flat-screen TVs I'd ever seen.

"But why?" She sounded puzzled. "Neither of them killed Inman."

"Yes, but Mr. Brownlow is still a convicted embezzler," I said. "That's why they left Richmond, you know."

"Because everyone there knew he was a crook." She nodded. "And now everyone here does, too. Still, if they'd just brazen it out, people would get over it in time, you know. That's what I'd do."

Yes, she would. I liked her a little better for that.

"I think that's what I'd do, too," I said. "But I don't think she's the brazening type. And his health's not good." And as I said it, I felt a surprising twinge of pity for the Brownlows. Who, after all, weren't murderers.

"That makes sense." She nodded. "And I still can't get over how that witch Britni turned out to be a killer on top of the blackmail. It figures."

She nodded her head, and I got the distinct impression that over time, her account of the last few days' events would slowly morph in the telling until she was the hero of the tale, whose prescient warnings about Britni's evil nature could have saved Walter Inman's life, if only someone had listened to her.

"Oh, by the way." She frowned, looked distinctly uncomfortable, and seemed to brace herself before continuing. "Thanks for the suggestion."

"Suggestion?" I groped to remember any suggestions I might have made to her and could come up with only a great number of rude ones that I'd stifled unsaid.

"That I show Kimberly proof that I had artificial insemination." Her frown gave way to a slight smile. "She's still kind of ticked at me for not telling her sooner. But she's speaking to me again. And coming down for a visit this weekend. Probably won't be a quiet visit, but it's better than it was. No idea why I didn't think of that myself."

"You'd been keeping the secret from your husband for so long," I said. "And for his own good, of course," I added, hastily, seeing her sharp glance at me. "And since you're still not recovered from his death, it's no wonder you hadn't yet realized that you could finally tell her."

"That's true." The idea that she'd eventually have thought of leveling with Kimberly seemed to hearten her. She turned to go.

"Mrs. Anstruther," I called. "By the way—"

"Just Mavis," she said, as she turned around. "It's not as if we haven't butted heads enough to get to know each other."

I could get to like that blunt tongue of hers. And now that I thought about it, I hadn't seen the needlepoint Confederate pillows when I'd visited her. Maybe they'd been her husband's idea and she'd gotten rid of them since his death. I could always hope.

"Do you still want me to remind you to cancel your subscription to *Sweet Tea and Sassafras?*" I asked.

"Already did it yesterday," she said. "I suppose I should have stayed until after they did the feature on your gran, but it was time."

"They're no longer doing a feature on Cordelia," I said. "She called them up yesterday and canceled it. Gave them an earful about inflicting someone on her who turned out to be a blackmailer and a killer."

"Good," she said. "Probably not their fault they hired a blackmailer, of course. But definitely their fault for running a really stupid rag."

With that she strode off toward her own house.

And I noticed four cars entering the cul-de-sac—the Twinmobile, Chief Burke's sedan, Aida's cruiser, and Isaac Washington's huge pickup. They all pulled to a stop in front of the Inman house and disgorged a small herd of boys and dogs. Josh, Jamie, Adam, Isaac Junior, and several more of their friends, holding on to the leashes of Spike, Tinkerbell, five of the seven Pomeranians, and several other canine friends.

"Come on, Mom," Jamie said as they raced past me toward Inman's backyard. "We're going to watch the bees!"

Josh and the rest just ran past—well, except for a couple of the Pomeranians, who insisted on greeting me with their muddy paws before rejoining the herd.

Isaac, Aida, Cordelia—who had been driving the Twinmobile—and the chief stopped to greet us.

"What are the bees doing that we should be watching?" I asked.

"It's the return of the bees," Cordelia explained. "A bunch of Edgar's beekeeper friends have joined forces to help him re-build his backyard apiary. They're going to be bringing over new hives to replace the contaminated ones, and they've even managed to round up nine batches of bees. Your father's going over to Edgar's to help, but we decided it would be safer for the boys to watch from over here."

She strode toward the backyard.

"Actually, Edgar's friends found ten batches of bees," Aida said. "One's going over to the middle school for the kids to en-joy. Can you come over this afternoon to help with it?"

"Dad and Grandfather are the bee experts," I said.

"Yeah, but you're better at construction projects," she said. "We're going to build an all-glass hive inside the classroom, with tubes to the outside to let the bees come and go. Let the kids watch everything the bees do."

"Cool," I said. "Count me in."

"Great!" Aida strode off toward the backyard.

"And while you're planning your week," Isaac said, "I'm taking Grandad back out to Muddy Hollow Cemetery Thursday. Bring-ing along some people from the Virginia Board of Historic Re-sources to see it so we can start the process of getting it listed in the Virginia Landmarks Register. If you'd like to come along—"

"I'd love to," I said. "Just let me know when. And if Cordelia's still in town, I bet she'll want to come, too."

He nodded and dashed off after the boys. The chief and I followed more slowly.

"Recovered from your ordeal, I hope," he said.

"Mostly," I replied. "It would contribute to my full recovery to know that Britni will be spending a very long time behind bars."

"Odds are good," he said. "She wasn't nearly as smart about covering her tracks as she thought she was. The circumstantial evidence is mounting up. We've got video of Walter Inman get-ting into her rental car at a little after ten Thursday evening."

"From Inman's security system?" I asked. "That was pretty careless."

"No, from Mrs. Anstruther's security system." He shook his head. "All of a sudden she's being really helpful. No idea why, but I hope it continues. And we seized a half-empty box of nine-millimeter cartridges from Britni's room at the Inn—same brand as the ones that killed Inman."

"Okay, that was careless."

"Again, not really." He chuckled. "She'd tucked it behind some of the molding in the coffered ceiling in her room. In most hotels, that would have been a perfect hiding place, but it didn't escape the housekeeping staff at the Inn."

I tried to imagine how my friend Ekaterina, manager of the Inn, would have reacted to discovering that a murderer had been staying under her roof—and had tried to take advantage of the Inn's architectural splendor to conceal evidence. She was probably having that entire wing of the hotel fumigated.

"And while I'm sure her attorney will try to have everything she's said suppressed, in spite of her Miranda warning Ms. Colleton has been very vocal about her indignation at the way in which Mr. Inman was attempting to extort from her a portion of the money she had extorted from her victims." He shook his head as if puzzled. "It's almost as if she thinks this justifies her crime, or at least counts as a mitigating factor. Well, she'll find out at trial. Oh, and thanks for the list of women she wrote articles about. I've already found several of them willing to testify against her. Yes, I think Ms. Colleton will be far too busy with her legal woes to be much of a danger to anyone for a good long while."

We had reached Inman's backyard. The boys and dogs were all sitting or leaning on the stone wall at the far end, while the various adults who had accompanied them were seated on some of the lower terraces. I wondered how Wally the Weird would have felt if he could see his pricey stone hardscaping used like a set of bleachers to watch the reversal of his bee extermination.

I took a seat beside Cordelia.

As we watched, a troop of a dozen or so figures, all clad in bee-keepers' clothing, began marching down from Edgar's house toward his beehives. Several of them were carrying beehives, and one was pulling a garden cart laden with half a dozen bee-hives. Others seemed to be carrying boxes like the one Dad's bees had come in. As we watched, a short, roundish figure in a beekeeping outfit ran out of Inman's backyard, down the vari-ous levels of deck, and across the plank bridge.

"Oh, good," Cordelia said. "I know your dad was very eager to help."

"Let's just hope he keeps his outfit on this time," I said.

"And let's hope he remembers to take the seal off the candy plug so the worker bees can eventually eat their way in to care for their queen. He forgot with your hive, you know."

"Oh, no." I leaped to my feet. "The queen will eventually die if they can't get to her—isn't that right? We need to go home and—"

"Relax," she said. "I fixed it already. I noticed the next morn-ing that the bees were behaving strangely, and I went out to the hive to see what was up. That was one of the problems I checked for—and an easy one to fix."

And I'd bet she didn't even wear a beekeeper's outfit to do it.

"But let's not tell your father," she said. "He'd be mortified. This crew seems to have a checklist they go through—look, they have at least two people checking on the queen cage with each hive. I'm going to suggest that to your father for future instal-lations."

And he'd probably welcome the suggestion, since it would mean he could sweep other people into his beekeeping activ-ities. I resigned myself to taking my turn wearing the veil and the gauntlets.

I suspected Cordelia was taking a few other notes as she watched this crew of seasoned beekeepers. They were certainly operating efficiently. Several of them were collecting the contaminated beehives and hauling them to the cart, while others replaced them with new beehives. Six of the hives seemed to have come preloaded with bees—they were wrapped in tulle, and the beekeepers carried them with great care, making sure to keep them level. The other three were presumably new hives—after setting them in place and making sure they were level and on solid ground, the beekeepers produced boxes of bees and poured them in—much more efficiently than Dad had done in setting up our hives.

"Why are they setting up pine branches in front of the hives?" I asked.

"To make sure the bees notice that they're in a new place," Cordelia said. "They have a fabulous navigation system—rather like GPS—but they're creatures of habit. If you move the hive, they tend to zoom out and start gathering nectar, and then when they've got a full load, they try to fly home, but their navigation systems will still be set to where the hive used to be. But when they fly out now, they'll see branches that they're not used to seeing right outside the hive entrance. It will clue them in to reset their location coordinates."

"Wonderful," I said.

"Your grandfather had a rather useful idea." Clearly their truce was working well. "He's going to take the contaminated hives and do an ongoing study to see how long it takes before they're safe to use again."

"He can be useful sometimes, can't he?" I said.

"Hmph," she replied. "I see there's some hope for your NIMBYs." She pointed over to the Griswolds' yard. There, hanging from one of the pergolas, was a hummingbird feeder. Quite possibly the hummingbird feeder we'd last seen in the Brownlows' yard. I wondered if Mrs. Brownlow had given it to Shane or if he'd merely appropriated it. Clearly it was no longer filled with mere red-colored water. Two hummingbirds were hovering by it, sipping what was obviously sugar water.

And then a slightly larger hummingbird darted over and chased the first two away.

"Oh, poor Shane," I said. "He's got a bully hummingbird already."

"We'll introduce him to Kevin," Cordelia said. "They'll manage. Look! They're taking the covering off some of the hives."

Most of the beekeepers had retreated to the bank of the little stream. But a pair of them were gently removing the tulle covers from the beehives. Clouds of bees rose over each hive and hovered there for a little while. Maybe it was my imagination, but I thought I could hear their buzzing—not angry so much as confused and a little annoyed. And then the clouds began dissipating as the bees began exploring their surroundings—the blossoming fruit trees, the beds of annuals, and especially the huge field of purple clover.

If any of the Westlakers were watching they'd probably be horrified. But the assembled beekeepers were waving their hive tools in what I gathered was a quiet salute to the success of their mission. The boys, not being close enough to disturb the bees, set up a loud cheer.

"Your bees could use some clover, too," Cordelia observed. "Now we don't have Britni underfoot, we should have plenty of time to plant some this afternoon."

"I can taste the honey already," I said.

Acknowledgments

Thanks once again to everyone at St. Martin's/Minotaur, including (but not limited to) Claire Cheek, Hector DeJean, Stephen Erickson, Nicola Ferguson, Meryl Gross, Paul Hochman, Kayla Janas, Andrew Martin, Sarah Melnyk, and especially my editor, Pete Wolverton. And thanks also to the Art Department for another beautiful cover.

More thanks to my agent, Ellen Geiger, and all the folks at the Frances Goldin Literary Agency for taking care of the business side of things so I can concentrate on writing.

Special thanks this time to Michael Thomas Ford, for tidbits on beekeeping, and to Cat Warren, whose book *What the Dog Knows: Scent, Science, and the Amazing Ways Dogs Perceive the World* helped inspire the Pomeranians' latest adventure. I hasten to add that I'm to blame, not them, for any inaccuracies in the dog and bee lore.

Many thanks to the friends who brainstorm and critique with me, give me good ideas, or help keep me sane while I'm writing: Stuart, Aidan, and Liam Andrews; Deborah Blake; Chris Cowan; Ellen Crosby; Kathy Deligianis; Margery Flax; Suzanne Frisbee; John Gilstrap; Barb Goffman; Joni Langevoort; David Niemi;

Alan Orloff; Dan Stashower, Art Taylor; Robin Templeton; and Dina Willner. And thanks to all the TeaBuds for two decades of friendship.

Above all, thanks to the readers who make all of this possible.